James Anthony Froude

History of England from the Fall of Wolsey to the Death of Elizabeth by James Anthony Froude

James Anthony Froude

History of England from the Fall of Wolsey to the Death of Elizabeth by James Anthony Froude

ISBN/EAN: 9783742848390

Manufactured in Europe, USA, Canada, Australia, Japa

Cover: Foto ©Andreas Hilbeck / pixelio.de

Manufactured and distributed by brebook publishing software (www.brebook.com)

James Anthony Froude

History of England from the Fall of Wolsey to the Death of Elizabeth by James Anthony Froude

HISTORY OF ENGLAND.

VOL. I.

HISTORY OF ENGLAND

FROM

THE FALL OF WOLSEY

TO

THE DEATH OF ELIZABETH.

BY

JAMES ANTHONY FROUDE, M.A.

LATE FELLOW OF EXETER COLLEGE, OXFORD.

AUTHORIZED EDITION.

VOLUME I.

LEIPZIG:

F. A. BROCKHAUS.

1861.

CONTENTS OF VOLUME I.

CHAPTER I.

In periods like the present, when knowledge is every
day extending, and the habits and thoughts of mankind
are perpetually changing under the influence of new discoveries, it is no easy matter to throw ourselves back
into a time in which for centuries the European world
grew upon a single type, in which the forms of
the father's thoughts were the forms of the son's, and
the late descendant was occupied in treading into paths
the footprints of his distant ancestors. So absolutely has
change become the law of our present condition, that it
is identified with energy and moral health; to cease to
change is to lose place in the great race; and to pass
away from off the earth with the same convictions which
we found when we entered it, is to have missed the best
object for which we now seem to exist.

It has been, however, with the race of men as it has
been with the planet which they inhabit. As we look
back over history, we see times of change and progress
alternating with other times when life and thought have
settled into permanent forms; when mankind, as if by
common consent, have ceased to seek for increase of knowledge, and, contented with what they possess, have endeavoured to make use of it for purposes of moral culti-
vation. Such was the condition of the Greeks through
many ages before the Persian war; such was that of the
Romans till the world revenged itself upon its conquerors
by the introduction among them of the habits of the conquered; and such again became the condition of Europe
when the Northern nations grafted the religion and the
laws of the Western empire on their own hardy natures,
and shaped out that wonderful spiritual and political organization which remained unshaken for a thousand years.

The aspirant after sanctity in the fifteenth century of the Christian era found a model which he could imitate in detail in the saint of the fifth. The gentleman at the court of Edward IV. or Charles of Burgundy could imagine no nobler type of heroism than he found in the stories of King Arthur's knights. The forms of life had become more elaborate—the surface of it more polished—but the life itself remained essentially the same; it was the development of the same conception of human excellence; just as the last orders of Gothic architecture were the development of the first, from which the idea had worked its way till the force of it was exhausted.

A condition of things differing alike both outwardly and inwardly from that into which a happier fortune has introduced ourselves, is necessarily obscure to us. In the alteration of our own character, we have lost the key which would interpret the characters of our fathers, and the great men even of our own English history before the Reformation seem to us almost like the fossil skeletons of another order of beings. Some broad conclusions as to what they were are at least possible to us, however; and we are able to determine, with tolerable certainty, the social condition of the people of this country, such as it was before the movements of the sixteenth century, and during the process of those movements.

The extent of the population can only be rudely conjectured. A rough census was taken at the time of the Armada, when it was found to be something under five millions; but anterior to this I can find no authority on which I can rely with any sort of confidence. It is my impression, however, from a number of reasons—each in itself insignificant, but which taken together leave little doubt upon my mind—that it had attained that number by a growth so slow as to be scarcely perceptible, and had nearly approached to it many generations before. Simon Fish, in *The Supplication of Beggars*,[1] says that the number of households in England in 1531 was 520,000. His calculation is of the most random kind; for he rates the number of parishes at 52,000, with ten households on an average in each parish. A mistake so preposterous respecting the number of parishes shows the great ignorance of educated men upon the subject. The ten households in each parish may, probably (in some parts of the country), have been a correct computation; but this tells us little with respect to the aggregate numbers, for the

---

[1] Printed in Foxe, vol. iv. p. 659, Townsend's edition.

households were very large—the farmers, and the gentlemen also, usually having all the persons whom they employed residing under their own roof. Neither from this, therefore, nor from any other positive statement which I have seen, can I gather any conclusion that may be depended upon. But when we remember the exceeding slowness with which the population multiplied in a time in which we can accurately measure it—that is to say, from 1588 to the opening of the last century—under circumstances in every way more favourable to an increase, I think we may assume that the increase was not so great between 1500 and 1588, and that, previous to 1500, it did not more than keep pace with the waste from civil and foreign war. The causes, indeed, were wholly wanting which lead to a rapid growth of numbers. Numbers now increase with the increase of employment and with the facilities which are provided by the modern system of labour for the establishment of independent households. At present, any able-bodied unskilled labourer earns, as soon as he has arrived at man's estate, as large an amount of wages as he will earn at any subsequent time; and having no connexion with his employer beyond the receiving the due amount of weekly money from him, and thinking himself as well able to marry as he is likely to be, he takes a wife, and is usually the father of a family before he is thirty. Before the Reformation, not only were early marriages determinately discouraged, but the opportunity for them did not exist. A labourer living in a cottage by himself was a rare exception to the rule; and the work of the field was performed generally, as it now is in the large farms in America and Australia, by servants who lived in the families of the squire or the farmer, and who, while in that position, commonly remained single, and married only when by prudence they had saved a sufficient sum to enable them to enter some other position.

Checked by circumstances of this kind, population would necessarily remain almost stationary, and a tendency to an increase was not of itself regarded by the statesmen of the day as any matter for congratulation or as any evidence of national prosperity. Not an increase of population, which would facilitate production and beat down wages by competition, but the increase of the commonwealth, the sound and healthy maintenance of the population already existing, were the chief objects which the government proposed to itself; and although Henry VIII. nursed his manufactures with the utmost care, in order to keep the people well employed, there is sufficient proof

in the grounds alleged for the measures to which he resorted, that there was little redundancy of occupation.

In the statute, for instance, for the encouragement of
the linen manufactures, it is said[1] that—'The King's
Highness, calling to his most blessed remembrance the
great number of idle people daily increasing throughout
this his Realm, supposeth that one great cause thereof is
by the continued bringing into the same the great number
of wares and merchandize made, and brought out and
from, the parts beyond the sea into this his Realm, ready
wrought by manual occupation; amongst the which wares
one kind of merchandize in great quantity, which is linen
cloth of divers sorts made in divers countries beyond the
sea, is daily conveyed into this Realm; which great quantity of linen cloth so brought is consumed and spent
within the same; by reason whereof not only the said
strange countries where the said linen cloth is made, by
the policy and industry of making and vending the same
are greatly enriched; and a marvellous great number o
their people, men, women, and children, are set on work
and occupation, and kept from idleness, to the great
furtherance and advancement of their commonwealth; but
also contrarywise the inhabitants and subjects of this
Realm, for lack of like policy and industry, are compelled
to buy all or most part of the linen cloth consumed in
the same, amounting to inestimable sums of money. And
also the people of this Realm, as well men as women,
which should and might be set on work, by exercise of
like policy and craft of spinning, weaving, and making of
cloth, lies now in idleness and otiosity, to the high displeasure of Almighty God, great diminution of the King's
people, and extreme ruin, decay, and impoverishment of
this Realm. Therefore, for reformation of these things,
the King's most Royal Majesty intending, like a most
virtuous Prince, to provide remedy in the premises; nothing so much coveting as the increase of the Commonwealth of this his Realm, with also the virtuous exercise
of his most loving subjects and people, and to avoid that
most abominable sin of idleness out of the Realm, hath,
by the advice and consent of his Lords and Commons in
Parliament assembled, ordained and enacted that every
person occupying land for tillage, shall for every sixty
acres which he hath under the plough, sow one quarter
of an acre in flax or hemp.'

This Act was designed immediately to keep the wives

---

[1] 24 Hen. VIII. cap. 4.

and children of the poor in work in their own houses;[1] but it leaves no doubt that manufactures in England had not of themselves that tendency to self-development which would encourage an enlarging population. The woollen manufactures similarly appear, from the many statutes upon them, to have been vigorous at a fixed level, but to have shown no tendency to rise beyond that level. With a fixed market and a fixed demand, production continued uniform.

A few years subsequent, indeed, to the passing of the Act which I have quoted, a very curious complaint is entered in the statute book, from the surface of which we should gather, that so far from increasing, manufactures had alarmingly declined. The fact mentioned may bear another meaning, and a meaning far more favourable to the state of the country; although, if such a phenomenon were to occur at the present time, it could admit of but one interpretation. In the 18th and 19th of the 32nd of Henry VIII., all the important towns in England, from the Tweed to the Land's End, are stated, one by one, to have fallen into serious decay. Usually when we meet with language of this kind, we suppose it to mean nothing more than an awakening to the consciousness of evils which had long existed, and which had escaped notice only because no one was alive to them. In the present instance, however, the language was too strong and too detailed to allow of this explanation; and the great body of the English towns undoubtedly were declining in wealth and in the number of their inhabitants. The statutes speak of 'divers and many beautiful houses of habitation, built in tyme past within their walls and liberties, which now are fallen down and decayed, and at this day remain unre-edified, and do lie as desolate and vacant grounds, many of them nigh adjoining to the High-streets, replenished with much uncleanness and filth, with pits, sellars, and vaults lying open and uncovered, to the great perill and danger of the inhabitants and other the King's subjects passing by the same. And some houses be very weak and feeble, ready to fall down, and therefore danger-

---

[1] Bishop Latimer, in a sermon at Paul's Cross, suggested another purpose which this act might answer. One of his audience, writing to the Mayor of Plymouth, after describing the exceedingly disrespectful language in which he spoke of the high church dignitaries, continues, 'The king,' quoth he, 'made a marvellous good act of parliament that certain men should sow every of them two acres of hemp; but it were all too little were it so much more to hang the thieves that be in England.'—*Suppression of the Monasteries*, Camden Society's publications, p. 38.

ous to pass by, to the great decay and hinderance of the said boroughs and towns.'[1]

At present, the decay of a town implies the decay of the trade of the town; and the decay of all towns simultaneously would imply a general collapse of the trade of the whole country. Walled towns, however, before the Reformation, existed for other purposes than as the centre points of industry: they existed for the protection of property and life: and although it is not unlikely that the agitation of the Reformation itself did to some degree interrupt the occupation of the people, yet I believe that the true account of the phenomenon which then so much disturbed the parliament, is, that one of their purposes was no longer required; the towns flagged for a time, because the country had become secure. The woollen manufacture in Worcestershire was spreading into the open country,[2] and, doubtless, in other counties as well; and the 'beautiful houses' which had fallen into decay, were those which, in the old times of insecurity, had been occupied by wealthy merchants and tradesmen, who were now enabled, by a strong and settled government, to dispense with the shelter of locked gates and fortified walls, and remove their residences to more convenient situations. It was, in fact, the first symptom of the impending social revolution. Two years before the passing of this Act, the magnificent Hengrave Hall, in Suffolk, had been completed by Sir Thomas Kitson, 'mercer of London,'[3] and Sir Thomas Kitson was but one of many of the rising merchants who were now able to root themselves on the land by the side of the Norman nobility, first to rival, and then slowly to displace them.

This mighty change, however, was long in silent progress before it began to tell on the institutions of the country. When city burghers bought estates, the law insisted jealously on their accepting with them all the feudal obligations. Attempts to use the land as 'a commodity' were, as we shall presently see, angrily repressed; while, again, in the majority of instances, such persons endeavoured, as they do at present, to cover the recent origin of their families by adopting the manners of the nobles, rather than to transfer the habits of the towns among the parks and chases of the English counties. The old English organization maintained its full activity; and the duties of property continued to be for another century more considered than its rights.

[1] 32 Hen. VIII. cap. 18.　[2] 25 Hen. VIII. cap. 13.
[3] *Antiquities of Hengrave*, by Sir T. Gage.

Turning, then, to the tenure of land—for if we would
understand the condition of the people, it is to this point
that our first attention must be directed—we find that
through the many complicated varieties of it there was
one broad principle which bore equally upon every class,
that the land of England must provide for the defence
of England. The feudal system was still the organizing
principle of the nation, and whoever owned land, was
bound to military service for his country whenever occasion required. Further, the land was to be so administered,
that the accustomed number of families supported by it
should not be diminished, and that the State should suffer
no injury from the carelessness or selfishness of the owners.[1]
Land never was private property in that personal sense of
property in which we speak of a thing as our own, with
which we may do as we please; in the administration of
estates, as indeed in the administration of all property
whatsoever, duty to the State was at all times supposed
to override private interest or inclination. Even tradesmen, who took advantage of the fluctuations of the market,
were rebuked by parliament for 'their greedy and covetous
minds,' 'as more regarding their own singular lucre and
profit than the commonweal of the Realm,'[2] and although
in an altered world, neither industry nor enterprise will
thrive except under the stimulus of self-interest, we may
admire the confidence which in another age expected
every man to prefer the advantage of the community to
his own. All land was held upon a strictly military principle. It was the representative of authority, and the
holder or the owner took rank in the army of the State
according to the nature of his connexion with it. It was
first broadly divided among the great nobility holding immediately under the crown, who, above and beyond the
ownership of their private estates, were the Lords of the
Fee throughout their presidency, and possessed in right
of it the services of knights and gentlemen who held their
manors under them, and who followed their standard in
war. Under the lords of manors, again, small freeholds
and copyholds were held of various extent, often forty
shilling and twenty shilling value, occupied by peasant
occupiers, who thus, on their own land, lived as free Englishmen, maintaining by their own free labour themselves
and their families. There was thus a descending scale of
owners, each of whom possessed his separate right, which
the law guarded and none might violate; yet no one of

[1] See especially 2 Hen. VII. capp. 16 and 19.
[2] 24 Hen. VIII. cap. 9.

whom, again, was independent of an authority higher than himself; and the entire body of the English free possessors of the soil was interpenetrated by a coherent organization which converted them into a perpetually subsisting army of soldiers. The extent of land which was held by the petty freeholders was very large, and the possession of it was jealously treasured; the private estates of the nobles and gentlemen were either cultivated by their own servants, or let out, as at present, to free tenants; or (in earlier times) were occupied by villains, a class who, without being bondmen, were expected to furnish further services than those of the field, services which were limited by the law, and recognised by an outward ceremony, a solemn oath and promise from the villain to his lord. Villanage, in the reign of Henry VIII., had for some time ceased. The name of it last appears upon the statute book in the early years of the reign of Richard II., when the disputes between villains and their liege lords on their relative rights had furnished matter for cumbrous lawsuits, and by general consent the relation had merged of itself into a more liberal form. Thus serfdom had merged or was rapidly merging into free servitude; but it did not so merge that labouring men, if they pleased, were allowed to live in idleness. Every man was regimented somewhere; and although the peasantry, when at full age, were allowed, under restrictions, their own choice of masters, yet the restrictions both on masters and servants were so severe as to prevent either from taking advantage of the necessities of the other, or from terminating through caprice or levity, or for any insufficient reason, a connexion presumed to be permanent.[1]

Through all these arrangements a single aim is visible, that every man in England should have his definite place and definite duty assigned to him, and that no human being should be at liberty to lead at his own pleasure an unaccountable existence. The discipline of an army was transferred to the details of social life, and it issued in a chivalrous perception of the meaning of the word duty, and in the old characteristic spirit of English loyalty.

From the regulations with respect to land, a coarser advantage was also derived, of a kind which at the present time will be effectively appreciated. It is a common matter of dispute whether landed estates should be large or small; whether it is better that the land should be divided among small proprietors, cultivating their own

---

[1] See especially the 4th of the 5th of Elizabeth.

ground, or that it should follow its present tendency, and be shared by a limited and constantly diminishing number of wealthy landlords. The advocates for a peasant proprietary tell us truly, that a landed monopoly is dangerous; that the possession of a spot of ground, though it be but a few acres, is the best security for loyalty, giving the state a pledge for its owner, and creating in the body of the nation a free, vigorous, and manly spirit. The advocates for the large estates tell us, that the masses are too ill-educated to be trusted with independence; that without authority over them, these small proprietors become wasteful, careless, improvident; that the free spirit becomes a democratic and dangerous spirit; and finally, that the resources of the land cannot properly be brought out by men without capital to cultivate it. Either theory is plausible. The advocates of both can support their arguments with an appeal to experience; and the verdict of fact has not as yet been pronounced emphatically.

The problem will be resolved in the future history of this country. It was also nobly and skilfully resolved in the past. The knights and nobles retained the authority and power which was attached to the lordships of the fees. They retained extensive estates in their own hands or in the occupation of their immediate tenants; but the large proportion of the lands was granted out by them to smaller owners, and the expenditure of their own incomes in the wages and maintenance of their vast retinues left but a small margin for indulgence in luxuries. The necessities of their position obliged them to regard their property rather as a revenue to be administered in trust, than as 'a fortune' to be expended in indulgence. Before the Reformation, while the differences of social degree were enormous, the differences in habits of life were comparatively slight, and the practice of men in these things was curiously the reverse of our own. Dress, which now scarcely suffices to distinguish the master from his servant, was then the symbol of rank, prescribed by statute to the various orders of society as strictly as the regimental uniform to officers and privates; diet also was prescribed, and with equal strictness; but the diet of the nobleman was ordered down to a level which was then within the reach of the poorest labourer. In 1336, the following law was enacted by the Parliament of Edward III.:[1] 'Whereas, heretofore through the excessive and over-many sorts of costly meats which the people of

---

[1] 10 Ed. III. cap. 3.

this Realm have used more than elsewhere, many mischiefs have happened to the people of this Realm; for the great men by these excesses have been sore grieved, and the lesser people, who only endeavour to imitate the great ones in such sort of meats, are much impoverished, whereby they are not able to aid themselves, nor their liege lord, in time of need, as they ought; and many other evils have happened, as well to their souls as their bodies; our Lord the King, desiring the common profit as well of the great men as of the common people of his Realm, and considering the evils, grievances, and mischiefs aforesaid, by the common assent of the prelates, earls, barons, and other nobles of his said Realm, and of the commons of the same Realm, hath ordained and established that no man, of what estate or condition soever he be, shall cause himself to be served, in his house or elsewhere, at dinner, meal, or supper, or at any other time, with more than two courses, and each mess of two sorts of victuals at the utmost, be it of flesh or fish, with the common sorts of pottage, without sauce or any other sort of victuals. And if any man choose to have sauce for his mess, he may, provided it be not made at great cost; and if fish or flesh be to be mixed therein, it shall be of two sorts only at the utmost, either fish or flesh, and shall stand instead of a mess, except only on the principal feasts of the year, on which days every man may be served with three courses at the utmost, after the manner aforesaid.'

Sumptuary laws are among the exploded fallacies which we have outgrown, and we smile at the unwisdom which could expect to regulate private habits and manners by statute. Yet some statutes may be of moral authority when they cannot be actually enforced, and may have been regarded, even at the time at which they were issued, rather as an authoritative declaration of what wise and good men considered to be right, than as laws to which obedience could be compelled. This act, at any rate, witnesses to what was then thought to be right by 'the great persons' of the English realm; and when great persons will submit themselves of their free will to regulations which restrict their private indulgence, they are in little danger of disloyalty from those whom fortune has placed below them.

Such is one aspect of these old arrangements; it is unnecessary to say that with these, as with all other institutions created and worked by human beings, the picture admits of being reversed. When by the accident of birth men are placed in a position of authority, no care in their training will prevent it from falling often to singularly unfit persons. The command of a permanent military force was a temptation to ambition, to avarice or hatred, to the indulgence of private piques and jealousies, to political discontent on private and personal grounds. A combination of three or four of the leading nobles was sufficient, when an incapable prince sate on the throne, to effect a revolution; and the rival claims of the houses of York and Lancaster to the crown, took the form of a war unequalled in history for its fierce and determined malignancy, the whole nation tearing itself in pieces in a quarrel in which no principle was at stake, and no national object was to be gained. A more terrible misfortune never befel either this or any other country, and it was made possible only in virtue of that loyalty with which the people followed the standard, through good and evil, of their feudal superiors. It is still a question, however, whether the good or the evil of the system predominated; and the answer to such question is the more difficult because we have no criterion by which, in these matters, degrees of good and evil admit of being measured. Arising out of the character of the nation, it reflected this character in all its peculiarities; and there is something truly noble in the coherence of society upon principles of fidelity. Fidelity of man to man is among the rarest excellences of humanity, and we can tolerate large evils which arise out of such a cause. Under the feudal system men were held together by oaths, free acknowledgments, and reciprocal obligations, entered into by all ranks, high and low, binding servants to their masters, as well as nobles to their kings; and in the beautiful roll of the old language in which the oaths were sworn we cannot choose but see that we have lost something in exchanging these ties for the harsher connecting links of mutual self-interest. .

'When a freeman shall do fealty to his lord,' the statute says, 'he shall hold his right hand upon the book, and shall say thus:—Hear you, my lord, that I shall be to you both faithful and true, and shall owe my faith to you for the land that I hold, and lawfully shall do such customs and services as my duty is to you, at the times assigned, so help me God and all his saints.'

'The villain,' also, 'when he shall do fealty to his lord, shall hold his right hand over the book, and shall say:— Hear you, my lord, that I from this day forth unto you shall be true and faithful, and shall owe you fealty for

the land which I hold of you in villanage; and that no
evil or damage will I see concerning you, but I will
defend and warn you to my power. So help me God and
all his saints.'[1]

Again, in the distribution of the produce of land, men
dealt fairly and justly with each other; and in the material
condition of the bulk of the people there is a fair evidence that the system worked efficiently and well. It
worked well for the support of a sturdy high-hearted
race, sound in body and fierce in spirit, and furnished
with thews and sinews which, under the stimulus of those
'great shins of beef,'[2] their common diet, were the wonder
of the age. 'What comyn folke in all this world,' says a
state paper in 1515,[3] 'may compare with the comyns of
England in riches, freedom, liberty, welfare, and all prosperity? What comyn folke is so mighty, so strong in
the felde, as the comyns of England?' The relative numbers of the French and English armies which fought at
Cressy and Agincourt may have been exaggerated, but no
allowance for exaggeration will affect the greatness of
those exploits; and in stories of authentic actions under
Henry VIII., where the accuracy of the account is undeniable, no disparity of force made Englishmen shrink from
enemies wherever they could meet them. Again and again
a few thousands of them carried dismay into the heart
of France. Four hundred adventurers, vagabond apprentices from London,[4] who formed a volunteer corps in
the Calais garrison, were for years the terror of Normandy. In the very frolic of conscious power they fought
and plundered, without pay, without reward, except what
they could win for themselves; and when they fell at last,
they fell only when surrounded by six times their number,
and were cut to pieces in careless desperation. Invariably,
by friend and enemy alike, the English are described as

[1] *Statutes of the Realm*, vol. i. (edit. 1817). pp. 227-8.
[2] 'The artificers and husbandmen make most account of such meat
as they may soonest come by and have it quickliest ready. Their food
consisteth principally in beef, and such meat as the butcher selleth,
that is to say, mutton, veal, lamb, pork, whereof the one findeth great
store in the markets adjoining; besides souse, brawn, bacon, fruit, pies
of fruit, fowls of sundry sorts, as the other wanteth it not at home
by his own provision, which is at the best hand and commonly least
charge. In feasting, this latter sort—I mean the husbandmen—do exceed after their manner, especially at bridals and such odd meetings,
where it is incredible to tell what meat is consumed and spent.'—
HARRISON's *Description of England*, p. 282.

The Spanish nobles who came into England with Philip were
astonished at the diet which they found among the poor.

'These English,' said one of them, 'have their houses made of sticks
and dirt, but they fare commonly so well as the king.'—Ibid. p. 313.
[3] *State Papers*, Hen. VIII. vol. ii. p. 10.   [4] HALL, p. 646.

the fiercest people in all Europe (the English wild beasts,
Benvenuto Cellini calls them): and this great physical
power they owed to the profuse abundance in which they
lived, and to the soldier's training in which every man
of them was bred from childhood.

The state of the working classes can, however, be more
certainly determined by a comparison of their wages with
the prices of food. Both were regulated, so far as regu-
lation was possible, by act of parliament, and we have
therefore data of the clearest kind by which to judge.
The majority of agricultural labourers lived, as I have
said, in the houses of their employers; this, however, was
not the case with all, and if we can satisfy ourselves as
to the rate at which those among the poor were able to
live who had cottages of their own, we may be assured
that the rest did not live worse at their masters' tables.

Wheat, the price of which necessarily varied, averaged
in the middle of the fourteenth century tenpence the
bushel;[1] barley averaging at the same time three shillings
the quarter. With wheat the fluctuation was excessive; a
table of its possible variations describes it as ranging from
eighteenpence the quarter to twenty shillings; the average,
however, being six and eightpence.[2] When the price was
above this sum, the merchants might import to bring it
down;[3] when it was below this price the farmers were
allowed to export to the foreign markets.[4] The same
scale, with a scarcely appreciable tendency to rise, continued to hold until the disturbance in the value of the
currency. In the twelve years from 1551 to 1562, although
once before harvest wheat rose to the extraordinary price
of forty-five shillings a quarter, it fell immediately after
to five shillings and four.[5] Six and eightpence continued
to be considered in parliament as the average;[6] and on
the whole it seems to have been maintained for that time
with little variation.[7]

[1] 25 Ed. III. cap. 1. [2] *Statutes of the Realm*, vol. i. p. 199.
[3] 3 Ed. IV. cap. 2. [4] 10 Hen. VI. cap. 2. [5] STOWE's *Chronicle.*
[6] *Statutes of Philip and Mary.*
[7] From 1565 to 1575 there was a rapid and violent rise in the prices
of all kinds of grain. Wheat stood at four and five times its earlier
rates; and in 1576, when Harrison wrote, was entirely beyond the reach
of the labouring classes. 'The poor in some shires,' he says, 'are enforced to content themselves with rye or barley, yea, and in time of
dearth many with bread made either of peas, beans, or oats, or of
altogether and some acorns among, of which scourge the poorest do
soonest taste sith they are least able to provide themselves of better.
I will not say that this extremity is oft so well seen in time of plenty
as of dearth, but if I should I could easily bring my trial. For, albeit that there be much more ground eared now almost in every place
than hath been of late years, yet such a price of corn continues in

Beef and pork were a halfpenny a pound—mutton was three farthings. They were fixed at these prices by the 3rd of the 24th of Hen. VIII. But the act was unpopular both with buyers and with sellers. The old practice had been to sell in the gross, and under that arrangement the rates had been generally lower. Stowe says,[1] 'It was this year enacted that butchers should sell their beef and mutton by weight—beef for a halfpenny the pound, and mutton for three farthings; which being devised for the great commodity of the realm (as it was thought), hath proved far otherwise: for at that time fat oxen were sold for six and twenty shillings and eightpence the piece; fat wethers for three shillings and fourpence the piece; fat calves at a like price; and fat lambs for twelvepence. The butchers of London sold penny pieces of beef for the relief of the poor—every piece two pound and a half, sometimes three pound for a penny; and thirteen and sometimes fourteen of these pieces for twelvepence; mutton eightpence the quarter, and an hundred weight of beef for four shillings and eightpence.' The act was repealed in consequence of the complaints against it,[2] but the prices never fell again to what they had been, although beef sold in the gross could still be had for a halfpenny a pound in 1570.[3] Other articles of food were in the same proportion. The best pig or goose in a country market could

each town and market, that the artificer and poor labouring man is not able to reach to it, but is driven to content himself with beans, peas, oats, tares. and lentils.'—HARRISON, p. 283. The condition of the labourer was at this period deteriorating rapidly. The causes will be described in the progress of this history.

[1] *Chronicle*, p. 568.

[2] 33 Hen. VIII. cap. 11. The change in the prices of such articles commenced in the beginning of the reign of Edward VI., and continued till the close of the century. A discussion upon the subject, written in 1581 by a Mr. Edward Stafford. and containing the clearest detailed account of the alteration. is printed in the *Harleian Miscellany*, vol. ix. p. 139, &c.

[3] Leland, *Itin.*, vol. vi. p. 17. In large households beef used to be salted in great quantities for winter consumption. The art of fatting cattle in the stall was imperfectly understood, and the loss of substance in the destruction of fibre by salt was less than in the falling off of flesh on the failure of fresh grass. The *Northumberland Household Book* describes the storing of salted provision for the earl's establishment at Michaelmas; and men now living can remember the array of salting tubs in old-fashioned country houses. So long as pigs, poultry, and other articles of food, however, remained cheap and abundant, the salt diet could not, as Hume imagines. have been carried to an extent injurious to health; and fresh meat, beef as well as mutton, was undoubtedly sold in all markets the whole year round in the reign of Henry VIII.. and sold at a uniform price, which it could not have been if there had been so much difficulty in procuring it. Latimer (*Letters*, p. 412). writing to Cromwell on Christmas Eve. 1538, speaks of his winter stock of 'beeves' and muttons as a thing of course.

be bought for fourpence; a good capon for threepence or fourpence; a chicken for a penny; a hen for twopence.[1]

Strong beer, such as we now buy for eighteenpence a gallon, was then a penny a gallon;[2] and table-beer less than a halfpenny. French and German wines were eightpence the gallon. Spanish and Portuguese wines a shilling. This was the highest price at which the best wines might be sold; and if there was any fault in quality or quantity, the dealers forfeited four times the amount.[3] Rent, another important consideration, cannot be fixed so accurately, for parliament did not interfere with it. Here, however, we are not without very tolerable information. 'My father,' says Latimer,[4] 'was a yeoman, and had no lands of his own; only he had a *farm of three or four pounds by the year* at the uttermost, and hereupon he tilled so much as kept half-a-dozen men. He had walk for a hundred sheep, and my mother milked thirty kine. He was able, and did find the king a harness with himself and his horse. I remember that I buckled on his harness when he went to Blackheath field. He kept me to school, or else I had not been able to have preached before the King's Majesty now. He married my sisters with five pounds, or twenty nobles, each, having brought them up in godliness and fear of God. He kept hospitality for his poor neighbours, and some alms he gave to the poor; and all this he did of the said farm.' If 'three or four pounds at the uttermost' was the rent of a farm yielding such results. the rent of labourers' cottages is not likely to have been considerable.[5]

Some uncertainty is unavoidable in all calculations of the present nature; yet, after making the utmost allowances for errors, we may conclude from such a table of prices that a penny, in terms of the labourer's necessities, must have been nearly equal in the reign of Henry VIII. to the

---

[1] STAFFORD's *Discourse on the State of the Realm*. It is to be understood. however, that these rates applied only to articles of ordinary consumption. Capons fatted for the dinners of the London companies were sometimes provided at a shilling a piece. Fresh fish was also extravagantly dear.

[2] 'When the brewer buyeth a quarter of malt for two shillings, then he shall sell a gallon of the best ale for two farthings; when he buyeth a quarter malt for four shillings, the gallon shall be four farthings. and so forth . . . and that he sell a quart of ale upon his table for a farthing.'—Assize of Brewers: from a MS. in Balliol College, Oxford.

[3] 28 Hen. VIII. cap. 14.   [4] *Sermons*, p. 101.

[5] See HARRISON, p. 315. At the beginning of the century farms let for four pounds a year which in 1576 had been raised to forty. fifty, or a hundred. The price of produce kept pace with the rent. The large farmers prospered; the poor forfeited their tenures.

present shilling. For a penny, at the time of which I write, the labourer could buy as much bread, beef, beer, and wine—he could do as much towards finding lodging for himself and his family—as the labourer of the nineteenth century can for a shilling. I do not see that this admits of question. Turning, then, to the table of wages, it will be easy to ascertain his position. By the 3rd of the 6th of Henry VIII. it was enacted that master carpenters, masons, bricklayers, tylers, plummers, glaziers, joiners, and other employers of such skilled workmen, should give to each of their journeymen, if no meat or drink was allowed, sixpence a day for the half year, fivepence a day for the other half; or fivepence halfpenny for the yearly average. The common labourers were to receive fourpence a day for half the year, for the remaining half, threepence.[1] In the harvest months they were allowed to work by the piece, and might earn considerably more;[2] so that, in fact (and this was the rate at which their wages were usually estimated), the day labourer, if in full employment, received on an average fourpence a day for the whole year. Allowing a deduction of one day in a fortnight for a saint's day or a holiday, he received, therefore, steadily and regularly, if well conducted, an

[1] The wages were fixed at a maximum, showing that labour was scarce, and that its natural tendency was towards a higher rate of remuneration. Persons not possessed of other means of subsistence were punishable if they refused to work at the statutable rate of payment; and a clause in the act of Hen. VIII. directed that where the practice had been to give lower wages, lower wages should be taken. This provision was owing to a difference in the value of money in different parts of England. The price of bread at Stratford, for instance, was permanently twenty-five per cent. below the price in London. (Assize of Bread in England: *Balliol MS.*) The statute, therefore, may be taken as a guide sufficiently conclusive as to the practical scale. It is of course uncertain how far work was constant. The ascending tendency of wages is an evidence, so far as it goes, in the labourer's favour; and the proportion between the wages of the household farm servant and those of the day labourer. which furnishes a further guide, was much the same as at present. By the same statute of Henry VIII. the common servant of husbandry, who was boarded and lodged at his master's house, received 16s. 8d. a year in money. with 4s. for his clothes; while the wages of the out-door labourer, supposing his work constant, would have been 5l. a year. Among ourselves, on an average of different counties, the labourer's wages are 25l. to 30l. a year, supposing his work constant. The farm servant. unless in the neighbourhood of large towns, receives about 6l., or from that to 8l.

Where meat and drink was allowed it was calculated at 2d. at day, or 1s. 2d. a week. In the household of the Earl of Northumberland the allowance was 2½d. Here, again. we observe an approach to modern proportions. The estimated cost of the board and lodging of a man servant in an English gentleman's family is now about 25l. a year.

[2] Mowers. for instance, were paid 8d. a day.—*Privy Purse Expenses of Henry VIII.*

equivalent of something near to twenty shillings a week, the wages at present paid in English colonies: and this is far from being a full account of his advantages. Except in rare instances, the agricultural labourer held land in connexion with his house, while in most parishes, if not in all, there were large ranges of common and unenclosed forest land, which furnished his fuel to him gratis, where pigs might range, and ducks and geese; where, if he could afford a cow, he was in no danger of being unable to feed it; and so important was this privilege considered, that when the commons began to the largely enclosed, parliament insisted that the working man should not be without some piece of ground on which he could employ his own and his family's industry.[1] By the 7th of the 31st of Elizabeth, it was ordered that no cottage should be built for residence without four acres of land at lowest being attached to it for the sole use of the occupants of such cottage.

It will, perhaps, be supposed that such comparative prosperity of labour was the result of the condition of the market in which it was sold, that the demand for labour was large and the supply limited, and that the state of England in the sixteenth century was analogous to that of Australia or Canada at the present time. And so long as we confine our view to the question of wages alone, it is undoubted that legislation was in favour of the employer. The Wages Act of Henry VIII. was unpopular with the labourers, and was held to deprive them of an opportunity of making better terms for themselves.[2] But we shall fall into extreme error if we translate into the language of modern political economy the social features of a state of things which in no way corresponded to our

[1] In 1581 the agricultural labourer, as he now exists, was only beginning to appear. 'There be such in the realm,' says Stafford, 'as live only by the labour of their hands and the profit which they can make upon the commons.'—STAFFORD'S *Discourse*. This novel class had been called into being by the general raising of rents, and the wholesale evictions of the smaller tenantry which followed the Reformation. The progress of the causes which led to the change can be traced from the beginning of the century. Harrison says he knew old men who, comparing things present with things past, 'spoke of two things grown to be very grievous—to wit, the enhancing of rents, and the daily oppression of copyholders, whose lords seek to bring their poor tenants almost into plain servitude and misery, daily devising new means, and seeking up all the old, how to cut them shorter and shorter; doubling, trebling, and now and then seven times increasing their fines; driving them also for every trifle to lose and forfeit their tenures, by whom the greatest part of the realm doth stand and is maintained, to the end they may fleece them yet more: which is a lamentable hearing.'—*Description of England*, p. 318.

[2] HALL, p. 581.

own. There was this essential difference, that labour was not looked upon as a market commodity; the government (whether wisely or not, I do not presume to determine) attempting to portion out the rights of the various classes of society by the rule, not of economy, but of equity. Statesmen did not care for the accumulation of capital; they desired to see the physical well-being of all classes of the commonwealth maintained at the highest degree which the producing power of the country admitted; and population and production remaining stationary, they were able to do it. This was their object, and they were supported in it by a powerful and efficient majority of the nation. On the one side parliament interfered to protect employers against their labourers; but it was equally determined that employers should not be allowed to abuse their opportunities; and this directly appears from the 4th of the 5th of Elizabeth, by which, on the most trifling appearance of a depreciation in the currency, it was declared that the labouring man could no longer live on the wages assigned to him by the act of Henry; and a sliding scale was instituted by which, for the future, wages should be adjusted to the price of food.

The same conclusion may be gathered also, indirectly, from other acts, interfering imperiously with the rights of property where a disposition showed itself to exercise them selfishly. The city merchants, as I have said, were becoming landowners; and some of them attempted to apply their rules of trade to the management of landed estates. While wages were ruled so high, it answered better as a speculation to convert arable land into pasture; but the law immediately stepped in to prevent a proceeding which it regarded as petty treason to the commonwealth. Self-protection is the first law of life; and the country relying for its defence on an able-bodied population, evenly distributed, ready at any moment to be called into action, either against foreign invasion or civil disturbance, it could not permit the owners of land to pursue for their own benefit a course of action which threatened to weaken its garrisons. It is not often that we are able to test the wisdom of legislation by specific results so clearly as in this present instance. The first attempts of the kind which I have described were made in the Isle of Wight, early in the reign of Henry VII. Lying so directly exposed to attacks from France, the Isle of Wight was a place which it was peculiarly important to keep in a state of defence, and the following act was therefore the consequence:—

'Forasmuch as it is to the surety of the Realm of England that the Isle of Wight, in the county of Southampton, be well inhabited with English people, for the defence as well of our antient enemies of the Realm of France as of other parties; the which Isle is late decayed of people by reason that many towns and villages have been let down, and the fields dyked and made pasture for beasts and cattle, and also many dwelling-places, farms, and farmholds have of late time been used to be taken into one man's hold and hands, that of old time were wont to be in many several persons' holds and hands, and many several households kept in them; and thereby much people multiplied, and the same Isle thereby well inhabited, which now, by the occasion aforesaid, is desolate and not inhabited, but occupied with beasts and cattle, so that if hasty remedy be not provided, that Isle cannot long be kept and defended, but open and ready to the hands of the king's enemies, which God forbid. For remedy hereof, it is ordained and enacted that no manner of person, of what estate, degree, or condition soever, shall take any several farms more than one, whereof the yearly value shall not exceed the sum of ten marks; and if any several leases afore this time have been made to any person or persons of divers and sundry farmholds, whereof the yearly value shall exceed that sum, then the said person, or persons shall choose one farmhold at his pleasure, and the remnant of his leases shall be utterly void.'[1]

An act, tyrannical in form, was singularly justified by its consequences. The farms were rebuilt, the lands re-ploughed, the island repeopled; and in 1546, when a French army of sixty thousand men attempted to effect a landing at St. Helen's, they were defeated and driven off by the militia of the island and a few levies transported from Hampshire and the adjoining counties.[2] The money-making spirit, however, lay too deep to be checked so readily. The trading classes were growing rich under the strong rule of the Tudors. Increasing numbers of them were buying or renting land; and the symptoms complained of broke out in the following reign in many parts of England. They could not choose but break out indeed; for they were the outward marks of a vital change, which was undermining the feudal constitution, and would by and bye revolutionize and destroy it. Such symptoms

---

[1] 4 Hen. VII. cap. 16. By the same parliament these provisions were extended to the rest of England. 4 Hen. VII. cap. 19.
[2] HALL, p. 863; and see vol. iv. of this work, chap. xxii.

it was impossible to extinguish; but the government wrestled
long and powerfully to hold down the new spirit; and
they fought against it successfully, till the old order of
things had finished its work, and the time was come for
it to depart. By the 1st of the 7th of Henry VIII., the
laws of feudal tenure were put in force against the landed
traders. Wherever lands were converted from tillage to
pasture, the lords of the fee had authority to seize half
of all profits until the farm-buildings were reconstructed.
If the immediate lord did not do his duty, the lord next
above him was to do it; and the evil still increasing, the
act, twenty years later, was extended further, and the king
had power to seize.[1] Nor was this all. Sheep-farming
had become an integral branch of business; and falling
into the hands of men who understood each other, it had
been made a monopoly, affecting seriously the prices of
wool and mutton.[2] Stronger measures were therefore now
taken, and the class to which the offenders belonged was
especially pointed out by parliament.

'Whereas,' says the 13th of the 25th of Henry VIII.,
'divers and sundry persons of the king's subjects of this
Realm, to whom God of his goodness hath disposed great
plenty and abundance of moveable substance, now of late,
within few years, have daily studied, practised, and invented ways and means how they might accumulate and
gather together into few hands, as well great multitude
of farms as great plenty of cattle, and in especial, sheep,
putting such lands as they can get to pasture and not to
tillage; whereby they have not only pulled down churches
and towns and enhanced the old rates of the rents of the
possessions of this Realm, or else brought it to such ex-

[1] 27 Hen. VIII. cap. 22.

[2] There is a cause of difficulty ·peculiar to England. the increase
of pasture. by which sheep may be now said to devour men and un-
people not only villages but towns. For wherever it is found that the
sheep yield a softer and richer wool than ordinary. there the nobility
and gentry. and even those holy men the abbots, not contented with
the old rents which their farms yielded, nor thinking it enough that
they, living at their ease, do no good to the public, resolve to do it
hurt instead of good. They stop the course of agriculture . . . . One
shepherd can look after a flock which will stock an extent of ground
that would require many hands if it were ploughed and reaped. And
this likewise in many places raises the price of corn. The price of
wool is also risen . . . . since. though sheep cannot be called a monopoly. because they are not engrossed by one person; yet they are in
so few hands, and these are so rich, that as they are not prest to sell
them sooner than they have a mind to it, so they never do it till they
have raised the price as high as possible.'—Sir THOMAS MORE's *Utopia*,
Burnet's Translation, pp. 17—19.

See, also. a petition to the crown, describing the extent and effects
of the enclosing system, which I have printed in a note to chapter 13,
in the third volume of this work.

cessive fines that no poor man is able to meddle with it, but also have raised and enhanced the prices of all manner of corn, cattle, wool, pigges, geese, hens, chickens, eggs, and such other commodities, almost double above the prices which hath been accustomed, by reason whereof a marvellous multitude of the poor people of this realm be not able to provide meat, drink and clothes necessary for themselves, their wives, and children, but be so discouraged with misery and poverty, that they fall daily to theft, robbery, and other inconveniences, or pitifully die for hunger and cold; and it is thought by the king's humble and loving subjects, that one of the greatest occasions that moveth those greedy and covetous people so to accumulate and keep in their hands such great portions and parts of the lands of this Realm from the occupying of the poor husbandmen, and so to use it in pasture and not in tillage, is the great profit that cometh of sheep which be now come into a few persons' hands, in respect of the whole number of the king's subjects; it is hereby enacted, that no person shall have or keep on lands not their own inheritance more than 2000 sheep; that no person shall occupy more than two farms; and that the 19th of the 4th of Henry VII., and those other acts obliging the lords of the fees to do their duty, shall be re-enacted and enforced.'[1]

By these measures the money-making spirit was for a time driven back, and the country resumed its natural course. I am not concerned to defend the economic wisdom of such proceedings; but they prove, I think, conclusively that the labouring classes owed their advantages not to the condition of the labour market, but to the care of the state; and that when the state relaxed its supervision, or failed to enforce its regulations, the labourers being left to the market chances, sank instantly in the unequal struggle with capital.

The government, however, remained strong enough to hold its ground (except during the discreditable interlude of the reign of Edward VI.) for the first three quarters of the century; and until that time the working classes

---

[1] I find scattered among the *State Papers* many loose memoranda, apparently of privy councillors, written on the backs of letters, or on such loose scraps as might be at hand. The following fragment on the present subject is curious. I do not recognise the hand:—

'Mem. That an act may be made that merchants shall employ their goods continually in the traffic of merchandise, and not in the purchasing of lands; and that craftsmen, also, shall continually use their crafts in cities and towns, and not leave the same and take farms in the country; and that no merchant shall hereafter purchase above 40*l.* lands by the year.'—*Cotton MS. Titus*, b. i. 160.

in this country remained in a condition more than prosperous. They enjoyed an abundance far beyond what in general falls to the lot of that order in long-settled countries; incomparably beyond what the same class were enjoying at that very time in Germany or France. The laws secured them; and that the laws were put in force we have the direct evidence of successive acts of the legislature justifying the general policy by its success: and we have also the indirect evidence of the contented loyalty of the great body of the people at a time when, if they had been discontented, they held in their own hands the means of asserting what the law acknowledged to be their right. The government had no power to compel submission to injustice, as was proved by the fate of an attempt to levy a 'benevolence' by force, in 1525. The people resisted with a determination against which the crown commissioners were unable to contend, and the scheme ended with an acknowledgment of fault by Henry, who retired with a good grace from an impossible position. If the peasantry had been suffering under any real grievances we should not have failed to have heard of them when the religious rebellions furnished so fair an opportunity to press them forward. Complaint was loud enough when complaint was just, under the Somerset protectorate.[1]

The incomes of the great nobles cannot be determined, for they varied probably as much as they vary now. Under Henry IV. the average income of an earl was estimated at 2000*l.* a year.[2] Under Henry VIII. the great Duke of Buckingham, the wealthiest English peer, had 6000*l.*[3] And the income of the Archbishop of Canterbury was rated at the same amount.[4] But the establishments of such

[1] When the enclosing system was carried on with greatest activity and provoked insurrection. In expressing a sympathy with the social policy of the Tudor government I have exposed myself to a charge of opposing the received and ascertained conclusions of political economy. I disclaim entirely an intention so foolish; but I believe that the science of political economy came into being with the state of things to which alone it is applicable. It ought to be evident that principles which answer admirably when a manufacturing system capable of indefinite expansion multiplies employment at home—when the soil of England is but a fraction of its empire, and the sea is a highway to emigration—would have produced far different effects, in a condition of things which habit had petrified into form, when manufactures could not provide work for one additional hand, when the first colony was yet unthought of, and where those who were thrown out of the occupation to which they had been bred could find no other. The tenants evicted, the labourers thrown out of employ, when the tillage lands were converted into pastures, had scarcely an alternative offered them except to beg, to rob, or to starve.

[2] *Landsdowne MS.* No. I. fol. 26.

[3] GIUSTINIANI'S *Letters from the Court of Henry VIII.* [4] Ibid.

men were enormous; their ordinary retinues in time of peace consisting of many hundred persons; and in war, when the duties of a nobleman called him to the field, although in theory his followers were paid by the crown, yet the grants of parliament were on so small a scale that the theory was seldom converted into fact, and a large share of the expenses were paid often out of private purses. The Duke of Norfolk, in the Scotch war of 1523, declared (not complaining of it, but merely as a reason why he should receive support) that he had spent all his private means upon the army; and in the sequel of this history we shall find repeated instances of knights and gentlemen voluntarily ruining themselves in the service of their country. The people, not universally, but generally, were animated by a true spirit of sacrifice; by a true conviction that they were bound to think first of England, and only next of themselves; and unless we can bring ourselves to understand this, we shall never understand what England was under the reigns of the Plantagenets and Tudors. The expenses of the court under Henry VII. were a little over 14,000*l.* a year, out of which were defrayed the whole cost of the king's establishment, the expenses of entertaining foreign ambassadors, the wages and maintenance of the yeomen of the guard, the retinues of servants, and all necessary outlay not incurred for public business. Under Henry VIII., of whose extravagance we have heard so much, and whose court was the most magnificent in the world, these expenses were 19,894*l.* 16*s.* 8*d.*,[1] a small sum when compared with the present cost of the royal establishment, even if we adopt the relative estimate of twelve to one, and suppose it equal to 240,000*l.* a year of our money. But indeed it was not equal to 240,000*l.*; for, although the proportion held in articles of common consumption, articles of luxury were very dear indeed.[2]

[1] 22 Hen. VIII. cap. 18.

[2] Under Hen. VI. the household expenses were 23,000*l.* a year. Cf. *Proceedings and Ordinances of the Privy Council*, vol. vi. p. 35. The particulars of the expenses of the household of Hen. VIII. are in an MS. in the Rolls House. They cover the entire outlay except the personal expenditure of the king, and the sum total amounts to 14,365*l.* 10*s.* 7*d.* This would leave above 5000*l.* a year for the privy purse, not, perhaps, sufficient to cover Henry's gambling extravagances in his early life. Curious particulars of his excesses in this matter will be found in a publication wrongly called *The Privy Purse Expenses of Henry the Eighth.* It is a diary of general payments, as much for purposes of state as for the king himself. The high play was confined for the most part to Christmas or other times of festivity, when the statutes against unlawful games were dispensed with for all classes.

Passing down from the king and his nobles, to the body of the people, we find that the income qualifying a country gentleman to be justice of the peace was 20*l.* a year,[1] and if he did his duty, his office was no sinecure. We remember Justice Shallow and his clerk Davy, with his novel theory of magisterial law; and Shallow's broad features have so English a cast about them, that we may believe there were many such, and that the duty was not always very excellently done. But the Justice Shallows were not allowed to repose upon their dignity. The justice of the peace was required not only to take cognizance of open offences, but to keep surveillance over all persons within his district, and over himself in his own turn there was a surveillance no less sharp, and penalties for neglect prompt and peremptory.[2] Four times a year he was to make proclamation of his duty, and exhort all persons to complain against him who had occasion. Twenty pounds a year, and heavy duties to do for it, represented the condition of the squire of the parish.[3] By the 2nd of the 2nd of Henry V., 'the wages' of a parish priest were limited to 5*l.* 6*s.* 8*d.*, except in cases where there was special licence from the bishop, when they might be raised as high as 6*l.* Priests were probably something better off under Henry VIII., but the statute remained in force, and marks an approach at least to their ordinary salary.[4] The priest had enough, being unmarried, to

[1] 18 Hen. VI. cap. 11.   [2] 4 Hen. VII. cap. 12.
[3] During the quarter sessions time they were allowed 4*s.* a day.— Ric. II. xii. 10.
[4] The rudeness of the furniture in English country houses has been dwelt upon with much emphasis by Hume and others. An authentic inventory of the goods and chattels in a parsonage in Kent proves that there has been much exaggeration in this matter. It is from an MS. in the Rolls House.

The Inventory of the Goods and Catales of Rich^d. Master, Clerk, Parson of Aldington, being in his Parsonage on the 20th Day of April, in the 25th Year of the Reign of our Sovereign Lord King Henry VIII.

Plate.
Silver spoons, twelve.

In the Hall.
Two tables and two forms.
Item, a painted cloth hanging at the upper end of the hall.
Item, a green banker hung on the bench in the hall.
Item, a laver of laten.

In the Parlour.
A hanging of old red and green saye.
Item, a banker of woven carpet of divers colours.
Item, two cushions.
Item, one table, two forms, one cupboard, one chair.
Item, two painted pictures and a picture of the names of kings of England pinned on the said hanging.

supply him in comfort with the necessaries of life. The squire had enough to provide moderate abundance for

In the Chamber on the North Side of the said Parlour.
A painted hauging.
Item, a bedstedyll with a feather bed, one bolster, two pillows, one blanket, one roulett of rough tapestry, a testner of green and red saye.
Item, two forms.
Item, one jack to set a basin on.

In the Chamber over the Parlour.
Two bedsteads.
Item, another testner of painted cloth.
Item. a painted cloth.
Item, two forms.

At the Stairs' Hed beside the Parson's Redchamber.
One table, two trestylls, four beehives.

In the Parson's Lodging-chamber.
A bedstedyll and a feather bed, two blankets. one payr of sheets, one coverlet of tapestry lined with canvas, one bolster, one pillow with a pillocote.
Item, one gown of violet cloth lined with red saye.
Item, a gown of black cloth, furred with lamb.
Item, two hoods of violet cloth, whereof one is lined with green earsenet.
Item, one jerkyn of tawny camlet.
Item, a jerkyn of cloth furred with white.
Item, a jacket of cloth furred.
Item, a sheet to put in cloth.
Item. one press.
Item, a leather mail.
Item. one table, two forms, four chairs, two trestylls.
Item, a tester of painted cloth.
Item, a pair of hangings of green saye, with two pictures thereupon.
Item, one cupboard. two chests.
Item. a little flock bed, with a bolster and a coverlet.
Item, one cushion, one mantell, one towel, and, by estimation, a pound of wax candles.
Item. Greek books covered with boards, 42.
Item, small books covered with boards, 33.
Item. books covered with leather and parchment, 38.

In the said Chest in the said Chamber.
Three pieces of red saye and green.
Item, one tyke for a bolster, two tykes for pillows.
Item, a typpett of cloth.
Item, diaper napkins, 4, diaper towels, 2.
Item, four pairs of sheets, and one shete, two tablecloths.

In the other Chest in the same Chamber.
One typpett of sarsenett.
Item. two cotes belonging to the crosse of Underhill, whereupon hang thirty-three pieces of money, rings, and other things, and three crystal stones closed in silver.

In the Study.
Two old boxes, a wicker hamper full of papers.

In the Chamber behind the Chimney.
One seam and a half of old malt.
Item. a trap for rats.
Item, a board of three yards length.

In the Chamber next adjoining westwards.
One bedstedyll, one flock bed, one bolster.
One form, two shelf boards, one little table, two trestylls. two awgyes, one nett, called a stalker. a well rope, five quarters of hemp.

himself and his family. Neither priest nor squire was able
to establish any steep differences in outward advantages
between himself and the commons among whom he lived.

In the Butlery.
Three basins of pewter, five candlesticks, one ewer of latcen, one
chafing dish, two platters, one dish, one salter, three podingers
[? porringer], a saltseller of pewter, seven kilderkyns, three keelers,
one form, five shelves, one byn, one table, one glasse bottell.

In the Priest's Chamber.
One bedstedyll, one feather bed, two forms, one press.

In the Woman's Keeping.
Two tablecloths, two pairs of sheets.

In the Servants' Chamber.
One painted hanging, a bedstedyll, one feather bed, a press, and a shelf.

In the Kitchen.
Eight bacon flitches, a little brewing lead, three brass pots, three
kettles, one posnett, one frying-pan, a dripping-pan, a great pan,
two trivetts, a chopping knife, a skimmer, one fire rake, a pot-
hanger, one pothookes, one andiron, three spits, one gridiron, one
firepan, a coal rake of iron, two botts [? butts], three wooden
platters, six boldishes, three forms, two stools, seven platters, two
pewter dishes, four saucers, a covering of a salt-sellar, a podynger,
seven tubbs, a caldron, two syffs, a capon cope, a mustard quern,
a ladder, two pails, one beehive.

In the Mill-house.
Seven butts, two cheeses, an old sheet, an old brass pan, three po-
dyngers, a pewter dish.

In the Boulting-house.
One brass pan, one quern, a boulting hutch, a boulting tub, three
little tubbys, two keelers, a tolvett, two boulters, one tonnell.

In the Larder.
One sieve, one bacon trough, a cheese press, one little tub, eight
. shelves, one graper for a well.

Wood.
Of tall wood ten load, of ash wood a load and a half.

Poultry.
Nine hens, eight capons, one cock, sixteen young chickens, three old
geese, seventeen goslings, four ducks.

Cattle.
Five young hoggs, two red kyne, one red heifer two years old, one
bay gelding lame of spavins, one old grey mare having a mare colt.

In the Entries.
Two tubbs, one trough, one ring to bear water and towel, a chest to
keep cornes.

In the same House.
Five seams of lime.

In the Woman's Chamber.
One bedstedyll of hempen yarn, by estimation 20lbs.

Without the House.
Of tyles,   , of bricks,   , seven planks, three rafters, one ladder.

In the Gate-house.
One form, a leather sack, three bushels of wheat.

In the Still beside the Gate.
Two old road saddles, one bridle, a horse-cloth.

In the Barn next the Gate.
Of wheat unthrashed, by estimation, thirty quarters, of barley unthrashed, by estimation, five quarters.

The habits of all classes were open, free, and liberal. There are two expressions corresponding one to the other, which we frequently meet with in old writings, and which are used as a kind of index, marking whether the condition of things was or was not what it ought to be. We read of 'merry England,'—when England was not merry, things were not going well with it; we hear of 'the glory of hospitality,' England's pre-eminent boast,— by the rules of which all tables, from the table of the twenty-shilling freeholder to the table in the baron's hall and abbey refectory, were open at the dinner hour to all comers, without stint or reserve, or question asked.[1] To every man, according to his degree, who chose to ask for it, there was free fare and free lodging; bread, beef, and beer for his dinner; for his lodging, perhaps, only a mat of rushes in a spare corner of the hall, with a billet of wood for a pillow,[2] but freely offered and freely taken, the guest probably faring much as his host fared, neither worse nor better. There was little fear of an abuse of such licence, for suspicious characters had no leave to wander at pleasure; and for any man found at large, and unable to give a sufficient account of himself, there were the ever-ready parish stocks or town gaol. The 'glory of hospitality' lasted far down into Elizabeth's time; and then, as Camden says, 'came in great bravery of building, to the marvellous beautifying of the realm, but to the decay' of what he valued more.

In such frank style the people lived, hating three things with all their hearts: idleness, want, and cowardice; and for the rest, carrying their hearts high, and having their hands full. The[3] hour of rising, winter and summer,

In the Cartlage.
One weene with two whyles, one dung-cart without whyles, two shod-whyles, two yokes, one sledge.
In the Barn next the Church.
Of oats unthrashed, by estimation, one quarter.
In the Garden-house.
Of oats, by estimation, three seams four bushels.
In the Court.
Two racks, one ladder.

[1] Two hundred poor were fed daily at the house of Thomas Cromwell. This fact is perfectly authenticated. Stowe the historian, who did not like Cromwell, lived in an adjoining house, and reports it as an eye witness.—*See* STOWE'S *Survey of London.*

[2] HARRISON'S *Description of Britain.*

[3] The Earl and Countess of Northumberland breakfasted together alone at seven. The meal consisted of a quart of ale, a quart of wine, and a chine of beef: a loaf of bread is not mentioned, but we hope it may be presumed. On fast days the beef was exchanged for a dish of sprats or herrings, fresh or salt.—*Northumberland Household Book,* quoted by Hume.

was four o'clock, with breakfast at five, after which the labourers went to work and the gentlemen to business, of which they had no little. In the country every unknown face was challenged and examined—if the account given was insufficient, he was brought before the justice; if the village shopkeeper sold bad wares, if the village cobbler made 'unhonest' shoes, if servants and masters quarrelled, all was to be looked to by the justice; there was no fear lest time should hang heavy with him. At twelve he dined; after dinner he went hunting, or to his farm, or to what he pleased.[1] It was a life unrefined, perhaps, but coloured with a broad, rosy, English health.

Of the education of noblemen and gentlemen we have contradictory accounts, as might be expected. The universities were well filled, by the sons of yeomen chiefly. The cost of supporting them at the colleges was little, and wealthy men took a pride in helping forward any boys of promise.[2] It seems clear also, as the Reformation drew nearer, while the clergy were sinking lower and lower, a marked change for the better became perceptible in a portion at least of the laity. The more old-fashioned of the higher ranks were slow in moving; for as late as the reign of Edward VI.[3] there were peers of parliament unable to read; but on the whole, the invention of printing, and the general ferment which was commencing all over

---

[1] Some notion of the style of living sometimes witnessed in England in the old times may be gathered from the details of a feast given at the installation of George Neville, brother of Warwick the King Maker, when made Archbishop of York.

The number of persons present including servants was about 3500. The provisions were as follow—

Wheat, 300 quarters.	Fesants, 200.
Ale, 300 tuns.	Partridges, 500.
Wine, 104 tuns.	Woodcocks, 400.
Ipocras, 1 pipe.	Plovers, 400.
Oxen. 80.	Curlews, 100.
Wild bulls. 6.	Quails. 100.
Mutton. 1004.	Egrets, 1000.
Veal, 300.	Rees. 200.
Porkers, 300.	Harts, bucks, and roes, 400 and odd.
Geese, 3000.	Pasties of venison, cold, 4000.
Capons. 2300.	Pasties of venison. hot, 1506.
Pigs. 2000.	Dishes of jelly, pasted. 1006.
Peacocks, 100.	Plain dishes of jelly, 4000.
Cranes, 200.	Cold tarts. baken, 4000.
Kids. 200.	Cold custards, 4000.
Chickens, 2000.	Custards. hot, 2000.
Pigeons, 4000.	Pikes, 300.
Conies, 4000.	Breams. 300.
Bitterns. 204.	Seals. 8.
Mallards and teals, 4000.	Porpoises. 4.
Heronshaws, 4000.	

[2] LATIMER'S *Sermons*, p. 64.
[3] *Statutes of the Realm.* 1 Ed. VI. cap. 12.

the world, had produced marked effects in all classes.
Henry VIII. himself spoke four languages, and was well
read in theology and history; and the high accomplishments of More and Sir T. Elliott, of Wyatt and Cromwell,
were but the extreme expression of a temper which was
rapidly spreading, and which gave occasion, among other
things, to the following reflection in Erasmus. 'Oh,
strange vicissitudes of human things,' exclaims he. 'Heretofore the heart of learning was among such as professed
religion. Now, while they for the most part give themselves up, *ventri luxui pecuniæque*, the love of learning
is gone from them to secular princes, the court, and the
nobility. May we not justly be ashamed of ourselves?
The feasts of priests and divines are drowned in wine,
are filled with scurrilous jests, sound with intemperate
noise and tumult, flow with spiteful slanders and defamation of others; while at princes' tables modest disputations
are held concerning things which make for learning and
piety.'

A letter to Thomas Cromwell from his son's tutor will
not be without interest on this subject; Cromwell was
likely to have been unusually careful in his children's
training, and we need not suppose that all boys were
brought up as prudently. Sir Peter Carew, for instance,
being a boy at about the same time, and giving trouble at
the High School at Exeter, was led home to his father's
house at Ottery, coupled between two foxhounds.[1] Yet
the education of Gregory Cromwell is probably not far
above what many young men of the middle and higher
ranks were beginning to receive. Henry Dowes was the
tutor's name, beyond which fact I know nothing of him.
His letter is as follows:—

'After that it pleased your mastership to give me in
charge, not only to give diligent attendance upon Master
Gregory, but also to instruct him with good letters, honest
manners, pastyme of instruments, and such other qualities
as should be for him meet and convenient, pleaseth it you
to understand that for the accomplishment thereof I have
endeavoured myself by all ways possible to excogitate how
I might most profit him. In which behalf, through his
diligence, the success is such as I trust shall be to your
good contentation and pleasure, and to his no small profit.
But for cause the summer was spent in the service of the
wild gods, [and] it is so much to be regarded after what
fashion youth is brought up, in which time that that is

---

[1] HOOKER's *Life of Sir Peter Carew.*

learned for the most part will not be wholly forgotten in
the older years, I think it my duty to ascertain your
mastership how he spendeth his time.   And first after
he hath heard mass he taketh a lecture of a dialogue of
Erasmus' *Colloquies*, called *Pietas Puerilis*, wherein is
described a very picture of one that should be virtuously
brought up; and for cause it is so necessary for him, I
do not only cause him to read it over, but also to practise the precepts of the same.   After this he exerciseth
his hand in writing one or two hours, and readeth upon
Fabyan's *Chronicle* as long.   The residue of the day he
doth spend upon the lute and virginals.   When he rideth,
as he doth very oft, I tell him by the way some history
of the Romans or the Greeks, which I cause him to re-
hearse again in a tale.   For his recreation he useth to
hawk and hunt and shoot in his long bow, which frameth
and succeedeth so well with him that he seemeth to be
thereunto given by nature.'[1]

I have spoken of the organization of the country population, I have now to speak of that of the towns, of the
trading classes and manufacturing classes, the regulations
respecting which are no less remarkable and no less
illustrative of the national character.   If the tendency of
trade to assume at last a form of mere self-interest be
irresistible, if political economy represent the laws to which
in the end it is forced to submit itself, the nation spared
no efforts, either of art or policy, to defer to the last
moment the unwelcome conclusion.

The names and shadows linger about London of certain ancient societies, the members of which may still
occasionally be seen in quaint gilt barges pursuing their
now difficult way among the swarming steamers; when on
certain days, the traditions concerning which are fast dying
out of memory, the Fishmongers' Company, the Goldsmiths'
Company, the Mercers' Company, make procession down
the river for civic feastings at Greenwich or Blackwall.
The stately tokens of ancient honour still belong to them,
and the remnants of ancient wealth and patronage and
power.   Their charters may still be read by curious antiquaries, and the bills of fare of their ancient entertain-
ments.   But for what purpose they were called into being,
what there was in these associations of common trades to
surround with gilded insignia, and how they came to be
possessed of broad lands and church preferments, few

---

[1] In a subsequent letter he is described as learning French, ety-
mology, casting of accounts, playing at weapons, and other such exer-
cises.—ELLIS, third series, vol. i. p. 349-3.

people now care to think or to inquire. Trade and traders
have no dignity any more in the eyes of any one, except
what money lends to them; and these outward symbols
scarcely rouse even a passing feeling of curiosity. And
yet these companies were once something more than
names. They are all which now remain of a vast organization which once penetrated the entire trading life of
England—an organization set on foot to realize that most
necessary, if most difficult, condition of commercial excellence under which man should deal faithfully with his
brother, and all wares offered for sale, of whatever kind,
should honestly be what they pretend to be.[1] I spoke of
the military principle which directed the distribution and
the arrangements of land. The analogy will best explain
a state of things in which every occupation was treated
as the division of an army; regiments being quartered
in every town, each with its own self-elected officers,
whose duty was to exercise authority over all persons professing the business to which they belonged, who were to
see that no person undertook to supply articles which he
had not been educated to manufacture, who were to determine the prices at which such articles ought justly to
be sold; above all, who were to take care that the common people really bought at shops and stalls what they
supposed themselves to be buying; that cloth put up for
sale was true cloth, of true texture and full weight: that
leather was sound and well tanned; wine pure, measures
honest; flour unmixed with devil's dust;—who were generally to look to it that in all contracts between man and
man for the supply of man's necessities, what we call
honesty of dealing should be truly and faithfully observed.
An organization for this purpose did once really exist in
England,[2] really trying to do the work which it was intended to do, as half the pages of our early statutes
witness. In London, as the metropolis, a central council
sate for every branch of trade, and this council was in
communication with the Chancellor and the Crown. It
was composed of the highest and most respectable members
of the profession, and its office was to determine prices,

---

[1] It has been objected that inasmuch as the Statute Book gives
evidence of extensive practices of adulteration, the guild system was
useless, nay, it has been even said that it was the cause of the evil.
Cessante causâ cessat effectus;—when the companies lost their authority, the adulteration ought to have ceased, which in the face of recent
exposures will be scarcely maintained. It would be as reasonable to
say that the police are useless because we have still burglars and
pickpockets among us.

[2] And not in England alone, but throughout Europe.

fix wages, arrange the rules of apprenticeship, and discuss all details connected with the business on which legislation might be required. Further, this council received the reports of the searchers—high officers taken from their own body, whose business was to inspect, in company with the lord mayor or some other city dignitary, the shops of the respective traders; to receive complaints, and to examine into them. In each provincial town local councils sate in connexion with the municipal authorities, who fulfilled in these places the same duties; and their reports being forwarded to the central body, and considered by them, representations on all necessary matters were then made to the privy council; and by the privy council, if requisite, were submitted to parliament. If these representations were judged to require legislative interference, the statutes which were passed in consequence were returned through the Chancellor to the mayors of the various towns and cities, by whom they were proclaimed as law. No person was allowed to open a trade or to commence a manufacture, either in London or the provinces, unless he had first served his apprenticeship; unless he could prove to the satisfaction of the authorities that he was competent in his craft; and unless he submitted as a matter of course to their supervision. The legislature had undertaken not to let that indispensable task go wholly unattempted, of distributing the various functions of society by the rule of capacity; of compelling every man to do his duty in an honest following of his proper calling, securing to him that he in his turn should not be injured by his neighbour's misdoings.

The state further promising for itself that all able-bodied men should be found in work,[1] and not allowing any man to work at a business for which he was unfit, insisted as its natural right that children should not be allowed to grow up in idleness, to be returned at mature age upon its hands. Every child, so far as possible, was to be trained up in some business or calling,[2] idleness 'being the mother of all sin,' and the essential duty of every man being to provide honestly for himself and his family. The educative theory, for such it was, was simple but effective: it was based on the single principle that, next to the knowledge of a man's duty to God, and as a means towards doing that duty, the first condition of a worthy life was the ability to maintain it in independence. Varieties of inapplicable knowledge might be good, but

---

[1] 27 Hen. VIII. cap. 25.   [2] Ibid.

they were not essential; such knowledge might be left to the leisure of after years, or it might be dispensed with without vital injury. Ability to labour could not be dispensed with, and this, therefore, the state felt it to be its own duty to see provided; so reaching, I cannot but think, the heart of the whole matter. The children of those who could afford the small entrance fees were apprenticed to trades, the rest were apprenticed to agriculture; and if children were found growing up idle, and their fathers or their friends failed to prove that they were able to secure them an ultimate maintenance, the mayors in towns and the magistrates in the country had authority to take possession of such children, and apprentice them as they saw fit, that when they grew up 'they might not be driven' by want or incapacity 'to dishonest courses.'[1]

Such is an outline of the organization of English society under the Plantagenets and Tudors. A detail of the working of the trade laws would be beyond my present purpose. It is obvious that such laws could be enforced only under circumstances when production and population remained (as I said before) nearly stationary; and it would be madness to attempt to apply them to the changed condition of the present. It would be well if some competent person would make these laws the subject of a special treatise. I will run the risk, however, of wearying the reader with two or three illustrative statutes, which I have chosen, not as being more significant than many others, but as specimens merely of the discipline under which, for centuries, the trade and manufactures of England contrived to move; showing on one side the good which the system effected, on the other the inevitable evils under which it finally sank.

The first which I shall quote concerns simply the sale of specific goods and the means by which tradesmen were prevented from enhancing prices. The Act is the 6th of the 24th of Henry VIII., and concerns the sale of wines, the statute prices of which I have already mentioned.

'Because,' says this Act, 'that divers merchants inhabiting within the city of London have of late not only presumed to bargain and sell in gross to divers of the king's subjects great quantities of wines of Gascony, Guienne, and French wines, some for five pounds per tonne, some for more and some for less, and so after the

---

[1] 27 Hen. VIII. cap. 25.

rate of excessive prices contrary to the effect of a good and laudable statute lately made in this present parliament; that is to say, contrary to and above the prices thereof set by the Right Honourable the Lord Chancellor, Lord Treasurer, Lord President of the King's most honourable Council, Lord Privy Seal, and the two Chief Justices of either bench, whereby they be fallen into the penalties limited by the said statute; as by due proof made by examination taken is well known—but also having in their hands great abundance of wine, by them acquired and bought to be sold, obstinately and maliciously, since their said attemptate and defaults proved, have refused to bargain and sell to many of the king's subjects any of their said wines remaining and being in their hands; purposing and intending thereby their own singular and unreasonable lucres and profits, to have larger and higher prices of their said wines, to be set according to their insatiable appetites and minds; it is therefore ordained and enacted, by authority of this present parliament, that every merchant now having, or which shall hereafter have, wines to be sold, and refusing to sell or deliver, or not selling and delivering any of the said wines for ready money therefore to be paid, according to the price or prices thereof being set, shall forfeit and lose the value of the wine so required to be bought. . . . For due execution of which provision, and for the relief of the king's subjects, it shall be lawful to all and singular justices of the peace, mayors, bailiffs, and other head officers in shires, cities, boroughs, towns, &c., at the request of any person to whom the said merchant or merchants have refused to sell, to enter into the cellars and other places where such wines shall lie or be, and to sell and deliver the same wine or wines desired to be bought to the person or persons requiring to buy the same; taking of the buyer of the wine so sold to the use and satisfaction of the proprietor aforesaid, according to the prices determined by the law.'

The next which I select is the eleventh of the second and third of Philip and Mary; and falling in the midst of the smoke of the Smithfield fires, and the cruelties of that melancholy time, it shines like a fair gleam of humanity, which will not lose anything of its lustre because the evils against which it contends have in our times, also, furnished matter for sorrow and calamity—calamity which we unhappily have been unable even to attempt to remedy. It is termed 'An Act touching Weavers,' and runs:

'Forasmuch as the weavers of this realm have, as well at this present parliament as at divers other times, complained that the rich and wealthy clothiers do in many ways oppress them—some by setting up and keeping in their houses divers looms, and keeping and maintaining them by journeymen and persons unskilful, to the decay of a great number of artificers which were brought up in the said science of weaving, with their families and their households—some by engrossing of looms into their hands and possession, and letting them out at such unreasonable rents, as the poor artificers are not able to maintain themselves, much less to maintain their wives, families, and children—some also by giving much less wages and hire for weaving and workmanship than in times past they did, whereby they are enforced utterly to forsake their art and occupation wherein they have been brought up; It is, therefore, for remedy of the premises, and for the avoiding of a great number of inconveniences which may grow if in time it be not foreseen, ordained and enacted by authority of this present parliament, that no person using the feat or mystery of cloth-making, and dwelling out of a city, borough, market-town, or corporate town, shall keep, or retain, or have in his or their houses or possession, any more than one woollen loom at a time; nor shall by any means, directly or indirectly, receive or take any manner of profit, gain, or commodity, by letting or setting any loom, or any house wherein any loom is or shall be used or occupied, which shall be together by him set or let, upon pain of forfeiture for every week that any person shall do the contrary to the tenor and true meaning hereof, twenty shillings.'

A provision then follows, limiting weavers living in towns to two looms—the plain intention being to prevent the cloth manufacture from falling into the power of large capitalists employing 'hands;' and to enable as many persons as possible to earn all in their own homes their own separate independent living. I suppose that the parliament was aware that by pursuing this policy, the cost of production was something increased; that cloth was thus made dearer than it would have been if trade had been left to follow its own course. It considered, however, that the loss was compensated to the nation by retaining its people in the condition not of 'hands,' but of men; by rendering them independent of masters, who only sought to make their own advantage at the expense of labour; and enabling them to continue to maintain themselves in manly freedom. The weak point of all such provisions did not lie, I think, in the economic aspect of them, but in a far deeper difficulty. The details of trade legislation, it is obvious, could only be determined by persons professionally conversant with those details; and the indispensable condition of success with such legislation is, that it be conducted under the highest sense of the obligations of honesty. No laws are of any service which are above the working level of public morality; and the deeper they are carried down into life, the larger become the opportunities of evasion. That the system succeeded for centuries is evident from the organization of the companies remaining so long in its vitality; but the efficiency of this organization for the maintenance of fair dealing could exist only so long as the companies themselves—their wardens and their other officials, who alone, *quisque in suâ arte*, were competent to judge what was right and what was wrong, could be trusted, at the same time being interested parties, to give a disinterested judgment. The largeness of the power inevitably committed to the councils was at once a temptation and an opportunity to abuse those powers; and slowly through the statute book we find the traces of the poison as it crept in and in. Already in the 24th of Henry VIII., we meet with complaints in the leather trade of the fraudulent conduct of the searchers, whose duty was to affix their seal upon leather ascertained to be sound, before it was exposed for sale, 'which mark or print, for corruption and lucre, is commonly set and put by such as take upon them the search and sealing, as well upon leather insufficiently tanned, as upon leather well tanned, to the great deceit of the buyers thereof.' About the same time, the 'craft wardens' of the various fellowships, 'out of sinister mind and purpose,' were levying excessive fees on the admission of apprentices; and when parliament interfered to bring them to order, they 'compassed and practised by cautill and subtle means to delude the good and wholesome statutes passed for remedy.'[1] The old proverb, *Quis custodiat custodes*, had begun to verify itself, and the symptom was a fatal one. These evils, for the first half of the century, remained within compass; but as we pass on we find them increasing steadily. In the 7th and the 8th of Elizabeth, there are indications of the truck system; and towards her later years, the multiplying statutes and growing complaints and difficulties show plainly that the companies had lost their healthy

---

[1] 22 Hen. VIII. cap. 4; 28 Hen. VIII. cap. 5.

vitality, and, with other relics of feudalism, were fast taking themselves away. There were no longer tradesmen to be found in sufficient numbers who were possessed of the necessary probity; and it is impossible not to connect such a phenomenon with the deep melancholy which in those years settled down on Elizabeth herself.

For, indeed, a change was coming upon the world, the meaning and direction of which even still is hidden from us, a change from era to era. The paths trodden by the footsteps of ages were broken up; old things were passing away, and the faith and the life of ten centuries were dissolving like a dream. Chivalry was dying; the abbey and the castle were soon together to crumble into ruins; and all the forms, desires, beliefs, convictions of the old world were passing away, never to return. A new continent had risen up beyond the western sea. The floor of heaven, inlaid with stars, had sunk back into an infinite abyss of immeasurable space; and the firm earth itself, unfixed from its foundations, was seen to be but a small atom in the awful vastness of the universe. In the fabric of habit in which they had so laboriously built for themselves, mankind were to remain no longer.

And now it is all gone—like an unsubstantial pageant faded; and between us and the old English there lies a gulf of mystery which the prose of the historian will never adequately bridge. They cannot come to us, and our imagination can but feebly penetrate to them. Only among the aisles of the cathedrals, only as we gaze upon their silent figures sleeping on their tombs, some faint conceptions float before us of what these men were when they were alive; and perhaps in the sound of church bells, that peculiar creation of mediæval age, which falls upon the ear like the echo of a vanished world.

The transition out of this old state is what in this book I have undertaken to relate. As yet there were uneasy workings below the surface; but the crust was unbroken, and the nation remained outwardly unchanged as it had been for centuries. I have still some few features to add to my description.

Nothing, I think, proves more surely the mutual confidence which held together the government and the people, than the fact that all classes were armed. Every man, as I have already said, was a soldier; and every man was ready equipped at all times with the arms which corresponded to his rank. By the great statute of Winchester,[1] which was repeated and expanded on many oc-

_____
[1] *Statut. Winton.* 13 Edw. I. cap. 6.

casions in the after reigns, it was enacted, 'That every
man have harness in his house to keep the peace after
the antient assise—that is to say, every man between fifteen years of age and sixty years shall be assessed and
sworn to armour according to the quantity of his lands
and goods—that is, to wit, for fifteen pounds lands and
forty marks goods, a hauberke, a helmet of iron, a sword,
a dagger, and a horse. For ten pounds of lands and
twenty marks goods, a hauberke, a helmet, a sword, and
a dagger. For five pounds lands, a doublet, a helmet of
iron, a sword, and a dagger. For forty shillings lands, a
sword, a bow and arrows, and a dagger. And all others
that may shall have bows and arrows. Review of armour
shall be made every year two times, by two constables
for every hundred and franchise thereunto appointed; and
the constables shall present, to justices assigned for that
purpose, such defaults as they do find.'

As the archery was more developed, and the bow became the peculiar weapon of the English, regular practice
was ordered, and shooting became at once the drill and
the amusement of the people. Every hamlet had its pair
of butts; and on Sundays and holidays[1] all able-bodied
men were required to appear in the field, to employ their
leisure hours 'as valyant Englishmen ought to do,' 'utterly leaving the play at the bowls, quoits, dice, knils,
and other unthrifty games;' magistrates, mayors, and
bailiffs being responsible for their obedience, under penalty, if these officers neglected their duty, of a fine of
twenty shillings for each offence. On the same days, the
tilt-yard at the Hall or Castle was thrown open, and the
young men of rank amused themselves with similar exer-
cises. Fighting, or mock fighting—and the imitation was
not unlike the reality—was at once the highest enjoyment
and the noblest accomplishment of all ranks in the state;
and over that most terrible of human occupations they
had flung the enchanted halo of chivalry, decorating it
with all the fairest graces, and consecrating it with the
most heroic aspirations.

The chivalry, with much else, was often perhaps something ideal. In the wars of the Roses it had turned into
mere savage ferocity; and in forty years of carnage the
fighting propensities had glutted themselves. A reaction
followed, and in the early years of Henry VIII. the statutes were growing obsolete, and 'the unlawful games'
rising again into favour. The younger nobles, or some

---

[1] 12 Rich. II. cap. 6: 11 Hen. IV. cap. 4.

among them, were shrinking from the tilt-yard, and were backward on occasions even when required for war. Lord Surrey, when waiting on the Border, expecting the Duke of Albany to invade the northern counties, in 1523, complained of the growing 'slowness' of the young lords 'to be at such journeys,'[1] and of their 'inclination to dancing, carding, and dicing.' The people had followed the example, and were falling out of archery practice, exchanging it for similar amusements. Henry VIII., in his earlier days an Englishman after the old type, set himself resolutely to oppose these downward tendencies, and to brace again the slackened sinews of the nation. In his own person he was the best rider, the best lance, and the best archer in England; and while a boy he was dreaming of fresh Agincourts, and even of fresh crusades. In 1511, when he had been king only three years, parliament re-enacted the Winchester statute, with new and remarkable provisions; and twice subsequently in the course of his reign he returned back upon the subject, insisting upon it with increasing stringency. The language of the Act of 1511 is not a little striking. 'The King's Highness,' so the words run, 'calling to his gracious remembrance that by the feats and exercise of the subjects of his realm in shooting in long bows, there had continually grown and been within the same great numbers and multitudes of good archers, which hath not only defended the realm and the subjects thereof against the cruel malice and dangers of their enemies in times heretofore past, but also, with little numbers and puissance in regard of their opposites, have done many notable acts and discomfitures of war against the infidels and others; and furthermore reduced divers regions and countries to their due obeysance, to the great honour, fame, and surety of this realm and subjects, and to the terrible dread and fear of all strange nations, anything to attempt or do to the hurt or damage of them: Yet nevertheless that archery and shooting in long bows is but little used, but daily does minish and decay, and abate more and more; for that much part of the commonalty and poor people of this realm, whereby of old time the great number and substance of archers had grown and multiplied, be not of power nor ability to buy them long bows of yew to exercise shooting in the same, and to sustain the continual charge thereof; and also because, by means and occasions of customable usage of tennis play, bowles,

---

[1] ELLIS's *Original Letters*, first series, vol. i. p. 226.

claish, and other unlawful games, prohibited by many good and beneficent statutes, much impoverishment hath ensued: Wherefore, the King's Highness, of his great wisdom and providence, and also for zeal to the public weal, surety, and defence of this his realm, and the antient fame in this behalf to be revived, by the assent of his Lords Spiritual and Temporal, and his Commons, in this present parliament assembled, hath enacted and established that the statute of Winchester for archers be put in due execution; and over that, that every man being the king's subject, not lame, decrepit, or maimed, being within the age of sixty years, except spiritual men, justices of the one bench and of the other, justices of the assize, and barons of the exchequer, do use and exercise shooting in long bows, and also do have a bow and arrows ready continually in his house, to use himself in shooting, And that every man having a man child or men children in his house, shall provide for all such, being of the age of seven years and above, and till they shall come to the age of seventeen years, a bow and two shafts, to learn them and bring them up in shooting; and after such young men shall come to the age of seventeen years, every of them shall provide and have a bow and four arrows continually for himself, at his proper costs and charges, or else of the gift and provision of his friends, and shall use the same as afore is rehearsed.' Other provisions are added, designed to suppress the games complained of, and to place the bows more within the reach of the poor, by cheapening the prices of them.

The same statute[1] (and if this be a proof that it had imperfectly succeeded. it is a proof also of Henry's confidence in the general attachment of his subjects) was re-enacted thirty years later, at the crisis of the Reformation, when the northern counties were fermenting in a half-suppressed rebellion, and the catholics at home and abroad were intriguing to bring about a revolution. In this subsequent edition of it[2] some particulars are added which demand notice. In the directions to the villages for the maintaining each 'a pair of buttes,' it is ordered that no person above the age of twenty-four shall shoot

---

[1] It has been stated again and again that the policy of Henry the Eighth was to make the crown despotic by destroying the remnants of the feudal power of the nobility. How is such a theory to be reconciled with statutes the only object of which was the arming and training of the country population, whose natural leaders were the peers. knights, and gentlemen? We have heard too much of this random declamation.

[2] 33 Hen. VIII. cap. 9.

with the light flight arrow at a distance under two hundred and twenty yards. Up to two hundred and twenty yards, therefore, the heavy war arrow was used, and this is to be taken as the effective range for fighting purposes of the old archery.[1] No measures could have been invented more effective than this vigorous arming to repress the self-seeking tendencies in the mercantile classes which I have mentioned as beginning to show themselves. Capital supported by force may make its own terms with labour; but capital lying between a king on one side resolved to prevent oppression, and a people on the other side in full condition to resist, felt even prudence dictate moderation, and reserved itself for a more convenient season.

Looking, therefore, at the state of England as a whole, I cannot doubt that under Henry the body of the people were prosperous, well-fed, loyal, and contented. In all points of material comfort they were as well off as they had ever been before; better off than they have ever been in later times.

Their amusements, as prescribed by statute, consisted in training themselves as soldiers. In the prohibitions of the statutes we see also what their amusements were inclined to be. But besides 'the bowles and the claish,' field sports, fishing, shooting, hunting, were the delight of every one, and although the forest laws were terrible, they served only to enhance the excitement by danger. Then, as now, no English peasant could be convinced that there was any moral crime in appropriating the wild game. It was an offence against statute law, but no offence against natural law; and it was rather a trial of skill between the noble who sought to monopolize a right which seemed to be common to all, and those who would succeed, if they could, in securing their own share of it. The Robin Hood ballads reflect the popular feeling

[1] From my experience of modern archery I found difficulty in believing that these figures were accurately given. Few living men could send the lightest arrow 220 yards, even with the greatest elevation, and for effective use it must be delivered nearly point blank. A passage in HOLLINSHED's *Description of Britain*, however, prevents me from doubting that the words of the statute are correct. In his own time, he says that the strength of the English archers had so notoriously declined that the French soldiers were in the habit of disrespectfully turning their backs, at long range, 'bidding them shoot.' whereas, says Hollinshed, 'had the archers been what they were wont to be, these fellows would have had their breeches nailed unto their buttocks.' In an order for bowstaves, in the reign of Henry the Eighth, I find this direction: 'Each bowstave ought to be *three fingers thick* and squared, and *seven feet long;* to be got up well polished and without knots.'—Butler to Bullinger: *Zurich Letters.*

and breathe the warm genial spirit of the old greenwood adventurers. If deer stealing was a sin, it was more than compensated by the risk of the penalty to which those who failed submitted, when no other choice was left. They did not always submit, as the old northern poem shows of *Adam Bell, Clym of the Clough, and William of Cloudislee,* with its most immoral moral; yet I suppose there was never pedant who could resist the spell of those ringing lines, or refuse with all his heart to wish the rogues success, and confusion to the honest men.

But the English peasantry had pleasures of less ambiguous propriety, and less likely to mislead our sympathies. The chroniclers have given us many accounts of the masques and plays which were acted in the court, or in the castles of the noblemen. Such pageants were but the most splendid expression of a taste which was national and universal. As in ancient Greece, generations before the rise of the great dramas of Athens, itinerant companies wandered from village to village, carrying their stage furniture in their little carts, and acted in their booths and tents the grand stories of the mythology; so in England the mystery players haunted the wakes and fairs, and in barns or taverns, taprooms, or in the farm-house kitchen, played at saints and angels, and transacted on their petty stage the entire drama of the Christian faith. To us, who can measure the effect of such scenes only by the impression which they would now produce upon ourselves, these exhibitions can seem but unspeakably profane: they were not profane when tendered in simplicity, and received as they were given. They were no more profane than those quaint monastic illuminations which formed the germ of Italian art; and as out of the illuminations arose those paintings which remain unapproached and unapproachable in their excellence, so out of the mystery plays arose the English drama, represented in its final completeness by the creations of a poet who, it now begins to be supposed, stands alone among mankind. We allow ourselves to think of Shakspeare or of Raphael or of Phidias, as having accomplished their work by the power of their own individual genius; but greatness like theirs is never more than the highest degree of an excellence which prevails widely round it, and forms the environment in which it grows. No single mind in single contact with the facts of nature could have created out of itself a Pallas, a Madonna, or a Lear; such vast conceptions are the growth of ages, the creations of a nation's spirit; and artist and poet, filled full with the power of that spirit, have but given them form, and nothing more than form. Nor would the form itself have been attainable by any isolated talent. No genius can dispense with experience; the aberrations of power, unguided or ill-guided, are ever in proportion to its intensity, and life is not long enough to recover from inevitable mistakes. Noble conceptions already existing, and a noble school of execution which will launch mind and hand at once upon their true courses, are indispensable to transcendent excellence; and Shakspeare's plays were as much the offspring of the long generations who had pioneered his road for him, as the discoveries of Newton were the offspring of those of Copernicus.

No great general ever arose out of a nation of cowards; no great statesman or philosopher out of a nation of fools; no great artist out of a nation of materialists; no great dramatist except when the drama was the passion of the people. Acting was the especial amusement of the English, from the palace to the village green. It was the result and expression of their strong tranquil possession of their lives, of their thorough power over themselves, and power over circumstances. They were troubled with no subjective speculations; no social problems vexed them with which they were unable to deal; and in the exuberance of vigour and spirits they were able, in the strict and literal sense of the word, to play with the materials of life. The mystery plays came first; next the popular legends; and then the great figures of English history came out upon the stage, or stories from Greek and Roman writers; or sometimes it was an extemporized allegory. Shakspeare himself has left us many pictures of the village drama. Doubtless he had seen many a Bottom in the old Warwickshire hamlets; many a Sir Nathaniel playing 'Alissander' and finding himself 'a little o'erparted.' He had been with Snug the joiner, Quince the carpenter, and Flute the bellows-mender, when a boy, we will not question, and acted with them, and written their parts for them; had gone up with them in the winter's evenings to the Lucys' Hall, before the sad trouble with the deer-stealing; and afterwards, when he came to London and found his way into great society, he had not failed to see Polonius burlesquing Cæsar on the stage, as in his proper person Polonius burlesqued Sir William Cecil. The strolling players in *Hamlet* might be met at every country wake or festival; it was the direction in which the especial genius of the people delighted to revel. As I desire in this chapter not only to relate what were the habits of the people, but to illustrate them also, within such compass as I can allow myself, I shall transcribe out of Hall[1] a description of a play which was acted by the boys of St. Paul's School, in 1527, at Greenwich, adding some particulars, not mentioned by Hall, from another source.[2] It is a good instance of the fantastic splendour with which exhibitions of this kind were got up, and it possesses also a melancholy interest of another kind, as showing how little the wisest among us can foresee our own actions, or assure ourselves that the convictions of to-day will alike be the convictions of to-morrow. The occasion was the despatch of a French embassy to England, when Europe was outraged by the Duke of Bourbon's capture of Rome, when the children of Francis I. were prisoners in Spain, and Henry, with the full energy of his fiery nature, was flinging himself into a quarrel with Charles V. as the champion of the Holy See.

At the conclusion of a magnificent supper 'the king led the ambassadors into the great chamber of disguisings; and in the end of the same chamber was a fountain, and on one side was a hawthorne tree, all of silk, with white flowers, and on the other side was a mulberry tree full of fair berries, all of silk. On the top of the hawthorne was the arms of England, compassed with the collar of the order[3] of St. Michael, and in the top of the mulberry tree stood the arms of France within a garter. The fountain was all of white marble, graven and chased; the bases of the same were balls of gold, supported by ramping beasts wound in leaves of gold. In the first work were gargoylles of gold, fiercely faced with spouts running. The second receit of this fountain was environed with winged serpents, all of gold, which griped it; and on the summit of the same was a fair lady, out of whose breasts ran abundantly water of marvellous delicious savour. About this fountain were benches of rosemary, fretted in braydes laid on gold, all the sides set with roses, on branches as they were growing about this fountain. On the benches sate eight fair ladies in strange attire, and so richly apparelled in cloth of gold, embroidered and cut over silver, that I cannot express the cunning workmanship thereof. Then when the king and queen were set there was played before them, by children, in the

---

[1] Page 735, quarto edition.

[2] The Personages, Dresses, and Properties of a Mystery Play, acted at Greenwich, by command of Henry VIII. *Rolls House MS.*

[3] Hall says, 'collar of the *garter* of St. Michael,' which, however, I venture to correct.

Latin tongue, a manner of tragedy, the effect whereof
was that the pope was in captivity and the church brought
under foot. Whereupon St. Peter appeared and put the
cardinal (Wolsey) in authority to bring the pope to his
liberty, and to set up the church again. And so the cardinal made intercession with the kings of England and
France that they took part together, and by their means
the pope was delivered. Then in came the French king's
children, and complained to the cardinal how the emperour
kept them as hostages, and would not come to reasonable
point with their father, whereupon they desired the cardinal to help for their deliverance; which wrought so with
the king his master and the French king that he brought
the emperour to a peace, and caused the two young
princes to be delivered.' So far Hall relates the scene,
but there was more in the play than he remembered or
cared to notice, and I am able to complete this curious
picture of a pageant once really and truly a living spectacle in the old palace at Greenwich, by an inventory of
the dresses worn by the boys and a list of the dramatis
personæ.

The school-boys of St. Paul's were taken down the
river with the master in six boats, at the cost of a shilling a boat—the cost of the dresses and the other expenses amounting in all to sixty-one shillings.

The characters were—

An orator in apparel of cloth of gold.

Religio, Ecclesia, Veritas, like three widows, in gar-
ments of silk, and suits of lawn and cypress.

Heresy and False Interpretation, like sisters of Bohemia,
apparelled in silk of divers colours.

The heretic Luther, like a party friar, in russet damask and black taffety.

Luther's wife, like a frow of Spiers in Almayn, in
red silk.

Peter, Paul, and James, in habits of white sarsnet,
and three red mantles, and lace of silver and damask,
and pelisses of scarlet.

A Cardinal in his apparel.

Two Sergeants in rich apparel.

The Dolphin and his brother in coats of velvet
embroidered with gold, and capes of satin bound with
velvet.

A Messenger in tinsel satin.

Six men in gowns of grey sarsnet.

Six women in gowns of crimson velvet.

War, in rich cloth of gold and feathers, armed.

Three Almeyns, in apparel all cut and holed in silk.
Lady Peace in lady's apparel white and rich.
Lady Quietness and Dame Tranquillity richly beseen
in lady's apparel.

It is a strange world. This was in November, 1527.
In November, 1530, but three brief years after, Wolsey
lay dying in misery, a disgraced man, at Leicester Abbey;
'the Pope's Holiness' was fast becoming in English eyes
plain Bishop of Rome, held guilty towards this realm of
unnumbered enormities, and all England was sweeping
with immeasurable velocity towards the heretic Luther.
So history repeats the lesson to us, not to boast ourselves of the morrow, for we know not what a day may
bring forth.

Before I conclude this survey, it remains for me to
say something of the position of the poor, and of the
measures which were taken for the solution of that most
difficult of all problems, the distinguishing the truly deserving from the worthless and the vagaboud. The subject is one to which in the progress of this work I shall
have more than one occasion to return; but inasmuch as
a sentimental opinion prevails that an increase of poverty
and the consequent enactment of poor-laws was the result
of the suppression of the religious houses, and that adequate relief had been previously furnished by these establishments, it is necessary to say a few words for the
removal of an impression which is as near as possible the
reverse of the truth. I do not doubt that for many centuries these houses fulfilled honestly the intentions with
which they were established; but as early as the reign of
Richard II. it was found necessary to provide some other
means for the support of the aged and impotent; the
monasteries not only having then begun to neglect their
duty; but by the appropriation of benefices having actually
deprived the parishes of their local and independent means
of charity.[1] Licences to beg were at that time granted
to deserving persons; and it is noticeable that this measure
was in a few years followed by the petition to Henry IV.
for the secularization of ecclesiastical property.[2] Thus
early in our history had the regular clergy forgotten the
nature of their mission, and the object for which the administration of the nation's charities had been committed
to them. Thus early, while their houses were the nurseries

---

[1] Rich. II. 12, cap. 7, 8, 9; Rich. II. 15, cap. 6.
[2] *Bib. Lansd.* I, fol. 26.

of dishonest mendicancy,[1] they had surrendered to lay compassion, those who ought to have been their especial care. I shall unhappily have occasion hereafter to illustrate these matters in detail. I mention them in this place only in order to dissipate at once a foolish dream. At the opening of the sixteenth century, before the suppression of the monasteries had suggested itself in a practical form, pauperism was a state question of great difficulty, and as such I have at present to consider it.

For the able-bodied vagrant, it is well known that the old English laws had no mercy. When wages are low, and population has outgrown the work which can be provided for it, idleness may be involuntary and innocent; at a time when all industrious men could maintain themselves in comfort and prosperity, 'when a fair day's wages for a fair day's work' was really and truly the law of the land, it was presumed that if strong capable men preferred to wander about the country, and live upon the labour of others, mendicancy was not the only crime of which they were likely to be guilty; while idleness itself was justly looked upon as a high offence and misdemeanour. The penalty of God's laws against idleness, as expressed in the system of nature, was starvation; and it was held intolerable that any man should be allowed to escape a divine judgment by begging under false pretences, and robbing others of their honest earnings.

In a country also the boast of which was its open-handed hospitality, it was necessary to take care that hospitality was not brought to discredit by abuse; and when every door was freely opened to a request for a meal or a night's lodging, there was an imperative duty to keep a strict eye on whatever persons were on the move. We shall therefore be prepared to find 'sturdy and valiant beggars' treated with summary justice as criminals of a high order; the right of a government so to treat them being proportioned to the facilities with which the honestly disposed can maintain themselves. It might have been expected, also, that when wages were so high, and work so constant, labourers would have been left to themselves to make provision against sickness and old age. To modern ways of thinking on these subjects, there would have seemed no hardship in so leaving them; and their sufferings, if they had suffered, would have appeared but as a deserved retribution. This, however, was not the temper of earlier times. Charity has ever been the

---

[1] Injunctions to the Monasteries: BURNET's *Collect.* pp. 77-8.

especial virtue of Catholic States, and the aged and the impotent were always held to be the legitimate objects of it. Men who had worked hard while they were able to work were treated like decayed soldiers, as the discharged pensionaries of society; they were held entitled to wear out their age (under restrictions) at the expense of others; and so readily did society acquiesce in this aspect of its obligations, that on the failure of the monasteries to do their duty, it was still sufficient to leave such persons to voluntary liberality, and legislation had to interfere only to direct such liberality into its legitimate channels. In the 23rd of Edw. III. cap. 7, a prohibition was issued against giving alms to 'valiant beggars,' and this proving inadequate, and charity being still given indiscriminately, in the twelfth year of Richard II. the system of licences was introduced, and a pair of stocks were erected by order in every town or village, to 'justify' persons begging unpermitted. The monasteries growing more and more careless, the number of paupers continued to multiply, and this method received successive expansions, till at length, when the Reformation was concluded, it terminated, after many changes of form, in the famous Act of Elizabeth. We can thus trace our poor law in the whole course of its growth, and into two stages through which it passed I must enter with some minuteness. The 12th of the 22nd of Henry VIII., and the 25th of the 27th, are so remarkable in their tone, and so rich in their detail, as to furnish a complete exposition of English thought at that time upon the subject; while the second of these two acts, and probably the first also, has a further interest for us, as being the composition of Henry himself, and the most finished which he has left to us.[1]

'Whereas,' says the former of these two Acts, 'in all places throughout this realm of England, vagabonds and beggars have of long time increased, and daily do increase in great and excessive numbers, by the occasion of idleness, mother and root of all vices; whereby hath insurged and sprung, and daily insurgeth and springeth, continual thefts, murders, and other heinous offences and great enormities, to the high displeasure of God, the inquietation and damage of the king's people, and to the marvellous disturbance of the common weal of this realm; and whereas, strait statutes and ordinances have been before this time devised and made, as well by the king our sovereign lord, as also by divers his most noble progenitors, kings of

---

[1] Letter of Thomas Dorset to the Mayor of Plymouth: *Suppression of the Monasteries*, p. 36.

England, for the most necessary and due reformation of the premises; yet that notwithstanding, the said number of vagabonds and beggars be not seen in any part to be diminished, but rather daily augmented and increased into great routs or companies, as evidently and manifestly it doth and may appear: Be it therefore enacted by the king, our sovereign lord, and by the Lords Spiritual and Temporal, and the Commons, in this present parliament assembled, that the justices of the peace of all and singular shires of England within the limits of their commission, and all other justices of the peace, mayors, sheriffs, bailiffs, and other officers of every city, borough, or franchise, shall from time to time, as often as need shall require, make diligent search and inquiry of all aged, poor, and impotent persons, which live, or of necessity be compelled to live by alms of the charity of the people; and such search made, the said officers, every of them within the limits of their authorities, shall have power, at their discretions, to enable to beg within such limits as they shall appoint, such of the said impotent persons as they shall think convenient; and to give in commandment to every such impotent beggar (by them enabled) that none of them shall beg without the limits so appointed to them. And further, they shall deliver to every such person so enabled a letter containing the name of that person, witnessing that he is authorized to beg, and the limits within which he is appointed to beg, the same letter to be sealed with the seal of the hundred, rape, wapentake, city, or borough, and subscribed with the name of one of the said justices or officers aforesaid. And if any such impotent person do beg in any other place than within such limits, then the justices of the peace, and all other the king's officers and ministers, shall by their discretions punish all such persons by imprisonment in the stocks, by the space of two days and two nights, giving them only bread and water.'

Further, 'If any such impotent person be found begging without a licence, at the discretion of the justices of the peace, he shall be stripped naked from the middle upwards, and whipped within the town in which he be found, or within some other town, as it shall seem good. Or if it be not convenient so to punish him, he shall be set in the stocks by the space of three days and three nights.'

Such were the restrictions under which impotency was allowed support. Though not in itself treated as an offence, and though its right to maintenance by society

was not denied, it was not indulged, as we may see, with
unnecessary encouragement. The Act then proceeds to
deal with the genuine vagrant.

'And be it further enacted, that if any person or persons, being whole and mighty in body and able to labour,
be taken in begging in any part of this realm; and if any
man or woman, being whole and mighty in body, having
no land, nor master, nor using any lawful merchandry,
craft, or mystery whereby he might get his living, be
vagrant, and can give none account how he doth lawfully
get his living, then it shall be lawful to the constables
and all other king's officers, ministers, and subjects of
every town, parish, and hamlet, to arrest the said vagabonds and idle persons, and bring them to any justice of
the peace of the same shire or liberty, or else to the high
constable of the hundred; and the justice of the peace,
high constable, or other officer, shall cause such idle person so to him brought, to be had to the next market
town or other place, and there to be tied to the end of
a cart, naked, and be beaten with whips throughout the
same town till his body be bloody by reason of such
whipping; and after such punishment of whipping had,
the person so punished shall be enjoined upon his oath
to return forthwith without delay, in the next and straight
way, to the place where he was born, or where he last
dwelled before the same punishment, by the space of
three years; and then put himself to labour, like a true
man ought to do; and after that done, every such person
so punished and ordered shall have a letter, sealed with
the seal of the hundred, rape, or wapentake, witnessing
that he hath been punished according to this estatute, and
containing the day and place of his punishment, and the
place whereunto he is limited to go, and by what time
he is limited to come thither: for that within that time,
showing the said letter, he may lawfully beg by the way,
and otherwise not; and if he do not accomplish the order
to him appointed by the said letter, then to be eftsoons
taken and whipped; and so often as there be fault found
in him, to be whipped till he has his body put to labour
for his living, or otherwise truly get his living, so long
as he is able to do so.'

Then follow the penalties against the justices of the
peace, constables, and all officers who neglect to arrest
such persons; and a singularly curious catalogue is added
of certain forms of 'sturdy mendicancy,' which, if un-
specified, might have been passed over as exempt, but to
which Henry had no intention of conceding further licence.

It seems as if, in framing the Act, he had Simon Fish's petition before him, and was commencing at last the rough remedy of the cart's-tail, which Fish had dared to recommend for a very obdurate evil.[1] The friars of the mendicant orders were tolerated for a few years longer; but many other spiritual persons may have suffered seriously under the provisions of the present statute.

'Be it further enacted,' the Act continues, 'that scholars of the Universities of Oxford and Cambridge, that go about begging, not being authorized under the seal of the said universities, by the commissary, chancellor, or vice-chancellor of the same; and that all and singular shipmen pretending losses of their ships and goods, going about the country begging without sufficient authority, shall be punished and ordered in manner and form as is above rehearsed of strong beggars; and that all proctors and pardoners, and all other idle persons going about in countries or abiding in any town, city, or borough, some of them using divers subtle, crafty, and unlawful games and plays, and some of them feigning themselves to have knowledge in physick, physnamye, and palmistry, or other crafty science, whereby they bear the people in hand that they can tell their destinies, dreams, and fortunes, and such other like fantastical imaginations, to the great deceit of the king's subjects, shall, upon examination had before two justices of the peace, if by provable witness they be found guilty of such deceits, be punished by whipping at two days together, after the manner before rehearsed. And if they eftsoons offend in the same or any like offence, to be scourged two days, and the third day to be put upon the pillory, from nine o'clock till eleven the forenoon of the same day, and to have the right ear cut off; and if they offend the third time, to have like punishment with whipping and the pillory, and to have the other ear cut off.'

It would scarcely have been expected that this Act would have failed for want of severity in its penalties; yet five years later, for this and for some other reasons, it was thought desirable to expand the provisions of it,

[1] 'Divers of your noble predecessors, kings of this realm, have given lands to monasteries, to give a certain sum of money yearly to the poor people, whereof for the ancienty of the time they never give one penny. Wherefore, if your Grace will build to your poor bedemen a sure hospital that shall never fail, take from them these things. . . . Tie the holy idle thieves to the cart to be whipped, naked, till they fall to labour, that they, by their importunate begging take not away the alms that the good charitable people would give unto us sore, impotent, miserable people, your bedemen.'—FISH's *Supplication;* FOXE, vol. iv. p. 664.

enhancing the penalties at the same time to a degree which has given a bloody name in the history of English law to the statutes of Henry VIII. Of this expanded statute[1] we have positive evidence, as I said, that Henry was himself the author. The merit of it, or the guilt of it—if guilt there be—originated with him alone. The early clauses contain practical amendments of an undoubtedly salutary kind. The Act of 1531 had been defective in that no specified means had been assigned for finding vagrants in labour, which, with men of broken character, was not immediately easy. The smaller monasteries having been suppressed in the interval, and sufficient funds being thus placed at the disposal of the government, public works[2] were set on foot throughout the kingdom, and this difficulty was obviated.

Another important alteration was a restriction upon private charity. Private persons were forbidden, under heavy penalties, to give money to beggars, whether deserving or undeserving. The poor of each parish might call at houses within the boundaries for broken meats; but this was the limit of personal almsgiving; and the money which men might be disposed to offer was to be collected by the churchwardens on Sundays and holidays in the churches. The parish priest was to keep an account of receipts and of expenditure, and relief was administered with some approach to modern formalities. A further excellent but severe enactment empowered the parish officers to take up all idle children above the age of five years, 'and appoint them to masters of husbandry or other craft or labour to be taught;' and if any child should refuse the service to which he was appointed, or run away 'without cause reasonable being shown for it,' he might be publicly whipped with rods, at the discretion of the justice of the peace before whom he was brought.

So far, no complaint can be urged against these provisions: they display only that severe but true humanity, which, in offering fair and liberal maintenance for all who will consent to be honest, insists, not unjustly, that its offer shall be accepted, and that the resources of charity shall not be trifled away. On the clause, however, which gave to the Act its especial and distinguishing character, there will be large difference of opinion. The 'sturdy vagabond' who by the earlier statute was condemned, on

[1] 27 Hen. VIII. cap. 25.
[2] Roads, harbours, embankments, fortifications at Dover and at Berwick, &c.—STRYPE'S *Memorials*, vol. i., p. 326 and 419; and see vol. iii. of this work, pp. 254—257.

his second offence, to lose the whole or a part of his right ear, was condemned by the amended Act, if found a third time offending, with the mark upon him of his mutilation, 'to suffer pains and execution of death, as a felon and as an enemy of the commonwealth.' So the letter stands. For an able-bodied man to be caught a third time begging was held a crime deserving death, and the sentence was intended, on fit occasions, to be executed. The poor man's advantages, which I have estimated at so high a rate, were not purchased without drawbacks. He might not change his master at his will, or wander from place to place. He might not keep his children at his home unless he could answer for their time. If out of employment, preferring to be idle, he might be demanded for work by any master of the 'craft' to which he belonged, and compelled to work whether he would or no. If caught begging once, being neither aged nor infirm, he was whipped at the cart's tail. If caught a second time, his ear was slit, or bored through with a hot iron. If caught a third time, being thereby proved to be of no use upon this earth, but to live upon it only to his own hurt and to that of others, he suffered death as a felon. So the law of England remained for sixty years. First drawn by Henry, it continued unrepealed through the reigns of Edward and of Mary, subsisting, therefore, with the deliberate approval of both the great parties between whom the country was divided. Reconsidered under Elizabeth, the same law was again formally passed; and it was, therefore, the expressed conviction of the English nation, that it was better for a man not to live at all than to live a profitless and worthless life. The vagabond was a sore spot upon the commonwealth, to be healed by wholesome discipline if the gangrene was not incurable; to be cut away with the knife if the milder treatment of the cart-whip failed to be of profit.[1]

A measure so extreme in its severity was partly dictated by policy. The state of the country was critical; and the danger from questionable persons traversing it unexamined and uncontrolled was greater than at ordinary times. But in point of justice as well as of prudence, it

[1] It is to be remembered that the criminal law was checked on one side by the sanctuary system, on the other by the practice of benefit of clergy. Habit was too strong for legislation, and these privileges continued to protect criminals long after they were abolished by statute. There is abundant evidence that the execution of justice was as lax in practice as it was severe in theory. See vol. iii. of this work, chapter 16, where the subject is discussed at length. In a note will be found an account of the legend that 72,000 criminals were executed in the reign of Henry VIII.

harmonized with the iron temper of the age, and it answered well for the government of a fierce and powerful people, in whose hearts lay an intense hatred of rascality, and among whom no one need have lapsed into evil courses except by deliberate preference for them. The moral substance of the English must have been strong indeed when it admitted of such stringent treatment; but, on the whole, they were ruled as they preferred to be ruled; and if wisdom may be tested by success, the manner in which they passed the great crisis of the Reformation is the best justification of their princes. The era was great throughout Europe. The Italians of the age of Michael Angelo; the Spaniards who were the contemporaries of Cortez; the Germans who shook off the pope at the call of Luther; and the splendid chivalry of Francis I. of France, were no common men. But they were all brought face to face with the same trials, and none met them as the English met them. The English alone never lost their self-possession; and if they owed something to fortune in their escape from anarchy, they owed more to the strong hand and steady purpose of their rulers.

To conclude this chapter then.

In the brief review of the system under which England was governed, we have seen a state of things in which the principles of political economy were, consciously or unconsciously, contradicted; where an attempt, more or less successful, was made to bring the production and distribution of wealth under the moral rule of right and wrong; and where those laws of supply and demand, which we are now taught to regard as immutable ordinances of nature, were absorbed or superseded by a higher code. It is necessary for me to repeat that I am not holding up the sixteenth century as a model which the nineteenth might safely follow. The population has become too large, and employment too complicated and fluctuating, to admit of such control; while, in default of control, the relapse upon self-interest as the one motive principle is certain to ensue, and when it ensues is absolute in its operations. But as, even with us, these so-called ordinances of nature in time of war consent to be suspended, and duty to his country becomes with every good citizen a higher motive of action than the advantages which he may gain in an enemy's market; so it is not uncheering to look back upon a time when the nation was in a normal condition of militancy against social injustice; when the government was enabled by happy circumstances to pursue into detail a single and serious aim at the well-being—well-being in its widest sense—of all members of the commonwealth. There were difficulties and drawbacks at that time as well as this. Of liberty, in the modern sense of the word, of the supposed right of every man 'to do what he will with his own' or with himself, there was no idea. To the question, if ever it was asked, May I not do what I will with my own? there was the brief answer, No man may do what is wrong, either with that which is his own or with that which is another's. Workmen were not allowed to take advantage of the scantiness of the labour market to exact extravagant wages. Capitalists were not allowed to drive the labourers from their holdings, and destroy their healthy independence. The antagonism of interests was absorbed into a relation of which equity was something more than the theoretic principle, and employers and employed were alike amenable to a law which both were compelled to obey. The working man of modern times has bought the extension of his liberty at the price of his material comfort. The higher classes have gained in luxury what they have lost in power. It is not for the historian to balance advantages. His duty is with the facts.

CHAPTER II.

Times were changed in England since the second Henry walked barefoot through the streets of Canterbury, and knelt while the monks flogged him on the pavement in the Chapter-house, doing penance for Becket's murder. The clergy had won the battle then because they deserved to win it. They were not free from fault and weakness, but they felt the meaning of their profession. Their hearts were in their vows, their authority was exercised more justly, more nobly, than the authority of the crown; and therefore, with inevitable justice, the crown was compelled to stoop before them. The victory was great; but, like many victories, it was fatal to the conquerors. It filled them full with the vanity of power; they forgot their duties in their privileges; and when, a century later, the conflict recommenced, the altering issue proved the altering nature of the conditions under which it was fought. The laity were sustained in vigour by the practical obligations of life; the clergy sunk under the influence of a waning religion, the administration of the forms of which had become their sole occupation; and as character forsook them, the Mortmain Act,[1] the Acts of Premunire, and the repeatedly recurring Statutes of Provisors mark the successive defeats that drove them back from the high post of command which character alone had earned for them. If the Black Prince had lived, or if Richard II. had inherited the temper of the Plantagenets, the ecclesiastical system would have been spared the misfortune of a longer reprieve. Its worst abuses would have then terminated, and the reformation of *doctrine* in the sixteenth century

---

[1] 27 Ed. III. stat. 1; 38 Ed. III. stat. 2; 16 Rich. cap. 5.

would have been left to fight its independent way unsupported by the moral corruption of the church from which it received its most powerful impetus. The nation was ready for sweeping remedies. The people felt little loyalty to the pope, as the language of the Statutes of Provisors[1] conclusively prove, and they were prepared to risk the sacrilege of confiscating the estates of the religious houses —a complete measure of secularization being then, as I have already said, the expressed desire of the House of Commons.[2] With an Edward III. on the throne such a measure would very likely have been executed, and the course of English history would have been changed. It was ordered otherwise, and doubtless wisely. The church was allowed a hundred and fifty more years to fill full the measure of her offences, that she might fall only when time had laid bare the root of her degeneracy, and that faith and manners might be changed together.

The history of the time is too imperfect to justify a positive conclusion. It is possible, however, that the success of the revolution effected by Henry IV. was due in part to a reaction in the church's favour; and it is certain that this prince, if he did not owe his crown to the support of the church, determined to conciliate it. He confirmed the Statutes of Provisors,[3] but he allowed them to sink into disuse. He forbade the further mooting of the confiscation project; and to him is due the first permission of the bishops to—send heretics to the stake.[4] If English tradition is to be trusted, the clergy still felt insecure; and the French wars of Henry V. are said to have been undertaken, as we all know from Shakspeare, at the persuasion of Archbishop Chichele, who desired to distract his attention from reverting to dangerous subjects. Whether this be true or not, no prince of the house of Lancaster betrayed a wish to renew the quarrel with the church. The battle of Agincourt, the conquest and reconquest of France, called off the attention of the people; while the rise of the Lollards, and the intrusion of speculative questions, the agitation of which has ever been the chief aversion of English statesmen, contributed to change the current; and the reforming spirit must have lulled before the outbreak of the wars of the Roses, or one of the two parties in so desperate a struggle would have scarcely failed to have availed themselves of it. Edward IV.

---

[1] 25 Ed. III. stat. 4; stat. 5, cap. 22; 13 Rich. II. stat. 2, cap. 2; 2 Hen. IV. cap. 3; 9 Hen. IV. cap. 6.

[2] *Lansdowne MS.* 1, fol. 26; STOWE'S *Chron.* ed. 1630, p. 338.

[3] 2 Hen. IV. cap. 3; 9 Hen. IV. cap. 8.   [4] 2 Hen. IV. cap. 15.

is said to have been lenient towards heresy; but his toleration, if it was more than imaginary, was tacit only; he never ventured to avow it. It is more likely that the inveterate frenzy of those years had no leisure to remember that heresy existed.

The clergy were thus left undisturbed to go their own course to its natural end. The storm had passed over them without breaking; and they did not dream that it would again gather. The immunity which they enjoyed from the general sufferings of the civil war contributed to deceive them; and without anxiety for the consequences, and forgetting the significant warning which they had received, they sank steadily into that condition which is inevitable from the constitution of human nature, among men without faith, wealthy, powerful, and luxuriously fed, yet condemned to celibacy, and cut off from the common duties and common pleasures of ordinary life. On the return of a settled government, they were startled for a moment in their security; the conduct of some among them had become so unbearable, that even Henry VII., who inherited the Lancastrian sympathies, was compelled to notice it; and the following brief act was passed by his first parliament, proving by the very terms in which it is couched the existing nature of church discipline. 'For the more sure and likely reformation,' it runs, 'of priests, clerks, and religious men, culpable, or by their demerits openly noised of incontinent living in their bodies, contrary to their order, be it enacted, ordained, and established, that it be lawful to all archbishops and bishops, and other ordinaries having episcopal jurisdiction, to punish and chastise such religious men, being within the bounds of their jurisdiction, as shall be convict before them, by lawful proof, of adultery, fornication, incest, or other fleshly incontinency, by committing them to ward and prison, there to remain for such time as shall be thought convenient for the quality of their trespasses.'[1]

Previous to the passing of this act, therefore, the bishops, who had power to arrest laymen on suspicion of heresy, and detain them in prison untried,[2] had no power to imprison priests, even though convicted of adultery or incest. The legislature were supported by the Archbishop

---

[1] 1 Hen. VII. cap. 4. Among the miscellaneous publications of the Record Commission, there is a complaint presented during this reign, by the gentlemen and the farmers of Carnarvonshire. accusing the clergy of systematic seduction of their wives and daughters; and see a Petition of the Clergy of the Diocese of Bangor, vol. iii., chapter 16, of this work.

[2] 2 Hen. IV. cap. 15.

of Canterbury. Cardinal Morton procured authority from the pope to visit the religious houses, the abominations of which had become notorious.[1] In a provincial synod held on the 24th of February, 1486, he laid the condition of the secular clergy before the assembled prelates. Many priests, it was stated, spent their time in hawking or hunting, in lounging at taverns, in the dissolute enjoyment of the world. They wore their hair long as the laymen; they were to be seen lounging in the streets with cloak and doublet, sword and dagger. By the scandal of their lives they emperilled the stability of their order.[2] A number of the worst offenders, in London especially, were summoned before the synod and admonished;[3] certain of the more zealous among the learned (*complures docti*) who had preached against clerical abuses were advised to be more cautious, for the avoiding of scandal;[4] but the archbishop, taking the duty upon himself, sent round a circular among the clergy of his province, exhorting them to general amendment.[5]

[1] MORTON's *Register*, MS. Lambeth. See vol. ii. cap. 10, of this work for the results of Morton's investigation.

[2] MORTON's *Register;* and see WILKINS's *Concilia*, vol. iii. pp. 618—621.

[3] Quibus Dominus intimavit qualis infamia super illos in dictâ civitate crescit quod complures eorundem tabernas pandoxatorias, sive caupones indies exerceant ibidem expectando fere per totum diem. Quare Dominus consuluit et monuit eosdem quod in posterum talia dimittant, et quod dimittant suos longos crines et induantur togis non per totum apertis.

[4] The expression is remarkable. They were not to dwell on the offences of their brethren coram laicis qui semper clericis sunt infesti. —WILKINS, vol. iii. p. 618.

[5] Johannes permissione divinâ Cantuar. episcop. totius Angliæ primas cum in præsenti convocatione pie et salubriter consideratum fuit quod nonnulli sacerdotes et alii clerici ejusdem nostræ provinciæ in sacris ordinibus constituti honestatem clericalem in tantum abjecerint ac in comâ tonsurâque et superindumentis suis quæ in anteriori suf parte totaliter aperta existere dignoscuntur, sic sunt dissoluti et adeo insolescant quod inter eos et alios laicos et sæculares viros nulla vel modica comæ vel habituum sive vestimentorum distinctio esse videatur quo fiet in brevi ut a multis verisimiliter formidatur quod sicut populus ita et sacerdos erit, et nisi celeriori remedio tantæ lasciviæ ecclesiasticarum personarum quanto ocyus obviemus et clericorum mores hujusmodi maturius compescamus, *Ecclesia Anglicana quæ superioribus diebus citâ famâ et compositis moribus floruisse dignoscitur nostris temporibus quod Deus avertat, præcipitanter ruet;*

Desiring, therefore, to find some remedy for these disorders, lest the blood of those committed to him should be required at his hands, the archbishop decrees and ordains,—

Ne aliquis sacerdos vel clericus in sacris ordinibus constitutus togam gerat nisi clausam a parte anteriori et non totaliter apertam neque utatur ense nec sicâ nec zonâ aut marcipio deaurato vel auri ornatum habente. Incedent etiam omnes et singuli presbyteri et clerici ejusdem nostræ provinciæ coronas et tonsuras gerentes aures patentes ostendendo juxta canonicas sanctiones. —WILKINS, vol. iii. p. 619.

Yet this little cloud again disappeared. Henry VII. sat too insecurely on his throne to venture on a resolute reform, even if his feelings had inclined him towards it, which they did not. Morton durst not resolutely grapple with the evil. He rebuked and remonstrated; but punishment would have caused a public scandal. He would not invite the inspection of the laity into a disease which, without their assistance, he had not the strength to encounter; and his incipient reformation died away ineffectually in words. The church, to outward appearance, stood more securely than ever. The obnoxious statutes of the Plantagenets were in abeyance, their very existence, as it seemed, was forgotten; and Thomas à Becket never desired more absolute independence for the ecclesiastical order than Archbishop Warham found established when he succeeded to the primacy. He, too, ventured to repeat the experiment of his predecessor. In 1511 he attempted a second visitation of the monasteries, and again exhorted a reform; but his efforts were even slighter than Morton's, and in their results equally without fruit. The maintenance of his order in its political supremacy was of greater moment to him than its moral purity: a decent veil was cast over the clerical infirmities, and their vices were forgotten as soon. as they ceased to be proclaimed.[1] Henry VIII., a mere boy on his accession, was borne away with the prevailing stream; trained from his childhood by theologians, he entered upon his reign saturated with theological prepossessions. The intensity of his nature recognising no half measures, he was prepared to make them the law of his life; and so zealous was he, that it seemed as if the church had found in him a new Alfred or a Charlemagne. Unfortunately for the church, institutions may be restored in theory; but theory, be it never so perfect, will not give them back their life; and Henry discovered, at length, that the church of the sixteenth century as little resembled the church of the eleventh as Leo X. resembled Hildebrand, or Warham resembled St. Anselm.

If, however, there were no longer saints among the clergy, there could still arise among them a remarkable man; and in Cardinal Wolsey the king found an adviser who was able to retain him longer than would otherwise have been possible in the course which he had entered upon; who, holding a middle place between an English statesman and a catholic of the old order, was essentially a transition minister; and who was qualified, above all

---

[1] See WARHAM's *Register*, MS. Lambeth.

men then living, by a combination of talent, honesty, and arrogance, to open questions which could not again be closed when they had escaped the grasp of their originator. Under Wolsey's influence Henry made war with Louis of France, in the pope's quarrel, entered the polemic lists with Luther, and persecuted the English protestants. But Wolsey could not blind himself to the true condition of the church. He was too wise to be deceived with outward prosperity; he knew well that there lay before it, in Europe and at home, the alternative of ruin or amendment; and therefore he familiarized Henry with the sense that a reformation was inevitable; and, dreaming that it could be effected from within, by the church itself inspired with a wiser spirit, he himself fell the first victim of a convulsion which he had assisted to create, and which he attempted too late to stay.

His intended measures were approaching maturity, when all Europe was startled by the news that Rome had been stormed by the Imperial army, that the pope was imprisoned, the churches pillaged, the cardinals insulted, and all holiest things polluted and profaned. A spectator, judging only by outward symptoms, would have seen at that strange crisis in Charles V. the worst patron of heresy, and the most dangerous enemy of the Holy See; while the indignation with which the news of these outrages was received at the English court, would have taught him to look on Henry as the one sovereign in Europe on whom that See might calculate most surely for support in its hour of danger. If he could have pierced below the surface, he would have found that the pope's best friend was the prince who held him prisoner; that Henry was but doubtfully acquiescing in the policy of an unpopular minister; and that the English nation would have looked on with stoical resignation if pope and papacy had been wrecked together. They were not inclined to heresy; but the ecclesiastical system was not the catholic faith; and this system, ruined by prosperity, was fast pressing its excesses to the extreme limit, beyond which it could not be endured. Wolsey talked of reformation, but delayed its coming; and in the mean time, the persons to be reformed showed no fear that it would come at all. The monasteries grew worse and worse. The people were taught only what they could teach themselves. The consistory courts became more oppressive. Pluralities multiplied, and non-residence and profligacy. Favoured parish clergy held as many as eight benefices.[1] Bishops accumu-

[1] 21 Hen. VIII. cap. 13.

lated sees, and, unable to attend to all, attended to none.
Wolsey himself, the church reformer (so little did he really
know what a reformation meant), was at once Archbishop
of York, Bishop of Winchester, of Bath, and of Durham,
and Abbot of St. Alban's. In Latimer's opinion, even
twenty years later, and after no little reform in such
matters, there was but one bishop in all England who
was ever at his work and ever in his diocese. 'I would
ask a strange question,' he said, in an audacious sermon
at Paul's Cross, 'Who is the most diligent bishop and
prelate in all England, that passeth all the rest in doing
of his office?' I can tell, for I know him who it is; I
know him well. But now I think I see you listening and
hearkening that I should name him. There is one that
passeth all the others, and is the most diligent prelate and
preacher in all England. And will ye know who it is?
I will tell you. It is the devil. Among all the pack of
them that have cure, the devil shall go for my money,
for he applieth his business. Therefore, ye unpreaching
prelates, learn of the devil to be diligent in your office.
If ye will not learn of God, for shame learn of the devil.'[2]

Under such circumstances, we need not be surprised
to find the clergy sunk low in the respect of the English
people. Sternly intolerant of each other's faults, the laity
were not likely to be indulgent to the vices of men who

[1] Roy's *Satire against the Clergy*, written about 1528, is so plain-spoken, and goes so directly to the point of the matter, that it is difficult to find a presentable extract. The following lines on the bishops are among the most moderate in the poem:—

'What are the bishops divines—
Yea, they can best skill of wines
Better than of divinity;
Lawyers are they of experience,
And in cases against conscience
They are parfet by practice
To forge excommuuications,
For tythes and decimations
Is their continual exercise.
As for preaching they take no care,
They would rather see a course at a hare;
Rather than to make a sermon
To follow the chase of wild deer,
Passing the time with jolly cheer.
Among them all is common
To play at the cards and dice;
Some of them are nothing nice
Both at hazard and momchance;
They drink in golden bowls
The blood of poor simple souls
Perishing for lack of sustenance.
Their hungry cures they never teach,
Nor will suffer none other to preach.' &c.

[2] LATIMER'S *Sermons*, pp. 70, 71.

ought to have set an example of purity; and from time to time, during the first quarter of the century, there were explosions of temper which might have served as a warning if any sense or judgment had been left to profit by it.

In 1514 a London merchant was committed to the Lollards' Tower for refusing to submit to an unjust exaction of mortuary;[1] and a few days after was found dead in his cell. An inquest was held upon the body, when a verdict of wilful murder was returned against the chancellor of the Bishop of London; and so intense was the feeling of the city, that the bishop applied to Wolsey for a special jury to be chosen on the trial. 'For assured I am,' he said, 'that if my chancellor be tried by any twelve men in London, they be so maliciously set *in favorem hæreticæ pravitatis*, that they will cast and condemn any clerk, though he were as innocent as Abel.'[2] Fish's famous pamphlet also shows the spirit which was seething; and though we may make some allowance for angry rhetoric, his words have the clear ring of honesty in them; and he spoke of what he had seen and knew. The monks, he tells the king, 'be they that have made a hundred thousand idle dissolute women in your realm, who would have gotten their living honestly in the sweat of their faces had not their superfluous riches allured them to lust and idleness. These be they that when they have drawn men's wives to such incontinency, spend away their husbands' goods, make the women to run away from their husbands, bringing both man, wife, and children to idleness, theft, and beggary. Yea, who is able to number the great broad bottomless ocean sea full of evils that this mischievous generation may bring upon us if unpunished?'[3]

Copies of this book were strewed about the London streets; Wolsey issued a prohibition against it, with the effect which such prohibitions usually have. Means were found to bring it under the eyes of Henry himself; and the manner in which it was received by him is full of significance, and betrays that the facts of the age were already telling on his understanding. He was always easy of access and easy of manner; and the story, although it rests on Foxe's authority, has internal marks of authenticity.

---

[1] A peculiarly hateful form of clerical impost, the priests claiming the last dress worn in life by persons brought to them for burial.

[2] Fitz James to Wolsey, FOXE, vol. iv. p. 196.

[3] *Supplication of the Beggars*, FOXE, vol. iv. p. 661. The glimpses into the condition of the monasteries which had been obtained in the imperfect visitation of Morton, bear out the pamphleteer too completely. See chapter x. of this work, second edition.

'One Master Edmund Moddis, being with the king in talk of religion, and of the new books that were come from beyond the seas, said that if it might please his Highness to pardon him, and such as he would bring to Grace, he should see such a book as it was a marvel to hear of. The king demanded who they were? He said 'Two of your merchants—George Elliot and George Robinson.' The king appointed a time to speak with them. When they came before his presence in a privy closet, he demanded what they had to say or to shew him. One of them said that there was a book come to their hands which they had there to shew his Grace. When he saw it he demanded if any of them could read it. 'Yea,' said George Elliot, 'if it please your Grace to hear it.' 'I thought so,' said the king; 'if need were, thou couldst say it without book.'

'The whole book being read out, the king made a long pause, and then said, 'If a man should pull down an old stone wall, and should begin at the lower part, the upper part thereof might chance to fall upon his head.' Then he took the book, and put it in his desk, and commanded them, on their allegiance, that they should not tell any man that he had seen it.'[1]

Symptoms such as these boded ill for a self-reform of the church, and it was further imperilled by the difficulty which it is not easy to believe that Wolsey had forgotten. No measures would be of efficacy which spared the religious houses, and they would be equally useless unless the bishops, as well as the inferior clergy, were comprehended in the scheme of amendment. But neither with monks nor bishops could Wolsey interfere except by a commission from the pope, and the laws were unrepealed which forbade English subjects, under the severest penalties, to accept or exercise within the realm an authority which they had received from the Holy See. Morton had gone beyond the limits of the statute of provisors in receiving powers from Pope Innocent to visit the monasteries. But Morton had stopped short with inquiry and admonition. Wolsey, who was in earnest with the work, had desired and obtained a full commission as legate, but he could only make use of it at his peril. The statute slumbered, but it still existed.[2] He was exposing not

<hr>

[1] Foxe, vol. iv. p. 653.

[2] 13 Ric. II. stat. ii. c. 2; 2 Hen. IV. c. 3; 9 Hen. IV. c. 8. Lingard is mistaken in saying that the Crown had power to dispense with these statutes. A dispensing power was indeed granted by the 12th of the 7th of Ric. II. But by the 2nd of the 13th of the same reign, the king

himself only, but all persons, lay and clerical, who might recognise his legacy to a Premunire; and he knew well that Henry's connivance, or even expressed permission, could not avail him if his conduct was challenged. He could not venture to appeal to parliament. Parliament was the last authority whose jurisdiction a churchman would acknowledge in the concerns of the clergy; and his project must sooner or later have sunk, like those of his two predecessors, under its own internal difficulties, even if the accident had not arisen which brought the dispute to a special issue in its most vital point, and which, fostered by Wolsey for his own purposes, precipitated his ruin.

It is never more difficult to judge equitably the actions of public men than when private as well as general motives have been allowed to influence them, or when their actions may admit of being represented as resulting from personal inclination, as well as from national policy. In life, as we actually experience it, motives slide one into the other, and the most careful analysis will fail adequately to sift them. In history, from the effort to make our conceptions distinct, we pronounce upon these intricate matters with unhesitating certainty, and we lose sight of truth in the desire to make it truer than itself. The difficulty is further complicated by the different points of view which are chosen by contemporaries and by posterity. Where motives are mixed, men all naturally dwell most on those which approach nearest to themselves: contemporaries whose interests are at stake overlooking what is personal in consideration of what is to them of broader moment; posterity unable to realize political embarrassments which have ceased to concern them, concentrating their attention on such features of the story as touch their own sympathies, and attending exclusively to the private and personal passions of the men and women whose character they are considering.

These natural, and to some extent inevitable tendencies, explain the difference with which the divorce between Henry VIII. and Catherine of Arragon has been regarded by the English nation in the sixteenth and in the nineteenth centuries. In the former, not only did the parliament profess to desire it, urge it, and further it, but we are told by a contemporary[1] that 'all indifferent and discreet persons' judged that it was right and necessary.

is expressly and by name placed under the same prohibitions as all other persons.

[1] HALL, p. 784.

In the latter, perhaps, there is not one of ourselves who has not been taught to look upon it as an act of enormous wickedness. In the sixteenth century, Queen Catherine was an obstacle to the establishment of the kingdom, an incentive to treasonable hopes. In the nineteenth, she is an outraged and injured wife, the victim of a false husband's fickle appetite. The story is a long and painful one, and on its personal side need not concern us here further than as it illustrates the private character of Henry. Into the public bearing of it I must enter at some length, in order to explain the interest with which the nation threw itself into the question, and to remove the scandal with which, had nothing been at stake beyond the inclinations of a profligate monarch, weary of his queen, the complaisance on such a subject of the lords and commons of England would have coloured the entire complexion of the Reformation.

The succession to the throne, although determined in theory by the ordinary law of primogeniture, was nevertheless subject to repeated arbitrary changes. The uncertainty of the rule was acknowledged and deplored by the parliament,[1] and there was no order of which the nation, with any unity of sentiment, compelled the observance. An opinion prevailed—not, I believe, traceable to statute, but admitted by custom, and having the force of statute in the prejudices of the nation—that no stranger born out of the realm could inherit.[2] Although the descent in the female line was not formally denied, no female sovereign had ever, in fact, sat upon the throne.[3] Even Henry VII. refused to strengthen his title by advancing the claims of his wife: and the uncertainty of the laws of marriage, and the innumerable refinements of the Romish canon law, which affected the legitimacy of children,[4]

---

[1] 25 Hen. VIII. c. 22.

[2] 28 Hen. VIII. c. 24. Speech of Sir Ralph Sadler in parliament, *Sadler Papers*, vol. iii. p. 323.

[3] Nor was the theory distinctly admitted, or the claim of the house of York would have been unquestionable.

[4] 25 Hen. VIII. c. 22. Draft of the Dispensation to be granted to Henry VIII. *Rolls House MS*. It has been asserted by a writer in the *Tablet* that there is no instance in the whole of English history where the ambiguity of the marriage law led to a dispute of title. This was not the opinion of those who remembered the wars of the fifteenth century. 'Recens in quorundam vestrorum animis adhuc est illius cruenti temporis memoria,' said Henry VIII. in a speech in council, 'quod a Ricardo tertio cum avi nostri materni Edwardi quarti statum in controversiam vocâsset ejusque heredes regno atque vitâ privâsset illatum est.'—WILKINS's *Concilia*, vol. iii. p. 714. Richard claimed the crown on the ground that a precontract rendered his brother's marriage invalid, and Henry VII. tacitly allowed the same doubt to continue. The language of the 22nd of the 25th of Hen. VIII. is so clear

furnished, in connexion with the further ambiguities of clerical dispensations, perpetual pretexts, whenever pretexts were needed, for a breach of allegiance. So long, indeed, as the character of the nation remained essentially military, it could as little tolerate an incapable king as an army in a dangerous campaign can bear with an inefficient commander; and whatever might be the theory of the title, when the sceptre was held by the infirm hand of an Edward II., a Richard II., or a Henry VI., the difficulty resolved itself by force, and it was wrenched by a stronger arm from a grasp too feeble to retain it. The consent of the nation was avowed, even in the authoritative language of a statute,[1] as essential to the legitimacy of a sovereign's title; and Sir Thomas More, on examination by the Solicitor-General, declared as his opinion that parliament had power to depose kings if it so pleased.[2] So many uncertainties on a point so vital had occasioned various fearful episodes in English history; the most fearful of them, which had traced its character in blood in the private records of every English family, having been the long struggle of the preceding century, from which the nation was still suffering, and had but recovered sufficiently to be conscious of what it had endured. It had decimated itself for a question which involved no principle and led to no result, and perhaps the history of the world may be searched in vain for any parallel to a quarrel at once so desperate and so unmeaning.

This very unmeaning character of the dispute increased the difficulty of ending it. In wars of conquest or of principle, when something definite is at stake, the victory is either won, or it is lost; the conduct of individual men, at all events, is overruled by considerations external to themselves, which admit of being weighed and calculated. In a war of succession, where the great families were divided in their allegiance, and supported the rival claimants in evenly balanced numbers, the inveteracy of the conflict increased with its duration, and propagated itself from

as to require no additional elucidation; but another distinct evidence of the belief of the time upon the subject is in one of the papers laid before Pope Clement.

'Constat, in ipso regno quam plurima gravissima bella sæpe exorta, confingentes ex justis et legitimis nuptiis quorundam Angliæ regum procreatos illegitimos fore propter aliquod consanguinitatis vel affinitatis confictum impedimentum et propterea inhabiles esse ad regni successionem.'—*Rolls House MS.*; WILKINS's *Concilia*, vol. iii. p. 707.

[1] 28 Hen. VIII. c. 24.

[2] *Appendix 2 to the Third Report of the Deputy-Keeper of the Public Records*, p. 241.

generation to generation. Every family was in blood feud with its neighbour; and children, as they grew to manhood, inherited the duty of revenging their fathers' deaths.

No effort of imagination can reproduce to us the state of this country in the fatal years which intervened between the first rising of the Duke of York and the battle of Bosworth; and experience too truly convinced Henry VII. that the war had ceased only from general exhaustion, and not because. there was no will to continue it. He breathed an atmosphere of suspended insurrection, and only when we remember the probable effect upon his mind of the constant dread of an explosion, can we excuse or understand, in a prince not generally cruel, the execution of the Earl of Warwick. The danger of a bloody revolution may present an act of arbitrary or cowardly tyranny in the light of a public duty.

Fifty years of settled government, howéver, had not been without their effects. The country had collected itself; the feuds of the families had been chastened, if they had not been subdued; while the increase of wealth and material prosperity had brought out into obvious prominence those advantages of peace which a hot-spirited people, antecedent to experience, had not anticipated, and had not been able to appreciate. They were better fed, better cared for, more justly governed, than they had ever been before; and though abundance of unruly tempers remained, yet the wiser portion of the nation, looking back from their new vantage-ground, were able to recognise the past in its true hatefulness. Thenceforward a war of succession was the predominating terror with English statesmen, and the safe establishment of the reigning family bore a degree of importance which it is possible that their fears exaggerated, yet which in fact was the determining principle of their action.

It was therefore with no little anxiety that the council of Henry VIII. perceived his male children, on whom their hopes were centered, either born dead, or dying one after another within a few days of their birth, as if his family were under a blight. When the queen had advanced to an age which precluded hope of further offspring, and the heir presumptive was an infirm girl, the unpromising prospect became yet more alarming. The life of the Princess Mary was precarious, for her health was weak from her childhood. If she lived, her accession would be a temptation to insurrection; if she did not live, and the king had no other children, a civil war was inevitable. At present such a difficulty would be disposed of by an immediate and simple reference to the collateral branches of the royal family; the crown would descend with even more facility than the property of an intestate to the next of kin. At that time, if the rule had been recognised, it would only have increased the difficulty, for the next heir in blood was James of Scotland; and, gravely as statesmen desired the union of the two countries, in the existing mood of the people, the very stones in London streets, it was said,[1] would rise up against a king of Scotland who claimed to enter England as sovereign. Even the parliament itself declared in formal language that they would resist any attempt on the part of the Scottish king 'to the uttermost of their power.[2]

As little, however, as the English would have admitted James's claims, would James himself have acknowledged their right to reject them. He would have pleaded the sacred right of inheritance, refusing utterly the imaginary law which disentitled him: he would have pressed his title with all Scotland to back him, and probably with the open support of France. Centuries of humiliation remained unrevenged, which both France and Scotland had endured at English hands. It was not likely that they would waste an opportunity thrust upon them by Providence. The country might, it is true, have encountered this danger, serious as it would have been, if there had been hope that it would itself have agreed in any other choice. England had many times fought successfully against the same odds, and would have cared little for a renewal of the struggle, if united in itself: but the prospect on this side, also, was fatally discouraging. The elements of the old factions were dormant, but still smouldering. Throughout Henry's reign a White Rose agitation had been secretly fermenting; without open success, and without chance of success so long as Henry lived, but formidable in a high degree if opportunity to strike should offer itself. Richard de la Pole, the representative of this party, had been killed at Pavia, but his loss had rather strengthened their cause than weakened it, for by his long exile he was unknown in England; his personal character was without energy; while he made place for the leadership of a far more powerful spirit in the sister of the murdered Earl of Warwick, the Countess of Salisbury, mother of Reginald Pole. This lady had inherited, in no common degree, the fierce nature of the

---

[1] *Sadler Papers*, vol. iii. p. 323.　　[2] 28 Hen. VIII. c. 24.

Plantagenets; born to command, she had rallied round her the Courtenays, the Nevilles, and all the powerful kindred of Richard the King Maker, her grandfather. Her Plantagenet descent was purer than the king's; and on his death, without a male child, half England was likely to declare either for one of her sons, or for the Marquis of Exeter, the grandson of Edward IV.[1]

In 1515, when Giustiniani,[2] the Venetian ambassador, was at the court, the Dukes of Buckingham, of Suffolk, and of Norfolk, were also mentioned to him as having each of them hopes of the crown. Buckingham, meddling prematurely in the dangerous game, had lost his life for it; but in his death he had strengthened the chance of Norfolk, who had married his daughter. Suffolk was Henry's brother-in-law;[3] chivalrous, popular, and the ablest soldier of his day; and Lady Margaret Lennox, also, daughter of the Queen of Scotland by her second marriage, would not have wanted supporters, and early became an object of intrigue. Indeed, as she had been born in England, it was held in parliament that she stood next in order to the Princess Mary.[4]

Many of these claims were likely to be advanced if Henry died leaving a daughter to succeed him. They would all inevitably be advanced if he died childless; and no great political sagacity was required to foresee the probable fate of the country if such a moment was chosen for a French and Scottish invasion. The very worst disasters might be too surely looked for, and the hope of escape, precarious at the best, hung upon the frail thread of a single life. We may therefore imagine the dismay with which the nation saw this last hope failing them— and failing them even in a manner more dangerous than if it had failed by death; for it did but add another doubt, when already there were too many. In order to detach France from Scotland, and secure, if possible, its support for the claims of the princess, it had been proposed to marry the Princess Mary to a son of the French king. The negotiations were conducted through the Bishop of Tarbês,[5] and at their first opening he raised a question

[1] See vol. iii. of this work, chap. xv.
[2] *Four Years at the Court of Henry the Eighth,* vol. ii. pp. 315-16.
[3] Sir Charles Brandon, created Duke of Suffolk, and married to Mary Tudor, widow of Louis XII.
[4] 28 Hen. VIII. c. 24.
[5] The treaty was in progress from Dec. 24, 1526, to March 2, 1527 [LORD HERBERT, pp. 80, 81], and during this time the difficulty was raised. The earliest intimation which I find of an intended divorce was in June, 1527, at which time Wolsey was privately consulting the bishops.—*State Papers,* vol. i. p. 189.

in the name of his government, on the validity of the papal dispensation granted by Julius the Second, to legalize the marriage from which she was sprung. The abortive marriage scheme perished in its birth, but the doubt which had been raised could not perish with it. Doubt on such a subject once mooted might not be left unresolved, even if the raising it thus publicly had not itself destroyed the frail chance of an undisputed succession. If the relations of Henry with Queen Catherine had been of a cordial kind, it is possible that he would have been contented with resentment; that he would have refused to reconsider a question which touched his honour and his conscience; and, united with parliament, would have endeavoured to bear down all difficulties with a high hand. This at least he might have himself attempted. Whether the parliament, with so precarious a future before them, would have consented, is less easy to say. Fortunately or unfortunately, the interests of the nation pointed out another road, which Henry had no unwillingness to enter.

On the death of Prince Arthur, five months after his marriage, the interests of Henry VII. and of Ferdinand induced a desire that the bond between their families thus broken should again be united; and, as soon as it became clear that Catherine had not been left pregnant (a point which, tacitly at least, she allowed to be considered uncertain at the time of her husband's decease), it was proposed that she should be transferred, with the inheritance of the crown, to the new heir. A dispensation was reluctantly granted by the pope,[1] and reluctantly accepted by the English ministry. The Prince of Wales, who was no more than twelve years old at the time, was under the age at which he could legally sue for such an object; and a portion of the English council, the Archbishop of Canterbury among them, were unsatisfied,[2] both with the marriage itself, and with the adequacy of the forms observed in a matter of so dubious an import. The betrothal took place at the urgency of Ferdinand. In the year following Henry VII. became suddenly ill; Queen Elizabeth died; and superstition, working on the previous hesitation, misfortune was construed into an indication of the displeasure of Heaven. The intention was

---

[1] It was for some time delayed; and the papal agent was instructed to inform Ferdinand that a marriage which was at variance a jure et laudabilibus moribus could not be permitted nisi maturo consilio et necessitatis causâ.—Minute of a Brief of Julius the Second, dated March 13, 1504, *Rolls House MS.*

[2] LORD HERBERT, p. 114.

renounced, and the prince, as soon as he had completed his fourteenth year, was invited and required to disown, by a formal act, the obligations contracted in his name.[1] Again there was a change. The king lived on, the alarm yielded to the temptations of covetousness. Had he restored Catherine to her father he must have restored with her the portion of her dowry which had been already received; he must have relinquished the prospect of the moiety which had yet to be received. The negotiation was renewed. Henry VII. lived to sign the receipts for the first instalment of the second payment;[2] and on his death, notwithstanding much general murmuring,[3] the young Henry, then a boy of eighteen, proceeded to carry out his father's ultimate intentions. The princess-dowager, notwithstanding what had passed, was still on her side willing;—and the difference of age (she was six years older than Henry) seeming of little moment when both were comparatively young, they were married. For many years all went well; opposition was silenced by the success which seemed to have followed, and the original scruples were forgotten. Though the marriage was dictated by political convenience, Henry was faithful, with but one exception, to his wife's bed—no slight honour to him, if he is measured by the average royal standard in such matters; and, if his sons had lived to grow up around his throne, there is no reason to believe that the peace

[1] LORD HERBERT, p. 117, Kennett's edition. The act itself is printed in BURNET'S *Collectanea*, vol. iv. (Nares' edition) pp. 5, 6. It is dated June 27, 1505. Dr. Lingard endeavours to explain away the renunciation as a form. The language of Moryson, however, leaves no doubt either of its causes or its meaning. 'Non multo post sponsalia contrahuntur,' he says, 'Henrico plus minus tredecim annos jam nato. Sed rerum non recte inceptarum successus infelicior homines non prorsus oscitantes plerumque docet quid recte gestum quid perperam, quid factum superi volunt quid infectum. Nimirum Henricus Septimus nullâ ægritudinis prospectâ causâ repente in deteriorem valetudinem prolapsus est, nec unquam potuit affectum corpus pristinum statum recuperare. Uxor in aliud ex alio malum regina omnium laudatissima non multo post morbo periit. Quid mirum si Rex tot irati numinis indiciis admonitus cœperit cogitare rem male illis succedere qui vellent hoc nomine cum Dei legibus litem instituere ut diutius cum homine amicitiam gerere possent. Quid deinceps egit? Quid aliud quam quod decuit Christianissimum regem? Filium ad se accersiri jubet, accersitur. Adest, adsunt et multi nobilissimi homines. Rex filium regno natum hortatur ut secum una cum doctissimis ac optimis viris cogitavit nefarium esse putare leges Dei leges Dei non esse cum papa volet. Non ita longâ oratione usus filium patri obsequentissimum a sententiâ nullo negotio abduxit. Sponsalia contracta infirmantur, pontificiæque auctoritatis beneficio palam renunciatum est. Adest publicus tabellio—fit instrumentum. Rerum gestarum testes rogati sigilla apponunt. Postremo filius patri fidem se illam uxorem nunquam ducturum.'—*Apomaxis* RICARDI MORYSINI. Printed by Berthelet. 1537.

[2] See LINGARD, sixth edition, vol. iv. p. 164.

[3] HALL, p. 507.

of his married life would have been interrupted, or that, whatever might have been his private feelings, he would have appeared in the world's eye other than acquiescent in his condition.

But his sons had not lived; years passed on, bringing with them premature births, children born dead, or dying after a few days or hours;[1] and the disappointment was intense in proportion to the interests which were at issue. The especial penalty denounced against the marriage with a brother's wife[2] had been all but literally enforced; and the king found himself growing to middle life and his queen passing beyond it with his prayers unheard, and no hope any longer that they might be heard. The disparity of age also was more perceptible as time went by, while Catherine's constitution was affected by her misfortunes, and differences arose on which there is no occasion to dwell in these pages—differences which in themselves reflected no discredit either on the husband or the wife, but which were sufficient to extinguish between two infirm human beings an affection that had rested only upon mutual esteem, but had not assumed the character of love.

The circumstances in which Catherine was placed were of a kind which no sensitive woman could have endured without impatience and mortification; but her conduct, however natural, only widened the breach which personal

[1] He married Catherine, June 3, 1509. Early in the spring of 1510 she miscarried.—*Four Years at the Court of Henry VIII.* vol. i. p. 83.

Jan. 1, 1511. A prince was born, who died Feb. 22.—HALL.

Nov. 1513. Another prince was born, who died immediately.—LINGARD, vol. iv. p. 290.

Dec. 1514. Badoer, the Venetian ambassador, wrote that the queen had been delivered of a still-born male child, to the great grief of the whole nation.

May 3, 1515. The queen was supposed to be pregnant. If the supposition was right, she must have miscarried.—*Four Years at the Court of Henry VIII.* vol. i. p. 81.

Feb. 19, 1516. The Princess Mary was born.

July 3, 1518. 'The Queen declared herself quick with child.' (Pace to Wolsey: *State Papers*, vol. i. p. 2,) and again miscarried.

These misfortunes we are able to trace accidentally through casual letters, and it is probable that these were not all. Henry's own words upon the subject are very striking:—

'All such issue male as I have received of the queen died incontinent after they were born, so that I doubt the punishment of God in that behalf. Thus being troubled in waves of a scrupulous conscience, and partly in despair of any issue male by her, it drove me at last to consider the estate of this realm, and the danger it stood in for lack of issue male to succeed me in this imperial dignity.'—CAVENDISH, p. 220.

[2] 'If a man shall take his brother's wife it is an unclean thing. He hath uncovered his brother's nakedness. They shall be childless.'—*Leviticus* xx. 21.

repugnance and radical opposition of character had already made too wide. So far Henry and she were alike that both had imperious tempers, and both were indomitably obstinate; but Henry was hot and impetuous, she was cold and self-contained—Henry saw his duty through his wishes, she, in her strong Castilian austerity, measured her steps by the letter of the law; the more he withdrew from her, the more she insisted upon her relation to him as his wife; and continued with fixed purpose and immovable countenance[1] to share his table and his bed long after she was aware of his dislike for her.

If the validity of so unfortunate a connexion had never been questioned, or if no national interests had been dependent on the continuance or the abolition of it, I suppose that these discomforts were not too great to have been endured in silence. They were not originally occasioned, I am persuaded, by any latent inclination on the part of the king for another woman. They had arisen to their worst dimensions before he had ever seen Anne Boleyn, and were produced by causes of a wholly independent kind; and even if it had not been so, when we remember the tenor of his early life we need not think that he would have been unequal to the restraint which ordinary persons in similar circumstances are able to impose on their caprices. The legates spoke no more than the truth when they wrote to the pope, saying that 'it was mere madness to suppose that the king would act as he was doing merely out of dislike of the queen, or out of inclination for another person; he was not a man whom harsh manners and an unpleasant disposition *(duri mores et injucunda consuetudo)* could so far provoke; nor can any sane man believe him to be so infirm of character that sensual allurements would have led him to dissolve a connexion in which he has passed the flower of youth without stain or blemish, and in which he has borne himself in his present trial so reverently and honourably.'[2] I consider this entirely true in a sense which no great knowledge of human nature is required to understand. His personal dissatisfaction was great: if this had been all, however, it would have been extinguished or endured; but the interests of the nation, imperilled as they were by the maintenance of the marriage, entitled him to regard his position under another aspect. Even if the marriage in itself had never been questioned, he might justly have desired the dissolution of it; and when he recalled

<hr>

[1] *Letters of the Bishop of Bayonne*, LEGRAND, vol. iii.
[2] Legates to the Pope, printed in BURNET's *Collectanea*, p. 40.

the circumstances under which it was contracted, the hesitation of the council, the reluctance of the pope, the alarms and vacillation of his father, we may readily perceive how scruples of conscience must have arisen in a soil well prepared to receive them—how the loss of his children must have appeared as a judicial sentence on a violation of the Divine law. The divorce presented itself to him as a moral obligation, when national advantage combined with superstition to encourage what he secretly desired; and if he persuaded himself that those public reasons, without which, in truth and fact, he would not have stirred, were those that alone were influencing him, the self-deceit was of a kind with which the experience of most men will probably have made them too familiar. In those rare cases where inclination coincides with right, we cannot be surprised if mankind should deceive themselves with the belief that the disinterested motives weigh more with them than the personal.

A remarkable and very candid account of Henry's feelings is furnished by himself in one of the many papers of instructions[1] which he forwarded to his secretary at Rome. Hypocrisy was not among his faults, and in detailing the arguments which were to be laid before the pope he has exhibited a more complete revelation of what was passing in himself- and indirectly of his own nature in its strength and weakness—than he perhaps imagined while he wrote. The despatch is long and perplexed; the style that of a man who saw his end clearly, and was vexed with the intricate and dishonest trifling with which his way was impeded, and which nevertheless he was struggling to tolerate. The secretary was to say, 'that the King's Highness having above all other things his intent and mind ever founded upon such respect unto Almighty God as to a Christian and catholic prince doth appertain, knowing the fragility and uncertainty of all earthly things, and how displeasant unto God, how much dangerous to the soul, how dishonourable and damageable to the world it were to prefer vain and transitory things unto those that be perfect and certain, hath in this cause, doubt, and matter of matrimony, whereupon depend so high and manifold consequences of greatest importance, always cast from his conceit the darkness and blundering confusion of falsity, and specially hath had and put before his eyes the light and shining brightness of truth; upon which foundation as a most sure base for perpetual

---

[1] *State Papers,* vol. vii. p. 117.

tranquillity of his conscience his Highness hath expressly resolved and determined with himself to build and establish all his acts, deeds, and cogitations touching this matter. Without God do build the house, in vain they labour that go about to build it; and all our actions grounded upon that immovable fundament of truth, must needs therein be firm, sound, whole, perfect, and worthy of a Christian man. And if truth be put apart, they cannot for the same reason be but evil, vain, slipper, uncertain, and in nowise permanent or endurable.' He then laboured to urge on the pope the duty of straightforward dealing; and dwelt in words which have a sad interest for us (when we consider the manner in which the subject of them has been dealt with) on the judgment bar, not of God only, but of human posterity, at which his conduct would be ultimately tried. 'The causes of private persons dark and doubtful be sometimes,' he said, 'pretermitted and passed over as things more meet at some seasons to be dissimuled than by continual strife and plea to nourish controversies. Yet since all people have their eyes conject upon princes, whose acts and doings not only be observed in the mouths of them that now do live, but also remain in such perpetual memory to our posterity [so that] the evil, if any there be, cannot but appear and come to light, there is no reason for toleration, no place for dissimulation; but [there is reason] more deeply, highly, and profoundly to penetrate and search for the truth, so that the same may vanquish and overcome, and all guilt, craft, and falsehood clearly be extirpate and reject.' I am anticipating the progress of the story in making these quotations; for the main burden of the despatch concerns a forged document which had been introduced by the Roman lawyers to embarrass the process, and of which I shall by-and-bye have to speak directly; but I have desired to illustrate the spirit in which Henry entered upon the general question—assuredly a more calm and rational one than historians have usually represented it to be. In dealing with the obstacle which had been raised, he displayed a most efficient mastery over himself, although he did not conclude without touching the pith of the matter with telling clearness. The secretary was to take some opportunity of speaking to the pope privately; and of warning him, 'as of himself,' that there was no hope that the king would give way: he was to 'say plainly to his Holiness that the king's desire and intent *convolare ad secundas nuptias non patitur negativum;* and whatsoever should be found of bull, brief, or otherwise, his Highness found his conscience so inquieted, his succession in such danger, and his most royal person in such perplexity for things unknown and not to be spoken, that other remedy there was not but his Grace to come by one way or other, and specially at his hands, if it might be, to the desired end; and that all concertation to the contrary should be vain and frustrate.'

So peremptory a conviction and so determined a purpose were of no sudden growth, and had been probably maturing in his mind for years, when the gangrene was torn open by the Bishop of Tarbês, and accident precipitated his resolution. The momentous consequences involved, and the reluctance to encounter a probable quarrel with the emperor, might have long kept him silent, except for some extraneous casualty; but the tree being thus rudely shaken, the ripe fruit fell. The capture of Rome occurring almost at the same moment, Wolsey caught the opportunity to break the Spanish alliance; and the prospect of a divorce was grasped at by him as a lever by which to throw the weight of English power and influence into the papal scale, to commit Henry definitely to the catholic cause. Like his acceptance of legatine authority, the expedient was a desperate one, and if it failed it was ruinous. The nation at that time was sincerely attached to Spain. The alliance with the house of Burgundy was of old date; the commercial intercourse with Flanders was enormous, Flanders, in fact, absorbing all the English exports; and as many as 15,000 Flemings were settled in London. Charles himself was personally popular; he had been the ally of England in the late French war; and when in his supposed character of leader of the antipapal party in Europe he allowed a Lutheran army to desecrate Rome, he had won the sympathy of all the latent discontent which was fermenting in the population. France, on the other hand, was as cordially hated as Spain was beloved. A state of war with France was the normal condition of England; and the re-conquest of it the universal dream from the cottage to the castle. Henry himself, early in his reign, had shared in this delusive ambition; and but three years before the sack of Rome, when the Duke of Suffolk led an army into Normandy, Wolsey's purposed tardiness in sending reinforcements had alone saved Paris.[1]

There could be no doubt, therefore, that a breach with

---

[1] *Letters of the Bishop of Bayonne*, LEGRAND, vol. iii.; HALL, 669.

the emperor would in a high degree be unwelcome to the country. The king, and probably such members of the council as were aware of his feelings, shrank from offering an open affront to the Spanish people, and anxious as they were for a settlement of the succession, perhaps trusted that advantage might be taken of some political contingency for a private arrangement; and that Catherine might be induced by Charles himself to retire privately, sacrificing herself, of her free will, to the interests of the two countries. This, however, is no more than conjecture; I think it probable, because so many English statesmen were in favour at once of the divorce and of the Spanish alliance—two objects which, only on some such hypothesis, were compatible. The fact cannot be ascertained, however, because the divorce itself was not discussed at the council table until Wolsey had induced the king to change his policy by the hope of immediate relief. Wolsey has revealed to us fully his own objects in a letter to Sir Gregory Cassalis, his agent at Rome. He shared with half Europe in an impression that the emperor's Italian campaigns were designed to further the Reformation; and of this central delusion he formed the keystone of his conduct. 'First condoling with his Holiness,' he wrote, 'on the unhappy position in which, with the college of the most reverend cardinals, he is placed,[1] you shall tell him how, day and night, I am revolving by what means or contrivance I may bring comfort to the church of Christ, and raise the fallen state of our most Holy Lord. I care not what it may cost me, whether of expense or trouble; nay, though I have to shed my blood, or give my life for it, assuredly so long as life remains to me for this I will labour. And now let me mention the great and marvellous effects which have been wrought by my instrumentality on the mind of my most excellent master the king, whom I have persuaded to unite himself with his Holiness in heart and soul. I urged innumerable reasons to induce him to part him from the emperor, to whom he clung with much tenacity. The most effective of them all was the constancy with which I assured him of the good-will and affection which were felt for him by his Holiness, and the certainty that his Holiness would furnish proof of his friendship in conceding his said Majesty's requests, in such form as the church's treasure and the authority of the Vicar of Christ shall permit, or so far as that authority extends or may extend. I have

---

[1] They were shut up in the Castle of St. Angelo.

undertaken, moreover, for all these things in their utmost latitude, pledging my salvation, my faith, my honour and soul upon them. I have said that his demands shall be granted amply and fully, without scruple, without room or occasion being left for after-retractation; and the King's Majesty, in consequence, believing on these my solemn asseverations that the Pope's Holiness is really and indeed well inclined towards him, accepting what is spoken by me as spoken by the legate of the Apostolic See, and therefore as in the name of his Holiness, has determined to run the risk which I have pressed upon him; he will spare no labour or expense, he will disregard the wishes of his subjects, and the private interest of his Realm, to attach himself cordially and constantly to the Holy See.'[1]

These were the words of a man who loved England well, but who loved Rome better; and Wolsey has received but scanty justice from catholic writers, since he sacrificed himself for the catholic cause. His scheme was bold and well laid, being weak only in that it was confessedly in contradiction to the instincts and genius of the nation, by which, and by which alone, in the long run, either this or any other country has been successfully governed. And yet he might well be forgiven if he ventured on an unpopular course in the belief that the event would justify him; and that, in uniting with France to support the pope, he was not only consulting the true interest of England, but was doing what England actually desired, although blindly aiming at her object by other means. The French wars, however traditionally popular, were fertile-only in glory. The rivalry of the two countries was a splendid folly, wasting the best blood of both countries for an impracticable chimera; and though there was impatience of ecclesiastical misrule, though there was jealousy of foreign interference, and general irritation with the state of the church, yet the mass of the people hated protestantism even worse than they hated the pope, the clergy, and the consistory courts. They believed—and Wolsey was, perhaps, the only leading member of the privy council, except Archbishop Warham, who was not under the same delusion—that it was possible for a national church to separate itself from the unity of Christendom, and at the same time to crush or prevent innovation of doctrine; that faith in the sacramental system could still be maintained, though the priesthood by whom

---

[1] *State Papers*, vol. vii. pp. 18, 19.

those mysteries were dispensed should minister in gilded chains. This was the English historical theory handed down from William Rufus, the second Henry, and the Edwards; yet it was and is a mere phantasm, a thing of words and paper fictions, as Wolsey saw it to be. Wolsey knew well that an ecclesiastical revolt implied, as a certainty, innovation of doctrine; that plain men could not and would not continue to reverence the office of the priesthood, when the priests were treated as the paid officials of an earthly authority higher than their own. He was not to be blamed if he took the people at their word; if he believed that, in their doctrinal conservatism, they knew and meant what they were saying: and the reaction which took place under Queen Mary, when the Anglican system had been tried and failed, and the alternative was seen to be absolute between a union with Rome or a forfeiture of catholic orthodoxy, prove after all that he was wiser than in the immediate event he seemed to be; that if his policy had succeeded, and if, strengthened by success, he had introduced into the church those reforms which he had promised and desired,[1] he would have satisfied the substantial wishes of the majority of the nation.

Like other men of genius, Wolsey also combined practical sagacity with an unmeasured power of hoping. As difficulties gathered round him, he encountered them with the increasing magnificence of his schemes; and after thirty years' experience of public life, he was as sanguine as a boy. Armed with this little lever of the divorce, he saw himself, in imagination, the rebuilder of the catholic faith and the deliverer of Europe. The king being remarried, and the succession settled, he would purge the Church of England, and convert the monasteries into intellectual garrisons of pious and learned men, occupying the land from end to end. The feuds with France should cease for ever, and, united in a holy cause, the two countries should restore the papacy, put down the German heresies, depose the emperor, and establish in his place some faithful servant of the church: and Europe once more at peace, the hordes of the Crescent, which were threatening to settle the quarrels of Christians in the West as they had settled them in the East—by the extinction of Christianity itself,—were to be hurled back

---

[1] The fullest account of Wolsey's intentions on church reform will be found in a letter addressed to him by Fox, the old blind Bishop of Winchester, in 1528. The letter is printed in STRYPE's *Memorials Eccles.* vol. i. Appendix 10.

into their proper barbarism.[1] These magnificent visions fell from him in conversations with the Bishop of Bayonne, and may be gathered from hints and fragments of his correspondence. Extravagant as they seem, the prospect of realizing them was, humanly speaking, neither chimerical nor even improbable. He had but made the common mistake of men of the world who are the representatives of an old order of things at the time when that order is doomed and dying. He could not read the signs of the times; and confounded the barrenness of death with the barrenness of a winter which might be followed by a new spring and summer; he believed that the old life-tree of catholicism, which in fact was but cumbering the ground, might bloom again in its old beauty. The thing which he called heresy was the fire of Almighty God, which no politic congregation of princes, no state machinery, though it were never so active, could trample out; and as in the early years of Christianity the meanest slave who was thrown to the wild beasts for his presence at the forbidden mysteries of the gospel, saw deeper, in the divine power of his faith, into the future even of this earthly world than the sagest of his imperial persecutors, so a truer political prophet than Wolsey would have been found in the most ignorant of those poor men, for whom his myrmidons were searching in the purlieus of London, who were risking death and torture in disseminating the pernicious volumes of the English Testament.

If we look at the matter, however, from a more earthly point of view, the causes which immediately defeated Wolsey's policy were not such as human foresight could have anticipated. We ourselves, surveying the various parties in Europe with the light of our knowledge of the actual sequel, are perhaps able to understand their real relations; but if in 1527 a political astrologer had foretold that within two years of that time the pope and the emperor who had imprisoned him would be cordial allies,

<hr>

[1] *Letters of the Bishop of Bayonne*, LEGRAND, vol. iii. It is not uncommon to find splendid imaginations of this kind haunting statesmen of the 16th century; and the recapture of Constantinople always formed a feature in the picture. *A Plan for the Reformation of Ireland*, drawn up in 1515, contains the following curious passage: 'The prophecy is, that the King of England shall put this land of Ireland into such order that the wars of the land, whereof groweth the vices of the same, shall cease for ever; and after that God shall give such grace and fortune to the same king that he shall with the army of England and of Ireland subdue the realm of France to his obeysance for ever, and shall rescue the Greeks, and recover the great city of Constantinople, and shall vanquish the Turks, and win the Holy Cross and the Holy Land, and shall die Emperor of Rome, and eternal blisse shall be his end.'—*State Papers*, vol. ii. pp. 30, 31.

that the positions of England and Spain toward the papacy would be diametrically changed, and that the two countries were on the point of taking their posts, which they would ever afterwards maintain, as the champions respectively of the opposite principles to those which at that time they seemed to represent, the prophecy would have been held scarcely less insane than a prophecy six or even three years before the event, that in the year 1854 England would be united with an Emperor Napoleon for the preservation of European order.

Henry, then, in the spring of the year 1527, definitively breaking the Spanish alliance, formed a league with Francis I., the avowed object of which was the expulsion of the Imperialists from Italy; with a further intention—if it could be carried into effect—of avenging the outrage offered to Europe in the pope's imprisonment, by declaring vacant the imperial throne. Simultaneously with the congress at Amiens where the terms of the alliance were arranged, confidential persons were despatched into Italy to obtain an interview—if possible—with the pope, and formally laying before him the circumstances of the king's position, to request him to make use of his powers to provide a remedy. It is noticeable that at the outset of the negotiation, the king did not fully trust Wolsey. The latter had suggested, as the simplest method of proceeding, that the pope should extend his authority as legate, granting him plenary power to act as English vicegerent so long as Rome was occupied by the emperor's troops. Henry, not wholly satisfied that he was acquainted with his minister's full intentions in desiring so large a capacity, sent his own secretary, unknown to Wolsey, with his own private propositions—requesting simply a dispensation to take a second wife, his former marriage being allowed to stand with no definite sentence passed upon it; or, if that were impossible, leaving the pope to choose his own method, and settle the question in the manner least difficult and least offensive.[1]

Wolsey, however, soon satisfied the king that he had no sinister intentions. By the middle of the winter we find the private messenger associated openly with Sir Gregory Cassalis, the agent of the minister's communications;[2] and a series of formal demands were presented jointly by these two persons in the names of Henry and the legate; which, though taking many forms, resolved themselves substantially into one. The pope was required

[1] Knight to Henry: *State Papers*, vol. vii. pp. 2, 3.
[2] Wolsey to Cassalis: Ibid. p. 26.

to make use of his dispensing power to enable the King
of England to marry a wife who could bear him children,
and thus provide some better security than already existed
for the succession to the throne. This demand could not
be considered as in itself unreasonable; and if personal
feeling was combined with other motives to induce Henry
to press it, personal feeling did not affect the general
bearing of the question. His desire was publicly urged
on public grounds, and thus, and thus only, the pope was
at liberty to consider it. The marriages of princes have
ever been affected by other considerations than those which
influence such relations between private persons. Princes
may not, as 'unvalued persons' may, 'carve for themselves;' they pay the penalty of their high place, in submitting their affections to the welfare of the state; and
the same causes which regulate the formation of these
ties must be allowed to influence the continuance of them.
The case which was submitted to the pope was one of
those for which his very power of dispensing had been
vested in him; and being, as he called himself, the Father
of Christendom, the nation thought themselves entitled to
call upon him to make use of that power. A resource
of the kind must exist somewhere—the relation between
princes and subjects indispensably requiring it. It had
been vested in the Bishop of Rome, because it had been
presumed that the sanctity of his office would secure an
impartial exercise of his authority. And unless he could
have shown (which he never attempted to show) that the
circumstances of the succession were not so precarious
as to call for his interference, it would seem that the express contingency had arisen which was contemplated in
the constitution of the canon law;[1] and that where a
provision had been made by the church of which he was
the earthly head, for difficulties of this precise description,
the pope was under an obligation either to make the required concessions in virtue of his faculty, or, if he found
himself unable to make those concessions, to offer some
distinct explanation of his refusal. I speak of the question
as nakedly political. I am not considering the private injuries of which Catherine had so deep a right to complain,
nor the complications subsequently raised on the original

---

[1] The dispensing power of the popes was not formally limited.
According to the Roman lawyers, a faculty lay with them of granting
extraordinary dispensations in cases where dispensations would not
be usually admissible—which faculty was to be used, however, dum-
modo causa cogat urgentissima ne regnum aliquod funditus pereat;
the pope's business being to decide on the question of urgency.—Sir
Gregory Cassalis to Henry VIII., Dec. 26, 1532. *Rolls House MS.*

validity of the first marriage. A political difficulty, on which alone he was bound to give sentence, was laid before the pope in his judicial capacity, in the name of the nation; and the painful features which the process afterwards assumed are due wholly to his original weakness and vacillation.

Deeply, however, as we must all deplore the scandal and suffering which were occasioned by the dispute, it was in a high degree fortunate, that at the crisis of public dissatisfaction in England with the condition of the church, especially in the conduct of its courts of justice, a cause should have arisen which tested the whole question of church authority in its highest form; where the dispute between the laity and the ecclesiastics was represented in a process in which the pope sat as judge; in which the king was the appellant, and the most vital interests of the nation were at stake upon the issue. It was no accident which connected a suit for divorce with the reformation of religion. The ecclesiastical jurisdiction was upon its trial, and the future relations of church and state depended upon the pope's conduct in a matter which no technical skill was required to decide, but only the moral virtues of probity and courage. The time had been when the clergy feared only to be unjust, and when the functions of judges might safely be entrusted to them. The small iniquities of the consistory courts had shaken the popular faith in the continued operation of such a fear; and the experience of an Alexander VI., a Julius II., and a Leo X. had induced a suspicion that even in the highest quarters justice had ceased to be much considered. It remained for Clement VII. to disabuse men of their alarms, or by confirming them to forfeit for ever the supremacy of his order in England. Nor can it be said for him that the case was one in which it was unusually difficult to be virtuous. Justice, wounded dignity, and the interests of the See pointed alike to the same course. Queen Catherine's relationship to the emperor could not have recommended her to the tenderness of the pope, and the policy of assenting to an act which would infallibly alienate Henry from Charles, and therefore attach him to the Roman interests, did not require the eloquence of Wolsey to make it intelligible. If, because he was in the emperor's power, he therefore feared the personal consequences to himself, his cowardice of itself disqualified him to sit as a judge.

It does not fall within my present purpose to detail the first stages of the proceedings which followed. In substance they are well known to all readers of English history, and may be understood without difficulty as soon as we possess the clue to the conduct of Wolsey. I shall, however, in a few pages briefly epitomize what passed.

At the outset of the negotiation, the pope, although he would take no positive steps, was all, in words, which he was expected to be. Neither he nor the cardinals refused to acknowledge the dangers which threatened the country. He discussed freely the position of the different parties, the probabilities of a disputed succession, and the various claimants who would present themselves, if the king died without an heir of undisputed legitimacy.[1] Gardiner writes to Wolsey,[2] 'We did even more inculcate what speed and celerity the thing required, and what danger it was to the realm to have this matter hang in suspense. His Holiness confessed the same, and thereupon began to reckon what divers titles might be pretended by the King of Scots and others, and granted that, without an heir male, with provision to be made by consent of the state for his succession, and unless that what shall be done herein be established in such fashion as nothing may hereafter be objected thereto, the realm was like to come to dissolution.'

In stronger language the Cardinal-Governor of Bologna declared that 'he knew the gyze of England as well as few men did, and if the king should die without heirs male, he was sure it would cost two hundred thousand men's lives. Wherefore he thought, supposing his Grace should have no more children by the queen, and that by taking of another wife he might have heirs male, the bringing to pass that matter, and by that to avoid the mischiefs afore written, he thought would deserve Heaven.'[3] Whatever doubt there might be, therefore, whether the original marriage with Catherine was legal, it was universally admitted that there was none about the national desirableness of the dissolution of it; and if the pope had been free to judge only by the merits of the case, it is impossible to doubt that he would have cut the knot, either by granting a dispensation to Henry to marry a second wife—his first being formally, though not judicially, separated from him—or in some other way.[4] But the emperor was 'a lion in his path;' the question of strength

<hr>

[1] Knight and Cassalis to Wolsey: BURNET'S *Collect.* p. 12.

[2] STRYPE'S *Memorials*, vol. i., Appendix, p. 66.

[3] Sir F. Bryan and Peter Vannes to Henry: *State Papers*, vol. vii. p. 144.

[4] STRYPE'S *Memorials*, vol. i., Appendix, p. 100.

between the French and the Spaniards remained undecided, and Clement would come to no decision until he
was assured of the power of the allies to protect him
from the consequences. Accordingly he said and unsaid,
sighed, sobbed, beat his breast, shuffled, implored, threatened;[1] in all ways he endeavoured to escape from his
dilemma, to say yes and to say no, to do nothing, to
offend no one, and above all to gain time, with the weak
man's hope that 'something might happen' to extricate
him. Embassy followed embassy from England, each using
language more threatening than its predecessor. The thing,
it was said, must be done, and should be done. If it
was not done by the pope it would be done at home in
some other way, and the pope must take the consequences.[2] Wolsey warned him passionately of the rising storm,[3]
a storm which would be so terrible when it burst 'that
it would be better to die than to live.' The pope was
strangely unable to believe that the danger could be real,
being misled perhaps by other information from the friends
of Queen Catherine, and by an over-confidence in the attachment of the people to the emperor. He acted throughout in a manner natural to a timid amiable man, who
found himself in circumstances to which he was unequal;
and as long as we look at him merely as a man we can
pity his embarrassment. He forgot, however, that only
because he was supposed to be more than a man had
kings and emperors consented to plead at his judgment
seat — a fact of which Stephen Gardiner, then Wolsey's
secretary, thought it well to remind him in the following
striking language:—

'Unless,' said the future Bishop of Winchester in the
council, at the close of a weary day of unprofitable debating, 'unless some other resolution be taken than I
perceive you intend to make, hereupon shall be gathered

---

[1] STRYPE's *Memorials*, vol. i., Appendix, pp. 105-6; BURNET's *Collectanea*, p. 13.

[2] Wolsey to the Pope, BURNET's *Collectanea*, p. 16: Vereor quod
tamen nequeo tacere, ne Regia Majestas, humano divinoque jure quod
habet ex omni Christianitate suis his actionibus adjunctum freta, post-
quam viderit sedis Apostolicæ gratiam et Christi in terris Vicarii cle-
mentiam desperatam Cæsaris intuitu, in cujus manu neutiquam est tam
sanctos conatus reprimere, ea tunc moliatur, ea suæ causæ perquirat
remedia, quæ non solum huic Regno sed etiam aliis Christianis prin-
cipibus occasionem subministrarent sedis Apostolicæ auctoritatem et
jurisdictionem imminuendi et vilipendendi.

[3] BURNET's *Collectanea*, p. 20. Wolsey to John Cassalis: 'If his
Holyness, which God forbid, shall shew himself unwilling to listen to
the king's demands, to me assuredly it will be but grief to live longer,
for the innumerable evils which I foresee will then follow. One only
sure remedy remains to prevent the worst calamities. If that be
neglected, there is nothing before us but universal and inevitable ruin.'

a marvellous opinion of your Holiness, of the college of cardinals, and of the authority of this See. The King's Highness, and the nobles of the realm who shall be made privy to this, shall needs think that your Holiness and these most reverend and learned councillors either will not answer in this cause, or cannot answer. If you will not, if you do not choose to point out the way to an erring man, the care of whom is by God committed to you, they will say, 'Oh race of men most ungrateful, and of your proper office most oblivious! You who should be simple as doves are full of all deceit, and craft, and dissembling. If the king's cause be good, we require that you pronounce it good. If it be bad, why will you not say that it is bad, so to hinder a prince to whom you are so much bounden from longer continuing with it? We ask nothing of you but justice, which the king so loves and values, that whatever sinister things others may say or think of him, he will follow that with all his heart; that, and nothing else, whether it be for the marriage or against the marriage.'

'But if the King's Majesty,' continued Gardiner, hitting the very point of the difficulty, 'if the King's Majesty and the nobility of England, being persuaded of your good will to answer if you can do so, shall be brought to doubt of your ability, they will be forced to a harder conclusion respecting this See—namely, that God has taken from it the key of knowledge; and they will begin to give better ear to that opinion of some persons to which they have as yet refused to listen, that those papal laws which neither the pope himself nor his council can interpret, deserve only to be committed to the flames.' 'I desired his Holiness,' he adds, 'to ponder well this matter.'[1]

Clement was no hero, but in his worst embarrassments his wit never failed him. He answered that he was not learned, and 'to speak truth, albeit there was a saying in the canon law, that *Pontifex habet omnia jura in scrinio pectoris* (the pope has all laws locked within his breast), yet God had never given him the key to open that lock.' He was but 'seeking pretexts' for delay, as Gardiner saw, till the issue of the Italian campaign of the French in the summer of 1528 was decided. He had been liberated, or had been allowed to escape from Rome, in the fear that if detained longer he might nominate a vicegerent; and was residing at an old ruined castle at Orvieto, waiting upon events, leaving the Holy City still occupied by the

[1] Gardiner and Fox to Wolsey: STRYPE's *Memorials*, vol. i. Appendix, p. 92.

Prince of Orange. In the preceding autumn, immediately after the congress at Amiens, M. de Lautrec, accompanied by several English noblemen, had led an army across the Alps. He had defeated the Imperialists in the north of Italy in several minor engagements; and in January his success appeared so probable, that the pope took better heart, and told Sir Gregory Cassalis, that if the French would only approach near enough to enable him to plead compulsion, he would grant a commission to Wolsey, with plenary power to conclude the cause.[1] De Lautrec, however, foiled in his desire to bring the Imperialists to a decisive engagement, wasted his time and strength in ineffectual petty sieges; and finally, in the summer, on the unhealthy plains of Naples, a disaster more fatal in its consequences than the battle of Pavia, closed the prospects of the French to the south of the Alps; and with them all Wolsey's hopes of realizing his dream. Struck down, not by a visible enemy, but by the silent hand of fever, the French general himself, his English friends, and all his army melted away from off the earth. The pope had been wise in time. He had committed himself in words and intentions; but he had done nothing which he could not recal. He obtained his pardon from the emperor by promising to offend no more; and from that moment never again entertained any real thought of concession. Acting under explicit directions, he made it his object thence-

---

[1] His Holiness being yet in captivity, as he esteemed himself to be, so long as the Almayns and Spaniards continue in Italy, he thought if he should grant this commission that he should have the emperour his perpetual enemy without any hope of reconciliation. Notwithstanding he was content rather to put himself in evident ruin, and utter undoing, than the king or your Grace shall suspect any point of ingratitude in him; heartily desiring with sighs and tears that the king and your Grace which have been always fast and good to him, will not now suddenly precipitate him for ever: which should be done if immediately on receiving the commission your Grace should begin process. He intendeth to save all upright thus. If M. de Lautrec would set forwards, which he saith daily that he will do, but yet he doth not, at his coming the Pope's Holiness may have good colour to say, 'He was required of the commission by the ambassador of England, and denying the same, he was, eftsoons, required by M. de Lautrec to grant the said commission, inasmuch as it was but a letter of justice.' And by this colour he would cover the matter so that it might appear unto the emperour that the pope did it not as he that would gladly do displeasure unto the emperour, but as an indifferent judge, that could not nor might deny justice, specially being required by such personages; and immediately he would despatch a commission bearing date after the time that M. de Lautrec had been with him or was nigh unto him. The pope most instantly beseecheth your Grace to be a mean that the King's Highness may accept this in a good part, and that he will take patience for this little time, which, as it is supposed, will be but short.—Knight to Wolsey and the King. Jan. 1. 1527-8: BURNET *Collections.* 12, 13.

forward to delay and to procrastinate. Charles had no desire to press matters to extremities. War had not yet been declared[1] against him by Henry; nor was he anxious himself to precipitate a quarrel from which, if possible, he would gladly escape. He had a powerful party in England, which it was unwise to alienate by hasty, injudicious measures; and he could gain all which he himself desired by a simple policy of obstruction. His object was merely to protract the negotiation and prevent a decision, in the hope either that Henry would be wearied into acquiescence, or that Catherine herself would retire of her own accord, or, finally, that some happy accident might occur to terminate the difficulty. It is, indeed, much to the honour of Charles V. that he resolved to support the queen. She had thrown herself on his protection; but princes in such matters consider prudence more than feeling, and he could gain nothing by defending her: while, both for himself and for the church he risked the loss of much. He over-rated the strength of his English connexion, and mistook the English character; but he was not blind to the hazard which he was incurring, and would have welcomed an escape from the dilemma perhaps as warmly as Henry would have welcomed it himself. The pope, who well knew his feelings, told Gardiner, 'It would be for the wealth of Christendom if the queen were in her grave; and he thought the emperor would be thereof most glad of all;' saying, also, 'that he thought like as the emperor had destroyed the temporalities of the church, so shall she be the destruction of the spiritualities.'[2]

---

[1] Such at least was the ultimate conclusion of a curious discussion. When the French herald declared war, the English herald accompanied him into the emperor's presence, and when his companion had concluded, followed up his words with an intimation that unless the French demands were complied with, England would unite to enforce them. The Emperor replied to Francis with defiance. To the English herald he expressed a hope that peace on that side would still be maintained. For the moment the two countries were uncertain whether they were at war or not. The Spanish ambassador in London did not know, and the court could not tell him. The English ambassador in Spain did not leave his post, but he was placed under surveillance. An embargo on Spanish and English property was laid respectively in the ports of the two kingdoms; and the merchants and residents were placed under arrest. Alarmed by the outcry in London, the king hastily concluded a truce with the Regent of the Netherlands, the language of which implied a state of war; but when peace was concluded between France and Spain, England appeared only as a contracting party, not as a principal, and in 1542 it was decided that the antecedent treaties between England and the empire continued in force.—See LORD HERBERT; HOLLINSHED; *State Papers,* vols. vii. viii. and ix.; with the treaties in RYMER, vol. vi. part 2.

[2] Gardiner to the King: BURNET'S *Collectanea,* p. 426.

In the summer of 1528, before the disaster at Naples, Cardinal Campeggio had left Rome on his way to England, where he was to hear the cause in conjunction with Wolsey. An initial measure of this obvious kind it had been impossible to refuse; and the pretexts under which it was for many months delayed, were exhausted before the pope's ultimate course had been made clear to him. But Campeggio was instructed to protract his journey to its utmost length, giving time for the campaign to decide itself. He loitered into the autumn, under the excuse of gout and other convenient accidents, until the news reached him of De Lautrec's death, which took place on the 21st of August; and then at length proceeding, he betrayed to Francis I., on passing through Paris, that he had no intention of allowing judgment to be passed upon the cause.[1] Even Wolsey was beginning to tremble at what he had attempted, and was doubtful of success.[2] The seeming relief came in time, for Henry's patience was fast running out. He had been over-persuaded into a course which he had never cordially approved. The majority of the council, especially the Duke of Norfolk and the Duke of Suffolk, were traditionally imperial, and he himself might well doubt whether he might not have found a nearer road out of his difficulties by adhering to Charles. Charles, after all, was not ruining the papacy, and had no intention of ruining it; and his lightest word weighed more at the court of Rome than the dubious threats and prayers of France. The Bishop of Bayonne, resident French ambassador in London, whose remarkable letters transport us back into the very midst of that unquiet and stormy scene, tells us plainly that the French alliance was hated by the country, that the nobility were all for the emperor, and that among the commons the loudest discontent was openly expressed against Wolsey from the danger of the interruption of the trade with Flanders. Flemish ships had been detained in London, and English ships in retaliation had been arrested in the Zealand ports; corn was unusually dear, and the expected supplies from Spain and Germany were cut off;[3] while the derangement of the woollen trade, from the reluctance of the merchants to venture purchases, was causing distress all over the country, and Wolsey had been driven to the most arbitrary measures to prevent open disturbance.[4] He had set his hopes

---

[1] Duke of Suffolk to Henry the Eighth: *State Papers*, vol. vii. p. 183.
[2] Ibid.
[3] HALL, p. 744.
[4] When the clothiers of Essex, Kent, Wiltshire, Suffolk, and other

upon the chance of a single cast which he would not believe could fail him, but on each fresh delay he was compelled to feel his declining credit, and the Bishop of Bayonne writes, on the 20th of August, 1528, that the cardinal was in bad spirits, and had told him in confidence that 'if he could only see the divorce arranged, the king remarried, the succession settled, and the laws and the manners and customs of the country reformed, he would retire from the world and would serve God the remainder of his days.'[1] To these few trifles he would be contented to confine himself—only to these; he was past sixty, he was weary of the world, and his health was breaking, and he would limit his hopes to the execution of a work for which centuries imperfectly sufficed. It seemed as if he measured his stature by the lengthening shadow, as his sun made haste to its setting. Symptoms of misgiving may be observed in the many anxious letters which he wrote while Campeggio was so long upon his road; and the Bishop of Bayonne, whose less interested eyes could see more deeply into the game, warned him throughout that the pope was playing him false.[2] Only in a revulsion from violent despondency could he have allowed himself, on the mere arrival of the legate, and after a few soft words from him, to write in the following strain to Sir Gregory Cassalis :—

'You cannot believe the exultation with which at length I find myself successful in the object for which these many years, with all my industry, I have laboured. At length I have found means to bind my most excellent sovereign and this glorious realm to the holy Roman see in faith

---

shires which are clothmaking, brought clothes to London to be sold, as they were wont, few merchants or none bought any cloth at all. When the clothiers lacked sale, then they put from them their spinners, carders, tuckers, and such others that lived by clothworking, which caused the people greatly to murmur, and specially in Suffolk, for if the Duke of Norfolk had not wisely appeased them, no doubt but they had fallen to some rioting. When the king's council was advertised of the inconvenience, the cardinal sent for a great number of the merchants of London, and to them said, 'Sirs, the king is informed that you use not yourselves like merchants, but like graziers and artificers; for where the clothiers do daily bring clothes to the market for your ease, to their great cost, and then be ready to sell them, you of your wilfulness will not buy them, as you have been accustomed to do. What manner of men be you?' said the cardinal. 'I tell you that the king straightly commandeth you to buy their clothes as before time you have been accustomed to do, upon pain of his high displeasure.'—HALL, p. 746.

[1] LEGRAND, vol. iii. p. 157. By manners and customs he was referring clearly to his intended reformation of the church. See the letter of Fox, Bishop of Winchester (STRYPE's *Memorials*, vol. ii. p. 25), in which Wolsey's intentions are dwelt upon at length.

[2] Ibid. pp. 136-7.

and obedience for ever. Henceforth will this people become the most sure pillar of support to bear up the sacred fabric of the church. Henceforth, in recompense for that enduring felicity which he has secured to it, our most Holy Lord has all England at his devotion. In brief time will this noble land make its grateful acknowledgments to his clemency for the preservation of the most just, most wise, most excellent of princes, a prince endowed with every royal grace, and at the same time for the secure establishment of the realm and the protection of the royal succession.'[1]

This letter is dated on the fourth of October, and was written in the hope that the pope had collected his courage, and that the legate had brought powers to proceed to judgment. In a few days the prospect was again clouded, and Wolsey was once more in despair.[2] Campeggio had brought with him instructions if possible to arrange a compromise,—if a compromise was impossible, to make the best use of his ingenuity, and do nothing and allow nothing to be done. In one of two ways, however, it was hoped that he might effect a peaceful solution. He urged the king to give way and to proceed no further; and this failing, as he was prepared to find, he urged the same thing upon the queen.[3] He invited her, or he was directed to invite her, in the pope's name,[4] for the sake of the general interests of Christendom, to take the vows and enter what was called *religio lara*, a state in which she might live unincumbered by obligations except the easy one of chastity, and free from all other restrictions either of habit, diet, or order. The proposal was Wolsey's, and was formed when he found the limited nature of Campeggio's instructions;[5] but it was adopted by the latter; and I cannot but think (though I have no proof of it) that it was not adopted without the knowledge of the emperor. No portion of Charles's private correspondence with Queen Catherine has yet, I believe, been discovered, and we are left to form conjectures of its probable purport from hints and probabilities. He would seem generally, whatever were his own interests, to have declined to press her to consider anything except herself and her daughter; he made it his duty to support her in the ignominious position in which she was placed, and submitted his own conduct to be guided by her wishes. It

[1] *State Papers*, vol. ii. pp. 96-7.
[2] Wolsey to Cassalis: Ibid. p. 100.
[3] *State Papers*, vol. vii. pp. 106-7.   [4] Ibid. p. 118.
[5] Ibid. p. 113.

cannot be doubted, however, from the pope's words, and also from the circumstances of the case, that if she could have prevailed upon herself to yield, it would have relieved him from a painful embarrassment. As a prince, he must have felt the substantial justice of Henry's demand, and in refusing to allow the pope to pass a judicial sentence of divorce, he could not but have known that he was compromising the position of the Holy See: while Catherine herself, on the other hand, if she had yielded, would have retired without a stain; no opinion would have been pronounced upon her marriage; the legitimacy of the Princess Mary would have been left without impeachment; and her right to the succession, in the event of no male heir following from any new connexion which the king might form, would have been readily secured to her by act of parliament. It may be asked why she did not yield, and it is difficult to answer the question. She was not a person who would have been disturbed by the loss of a few court vanities. Her situation as Henry's wife could not have had many charms for her, nor can it be thought that she retained a personal affection for him. If she had loved him, she would have suffered too deeply in the struggle to have continued to resist, and the cloister would have seemed a paradise. Or if the cloister had appeared too sad a shelter for her, she might have gone back to the gardens of the Alhambra, where she had played as a child, carrying with her the affectionate remembrance of every English heart, and welcomed by her own people as an injured saint. Nor again can we suppose that the possible injury of her daughter's prospects from the birth of a prince by another marriage could have seemed of so vast moment to her. Those prospects were already more than endangered, and would have been rather improved than brought into further peril.

It is not for us to dictate the conduct which a woman smarting under injuries so cruel ought to have pursued. She had a right to choose the course which seemed the best to herself, and England especially could not claim of a stranger that readiness to sacrifice herself which she might have demanded and exacted of one of her own children. We may regret, however, what we are unable to censure; and the most refined ingenuity could scarcely have invented a more unfortunate answer than that which she returned to the legate's request. She seems to have said that she was ready to take vows of chastity if the king would do the same. It does not appear whether the request was *formally* made, or whether it was merely suggested to her in private conversation. That she told the legates, however, what her answer would be, appears certain from the following passage, sadly indicating the 'devices of policy' to which in this unhappy business honourable men allowed themselves to be driven:—

'Forasmuch as it is like that the queen shall make marvellous difficulty, and in nowise be conformable to enter religion[1] or take vows of chastity, but that to induce her thereunto, there must be ways and means of high policy used, and all things possible devised to encourage her to the same; wherein percase she shall resolve that she in no wise will condescend so to do, unless that the King's Highness also do the semblable for his part; the king's said orators shall therefore in like wise ripe and instruct themselves by their secret learned council in the court of Rome, if, for so great a benefit to ensue unto the king's succession, realm, and subjects, with the quiet of his conscience, his Grace should promise so to enter religion on vows of chastity for his part, only thereby to conduce the queen thereunto, whether in that case the Pope's Holiness may dispense with the King's Highness for the same promise, oath, or vow, discharging his Grace clearly of the same.'[2]

The explanation of the queen's conduct lies probably in regions into which it is neither easy nor well to penetrate; in regions of outraged delicacy and wounded pride, in a vast drama of passion which had been enacted behind the scenes. From the significant hints which are let fall of the original cause of the estrangement, it was of a kind more difficult to endure than the ordinary trial of married women, the transfer of a husband's affection to some fairer face; and a wife whom so painful a misfortune had failed to crush would be likely to have been moved by it to a deeper and more bitter indignation even, because while she could not blame herself, she knew not whom she might rightly allow herself to blame. And if this were so, the king is not likely to have allayed the storm when at length, putting faith in Wolsey's promises, he allowed himself openly to regard another person as his future wife, establishing her in the palace at Greenwich under the same roof with the queen, with reception rooms, and royal state, and a position openly acknowledged,[3] the gay court and courtiers forsaking the gloomy dignity of the

[1] Take the veil.
[2] Instruction to the Ambassadours at Rome: *State Papers*, vol. vii. p. 136.
[3] *Letters of the Bishop of Bayonne*, LEGRAND, vol. iii.

actual wife for the gaudy splendour of her brilliant rival. Tamer blood than that which flowed in the veins of a princess of Castile would have boiled under these indignities; and we have little reason to be surprised if policy and prudence were alike forgotten by Catherine in the bitterness of the draught which was forced upon her, and if her own personal wrongs outweighed the interests of the world. Henry had proceeded to the last unjustifiable extremity as soon as the character of Campeggio's mission had been made clear to him, as if to demonstrate to all the world that he was determined to persevere at all costs and hazards.[1] Taking the management of the negotiation into his own keeping, he sent Sir Francis Bryan, the cousin of Anne Boleyn, to the pope, to announce that what he required must be done, and to declare peremptorily, no more with covert hints, but with open menace, that in default of help from Rome, he would lay the matter before parliament, to be settled at home by the laws of his own country.

Meanwhile, the emperor, who had hitherto conducted himself with the greatest address, had fallen into his first error. He had retreated skilfully out of the embarrassment in which the pope's imprisonment involved him, and mingling authority and dictation with kindness and deference, he had won over the Holy See to his devotion, and neutralized the danger to which the alliance of France and England threatened to expose him. His correspondence with the latter country assured him of the unpopularity of the course which had been pursued by the cardinal; he was aware of the obstruction of trade which it had caused, and of the general displeasure felt by the people at the breach of an old friendship; while the league with France in behalf of the Roman church had been barren of results, and was made ridiculous by the obvious preference of the pope for the enemy from whom it was formed to deliver him. If Charles had understood the English temper, therefore, and had known how to avail himself of the opportunity, events might have run in a very different channel. But he was not aware of the earnestness with which the people were bent upon securing the succession, nor of their loyal attachment to Henry. He supposed that disapproval of the course followed by Wolsey to obtain the divorce implied an aversion to it altogether; and trusting to his interest in the privy council, and to his commercial connexion with the city,

---

[1] LEGRAND, vol. iii. p. 231.

he had attempted to meet menace with menace, and had
replied to the language addressed by Henry to the pope
with an attempt to feel the pulse of English disaffection.

The opportunity for a movement of this kind had not
yet arrived. There was as yet no wide disaffection; but
there was a chance of serious outbreaks; and Henry instantly threw himself upon the nation. He summoned the
peers by circular to London, and calling a general meeting, composed of the nobility, the privy council, the lord
mayor, and the great merchants of the city, he laid before
them a specific detail of his objects in desiring the divorce;[1]

[1] Henrici regis octavi de repudianda domina Catherina oratio Idibus
Novembris habita 1528.

Veneranda et chara nobis præsulum procerum atque consiliariorum
cohors quos communis reipublicæ atque regni nostri administrandi cura
conjunxit. Haud vos latet divina nos Providentia viginti jam ferme
annis hanc nostram patriam tanta felicitate rexisse ut in illa ab hosti-
libus incursionibus tuta semper interea fuerit et nos in his bellis quæ
suscepimus victores semper evasimus; et quanquam in eo gloriari jure
possumus majorem tranquillitatem opes et honores prioribus huc usque
ductis socculis, nunquam subditis a majoribus parentibusque nostris
Angliæ regibus quam a nobis provenisse, tamen quando cum hac gloria
in mentem una venit ac concurrit mortis cogitatio, veremur ne nobis
sine prole legitima decedentibus majorem ex morte nostra patiamini
calamitatem quam ex vita fructum ac emolumentum percepistis. Recens enim in quorundam vestrorum animis adhuc est illius cruenti
temporis memoria quod a Ricardo tertio cum avi nostri materni Edwardi Quarti statum in controversium vocasset ejusque heredes regno
atque vita privasset illatum est. Tum ex historiis notæ sunt illæ diræ
strages quæ a clarissimis Angliæ gentibus Eboracensi atque Lan-
castrensi, dum inter se de regno et imperio multis ævis contenderent,
populo evenerunt. Ac illæ ex justis nuptiis inter Henricum Septimum
et dominam Elizabetham clarissimos nostros parentes contractis in
nobis inde legitima nata sobole sopitæ tandem desierunt. Si vero
quod absit, regalis ex nostris nuptiis stirps quæ jure deinceps regnare
possit non nascatur, hoc regnum civilibus atque intestinis se versabit
tumultibus aut in exterorum dominationem atque potestatem veniet.
Nam quanquam forma atque venustate singulari, quæ magno nobis
solatio fuit filiam Dominam Mariam ex nobilissima fœmina Domina
Catherina procreavimus, tamen a piis atque eruditis theologis nuper
accepimus quia eam quæ Arturi fratris nostri conjux ante fuerat uxorem duximus nostras nuptias jure divino esse vetitas, partumque inde
editum non posse censeri legitimum. Id quod eo vehementius nos
angit et excruciat, quod cum superiori anno legatos ad conciliandas
inter Aureliensem ducem et filiam nostram Mariam nuptias ad Fran-
ciscum Gallorum regem misisissemus a quodam ejus consiliario respon-
sum est, 'antequam de hujusmodi nuptiis agatur inquirendum esse
prius an Maria fuerit filia nostra legitima; constat enim 'inquit,' quod
ex domina Catherina fratris sui vidua cujusmodi nuptiæ jure divino
interdictæ sunt suscepta est.' Quæ oratio quanto metu ac horrore
animum nostrum turbaverit quia res ipsa æternæ tam animi quam cor-
poris salutis periculum in se continet, et quum perplexis cogitationibus
conscientiam occupat, vos quibus et capitis aut fortunæ ac multo magis
animarum jactura immineret, remedium nisi adhibere velitis, ignorare
non posse arbitror. Hæc una res—quod Deo teste et in Regis oraculo
affirmamus—nos impulit ut per legatos doctissimorum per totum orbem
Christianum theologorum sententias exquireremus et Romani Pontificis
legatum verum atque æquum judicium de tanta causa laturum ut tran-
quilla deinceps et integra conscientia in conjugio licito vivere possimus

and informed them of the nature of the measures which had been taken.[1] This, the French ambassador informs us, gave wide satisfaction, and served much to allay the disquiet; but so great was the indignation against Wolsey, that disturbances in London were every day anticipated; and at one time the danger appeared so threatening, that an order of council was issued, commanding all strangers to leave the city, and a general search was instituted for arms.[2] The strangers aimed at were the Flemings, whose numbers made them formidable, and who were, perhaps, supposed to be ready to act under instructions from abroad. The cloud, however, cleared away; the order was not enforced; and the propitious moment for treason had not yet arrived. The emperor had felt so confident that, in the autumn of 1528, he had boasted that, 'before the winter was over, he would fling Henry from his throne by the hands of his own subjects.' The words had been repeated to Wolsey, who mentioned them openly at his table before more than a hundred gentlemen. A person present exclaimed, 'That speech has lost the emperor more than a hundred thousand hearts among us;'[3] an expression which reveals at once the strength and the weakness of the imperial party. England might have its own opinions of the policy of the government, but it was in no humour to tolerate treason, and the first hint of

accerseremus. In quo si ex sacris litteris hoc quo viginti jam fere annis gavisi sumus matrimonium jure divino permissum esse manifeste liquidoque constabit, non modo ob conscientiæ tranquillitatem, verum etiam ob amabiles mores virtutesque quibus regina prædita et ornata est. nihil optatius nihilque jucundius accidere nobis potest. Nam præterquam quod regali atque nobili genere prognata est, tantâ præterea comitate et obsequio conjugali tum cæteris animi morumque ornamentis quæ nobilitatem illustrant omnes fœminas his viginti annis sic mihi anteire visa est ut si a conjugio liber essem ac solutus, si jure divino liceret, hanc solam præ cæteris fœminis stabili mihi jure ac fœdere matrimoniali conjungerem. Si vero in hoc judicio matrimonium nostrum jure divino prohibitum, ideoque ab initio nullum irritumque fuisse pronuncietur, infelix hic meus casus multis lacrimis lugendus ac deplorandus erit. Non modo quod a tam illustris et amabilis mulieris consuetudine et consortio divertendum sit, sed multo magis quod specie ad similitudinem veri conjugii deocpti in amplexibus plusquam fornicariis tam multos annos trivimus nullâ legitimâ prognatâ nobis sobole quæ nobis mortuis hujus inclyti regni hereditatem capessat.

Hæ nostræ curæ istæque solicitudines sunt quæ mentem atque conscientiam nostram dies noctesque torquent et excruciant, quibus auferendis et profligandis remedium ex hâc legatione et judicio opportunum quærimus. Ideoque vos quorum virtuti atque fidei multum attribuimus rogamus ut certum atque genuinum nostrum de hâc re sensum quem ex nostro sermone percepistis populo declaretis: eumque excitetis ut nobiscum una oraret ut ad conscientiæ nostræ pacem atque tranquillitatem in hoc judicio veritas multis jam annis tenebris involuta tandem patefiat.—WILKINS's *Concilia*, vol. iii. p. 714.

[1] HALL. *Letters of the Bishop of Bayonne*, LEGRAND, vol. iii.

[2] LEGRAND, vol. iii.   [3] Ibid. pp. 232, 3.

revolt was followed by an instant recoil. The discovery of more successful intrigues in Scotland and Ireland completed the destruction of Charles's influence;[1] and the result of these ill-judged and premature efforts was merely to unite the nation in their determination to prosecute the divorce.

Thus were the various parties in the vast struggle which was about to commence gravitating into their places; and mistake combined with policy to place them in their true positions. Wolsey, in submitting 'the king's matter' to the pope, had brought to issue the question whether the papal authority should be any longer recognised in England; and he had secured the ruin of that authority by the steps through which he hoped to establish it; while Charles, by his unwise endeavours to foment a rebellion, severed with his own hand the links of a friendship which would have been seriously embarrassing if it had continued. By him, also, was dealt the concluding stroke in this first act of the drama; and though we may grant him credit for the ingenuity of his contrivance, he can claim it only at the expense of his probity. The pope, when the commission was appointed for the trial of the cause in England, had given a promise in writing that the commission should not be revoked. It seemed, therefore, that the legates would be compelled, in spite of themselves, to pronounce sentence; and that the settlement of the question, in one form or other, could not long be delayed. At the pressure of the crisis in the winter of 1528-9, a document was produced alleged to have been found in Spain, which furnished a pretext for a recal of the engagement, and opening new questions, indefinite and inexhaustible, rendered the passing of a sentence in England impossible. Unhappily, the weight of the king's claim (however it had been rested on its true merits in conversation and in letters) had, by the perverse ingenuity of the lawyers, been laid on certain informalities and defects in the original bull of dispensation, which had been granted by Julius II. for the marriage of Henry and Catherine. At the moment when the legates' court was about to be opened, a copy of a brief was brought forward, bearing the same date as the bull, exactly meeting the objection. The authenticity of this brief was open, on its own merits, to grave doubt; and suspicion becomes certainty when we find it was dropped out of the controversy so soon as the immediate object

---

[1] *State Papers*, vol. vii. p. 120; Ibid. p. 186.

was gained for which it was produced. But the legates'
hands were instantly tied by it. The 'previous question'
of authenticity had necessarily to be tried before they
could take another step; and the 'original' of the brief
being in the hands of the emperor, who refused to send
it into England, but offered to send it to Rome, the cause
was virtually transferred to Rome, where Henry, as he
knew, was unlikely to consent to plead, or where he could
himself rule the decision. He had made a stroke of political finesse, which answered not only the purpose that
he immediately intended, but answered, also, the purpose that he did not intend—of dealing the hardest
blow which it had yet received to the supremacy of the
Holy See.

The spring of 1529 was wasted in fruitless efforts to
obtain the brief. At length, in May, the proceedings were
commenced; but they were commenced only in form, and
were never more than an illusion. Catherine had been
instructed in the course which she was to pursue. She
appealed from the judgment of the legates to that of the
pope; and the pope, with the plea of the new feature
which had arisen in the case, declared that he could not
refuse to revoke his promise. Having consented to the
production of the brief, he had in fact no alternative; nor
does it appear what he could have urged in excuse of
himself. He may have suspected the forgery; nay, it is
certain that in England he was believed to be privy to
it; but he could not ignore an important feature of necessary evidence, especially when pressed upon him by
the emperor; and it was in fact no more than an absur-
dity to admit the authority of a papal commission, and
to refuse to permit an appeal from it to the pope in person. We may thank Clement for dispelling a chimera by
a simple act of consistency. The power of the See of
Rome in England was a constitutional fiction, acknowledged only on condition that it would consent to be
inert. So long as a legate's court sat in London, men
were able to conceal from themselves the fact of a foreign
jurisdiction, and to feel that, substantially, their national
independence was respected; when the fiction aspired to
become a reality, but one consequence was possible. If
Henry himself would have stooped to plead at a foreign
tribunal, the spirit of the nation would not have permitted him to inflict so great a dishonour on the free
majesty of England.

So fell Wolsey's great scheme, and with it fell the
last real chance of maintaining the pope's authority in

7 *

England under any form. The people were smarting under the long humiliation of the delay, and ill-endured to see the interests of England submitted, as they virtually were, to the arbitration of a foreign prince. The emperor, not the pope, was the true judge who sat to decide the quarrel; and their angry jealousy refused to tolerate longer a national dishonour.

'The great men of the realm,' wrote the legates, 'are storming in bitter wrath at our procrastination. Lords and commons alike complain that they are made to expect at the hands of strangers things of vital moment to themselves and their fortunes. And many persons here who would desire to see the pope's authority in this country diminished or annulled, are speaking in language which we cannot repeat without horror.'[1]

And when, being in such a mood, they were mocked, after two weary years of negotiation, by the opening of a fresh vista of difficulties, when they were informed that the further hearing of the cause was transferred to Italy, even Wolsey, with certain ruin before him, rose in protest before such a dream of shame. He was no more the Roman legate, but the English minister.

'If the advocation be passed,' he wrote to Cassalis,[2] 'or shall now at any time hereafter pass, with citation of the king in person, or by proctor, to the court of Rome, or with any clause of interdiction or excommunication, *vel cum inrocatione brachii sæcularis*, whereby the king should be precluded from taking his advantage otherwise, the dignity and prerogative royal of the king's crown, whereunto all the nobles and subjects of this realm will adhere and stick unto the death, may not tolerate nor suffer that the same be obeyed. And to say the truth, in so doing the pope should not only show himself the king's enemy, but also as much as in him is, provoke all other princes and people to be the semblable. Nor shall it ever be seen that the king's cause shall be ventilated or decided in any place out of his own realm; *but that if his Grace should come at any time to the Court of Rome, he would do the same with such a main and army royal as should be formidable to the pope and all Italy.*'

Wolsey, however, failed in his protest; the advocation was passed, Campeggio left England, and he was lost. A crisis had arrived, and a revolution of policy was inevitable. From the accession of Henry VII., the country had been governed by a succession of ecclesiastical ministers, who being priests as well as statesmen, were essentially conservative; and whose efforts in a position of constantly increasing difficulty had been directed towards resisting the changing tendencies of the age, and either evading a reformation of the church while they admitted its necessity, or retaining the conduct of it in their own hands, while they were giving evidence of their inability to accomplish the work. It was now over; the ablest representative of this party, in a last desperate effort to retain power, had decisively failed. Writs were issued for a parliament when the legate's departure was determined, and the consequences were inevitable. Wolsey had known too well the unpopularity of his foreign policy, to venture on calling a parliament himself. He relied on success as an ultimate justification; and inasmuch as success had not followed, he was obliged to bear the necessary fate of a minister who, in a free country, had thwarted the popular will, and whom fortune deserted in the struggle. The barriers which his single hand had upheld suddenly gave way, the torrent had free course, and he himself was the first to be swept away. In modern language, we should describe what took place as a change of ministry, the government being transferred to an opposition, who had been irritated by long depression under the hands of men whom they despised, and who were borne into power by an irresistible force in a moment of excitement and danger. The king, who had been persuaded against his better judgment to accept Wolsey's schemes, admitted the rising spirit without reluctance, contented to moderate its action, but no longer obstructing or permitting it to be obstructed. Like all great English statesmen, he was constitutionally conservative, but he had the tact to perceive the conditions under which, in critical times, conservatism is possible; and although he continued to endure for himself the trifling of the papacy, he would not, for the sake of the pope's interest, delay further the investigation of the complaints of the people against the church; while in the future prosecution of his own cause, he resolved to take no steps except with the consent of the legislature, and in a question of national moment, to consult only the nation's wishes.

The new ministry held a middle place between the moving party in the commons and the expelled ecclesiastics, the principal members of it being the chief representatives of the old aristocracy, who had been Wolsey's fiercest opponents, but who were disinclined by constitution and sympathy from sweeping measures. An attempt was made, indeed, to conciliate the more old-fashioned of the churchmen, by an offer of the seals to Warham, Archbishop of Canterbury, probably because he originally opposed the marriage between the king and his sister-in-law, and because it was hoped that his objections remained unaltered. Warham, however, as we shall see, had changed his mind: he declined, on the plea of age, and the office of chancellor was given to Sir Thomas More, perhaps the person least disaffected to the clergy who could have been found among the leading laymen. The substance of power was vested in the Dukes of Norfolk and Suffolk, the great soldier-nobles of the age, and Sir William Fitz-William, lord admiral; to all of whom the ecclesiastical domination had been most intolerable, while they had each of them brilliantly distinguished themselves in the wars with France and Scotland. According to the French ambassador, we must add one more minister, supreme, if we may trust him, above them all. 'The Duke of Norfolk,' he writes, 'is made president of the council, the Duke of Suffolk vice-president, and above them both is Mistress Anne;'[1] this last addition to the council being one which boded little good to the interests of the See that had so long detained her in expectation. So confident were the destructive party of the temper of the approaching parliament, and of the irresistible pressure of the times, that the general burden of conversation at the dinner-tables in the great houses in London was an exulting expectation of a dissolution of the church establishment, and a confiscation of ecclesiastical property; the king himself being the only obstacle which was feared by them. 'These noble lords imagine,' continues the same writer, 'that the cardinal once dead or ruined, they will incontinently plunder the church, and strip it of all its wealth,' adding that there was no occasion for him to write this in cipher, for it was everywhere openly spoken of.[2]

Movements, nevertheless, which are pregnant with vital change, are slow in assuming their essential direction, even after the stir has commenced. Circumstances do not immediately open themselves; the point of vision alters gradually; and fragments of old opinions, and prepossessions, and prejudices remain interfused with the new, even in the clearest minds, and cannot at a moment be shaken off. Only the unwise change suddenly; and we can never too often remind ourselves, when we see men

---

[1] LEGRAND, vol. iii. p. 377.   [2] Ibid. p. 374.

stepping forward with uncertainty and hesitation over a road, where to us, who know the actual future, all seems so plain, that the road looked different to the actors themselves, who were beset with imaginations of the past, and to whom the gloom of the future appeared thronged with phantoms of possible contingencies. The hasty expectations of the noble lords were checked by Henry's prudence; and though parties were rapidly arranging themselves, there was still confusion. The city, though disinclined to the pope and the church, continued to retain an inclination for the emperor; and the pope had friends among Wolsey's enemies, who, by his overthrow, were pressed forward into prominence, and divided the victory with the reformers. The presence of Sir Thomas More in the council was a guarantee that no exaggerated measures against the church would be permitted so long as he held the seals; and Henry, perhaps, was anxious to leave room for conciliation, which he hoped that the pope would desire as much as himself, so soon as the meeting of parliament had convinced him that the mutinous disposition of the nation had not been overstated by his own and Wolsey's letters.

The impression conceived two years before of the hostile relations between the pope and Charles had not yet been wholly effaced; and even as late as September, 1529, after the closing of the legates' court, in the very heat of the public irritation, there were persons who believed that when Clement met his imperial captor face to face, and the interview had taken place which had been arranged for the ensuing January, his eyes would be opened, and that he would fall back upon England.[1] At the same time, the incongruities in the constitution of the council became so early apparent, that their agreement was thought impossible, and Wolsey's return to power was discussed openly as a probability[2]—a result which Anne Boleyn, who, better than any other person, knew the king's feelings, never ceased to fear, till, a year after his disgrace, the welcome news were brought to her that he had sunk into his long rest, where the sick load of office and of obloquy would gall his back no more.

There was a third party in the country, unconsidered as yet, who had a part to play in the historical drama: a party which, indeed, if any one had known it, was the most important of all; the only one which, in a true, high sense, was of importance at all; and for the sake of which,

<hr>

[1] LEGRAND, vol. iii. p. 355. [2] Ibid.

little as it then appeared to be so, the whole work was to be done—composed at that time merely of poor men, poor cobblers, weavers, carpenters, trade apprentices, and humble artisans, men of low birth and low estate, who might be seen at night stealing along the lanes and alleys of London, carrying with them some precious load of books which it was death to possess; and giving their lives gladly, if it must be so, for the brief tenure of so dear a treasure. These men, for the present, were likely to fare ill from the new ministry. They were the disturbers of order, the anarchists, the men disfigured *pravitate hereticâ*, by monstrous doctrines, and consequently by monstrous lives—who railed at authorities, and dared to read New Testaments with their own eyes—who, consequently, by their excesses and extravagances, brought discredit upon liberal opinions, and whom moderate liberals (as they always have done, and always will do while human nature remains itself) held it necessary for their credit's sake to persecute, that a censorious world might learn to make no confusion between true wisdom and the folly which seemed to resemble it. The Protestants had not loved Wolsey, and they had no reason to love him; but it was better to bear a fagot of dry sticks in a procession of symbolic punishment, than, lashed fast to a stake in Smithfield, amidst piles of the same fagots kindled into actual flames, to sink into a heap of blackened dust and ashes; and before a year had passed, they would gladly have accepted again the hated cardinal, to escape from the philosophic mercies of Sir Thomas More. The number of English Protestants at this time it is difficult to conjecture. The importance of such men is not to be measured by counting heads. In 1526, they were organized into a society, calling themselves 'the Christian brotherhood,'[1] with a central committee sitting in London; with subscribed funds, regularly audited, for the purchase of Testaments and tracts; and with paid agents, who travelled up and down the country to distribute them. Some of the poorer clergy belonged to the society;[2] and among the city merchants there were many well inclined to it, and who, perhaps, attended its meetings 'by night, secretly, for fear of the Jews.' But, as a rule, 'property and influence' continued to hold haughtily aloof, and the pioneers of the new opinions had yet to win their way along a scorched and blackened path of

[1] Memorandum relating to the Society of Christian Brethren: *Rolls House MS.*

[2] DALABER'S *Narrative*, printed in FOXE, vol. iv. Seeley's Ed.

suffering, before the State would consent to acknowledge them. We think bitterly of these things, and yet we are but quarrelling with what is inevitable from the constitution of the world. New doctrines ever gain readiest hearing among the common people; not only because the interests of the higher classes are usually in some degree connected with the maintenance of existing institutions; but because ignorance is itself a protection against the many considerations which embarrass the judgment of the educated. The value of a doctrine cannot be determined on its own apparent merits by men whose habits of mind are settled in other forms; while men of experience know well that out of the thousands of theories which rise in the fertile soil below them, it is but one here and one there which grows to maturity; and the precarious chances of possible vitality, where the opposite probabilities are so enormous, oblige them to discourage and repress opinions which threaten to disturb existing institutions, or which, by the rules of existing beliefs, imperil the souls of those who entertain them. Persecution has ceased among ourselves, because we do not any more believe that want of theoretic orthodoxy in matters of faith is necessarily fraught with the tremendous consequences which once were supposed to be attached to it. If, however, a school of Thugs were to rise among us, making murder a religious service; if they gained proselytes, and the proselytes put their teaching in execution, we should speedily begin again to persecute opinion—such opinion not being tolerable in a Christian state. What teachers of Thuggism would appear to ourselves, the teachers of heresy actually appeared to Sir Thomas More, only being as much more hateful as the eternal death of the soul is more terrible than the single and momentary separation of it from the body. There is, I think, no just ground on which to condemn conscientious Catholics on the score of persecution, except only this: that as we are now convinced of the injustice of the persecuting laws, so among those who believed them to be just, there were some who were led by an instinctive protest of human feeling to be lenient in the execution of those laws; while others of harder nature and more narrow sympathies enforced them without reluctance, and even with exultation. The heart, when it is rightly constituted, corrects the folly of the head; and wise good men, even though they entertain no conscious misgiving as to the soundness of their theories, may be delivered from the worst consequences of them, by trusting their more genial instincts. And thus, and

thus only, are we justified in consuring those whose names
figure largely in the persecuting lists. Their defence is
impregnable to logic. We blame them for the absence
of that humanity which is deeper than logic, and which
should have taught them to refuse the conclusions of their
speculative creed.

Such, then, was the state of parties in the autumn of
1529. The old conservatives, the political ecclesiastics,
had ceased to exist, and the clergy as a body were pa-
ralysed by corruption. There remained—

The English party, who had succeeded to power, and
who were bent upon a secular revolt.

The papal party, composed of theoretic theologians,
like Fisher, Bishop of Rochester, and represented on the
council by Sir Thomas More.

And both of these were united in their aversion to
the third party, that of the doctrinal Protestants, who
were still called heretics.

These three substantially divided what was sound in
England; the first composed of the mass of the people,
representing the principles of prudence, justice, good
sense, and the working faculties of social life: the two
last sharing between them the higher qualities of nobleness,
enthusiasm, self-devotion; but in their faith being without
discretion, and in their piety without understanding. The
problem of the Reformation was to reunite virtues which
could be separated only to their mutual confusion; and
to work out among them such inadequate reconciliation
as the weak wilfulness of human nature would allow.

Before I close this chapter, which is intended as a
general introduction, I have to say something of two pro-
minent persons whose character antecedent to the actions
in which we are to find them engaged it is desirable that
we should understand; I mean Henry VIII. himself, and
the lady whom he had selected to fill the place from which
Catherine of Arragon was to be deposed.

If Henry VIII. had died previous to the first agitation
of the divorce, his loss would have been deplored as one
of the heaviest misfortunes which had ever befallen the
country; and he would have left a name which would
have taken its place in history by the side of that of the
Black Prince or of the conqueror of Agincourt. Left at
the most trying age, with his character unformed, with
the means at his disposal of gratifying every inclination,
and married by his ministers when a boy to an unattrac-
tive woman far his senior, he had lived for thirty-six
years almost without blame, and bore through England

the reputation of an upright and virtuous king. Nature had been prodigal to him of her rarest gifts. In person he is said to have resembled his grandfather, Edward IV., who was the handsomest man in Europe. His form and bearing were princely; and amidst the easy freedom of his address, his manner remained majestic. No knight in England could match him in the tournament except the Duke of Suffolk; he drew with ease as strong a bow as was borne by any yeoman of his guard; and these powers were sustained in unfailing vigour by a temperate habit and by constant exercise. Of his intellectual ability we are not left to judge from the suspicious panegyrics of his contemporaries. His state papers and letters may be placed by the side of those of Wolsey or of Cromwell, and they lose nothing in the comparison. Though they are broadly different, the perception is equally clear, the expression equally powerful, and they breathe throughout an irresistible vigour of purpose. In addition to this he had a fine musical taste, carefully cultivated; he spoke and wrote in four languages; and his knowledge of a multitude of other subjects, with which his versatile ability made him conversant, would have formed the reputation of any ordinary man. He was among the best physicians of his age; he was his own engineer, inventing improvements in artillery, and new constructions in ship-building; and this not with the condescending incapacity of a royal amateur, but with thorough workmanlike understanding. His reading was vast, especially in theology, which has been ridiculously ascribed by Lord Herbert to his father's intention of educating him for the Archbishopric of Canterbury; as if the scientific mastery of such a subject could have been acquired by a boy of twelve years of age, for he was no more when he became Prince of Wales. He must have studied theology with the full maturity of his intellect; and he had a fixed and perhaps unfortunate interest in the subject itself.[1]

[1] All authorities agree in the early account of Henry, and his letters provide abundant proof that it is not exaggerated. The following description of him in the despatches of the Venetian ambassador shows the effect which he produced on strangers in 1515:—

'Assuredly, most serene prince, from what we have seen of him, and in conformity, moreover, with the report made to us by others, this most serene king is not only very expert in arms and of great valour and most excellent in his personal endowments, but is likewise so gifted and adorned with mental accomplishments of every sort, that we believe him to have few equals in the world. He speaks English, French, Latin, understands Italian well; plays almost on every instrument; sings and composes fairly; is prudent, and sage, and free from every vice.'—*Four Years at the Court of Henry VIII.* vol. i. p. 76.

Four years later, the same writer adds,—

In all directions of human activity Henry displayed natural powers of the highest order, at the highest stretch of industrious culture. He was 'attentive,' as it is called, 'to his religious duties,' being present at the services in chapel two or three times a day with unfailing regularity, and showing to outward appearance a real sense of religious obligation in the energy and purity of his life. In private he was good-humoured and good-natured. His letters to his secretaries, though never undignified, are simple, easy, and unrestrained; and the letters written by them to him are similarly plain and businesslike, as if the writers knew that the person whom they were addressing disliked compliments, and chose to be treated as a man. Again, from their correspondence with one another, when they describe interviews with him, we gather the same pleasant impression. He seems to have been always kind, always considerate; inquiring into their private concerns with genuine interest, and winning, as a consequence, their warm and unaffected attachment.

As a ruler he had been eminently popular. All his wars had been successful. He had the splendid tastes in which the English people most delighted, and he had substantially acted out his own theory of his duty which was expressed in the following words:—

'Scripture taketh princes to be, as it were, fathers and nurses to their subjects, and by Scripture it appeareth that it appertaineth unto the office of princes to see that right religion and true doctrine be maintained and taught, and that their subjects may be well ruled and governed by good and just laws; and to provide and care for them that all things necessary for them may be plenteous; and that the people and commonweal may increase; and to defend them from oppression and invasion, as well within the realm as without; and to see that justice be administered unto them indifferently; and to hear benignly all their complaints; and to show towards them, although they offend, fatherly pity. And, finally, so to correct them that be evil, that they had yet rather save them than lose them if it were not for respect of justice, and maintenance of peace and good order in the commonweal.'[1] These principles do really appear to have determined Henry's

---

'The king speaks good French, Latin, and Spanish; is very religious; hears three masses a day when he hunts, and sometimes five on other days; he hears the office every day in the queen's chamber—that is to say, vespers and complins.'—Ibid. vol. ii. p. 312.

[1] Exposition of the Commandments, set forth by Royal authority, 1536. This treatise was drawn up by the bishops, and submitted to, and revised by, the king.

conduct in his earlier years. His social administration
we have partially seen in the previous chapter. He had
more than once been tried with insurrection, which he
had soothed down without bloodshed, and extinguished
in forgiveness; and London long recollected the great
scene which followed 'evil May-day,' 1517, when the apprentices were brought down to Westminster Hall to receive their pardons. There had been a dangerous riot in
the streets, which might have provoked a mild government to severity; but the king contented himself with
punishing the five ringleaders, and four hundred other
prisoners, after being paraded down the streets in white
shirts with halters round their necks, were dismissed with
an admonition, Wolsey weeping as he pronounced it.[1]

It is certain that if, as I said, he had died before the
divorce was mooted, Henry VIII., like that Roman emperor said by Tacitus to have been *consensu omnium
dignus imperii nisi imperasset*, would have been considered by posterity as formed by Providence for the conduct of the Reformation, and his loss would have been
deplored as a perpetual calamity. We must allow him,
therefore, the benefit of his past career, and be careful
to remember it, when interpreting his later actions. Not
many men would have borne themselves through the same
trials with the same integrity; but the circumstances of
those trials had not tested the true defects in his moral
constitution. Like all princes of the Plantagenet blood,
he was a person of a most intense and imperious will.
His impulses, in general nobly directed, had never known
contradiction; and late in life, when his character was
formed, he was forced into collision with difficulties with
which the experience of discipline had not fitted him to
contend. Education had done much for him, but his nature required more correction than his position had permitted, whilst unbroken prosperity and early independence
of control had been his most serious misfortune. He had
capacity, if his training had been equal to it, to be one
of the greatest of men. With all his faults about him,
he was still perhaps the greatest of his contemporaries;
and the man best able of all living Englishmen to go-
vern England, had been set to do it by the conditions
of his birth.

The other person whose previous history we have to
ascertain is one, the tragedy of whose fate has blotted
the remembrance of her sins—if her sins were, indeed,

---

[1] SAGUDINO's *Summary. Four Years at the Court of Henry VIII.*
vol. ii. p. 75.

and in reality, more than imaginary. Forgetting all else in shame and sorrow, posterity has made piteous reparation for her death in the tenderness with which it has touched her reputation; and with the general instincts of justice, we have refused to qualify our indignation at the wrong which she experienced, by admitting either stain or shadow on her fame. It has been with Anne Boleyn as it has been with Catherine of Arragon—both are regarded as the victims of a tyranny which catholics and protestants unite to remember with horror; and each has taken the place of a martyred saint in the hagiology of the respective creeds. Catholic writers have, indeed, ill repaid, in their treatment of Anne, the admiration with which the mother of Queen Mary has been remembered in the Church of England; but the invectives which they have heaped upon her have defeated their object by their extravagance. It has been believed that matter failed them to sustain a just accusation, when they condescended to outrageous slander. Inasmuch, however, as some natural explanation can usually be given of the actions of human beings in this world without supposing them to have been possessed by extraordinary wickedness, and if we are to hold Anne Boleyn entirely free from fault, we place not the king only, but the privy council, the judges, the Lords and Commons, and the two Houses of Convocation, in a position fatal to their honour and degrading to ordinary humanity; we cannot without inquiry acquiesce in so painful a conclusion. The English nation also, as well as she, deserves justice at our hands; and it must not be thought uncharitable if we look with some scrutiny at the career of a person who, except for the catastrophe with which it was closed, would not so readily have obtained forgiveness for having admitted the addresses of the king, or for having received the homage of the court as its future sovereign, while the king's wife, her mistress, as yet resided under the same roof, with the title and the position of queen, and while the question was still undecided of the validity of the first marriage. If in that alone she was to blame, her fault was, indeed, revenged a thousandfold,—and yet no lady of true delicacy would have accepted such a position. Feeling for Queen Catherine ought to have forbidden it, if she was careless of respect for herself. It must, therefore, be permitted me, out of such few hints and scattered notices as remain, to collect such information as may be trusted respecting her early life before her appearance upon the great stage. These hints are but slight, since I shall not even mention

the scandals of Sanders, any more than I shall mention
the panegyrics of Foxe; stories which, as far as I can
learn, have no support in evidence, and rest on no stronger
foundation than the credulity of passion.

Anne Boleyn was the second daughter of Sir Thomas
Boleyn, a gentleman of noble family, though moderate
fortune;[1] who, by a marriage with the daughter of the
Duke of Norfolk, was brought into connexion with the
highest blood in the realm. The year of her birth has
not been certainly ascertained, but she is supposed to
have been seven years old[2] in 1514, when she accompanied
the Princess Mary into France, on the marriage of that
lady with Louis XII. Louis dying a few months subsequently, the princess married Sir Charles Brandon, afterwards created Duke of Suffolk, and returned to England.
Anne Boleyn did not return with her; she remained in
Paris to become accomplished in the graces and elegan-
cies, if she was not contaminated by the vices, of that
court, which, even in those days of royal licentiousness,
enjoyed an undesirable preeminence in profligacy. In the
French capital she could not have failed to see, to hear,
and to become familiar with occurrences with which no
young girl can be brought in contact with impunity, and
this poisonous atmosphere she continued to breathe for
nine years. She came back to England in 1525, to be
maid of honour to Queen Catherine, and to be distinguished
at the court, by general consent, for her talents, her accomplishments, and her beauty. Her portraits, though all
professedly by Holbein, or copied from pictures by him,
are singularly unlike each other. The profile in the picture
which is best known is pretty, innocent, and piquant, though
rather insignificant: there are other pictures, however, in
which we see a face more powerful, though less prepos-
sessing. In these the features are full and languid. The
eyes are large; but the expression, though remarkable, is
not pleasing, and indicates cunning more than thought,
and passion more than feeling; while the heavy lips and
massive chin wear a look of sensuality which is not to
be mistaken. Possibly all are like the original, but represented her under different circumstances, or at different
periods of her life. Previous to her engagement with the
king, she was the object of floating attentions from the

<hr>

[1] 'The truth is, when ¡I married my wife, I had but fifty pounds
to live on for me and my wife so long as my father lived, and yet
she brought me forth every year a child.'—Earl of Wiltshire to Cromwell: ELLIS, third series, vol. iii. pp. 22, 3.

[2] BURNET, vol. i. p. 69.

young noblemen about the court. Lord Percy, eldest son of Lord Northumberland, as we all know, was said to have been engaged to her. He was in the household of Cardinal Wolsey; and Cavendish, who was with him there, tells a long romantic story of the affair, which, if his account be true, was ultimately interrupted by Lord Northumberland himself. The story is not without its difficulties, since Lord Percy had been contracted, several years previously, to a daughter of the Earl of Shrewsbury,[1] whom he afterwards married, and by the law he could not have formed a second engagement so long as the first was undissolved. And again, he himself, when subsequently examined before the privy council, denied solemnly on his oath that any contract of the kind had existed.[2] At the same time, we cannot suppose Cavendish to have invented so circumstantial a narrative, and Percy would not have been examined if there had been no reason for suspicion. Something, therefore, probably had passed between him and the young maid of honour, though we cannot now conjecture of what nature; and we can infer only that it was not openly to her discredit, or she would not have obtained the position which cost her so dear. She herself confessed subsequently, before Archbishop Cranmer, to a connexion of some kind into which she had entered before her acquaintance with Henry. No evidence survives which will explain to what she referred, for the act of parliament which mentions the fact furnishes no details.[3] But it was of a kind which made her marriage with the king illegal, and illegitimatized the offspring of it; and it has been supposed, therefore, that, in spite of Lord Percy's denial, he had really engaged himself to her, and was afraid to acknowledge it. This supposition, however, is irreconcilable with the language of the act, which speaks of the circumstance, whatever it was, as only 'recently known;' nor could a contract with Percy have invalidated her marriage with the king, when Percy having been pre-contracted to another person, it would have been itself invalid. A light is thrown upon the subject by a letter found among Cromwell's papers, addressed by some unknown person to a Mr. Melton, also unknown, but written obviously when 'Mistress Anne' was a young lady about the court, and before she had been the object of any open attention from Henry.

[1] Thomas Allen to the Earl of Shrewsbury: LODGE's *Illustrations*, vol. i. p. 20.

[2] Earl of Northumberland to Cromwell: printed by LORD HERBERT and by BURNET.

[3] 28 Hen. VIII. cap. 7.

'Mr. MELTON.—This shall be to advertise you that Mistress Anne is changed from that she was at when we three were last together. Wherefore I pray you that ye be no devil's sakke, but according to the truth ever justify, as ye shall make answer before God; and do not suffer her in my absence to be married to any other man. I must go to my master, wheresoever he be, for the Lord Privy Seal desireth much to speak with me, whom if I should speak with in my master's absence, it would cause me to lose my head: and yet I know myself as true a man to my prince as liveth, whom (as my friend informeth me) I have offended grievously in my words. No more to you, but to have me commended unto Mistress Anne, and bid her remember her promise, which none can loose, but God only, to whom I shall daily during my life commend her.'[1]

The letter must furnish its own interpretation: for it receives none from any other quarter. Being in the possession of Cromwell, however, it had perhaps been forwarded to him at the time of Queen Anne's trial, and may have thus occasioned the investigation which led to the annulling of her marriage.

From the account which was written of her by the grandson of Sir Thomas Wyatt the poet, we still gather the impression (in spite of the admiring sympathy with which Wyatt writes) of a person with whom young men took liberties,[2] however she might seem to forbid them. In her diet she was an epicure, fond of dainty and delicate eating, and not always contented if she did not obtain what she desired. When the king's attentions towards her became first marked, Thomas Heneage, afterwards lord chamberlain, wrote to Wolsey, that he had one night been 'commanded down with a dish for Mistress Anne for supper; she caused me,' he added, 'to sup with her, and she wished she had some of your good meat, as carps, shrimps, and others.'[3] And this was not said in jest, since Heneage related it as a hint to Wolsey, that he might know what to do, if he wished to please her. In the same letter he suggested to the cardinal that she was a little displeased at not having received a token or present from him; she was afraid she was forgotten, he said, and 'my lady, her mother, desired me to send unto your Grace, and desire your Grace to bestow a morsel of tunny upon her.' Wolsey made her presents also at times

---

[1] ELLIS, third series, vol. ii. p. 131.
[2] Wyatt's Memorials, printed in Singer's CAVENDISH, p. 420.
[3] ELLIS, third series, vol. ii. p. 132.

of a more valuable character, as we find her acknowledging in language of exaggerated gratitude;[1] and, perhaps
the most painful feature in all her earlier history lies in
the contrast between the servility with which she addresed
the cardinal so long as he was in power, and the bitterness
which with the Bishop of Bayonne (and, in fact, all contemporary witnesses) tells us, that she pressed upon his
decline. Wolsey himself spoke of her under the title of
'the night-crow,'[2] as the person to whom he owed all
which was most cruel in his treatment; as 'the enemy
that never slept, but studied and continually imagined,
both sleeping and waking, his utter destruction.'[3]

Taking these things together, and there is nothing to
be placed beside them of a definitely pleasing kind, except
beauty and accomplishments, we form, with the assistance
of her pictures, a tolerable conception of this lady; a conception of her as a woman not indeed questionable, but
as one whose antecedents might lead consistently to a future either of evil or of good; and whose character re-
moves the surprise which we might be inclined to feel at
the position with respect to Queen Catherine in which she
consented to be placed. A harsh critic would describe
her, on this evidence, as a self-indulgent coquette, indifferent to the obligations of gratitude, and something careless
of the truth. From the letter referring to her, preserved
by Cromwell, it appears that she had broken a definite
promise at a time when such promises were legally binding, and that she had really done so was confirmed by
her subsequent confession. The breach of such promises
by a woman who could not be expected to understand the
grounds on which the law held them to be sacred, implies
no more than levity, and levity of this kind has been found
compatible with many other high qualities. Levity, however, it does undoubtedly imply, and the symptom, if a
light one, must be allowed the weight which is due to it.

It is a miserable duty to be compelled to search for
these indications of human infirmities; above all, when
they are the infirmities of a lady whose faults, let them
have been what they would, were so fearfully and terribly

---

[1] ELLIS, first series, vol. i. p. 135. 'My Lord, in my most humblest
wise that my poor heart can think, I do thank your Grace for your
kind letter, and for your rich and goodly present; the which I shall
never be able to deserve without your great help; of the which I have
hitherto had so great plenty, that all the days of my life I am most
bound of all creatures, next to the King's Grace, to love and serve
your Grace. Of the which I beseech you never to doubt that ever I
shall vary from this thought as long as any breath is in my body.'
[2] CAVENDISH: *Life of Wolsey*, p. 316. Singer's edition.
[3] CAVENDISH, pp. 364, 5.

expiated; and, if there were nothing else at issue but poor questions of petty scandal, it were better far that they perished in forgetfulness, and passed away out of mind and memory for ever. The fortunes of Anne Boleyn were unhappily linked with those of men to whom the greatest work ever yet accomplished in this country was committed; and the characters of a king of England, and of the three estates of the realm, are compromised in the treatment which she received from them.

CHAPTER III.

No Englishman can look back uninterested on the meeting of the parliament of 1529. The era at which it assembled is the most memorable in the history of this country, and the work which it accomplished before its dissolution was of larger moment politically and spiritually than the achievements of the Long Parliament itself. For nearly seven years it continued surrounded by intrigue, confusion, and at length conspiracy, presiding over a people from whom the forms and habits by which they had moved for centuries were falling like the shell of a chrysalis. While beset with enemies within the realm and without, it effected a revolution which severed England from the papacy, yet it preserved peace unbroken and prevented anarchy from breaking bounds; and although its hands are not pure from spot, and red stains rest on them which posterity will bitterly and long remember; yet if we consider the changes which it carried through, and if we think of the price which was paid by other nations for victory in the same struggle, we shall acknowledge that the records of the world contain no instance of such a triumph, bought at a cost so slight and tarnished by blemishes so trifling.

The letters of the French Ambassador[1] describe to us the gathering of the members into London, and the hum of expectation sounding louder and louder as the day of the opening approached. In order that we may see distinctly what London felt on this occasion, that we may understand in detail the nature of those questions with which parliament was immediately to deal, we will glance at some of the proceedings which had taken place in the Bishops' Consistory Courts during the few preceding years.

----

[1] *Letters of the Bishop of Bayonne,* LEGRAND, vol. iii. pp. 368, 378, &c.

The duties of the officials of these courts resembled in
theory the duties of the censors under the Roman Republic. In the middle ages, a lofty effort had been made
to overpass the common limitations of government, to introduce punishment for sins as well as crimes, and to
visit with temporal penalties the breach of the moral law.
The punishment best adapted for such offences was some
outward expression of the disapproval with which good
men regard acts of sin; some open disgrace; some spiritual
censure; some suspension of communion with the church,
accompanied by other consequences practically inconvenient,
to be continued until the offender had made reparation,
or had openly repented, or had given confirmed proof of
amendment. The administration of such a discipline fell,
as a matter of course, to the clergy. The clergy were
the guardians of morality; their characters were a claim
to confidence, their duties gave them opportunities of
observation which no other men could possess; while their
priestly office gave solemn weight to their sentences.
Thus arose throughout Europe a system of spiritual surveillance over the habits and conduct of every man, extending from the cottage to the castle, taking note of all
wrong dealing, of all oppression of man by man, of all
licentiousness and profligacy, and representing upon earth,
in the principles by which it was guided, the laws of the
great tribunal of Almighty God.

Such was the origin of the church courts, perhaps the
greatest institutions ever yet devised by man. But to aim
at these high ideals is as perilous as it is noble; and
weapons which may be safely trusted in the hands of
saints become fatal implements of mischief when saints
have ceased to wield them. For a time, we need not
doubt, the practice corresponded to the intention. Had
it not been so, the conception would have taken no root,
and would have been extinguished at its birth. But a
system which has once established itself in the respect of
mankind will be tolerated long after it has forfeited its
claim to endurance, as the name of a great man remains
honoured though borne by worthless descendants; and the
Consistory courts had continued into the sixteenth century with unrestricted jurisdiction, although they had been
for generations merely perennially flowing fountains, feeding the ecclesiastical exchequer. The moral conduct of
every English man and woman remained subject to them.
Each private person was liable to be called in question
for every action of his life; and an elaborate network of
canon law perpetually growing, enveloped the whole sur-

face of society. But between the original design and the
degenerate counterfeit there was this vital difference,—
that the censures were no longer spiritual. They were
commuted in various gradations for pecuniary fines, and
each offence against morality was rated at its specific
money value in the episcopal tables. Suspension and excommunication remained as ultimate penalties; but they
were resorted to only to compel unwilling culprits to accept the alternative.

The misdemeanours of which the courts took cognizance[1] were 'offences against chastity,' 'heresy,' or 'matter
sounding thereunto,' 'witchcraft,' 'drunkenness,' 'scandal,'
'defamation,' 'impatient words,' 'broken promises,' 'un-
truth,' 'absence from church,' 'speaking evil of saints,'
'non-payment of offerings,' and other delinquencies incapable of legal definition; matters, all of them, on which
it was well, if possible, to keep men from going wrong;
but offering wide opportunities for injustice; while all
charges, whether well founded or ill, met with ready acceptance in courts where innocence and guilt alike contributed to the revenue.[2] 'Mortuary claims' were another
fertile matter for prosecution; and probate duties and
legacy duties; and a further lucrative occupation was the
punishment of persons who complained against the constitutions of the courts themselves; to complain against
the justice of the courts being to complain against the
church, and to complain against the church being heresy.
To answer accusations on such subjects as these, men were
liable to be summoned, at the will of the officials, to the
metropolitan courts of the archbishops, hundreds of miles
from their homes.[3] No expenses were allowed; and if
the charges were without foundation, it was rare that
costs could be recovered. Innocent or guilty, the accused
parties were equally bound to appear.[4] If they failed,
they were suspended for contempt. If after receiving
notice of their suspension, they did not appear, they were
excommunicated; and no proof of the groundlessness of
the original charge availed to relieve them from their
sentence, till they had paid for their deliverance.

Well did the church lawyers understand how to make
their work productive. Excommunication seems but a
light thing when there are many communions. It was no

---

[1] See HALE's *Criminal Causes from the Records of the Consistory
Court of London.*

[2] Petition of the Commons, infra, p. 191, &c.

[3] Reply of the Ordinaries to the petition of the Commons, infra,
p. 202, &c.

[4] Petition of the Commons: 23 Hen. VIII. c. 9.

light thing when it was equivalent to outlawry; when the person excommunicated might be seized and imprisoned at the will of the ordinary; when he was cut off from all holy offices; when no one might speak to him, trade with him, or show him the most trivial courtesy; and when his friends, if they dared to assist him, were subject to the same penalties. In the *Register* of the Bishop of London[1] there is more than one instance to be found of suspension and excommunication for the simple crime of offering shelter to an excommunicated neighbour; and thus offence begot offence, guilt spread like a contagion through the influence of natural humanity, and a single refusal of obedience to a frivolous citation might involve entire families in misery and ruin.

The people might have endured better to submit to so enormous a tyranny, if the conduct of the clergy themselves had given them a title to respect, or if equal justice had been distributed to lay and spiritual offenders. 'Benefit of clergy,' unhappily, as at this time interpreted, was little else than a privilege to commit sins with impunity. The grossest moral profligacy in a priest was passed over with indifference; and so far from exacting obedience in her ministers to a higher standard than she required of ordinary persons, the church extended her limits under fictitious pretexts as a sanctuary for lettered villany. Every person who could read was claimed by prescriptive usage as a clerk, and shielded under her protecting mantle; nor was any clerk amenable for the worst crimes to the secular jurisdiction, until he had been first tried and degraded by the ecclesiastical judges. So far was this preposterous exemption carried, that previous to the passing of the first of the 23rd of Henry the Eighth,[2] those who were within the degrees might commit murder with impunity, the forms which it was necessary to observe in degrading a priest or deacon being so complicated as to amount to absolute protection.[3]

Among the clergy, properly so called, however, the prevailing offence was not crime, but licentiousness. A

---

[1] HALE'S *Criminal Causes,* p. 4.

[2] An Act that no person committing murder, felony, or treason should be admitted to his clergy under the degree of sub-deacon.

[3] In May, 1528, the evil had become so intolerable, that Wolsey drew the pope's attention to it. Priests, he said, both secular and regular, were in the habit of committing atrocious crimes, for which, if not in orders, they would have been promptly executed; and the laity were scandalized to see such persons not only not degraded, but escaping with complete impunity. Clement something altered the law of degradation in consequence of this representation, but quite inadequately.—RYMER, vol. vi. part 2, p. 96.

doubt has recently crept in among our historians as to the credibility of the extreme language in which the contemporary writers spoke upon this painful topic. It will scarcely be supposed that the picture has been overdrawn in the act books of the Consistory courts; and as we see it there it is almost too deplorable for belief, as well in its own intrinsic hideousness and in the unconscious connivance of the authorities. Brothels were kept in London for the especial use of priests;[1] the 'confessional' was abused in the most open and abominable manner.[2] Cases occurred of the same frightful profanity in the service of the mass, which at Rome startled Luther into Pro-

[1] Thomas Cowper et ejus uxor Margarita pronubæ horribiles, et instigant mulieres ad fornicandum cum quibuscunque laicis, religiosis, fratribus minoribus, et nisi fornicant in domo suâ ipsi diffamabunt nisi voluerint dare eis ad voluntatem eorum; et vir est pronuba uxori, et vult relinquere eam apud fratres minores pro peccatis habendis.—HALE, *Criminal Causes*, p. 9.

Joanna Cutting communis pronuba at præsertim inter presbyteros fratres monachos et canonicos et etiam inter Thomam Peise et quandam Agnetam, &c.—HALE, *Criminal Causes*, p. 28.

See also Ibid. pp. 15, 22, 23, 39, &c.

In the first instance the parties accused 'made their purgation' and were dismissed. The exquisite corruption of the courts, instead of inviting evidence and sifting accusations, allowed accused persons to support their own pleas of not guilty by producing four witnesses, not to disprove the charges, but to swear that they believed the charges untrue. This was called 'purgation.'

Clergy, it seems, were sometimes allowed to purge themselves simply on their own word.—HALE, p. 22; and see the Preamble of the 1st of the 23rd of Henry VIII.

[2] Complaints of iniquities arising from confession were laid before Parliament as early as 1394.

'Auricularis confessio quæ dicitur tam necessaria ad salvationem hominis, cum fictâ potestate absolutionis exaltat superbiam sacerdotum, et dat illis opportunitatem secretarum sermocinationum quas nos nolumus dicere, quia domini et dominæ attestantur quod pro timore confessorum suorum non audent dicere veritatem; et in tempore confessionis est opportunum tempus procationis id est of wowing et aliarum secretarum conventionum ad peccata mortalia. Ipsi dicunt quod sunt commissarii Dei ad judicandum de omni peccato perdonandum et mundandum quemcunque eis placuerint. Dicunt quod habent claves cœli et inferni et possunt excommunicare et benedicere ligare et solvere in voluntatem eorum: in tantum quod pro bussello vel 12 denariis volunt vendere benedictionem cœli per chartam et clausulam de warrantiâ sigillatâ sigillo communi. Ista conclusio sic est in usu quod non eget probatione aliquâ.'—Extract from a Petition presented to Parliament: WILKINS, vol. iii. p. 221.

This remarkable paper ends with the following lines:—

> 'Plangunt Anglorum gentes crimen Sodomorum
> Paulus fert horum sunt idola causa malorum
> Surgunt ingrati Giezitæ Simone nati
> Nomine prælati hoc defensare parati
> Qui reges estis populis quicunque præestis
> Qualiter his gestis gladios prohibere potestis.'

See also HALE, p. 42, where an abominable instance is mentioned, and a still worse in the *Suppression of the Monasteries*, pp. 45—50.

testantism;[1] and acts of incest between nuns and monks were too frequently exposed to allow us to regard the detected instances as exceptions.[2] It may be said that the proceedings upon these charges prove at least that efforts were made to repress them. The bishops must have the benefit of the plea, and the two following instances will show how far it will avail their cause. In the Records of the London Court I find a certain Thomas Wyseman, priest, summoned for fornication and incontinency. He was enjoined for penance, that on the succeeding Sunday, while high mass was singing, he should offer at each of the altars in the Church of St. Bartholomew a candle of wax, value one penny, saying therewith five *Paternosters*, five *Ave Marys*, and five *Credos*. On the following Friday he was to offer a candle of the same price before the crucifix, standing barefooted, and one before the image of our Lady of Grace. This penance accomplished, he appeared again at the court and compounded for absolution, paying six shillings and eightpence.'[3]

An exposure too common to attract notice, and a fine of six and eightpence was held sufficient penalty for a mortal sin.

Even this, however, was a severe sentence compared with the sentence passed upon another priest who confessed to incest with the prioress of Kilbourn. The offender was condemned to bear a cross in a procession in his parish church, and was excused his remaining guilt for three shillings and fourpence.[4]

I might multiply such instances indefinitely; but there is no occasion for me to stain my pages with them.[5]

[1] HALE, p. 12.
[2] HALE, pp. 75. 83; *Suppression of the Monasteries*, p. 47.
[3] Ibid. p. 80.　[4] HALE. p. 83.
[5] I have been taunted with my inability to produce more evidence. For the present I will mention two additional instances only, and perhaps I shall not be invited to swell the list further.

1. In the State Paper Office is a report to Cromwell by Adam Bekenshaw, one of his diocesan visitors, in which I find this passage:—

'There be knights and divers gentlemen in the diocese of Chester who do keep concubines and do yearly compound with the officials for a small sum without monition to leave their naughty living.'

2. In another report I find also the following:—

'The names of such persons as be permitted to live in adultery and fornication for money:—

'The Vicar of Ledbury, the Vicar of Brasmyll, the Vicar of Stow, the Vicar of Cloune, the Parson of Wentnor, the Parson of Rusbury, the Parson of Plowden, the Dean of Pountsbury, the Parson of Stratton, Sir Matthew of Montgomery, Sir ―――― of Lauvange, Sir John Brayle, Sir Morris of Clone, Sir Adam of Clone, Sir Pierce of Norbury, Sir Gryffon ap Eymond, Sir John Orkeley, Sir John of Mynton, Sir John Reynolds, Sir Morris of Knighton, priest, Hugh Davis, Cadwallader ap Gern, Edward ap Meyrick. With many others of the diocese of Hereford.'

An inactive imagination may readily picture to itself the indignation likely to have been felt by a high-minded people, when they were forced to submit their lives, their habits, their most intimate conversations and opinions to a censorship conducted by clergy of such a character; when the offences of these clergy themselves were passed over with such indifferent carelessness. Men began to ask themselves who and what these persons were who retained the privileges of saints,[1] and were incapable of the most ordinary duties; and for many years before the burst of the Reformation the coming storm was gathering. Priests were hooted, or 'knocked down into the kennel,'[2] as they walked along the streets—women refused to receive the holy bread from hands which they thought polluted,[3] and the appear-

---

The originals of both these documents are in the State Paper Office. There are copies in the Bodleian Library.—*MS. Tanner*, 105.

[1] Skelton gives us a specimen of the popular criticism:—

'Thus I, Colin Clout,
As I go about,
And wondering as I walk,
I hear the people talk:
Men say for silver and gold
Mitres are bought and sold:
A straw for Goddys curse,
What are they the worse?

'What care the clergy though Gill sweat,
Or Jack of the Noke?
The poor people they yoke
With sumners and citacions,
And excommunications.
About churches and markets
The bishop on his carpets
At home soft doth sit.
This is a fearful fit,
To hear the people jangle.
How warily they wrangle!

'But Doctor Bullatus
Parum litteratus,
Dominus Doctoratus
At the broad gate-house.
Doctor Daupatus
And Bachelor Bacheleratus,
Drunken as a mouse
At the ale-house,
Taketh his pillion and his cap
At the good ale-tap,

For lack of good wine.
As wise as Robin Swine,
Under a notary's sign,
Was made a divine;
As wise as Waltham's calf,
Must preach in Goddys half;
In the pulpit solemnly;
More meet in a pillory;
For by St. Hilary
He can nothing smatter
Of logic nor school matter.

'Such temporal war and bate
As now is made of late
Against holy church estate,
Or to maintain good quarrels;
The laymen call them barrels
Full of gluttony and of hypocrisy,
That counterfeits and paints
As they were very saints.

'By sweet St. Marke,
This is a wondrous warke,
That the people talk this.
Somewhat there is amiss.
The devil cannot stop their mouths,
But they will talk of such uncouths
All that ever they ken
Against spiritual men.'

I am unable to quote more than a few lines from Roy's *Satire*. At the close of a long paragraph of details an advocate of the clergy ventures to say that the bad among them are a minority. His friend answers:—

'Make the company great or small,
Among a thousand find thou shall
Scant one chaste of body or mind.'

[2] Answer of the Bishops to the Commons' Petition: *Rolls House MS.*

[3] Joanna Leman notatur officio quod non venit ad ecclesiam parochialem; et dicit se nolle accipere panem benedictum a manibus rectoris; et vocavit eum 'horsyn preste.'—HALE, p. 99.

ance of an apparitor of the courts to serve a process or a citation in a private house was a signal for instant explosion. Violent words were the least which these officials had to fear, and they were fortunate if they escaped so lightly. A stranger had died in a house in St. Dunstan's belonging to a certain John Fleming, and an apparitor had been sent 'to seal his chamber and his goods' that the church might not lose her dues. John Fleming drove him out, saying loudly unto him, 'Thou shalt seale no door here; go thy way, thou stynkyng knave, ye are but knaves and brybours everych one of you.'[1] Thomas Banister, of St. Mary Wolchurch, when a process was served upon him, 'did threaten to slay the apparitor.' 'Thou horson knave,' he said to him, 'without thou tell me who set thee awork to summon me to the court, by Goddis woundes, and by this gold, I shall brake thy head.'[2] A 'waiter, at the sign of the Cock,' fell in trouble for saying that 'the sight of a priest did make him sick,' also, 'that he would go sixty miles to indict a priest,' saying also in the presence of many—'horsyn priests, they shall be indicted as many as come to my handling.'[3] Often the officers found threats convert themselves into acts. The apparitor of the Bishop of London went with a citation into the shop of a mercer of St. Bride's, Henry Clitheroe by name, 'Who does cite me?' asked the mercer. 'Marry, that do I,' answered the apparitor, 'if thou wilt anything with it;' whereupon, as the apparitor deposeth, the said Henry Clitheroe did hurl at him from off his finger that instrument of his art called the 'thymmelle,' and he, the apparitor, drawing his sword, the said Henry did snatch up his virga, Anglice, his yard, and did pursue the apparitor into the public streets, and after multiplying of many blows did break the head of the said apparitor.'[4] These are light matters, but they were straws upon the stream; and such a scene as this which follows reveals the principles on which the courts awarded their judgment. One Richard Hunt was summoned for certain articles implying contempt, and for vilipending his lordship's jurisdiction. Being examined, he confessed to the words following: 'That all false matters were bolstered and clokyd in this court of Paul's Cheyne; moreover he called the apparitor, William Middleton, false knave in the full court, and his father's dettes, said he, by means of his mother-in-law and master commissary, be not payd; and this I will abide by that I have now in this place said no more

---

[1] HALE, p. 63.   [2] Ibid. p. 98.   [3] Ibid. p. 38.   [4] Ibid. p. 67.

but truth.' Being called on to answer further, he said he would not, and his lordship did therefore excommunicate him.[1] From so brief an entry we cannot tell on which side the justice lay; but at least we can measure the equity of a tribunal which punished complaints against itself with excommunication, and dismissed the confessed incest of a priest with a fine of a few shillings.

Such then were the English consistory courts. I have selected but a few instances from the proceedings of a single one of them. If we are to understand the weight with which the system pressed upon the people, we must multiply the proceedings at St. Paul's by the number of the English dioceses; the number of dioceses by the number of archdeaconries; we must remember that in proportion to the distance from London the abuse must have increased indefinitely from the absence of even partial surveillance; we must remember that appeals were permitted only from one ecclesiastical court to another; from the archdeacon's court to that of the bishop of the diocese, from that of the bishop to the Court of Arches; that any language of impatience or resistance furnished suspicion of heresy, and that the only security therefore was submission. We can then imagine what England must have been with an archdeacon's commissary sitting constantly in every town; exercising an undefined jurisdiction over general morality; and every court swarming with petty lawyers who lived upon the fees which they could extract. Such a system for the administration of justice was perhaps never tolerated before in any country.

But the time of reckoning at length was arrived; slowly the hand had crawled along the dial plate; slowly as if the event would never come; and wrong was heaped on wrong; and oppression cried, and it seemed as if no ear had heard its voice; till the measure of the circle was at length fulfilled, the finger touched the hour, and as the strokes of the great hammer rang out above the nation, in an instant the mighty fabric of iniquity was shivered into ruins. Wolsey had dreamed that it might still stand, self-reformed as he hoped to see it; but in his dread lest any hands but those of friends should touch the work, he had 'prolonged its sickly days,' waiting for the convenient season which was not to be; he had put off the meeting of parliament, knowing that if parliament were once assembled, he would be unable to resist the pressure which would be brought to bear upon him; and

---

[1] HALE, p. 100.

in the impatient minds of the people he had identified himself with the evils which he alone for the few last years had hindered from falling. At length he had fallen himself, and his disgrace was celebrated in London with enthusiastic rejoicing as the inauguration of the new era. On the eighteenth of October, 1529, Wolsey delivered up the seals. He was ordered to retire to Esher; and, 'at the taking of his barge,' Cavendish saw no less than a thousand boats full of men and women of the city of London, 'waffeting up and down in Thames,' to see him sent, as they expected, to the Tower.[1] A fortnight later the same crowd was perhaps again assembled on a wiser occasion, and with truer reason for exultation, to see the king coming up in his barge from. Greenwich to open parliament.

'According to the summons,' says Hall, 'the King of England began his high court of parliament the third day of November, on which day he came by water to his palace of Bridewell, and there he and his nobles put on their robes of Parliament, and so came to the Black Friars Church, where a mass of the Holy Ghost was solemnly sung by the king's chaplain; and after the mass, the king, with all his Lords and Commons which were summoned to appear on that day, came into the Parliament. The king sate on his throne or seat royal, and Sir Thomas More, his chancellor, standing on the right hand of the king, made an eloquent oration, setting forth the causes why at that time the king so had summoned them.'[2] 'Like as a good shepherd,' he said, 'which not only keepeth and attendeth well his sheep, but also foreseeth and provideth for all things which either may be hurtful or noysome to his flock; so the king, which is the shepherd, ruler, and governor of his realm, vigilantly foreseeing things to come, considers how that divers laws, before this time made, are now, by long continuance of time and mutation of things, become very insufficient and imperfect; and also, by the frail condition of man, divers new enormities are sprung amongst the people, for the which no law is yet made to reform the same. For this cause the king at this time has summoned his high court of parliament. And I liken the king to a shepherd or herdsman, because if a prince be compared to his riches, he is but a rich man; if a prince be compared to his honour, he is but an honourable man; but compare him to the multitude of his people, and the number of his flock, then

---

[1] CAVENDISH, *Life of Wolsey*, p. 251.   [2] HALL, p. 764.

he is a ruler, a governor of might and puissance; so that his people maketh him a prince, as of the multitude of sheep cometh the name of a shepherd.

'And as you see that amongst a great flock of sheep some be rotten and faulty, which the good shepherd sendeth from the good sheep; so the great wether which is of late fallen, as you all know, so craftily, so scabedly, yea, so untruly juggled with the king, that all men must needs guess that he thought in himself, either the king had no wit to perceive his crafty doings, or else that he would not see nor know them.

'But he was deceived, for his Grace's sight was so quick and penetrable that he saw him; yea, and saw through him, both within and without; and according to his desert he hath had a gentle correction, which small punishment the king will not to be an example to other offenders; but clearly declareth that whosoever hereafter shall make like attempt, or shall commit like offence, shall not escape with like punishment.

'And because you of the Commons House be a gross multitude, and cannot all speak at one time, the king's pleasure is, that you resort to the Nether House, and then amongst yourselves, according to the old and antient custom, choose an able person to be your common mouth and speaker.'[1]

The invective against 'the great wether' was not perhaps the portion of the speech to which the audience listened with least interest. In the minds of contemporaries, principles are identified with persons, who form, as it were, the focus on which the passions concentrate. At present we may consent to forget Wolsey, and fix our attention on the more permanently essential matter—the reform of the laws. The world was changing; how swiftly, how completely, no living person knew;—but a confusion no longer tolerable was a patent fact to all men; and with a wise instinct it was resolved that the grievances of the nation, which had accumulated through centuries, should be submitted to a complete ventilation, without reserve, check, or secrecy.

For this purpose it was essential that the Houses should not be interfered with, that they should be allowed full liberty to express their wishes and to act upon them. Accordingly, the practice then usual with ministers, of undertaking the direction of the proceedings, was clearly on this occasion foregone. In the House of Commons

---

[1] HALL, p. 764.

then, as much as now, there was in theory unrestricted
liberty of discussion, and free right for any member to
originate whatever motion he pleased. 'The discussions
in the English Parliament,' wrote Henry himself to the
pope, 'are free and unrestricted; the crown has no power
to limit their debates or to controul the votes of the
members. They determine everything for themselves, as
the interests of the commonwealth require.'[1] But so long
as confidence existed between the crown and the people,
these rights were in great measure surrendered. The
ministers prepared the business which was to be transacted;
and the temper of the Houses was usually so well understood, that, except when there was a demand for money,
it was rare that a measure was proposed the acceptance
of which was doubtful, or the nature of which would provoke debate. So little jealousy, indeed, was in quiet times
entertained of the power of the crown, and so little was
a residence in London to the taste of the burgesses and
the country gentlemen, that not only were their expenses
defrayed by a considerable salary, but it was found necessary to forbid them absenting themselves from their duties
by a positive enactment.[2]

In the composition of the House of Commons, however, which had now assembled, no symptoms appeared
of such indifference. The election had taken place in the
midst of great and general excitement; and the members
chosen, if we may judge from their acts and their peti-
tions, were men of that broad resolved temper, who only
in times of popular effervescence are called forward into
prominence. It would have probably been unsafe for the
crown to attempt dictation or repression at such a time,
if it had desired to do so. Under the actual circumstances,
its interest was to encourage the fullest expression of
public feeling.

The proceedings were commenced with a formal 'act
of accusation' against the clergy, which was submitted to
the king in the name of the Commons of England, and
contained a summary of the wrongs of which the people
complained. This remarkable document must have been
drawn up before the opening of parliament, and must have
been presented in the first week of the session,—probably
on the first day on which the House met to transact
business.[3] There is appearance of haste in the composition,
little order being observed in the catalogue of grievances;

---

[1] *State Papers*, vol. vii. p. 361.   [2] 6 Hen. VIII. cap. 16.
[3] The session lasted six weeks only, and several of the subjects of
the petition were disposed of in the course of it, as we shall see.

but inasmuch as it contains the germ of all the acts which
were framed in the following years for the reform of the
church, and is in fact the most complete exhibition which
we possess of the working of the church system at the
time when it ceased to be any more tolerable, I have
thought it well to insert it uncurtailed. Although the fact
of the presentation of this petition has been well known,
it has not been accurately described by any of our historians, none of them appearing to have seen more than
incorrect and imperfect epitomes of it.[1]

TO THE KING OUR SOVEREIGN LORD.

In most humble wise show unto your Highness and
your most prudent wisdom your faithful, loving, and most
obedient servants the Commons in this your present parliament assembled: that of late, as well through new fantastical and erroneous opinions grown by occasion of
frantic seditious books compiled, imprinted, published, and
made in the English tongue, contrary and against the
very true Catholic and Christian faith; as also by the
extreme and uncharitable behaviour and dealing of divers
ordinaries, their commissaries and summers, which have
heretofore had, and yet have the examination in and upon
the said errours and heretical opinions; much discord,
variance, and debate hath risen, and more and more daily
is like to increase and ensue amongst the universal sort
of your said subjects, as well spiritual as temporal, each
against the other—in most uncharitable manner, to the
great inquietation, vexation, and breach of your peace
within this your most Catholic Realm:

The special particular griefs whereof, which most principally concern your Commons and lay subjects, and which
are, as they undoubtedly suppose, the very chief fountains,
occasions, and causes that daily breedeth and nourisheth
the said seditious factions, deadly hatred, and most uncharitable part taking, of either part of said subjects spiritual
and temporal against the other, followingly do ensue.—

1. First the prelates and spiritual ordinaries of this
your most excellent Realm of England, and the clergy of
the same, have in their convocations heretofore made or
caused to be made, and also daily do make many and
divers fashions of laws, constitutions, and ordinances;
without your knowledge or most Royal assent, and without the assent and consent of any of your lay subjects;

---

[1] The MS. from which I have transcribed this copy is itself imperfect, as will be seen in the 'reply of the Bishops,' which supplies several omitted articles. See p. 204, et seq. It is in the Rolls House.

unto the which laws your said lay subjects have not only heretofore been and daily be constrained to obey, in their bodies, goods, and possessions; but have also been compelled to incur daily into the censures of the same, and been continually put to importable charges and expenses, against all equity, right, and good conscience. And yet your said humble subjects ne their predecessors could ever be privy to the said laws; ne any of the said laws have been declared unto them in the English tongue, or otherwise published, by knowledge whereof they might have eschewed the penalties, dangers, or censures of the same; which laws so made your said most humble and obedient servants, under the supportation of your Majesty, suppose to be not only to the diminution and derogation of your imperial jurisdiction and prerogative royal, but also to the great prejudice, inquietation, and damage of your said subjects.

II. Also now of late there hath been devised by the Most Reverend Father in God, William, Archbishop of Canterbury, that in the courts which he calleth his Courts of the Arches and Audience, shall only be ten proctors at his deputation, which be sworn to preserve and promote the only jurisdiction of his said courts; by reason whereof, if any of your lay subjects should have any lawful cause against the judges of the said courts, or any doctors or proctors of the same, or any of their friends and adherents, they can ne may in nowise have indifferent counsel: and also all the causes depending in any of the said courts may by the confederacy of the said few proctors be in such wise tracted and delayed, as your subjects suing in the same shall be put to importable charges, costs, and expence. And further, in case that any matter there being preferred should touch your crown, your regal jurisdiction, and prerogative Royal, yet the same shall not be disclosed by any of the said proctors for fear of the loss of their offices. Your most obedient subjects do therefore, under protection of your Majesty, suppose that your Highness should have the nomination of some convenient number of proctors to be always attendant upon the said Courts of Arches and Audience, there to be sworn to the preferment of your jurisdiction and prerogative, and to the expedition of the causes of your lay subjects repairing and suing to the same.

III. And also many of your said most humble and obedient subjects, and *specially those that be of the poorest sort,* within this your Realm, be daily convented and called before the said spiritual ordinaries, their commissaries and substitutes, *ex officio;* sometimes, at the pleasure of the said ordinaries, for malice without any cause; and some·times at the only promotion and accusement of their summoners and apparitors, being light and undiscreet persons; without any lawful cause of accusation, or credible fame proved against them, and without any presentment in the visitation: and your said poor subjects be thus inquieted, disturbed, vexed, troubled, and put to excessive and importable charges for them to bear—and many times be suspended and excommunicate for small and light causes upon the only certificate of the proctors of the adversaries, made under a feigned seal which every proctor hath in his keeping; whereas the party suspended or excommunicate many times never had any warning; and yet when he shall be absolved, if it be out of court, he shall be compelled to pay to his own proctor twenty[1] *pence;* to the proctor which is against him other twenty pence, and twenty pence to the scribe, besides a privy reward that the judge shall have, to the great impoverishing of your said poor lay subjects.

IV.   Also your said most humble and obedient servants find themselves grieved with the great and excessive fees taken in the said spiritual courts, and especially in the said Courts of the Arches and Audience; where they take for every citation two shillings and sixpence; for every inhibition six shillings and eightpence; for every proxy sixteen pence; for every certificate sixteen pence; for every libel three shillings and fourpence; four every answer for every libel three shillings and fourpence; for every act, if it be but two words according to the register, fourpence; for every personal citation or decree three shillings and fourpence; for every sentence or judgment, to the judge twenty-six shillings and eightpence; for every testament upon such sentence or judgment twenty-six shillings and eightpence; for every significavit twelve shillings; for every commission to examine witnesses twelve shillings, which charges be thought importable to be borne by your said subjects, and very necessary to be reformed.

V.   And also the said prelates and ordinaries daily do permit and suffer the parsons, vicars, curates, parish priests, and other spiritual persons having cure of souls within this your Realm, to exact and take of your humble servants divers sums of money for the sacraments and sacramentals of Holy Church, sometimes denying the same

---

[1] The penny, as I have shown, equalled, in terms of a poor man's necessities, a shilling. See chap. i.

without they be first paid[1] the said sums of money, which
sacraments and sacramentals your said most humble and
obedient subjects, under protection of your Highness, do
suppose and think ought to be in most reverend charitable
and godly wise freely ministered unto them at all times
requisite, without denial, or exaction of any manner sums
of money to be demanded or asked for the same.

VI. And also in the spiritual courts of the said prelates and ordinaries there be limited and appointed so
many judges, scribes, apparitors, summoners, appraysers,
and other ministers for the approbation of Testaments,
which covet so much their own private lucres, and the
satisfaction and appetites of the said prelates and ordinaries,
that when any of your said loving subjects do repair to
any of the said courts for the probate of any Testaments,
they do in such wise make so long delays, or excessively
do take of them so large fees and rewards for the same
as is importable for them to bear, directly against all
justice, law, equity, and good conscience. Therefore your
most humble and obedient subjects do, under your gracious correction and supportation, suppose it were very
necessary that the said ordinaries in their deputation of
judges should be bound to appoint and assign such discreet, gracious, and honest persons, having sufficient learning, wit, discretion, and understanding; and also being
endowed with such spiritual promotion, stipend, and salary;
as they being judges in their said courts might and may
minister to every person repairing to the same, justice—
without taking any manner of fee or reward for any manner
of sentence or judgment to be given before them.

VII. And also divers spiritual persons being presented
as well by your Highness as others within this your Realm
to divers benefices or other spiritual promotions, the said
ordinaries and their ministers do not only take of them
for their letters of institution and induction many large
sums of money and rewards; but also do pact and covenant
with the same, taking sure bonds for their indemnity to
answer to the said ordinaries for the firstfruits of their
said benefices after their institution—so as they, being
once presented or promoted, as aforesaid, are by the said
ordinaries very uncharitably handled to their no little
hindrance and impoverishment; which your said subjects

---

[1] See instances in HALE: p. 62, *Omnium Sanctorum in muro.*—M.
Gulielmus Edward curatus notatur officio quod recusat ministrare
sacramenta ecclesiastica ægrotantibus nisi prius habitis pecuniis pro
suo labore: p. 64, *St. Mary Magdalen.*—Curatus notatur officio propter
quod recusavit solemnizare matrimonium quousque habet pro hujusmodi solemnizatione, 3s. 8d.; and see pp. 62, 75.

suppose not only to be against all laws, right, and good conscieuce, but also to be simony, and contrary to the laws of God.

VIII. And also *the said spiritual ordinaries do daily confer and give sundry benefices unto certain young folks, calling them their nephews or kinsfolk*, being in their minority and within age, not apt ne able to serve the cure of any such benefice: whereby the said ordinaries do keep and detain the fruits and profits of the same benefices in their own hands, and thereby accumulate to themselves right great and large sums of money and yearly profits to the most pernicious example of your said lay subjects—and so the cures and promotions given unto such infants be only employed to the enriching of the said ordinaries; and the poor silly souls of your people, which should be taught in the parishes given as aforesaid, for lack of good curates [be left] to perish without doctrine or any good teaching.

IX. Also, a great number of holydays now at this present time, with very small devotion, be solemnized and kept throughout this your Realm, upon the which many great, abominable, and execrable vices, idle and wanton sports, be used and exercised, which holydays, if it may stand with your Grace's pleasure, and specially such as fall in the harvest, might, by your Majesty, with the advice of your most honourable council, prelates, and ordinaries, be made fewer in number; and those that shall be hereafter ordained to stand and continue, might and may be the more devoutly, religiously, and reverendly observed to the laud of Almighty God, and to the increase of your high honour and favour.

X. And furthermore the said spiritual ordinaries, their commissaries and substitutes, sometimes for their own pleasure, sometimes by the sinister procurement of other spiritual persons, use to make out process against divers of your said subjects, and thereby compel them to appear before themselves, to answer at a certain day and place to such articles as by them shall be, *ex officio*, then proposed; and that secretly and not in open places;[1] and forthwith upon their appearance without any declaration made or showed, commit and send them to ward, sometimes for [half] a year, sometimes for a whole year or

---

[1] I give many instances of this practice in my sixth chapter. It was a direct breach of the statute of Henry IV., which insists on all examinations for heresy being conducted in open court. 'The diocesan and his commissaries,' says that act, 'shall openly and judicially proceed against persons arrested.'—2 Hen. IV. c. 15.

more before they may in anywise know either the cause
of their imprisonment or the name of their accuser;[1] and
finally after their great costs and charges therein, when
all is examined and nothing can be proved against them,
but they clearly innocent for any fault or crime that can
be laid unto them, they be again set at large without
any recompence or amends in that behalf to be towards
them adjudged.

XI. And also if percase upon the said process and
appearance any party be upon the said matter, cause, or
examination, brought forth and named, either as party or
witness, and then upon the proof and trial thereof be not
able to prove and verify the said accusation and testimony
against the party accused, then the person so accused is
for the more part without any remedy for his charges and
wrongful vexation to be towards him adjudged and recovered.

XII. Also upon the examination of the said accusation,
if heresy be ordinarily laid unto the charge of the parties so accused, then the said ordinaries or their ministers
use to put to them such subtle interrogatories concerning
the high mysteries of our faith, as are able quickly to
trap a simple unlearned, or yet a well-witted layman
without learning, and bring them by such sinister intro-
ductions soon to their own confusion. And further, if
there chance any heresy to be by such subtle policy, by
any person confessed in words, and yet never committed
neither in thought nor deed, then put they, without further
favour, the said person either to make his purgation, and
so thereby to lose his honesty and credence for ever; or
else as some simple silly soul [may do] the said person
may stand precisely to the testimony of his own well-
known conscience, rather than confess his innocent truth
in that behalf [to be other than he knows it to be], and
so be utterly destroyed. And if it fortune the said party
so accused to deny the said accusation, and to put his
adversaries to prove the same as being untrue, forged and
imagined against him, then for the most part such witnesses as are brought forth for the same, be they but
two in number, never so sore diffamed, of little truth or
credence, they shall be allowed and enabled, only by
discretion of the said ordinaries, their commissaries or
substitutes; and thereupon sufficient cause be found to
proceed to judgment, to deliver the party so accused

---

[1] Again breaking the statute of Hen. IV., which limited the period
of imprisonment previous to public trial to three months.—2 Hen. IV.
c. 15.

either to secular hands, after abjuration,[1] without remedy; or afore if he submit himself, as best happeneth, he shall have to make his purgation and bear a faggot, to his extreme shame and undoing.

In consideration of all these things, most gracious Sovereign Lord, and forasmuch as there is at this present time, and by a few years past hath been outrageous violence on the one part and much default and lack of patient sufferance, charity, and good will on the other part; and consequently a marvellous disorder [hath ensued] of the godly quiet, peace, and tranquillity in which this your Realm heretofore, ever hitherto, has been through your politic wisdom, most honourable fame, and catholic faith inviolably preserved; it may therefore, most benign Sovereign Lord, like your excellent goodness for the tender and universally indifferent zeal, benign love and favour which your Highness beareth towards both the said parties, that the said articles (if they shall be by your most clear and perfect judgment, thought any instrument of the said disorders and factions), being deeply and weightily, after your accustomed ways and manner, searched and considered; graciously to provide (all violence on both sides utterly and clearly set apart) some such necessary and behoveful remedies as may effectually reconcile and bring in perpetual unity, your said subjects, spiritual and temporal; and for the establishment thereof, to make and ordain on both sides such strait laws against transgressors and offenders as shall be too heavy, dangerous, and weighty for them, or any of them, to bear, suffer, and sustain.

Whereunto your said Commons most humbly and entirely beseech your Grace, as the only Head, Sovereign Lord, and Protector of both the said parties, in whom and by whom the only and sole redress, reformation, and remedy herein absolutely resteth [of your goodness to consent]. By occasion whereof all your Commons in their conscience surely account that, beside the marvellous fervent love that your Highness shall thereby engender in their hearts towards your Grace, ye shall do the most princely feat, and show the most honourable and charitable precedent and mirrour that ever did sovereign lord upon his subjects; and therewithal merit and deserve of our merciful God eternal bliss — whose goodness grant your Grace in goodly, princely, and honourable estate long to

---

[1] To be disposed of at Smithfield. Abjuration was allowed once. For a second offence there was no forgiveness.

reign, prosper, and continue as the Sovereign Lord over all your said most humble and obedient servants.[1]

I need add but little comment in explanation of this petition, which, though drawn with evident haste, is no less remarkable for temper and good feeling, than for the masterly clearness with which the evils complained of are laid bare. Historians will be careful for the future how they swell the charges against Wolsey with quoting the lamentations of Archbishop Warham, when his Court of Arches was for a while superseded by the Legate's Court, and causes lingering before his commissaries were summarily dispatched at a higher tribunal.[2] The archbishop professed, indeed, that he derived no personal advantage from his courts,[3] and as we have only the popular impression to the contrary to set against his word, we must believe him; yet it was of small moment to the laity who were pillaged, whether the spoils taken from them filled the coffers of the master, or those of his followers and friends.

When we consider, also, the significant allusion[4] to the young folks whom the bishops called their nephews, we cease to wonder at their lenient dealing with the poor priests who had sunk under the temptations of frail humanity; and still less can we wonder at the rough handling which was soon found necessary to bring back these high dignitaries to a better mind.

The House of Commons, in casting their grievances into the form of a petition, showed that they had no desire to thrust forward of themselves violent measures of reform; they sought rather to explain firmly and decisively what the country required. The king, selecting out of the many points noticed those which seemed most immediately pressing, referred them back to the parliament, with a direction to draw up such enactments as in their own judgment would furnish effective relief. In the meantime he submitted the petition itself to the consideration of the bishops, requiring their immediate answer to the charges against them, and accompanied this request with a further important requisition. The legislative authority of con-

---

[1] Petition of the Commons: *Rolls House MS.*

[2] See STRYPE, *Eccles. Memorials*, vol. i. p. 191-2,—who is very eloquent in his outcries upon this subject.

[3] *Answer of the Bishops*, p. 204, &c.

[4] I need not enter into explanations; but the following passage may suggest the meaning of the House of Commons:—'The holy Father Prior of Maiden Bradley hath but six children, and but one daughter married yet of the goods of the monastery; trusting shortly to marry the rest.'—Dr. Leyton to Cromwell: *Suppression of the Monasteries*, p. 58.

vocation lay at the root of the evils which were most complained of. The bishops and clergy held themselves independent of either crown or parliament, and passed canons by their own irresponsible and unchecked will, irrespective of the laws of the land, and sometimes in direct violation of them; and to these canons the laity were amenable without being made acquainted with their provisions, learning them only in the infliction of penalties for their unintended breach. The king required that thenceforward the convocation should consent to place itself in the position of parliament, and that his own consent should be required and received before any law passed by convocation should have the force of statute.[1]

Little notion, indeed, could the bishops have possessed of the position in which they were standing. It seemed as if they literally believed that the promise of perpetuity which Christ had made to his church was a charm which would hold them free in the quiet course of their injustice; or else, under the blinding influence of custom, they did not really know that any injustice adhered to them. They could see in themselves only the ideal virtues of their saintly office, and not the vices of their fragile humanity; they believed that they were still holy, still spotless, still immaculate, and therefore that no danger might come near them. It cannot have been but that, before the minds of such men as Warham and Fisher, some visions of a future must at times have floated, which hung so plainly before the eyes of Wolsey and of Sir Thomas More.[2] They could not have been wholly deaf to the storm in Germany; and they must have heard something of the growls of smothered anger which for years had been audible at home, to all who had ears to hear.[3] Yet if any such thoughts at times did cross their imagination, they were thrust aside as an uneasy dream, to be shaken off like a nightmare, or with the coward's consolation, 'It will last my time.' If the bishops ever felt an uneasy moment, there is no trace of uneasiness in the answer which they sent in to the king, and which now, when we read it with the light which is thrown back out of the succeeding years, seems like the composition of mere lunacy. Perhaps they had confidence in the support of Henry. In their courts they were in the habit of identifying an attack upon themselves with an

<hr>

[1] Reply of the Bishops, infra.
[2] CAVENDISH, *Life of Wolsey*, p. 390. MORE'S *Life of More*, p. 109.
[3] Populus diu oblatrans. Fox to Wolsey. STRYPE, *Eccl. Mem.* vol. i. Appendix, p. 27.

attack upon the doctrines of the Church; and reading the king's feelings in their own, they may have considered themselves safe under the protection of a sovereign who had broken a lance with Luther, and had called himself the Pope's champion. Perhaps they thought that they had bound him to themselves by a declaration which they had all signed in the preceding summer in favour of the divorce.[1] Perhaps they were but steeped in the dulness of official lethargy. The defence is long, wearying the patience to read it; wearying the imagination to invent excuses for the falsehoods which it contains. Yet it is well to see all men in the light in which they see themselves; and justice requires that we allow the bishops the benefit of their own reply. It was couched in the following words:[2]—

'After our most humble wise, with our most bounden duty of honour and reverence to your excellent Majesty, endued from God with incomparable wisdom and goodness. Please it the same to understand that we, your orators and daily bounden bedemen, have read and perused a certain supplication which the Commons of your Grace's honourable parliament now assembled have offered unto your Highness, and by your Grace's commandment delivered unto us, that we should make answer thereunto. We have, as the time hath served, made this answer following, beseeching your Grace's indifferent benignity graciously to hear the same.

'And first for that discord, variance, and debate which, in the preface of the said supplication they do allege to have arisen among your Grace's subjects, spiritual and temporal, occasioned, as they say, by the uncharitable behaviour and demeanour of divers ordinaries: to this we, the ordinaries, answer, assuring your Majesty that in our hearts there is no such discord or variance on our part against our brethren in God and ghostly children your subjects, as is induced in this preface; but our daily prayer is and shall be that all peace and concord may increase among your Grace's true subjects our said children, whom God be our witness we love, have loved, and shall love ever with hearty affection; never intending any hurt ne harm towards any of them in soul or body; ne have we ever enterprised anything against them of trouble, vexation, or displeasure; but only have, with all charity, ex-

<hr>

[1] RYMER, vol. vi. part 2. p. 119.
[2] The answer of the Ordinaries to the supplication of the worshipful the Commons of the Lower House of Parliament offered to our Sovereign Lord the King's most noble Grace.—*Rolls House MS.*

ercised the spiritual jurisdiction of the Church, as we are bound of duty, upon certain evil-disposed persons infected with the pestilent poison of heresy. And to have peace with such had been against the Gospel of our Saviour Christ, wherein he saith, *Non veni mittere pacem sed gladium.* Wherefore, forasmuch as we know well that there be as well-disposed and well-conscienced men of your Grace's Commons in no small number assembled, as ever we knew at any time in parliament; and with that consider how on our part there is given no such occasion why the whole number of the spirituality and clergy should be thus noted unto your Highness; we humbling our hearts to God and remitting the judgment of this our inquietation to Him, and trusting, as his Scripture teacheth, that if we love him above all, *omnia cooperabuntur in bonum,* shall endeavour to declare to your Highness the innocency of us, your poor orators.

'And where, after the general preface of the same supplication, your Grace's Commons descend to special particular griefs, and first to those divers fashions of laws concerning temporal things, whereon, as they say, the clergy in their convocation have made and daily do make divers laws, to their great trouble and inquietation, which said laws be sometimes repugnant to the statutes of your Realm, with many other complaints thereupon:[1] To this we say, that forasmuch as we repute and take our authority of making of laws to be grounded upon the Sciptures of God and the determination of Holy Church, which must be the rule and square to try the justice and righteousness of all laws, as well spiritual as temporal, we verily trust that in such laws as have been made by us, or by our predecessors, the same being sincerely interpreted, and after the meaning of the makers, there shall be found nothing contained in them but such as may be well justified by the said rule and square. And if it shall otherwise appear, as it is our duty whereunto we shall always most diligently apply ourselves to reform our ordinances to God's commission, and to conform our statutes to the determination of Scripture and Holy Church; so *we hope in God, and shall daily pray for the same, that your Highness will, if there appear cause why, with the assent of your people, temper your Grace's laws accordingly; whereby shall ensue a most sure and hearty conjunction and agreement; God being lapis angularis.*

'And as concerning the requiring of your Highness's

---

[1] The terms of the several articles of complaint are repeated verbally from the petition. I condense them to spare recapitulation.

royal assent to the authorizing of such laws as have been made by our predecessors, or shall be made by us, in such points and articles as we have authority to rule and order; we knowing your Highness's wisdom, virtue, and learning, nothing doubt but that the same perceiveth how the granting thereunto dependeth not upon our will and liberty, *and that we may not submit the execution of our charges and duty certainly prescribed to us by God to your Highness's assent;* although, indeed, the same is most worthy for your most princely and excellent virtues, not only to give your royal assent, but also to devise and command what we should for good order or manners by statutes and laws provide in the church. Nevertheless, we considering we may not so nor in such sort restrain the doing of our office in the feeding and ruling of Christ's people, we most humbly desire your Grace (as the same hath done heretofore) to show your Grace's mind and opinion unto us, which we shall most gladly hear and follow if it shall please God to inspire us so to do; and with all humility we therefore beseech your Grace, following the steps of your most noble progenitors, to maintain and defend such laws and ordinances as we, according to our calling and by the authority of God, shall for his honour make to the edification of virtue and the maintaining of Christ's faith, whereof your Highness is defender in name, and hath been hitherto indeed a special protector.

'Furthermore, when there be found in the said supplication, with mention of your Grace's person, other griefs that some of the said laws extend to the goods and possessions of your said lay subjects, declaring the transgressors not only to fall under the terrible censure of excommunication, but also under the detestable crime of heresy:

'To this we answer that we remember no such, and yet if there be any such, it is but according to the common law of the Church, and also to your Grace's law, which determine and decree that every person spiritual or temporal condemned of heresy shall forfeit his moveables or immoveables to your Highness, or to the lord spiritual or temporal that by law hath right to them.[1] Other statutes we remember none that toucheth lands or goods. If there be, it were good that they were brought forth to be weighed and pondered accordingly.

'Item as touching the second principal article of the

---

[1] 2 Hen. IV. cap. 15; 2 Hen. V. cap. 7.

said supplication, where they say that divers and many of
your Grace's obedient subjects, and especially they that
be of the poorest sort, be daily called before us or before
our substitutes ex officio; sometimes at the pleasure of
us, the ordinaries, without any probable cause, and sometimes at the only promotion of our summoner, without
any credible fame first proved against them, and without
presentment in the visitation or lawful accusation:

'On this we desire your high wisdom and learning to
consider that albeit in the ordering of Christ's people,
your Grace's subjects, God of His spiritual goodness as-
sisteth his church, and inspireth by the Holy Ghost as
we verily trust such rules and laws as tend to the wealth
of his elect folk; yet upon considerations to man unknown,
his infinite wisdom leaveth or permitteth men to walk in
their infirmity and frailty; so that we cannot ne will ar-
rogantly presume of ourselves, as though being in name
spiritual men, we were also in all our acts and doings
clean and void from all temporal affections and carnality
of this world, or that the laws of the church made for
spiritual and ghostly purpose be not sometime applied to
worldly intent. This we ought and do lament, as becometh us, very sore. Nevertheless, as the evil deeds of
men be the mere defaults of those particular men, and
not of the whole order of the clergy, nor of the law
wholesomely by them made; our request and petition shall
be with all humility and reverence; that laws well made
be not therefore called evil because by all men and at
all times they be not well executed; and that in such defaults as shall appear such distribution may be used *ut
unusquisque onus suum portet*, and remedy be found to
reform the offenders; unto the which your Highness shall
perceive as great towardness in your said orators as can
be required upon declaration of particulars. And other
answer than this cannot be made in the name of your
whole clergy, for though *in multis offendimus omnes*, as
St. James saith, yet not 'in omnibus offendimus omnes;'
and the whole number can neither justify ne condemn
particular acts to them unknown but thus. He that calleth
a man ex officio for correction of sin, doeth well. He
that calleth men for pleasure or vexation, doeth evil.
Summoners should be honest men. If they offend in their
office, they should be punished. To prove first [their
faults] before men be called, is not necessary. He that
is called according to the laws ex officio or otherwise,
cannot complain. He that is otherwise ordered should
have by reason convenient recompence and so forth; that

is well to be allowed, and misdemeanour when it appeareth
to be reproved.

'Item where they say in the same article that upon
their appearance ex officio at the only pleasure of the
ordinaries, they be committed to prison without bail or
mainprize; and there they lie some half a year or more
before they come to their deliverance; to this we
answer,—

'That we use no prison before conviction but for sure
custody, and only of such as be suspected of heresy, in
which crime, thanked be God, there hath fallen no such
notable person in our time, or of such qualities as hath
given occasion of any sinister suspicion to be conceived of
malice or hatred to his person other than the heinousness
of their crime deserveth. *Truth it is that certain apostates,
friars, monks, lewd priests, bankrupt merchants, vagabonds,
and lewd idle fellows of corrupt intent, have embraced
the abominable and erroneous opinions lately sprung in
Germany;* and by them some have been seduced in simplicity and ignorance. Against these, if judgment has been
exercised according to the laws of the church, and con-
formably to the laws of this realm, we be without blame.
If we have been too remiss and slack, we shall gladly do
our duty from henceforth. If any man hath been, under
pretence of this [crime], particularly offended, it were pity
to suffer any man to be wronged; and thus it ought to
be, and otherwise we cannot answer, no man's special
case being declared in the said petition.

'Item where they say further that they so appearing
ex officio, be condemned to answer to many subtle questions by the which a simple, unlearned, or else a well-
witted layman without learning sometimes is, and commonly may be trapped and induced into peril of open
penance to their shame, or else [forced] to redeem their
penance for money, as is commonly used; to this we
answer that we should not use subtlety, for we should do
all things plainly and openly; and if we do otherwise, we
do amiss. We ought not to ask questions, but after the
capacities of the man. Christ hath defended his true
doctrine and faith in his Catholic church from all subtlety, and so preserved good men in the same, as they
have not (blessed be God) been vexed, inquieted, or
troubled in Christ's church. Thereupon evil men fall in
danger by their own subtlety; we protest afore God we
have neither known, read, nor heard of any one man
damaged or prejudiced by spiritual jurisdiction in this
behalf, neither in this realm nor any other, but only by

his own deserts. Such is the goodness of God in maintaining the cause of his Catholic faith.

'Item where they say they be compelled to do open penance, or else redeem the same for money; as for penance, we answer it consisteth in the arbitre of a judge who ought to enjoin such penance as might profit for correction of the fault. Whereupon we disallow that judge's doing who taketh money for penance for lucre or advantage, not regarding the reformation of sin as he ought to do. But when open penance may sometimes work in certain persons more hurt than good, it is commendable and allowable in that case to punish by the purse, and preserve the fame of the party; foreseeing always the money be converted *in usus pios et eleemosynam,* and thus we think of the thing, and that the offenders should be punished.

'Item where they complain that two witnesses be admitted, be they never so defamed, of little truth or credence, adversaries or enemies to the parties; yet in many cases they be allowed by the discretion of the ordinaries to put the party defamed, ex officio, to open penance, and then to redemption for money; so that every of your subjects, upon the only will of the ordinaries or their substitutes, without any accuser, proved fame, or presentment, is or may be infamed, vexed, and troubled, to the peril of their lives, their shames, costs, and expenses:

'To this we reply, *the Gospel of Christ teacheth us to believe two witnesses; and as the cause is, so the judge must esteem the quality of the witness; and in heresy no exception is necessary to be considered if their tale be likely; which hath been highly provided lest heretics without jeopardy might else plant their heresies in lewd and light persons, and taking exception to the witnesses, take boldness to continue their folly. This is the universal law of Christendom, and hath universally done good. Of any injury done to any man thereby we know not.*

'Item where they say it is not intended by them to take away from us our authority to correct and punish sins, and especially the detestable crime of heresy:

'To this we answer, in the prosecuting heretics we regard our duty and office whereunto we be called, and if God will discharge us thereof, or cease that plague universal, as, by directing the hearts of princes, and specially the heart of your Highness (laud and thanks be unto Him), His goodness doth commence and begin to do, we should and shall have great cause to rejoice; as being our authority therein, costly, dangerous, full of trouble and business, without any fruit, pleasure, or commodity, worldly, but a continued conflict and vexation with pertinacity, wilfulness, folly, and ignorance, whereupon followeth their bodily and ghostly destruction to our great sorrow.

'Item where they desire that by assent of your Highness (if the laws heretofore made be not sufficient for the repression of heresy) more dreadful and terrible laws may be made; this we think is undoubtedly a more charitable request than as we trust necessary, considering that by the aid of your Highness, and the pains of your Grace's statutes freely executed, your realm may be in short time clean purged from the few small dregs that do remain, if any do remain.

'Item where they desire some reasonable declaration may be made to your people, how they may, if they will, avoid the peril of heresy. No better declaration, we say, can be made than is already by our Saviour Christ, the Apostles, and the determination of the church, which if they keep, they shall not fail to eschew heresy.

'Item where they desire that some charitable fashion may be devised by your wisdom for the calling of any of your subjects before us, that it shall not stand in the only will and pleasure of the ordinaries at their own imagination, without lawful accusation by honest witness, according to your law; to this we say that a better provision cannot be devised than is already devised by the clergy in our opinion; and if any default appear in the execution, it shall be amended on declaration of the particulars, and the same proved.

'Item where they say that your subjects be cited out of the diocese which they dwell in, and many times be suspended and excommunicate for light causes upon the only certificate devised by the proctors, and that all your subjects find themselves grieved with the excessive fees taken in the spiritual courts:

'To this article for because it concerneth specially the spiritual courts of me the Archbishop of Canterbury, please it your Grace to understand that about twelve months past I reformed certain things objected here; and now within these ten weeks I reformed many other things in my said courts, as I suppose is not unknown unto your Grace's Commons; and some of the fees of the officers of my courts I have brought down to halves, some to the third part, and some wholly taken away and extincted; and yet it is objected to me as though I had taken no manner of reformation therein. Nevertheless I shall not cease yet; but in such things as I shall see your Commons

most offended I will set redress accordingly, so as, I trust,
they will be contented in that behalf. And I, the said
archbishop, beseech your Grace to consider what service
the doctors in civil law, which have had their practice in
my courts, have done your Grace concerning treaties,
truces, confederations, and leagues devised and concluded
with outward princes; and that without such learned men
in civil law your Grace could not have been so conveniently served as at all times you have been, which
thing, perhaps, when such learned men shall fail, will
appear more evident than it doth now. The decay whereof
grieveth me to foresee, not so greatly for any cause concerning the pleasure or profit of myself, being a man
spent, and at the point to depart this world, and having
no penny of any advantage by my said courts, but principally for the good love which I bear to the honour of
your Grace and of your realm. And albeit there is, by
the assent of the Lords Temporal and the Commons of
your Parliament, an act passed thereupon already, the
matter depending before your Majesty by way of supplication offered to your Highness by your said Commons;[1]
yet, forasmuch as we your Grace's humble chaplains, the
Archbishops of Canterbury and York, be bounden by oath
to be intercessors for the rights of our churches; and
forasmuch as the spiritual prelates of the clergy, being of
your Grace's parliament, consented to the said act for
divers great causes moving their conscience, we your
Grace's said chaplains show unto your Highness that it
hath appertained to the Archbishops of Canterbury and
York for the space of four hundred years or thereabouts
to have spiritual jurisdiction over all your Grace's subjects
dwelling within the provinces; and to have authority to
call before them, not only in spiritual causes devolved to
them by way of appeal, but also by way of querimony
and complaint; which right and privilege pertaineth not
only to the persons of the said archbishops, but also to
the preeminences of their churches. In so much that
when the archbishop of either of the sees dieth, the said
privileges do not only remain to his successor (by which
he is named Legatus natus), but also in the meantime of
vacation the same privilege resteth in the churches of
Canterbury and York; and is executed by the prior, dean
and chapter of the said churches; and so the said act is
directly against the liberty and privileges of the churches

---

[1] An Act that no person shall be cited out of the diocese in which
he dwells, except in certain cases. It received the Royal assent two
years later. See 23 Hen. VIII. cap. 9.

of Canterbury and York: and what dangers be to them
which study and labour to take away the liberties and
privileges of the church, whoso will read the general
councils of Christendom and the canons of the fathers of
the Catholic church ordained in that behalf, shall soon
perceive. And further, we think verily that our churches,
to whom the said privileges were granted, can give no
cause why the pope himself (whose predecessors granted
that privilege) or any other (the honour of your Grace
ever except) may justly take away the same privileges so
lawfully prescribed from our churches, though we [our-
selves] had greatly offended, abusing the said privileges.
But when in our persons we trust we have given no cause
why to lose that privilege, we beseech your Grace of your
goodness and absolute power to set such orders in this
behalf as we may enjoy our privileges lawfully admitted
so long.

'Item, when they complain that there is exacted and
demanded in divers parishes of this your realm, other
manner of tythes than hath been accustomed to be paid
this hundred years past; and in some parts of this your
realm there is exacted double tythes, that is to say, threepence, or twopence halfpenny, for one acre, over and
beside the tythe for the increase of cattle that pastureth
the same:

'To this we say, that tythes being due by God's law,
be so duly paid, (thanked be God) by all good men, as
there needeth not exaction in the most parts of this your
Grace's realm. As for double tythes, they cannot be
maintained due for one increase; whether in any place
they be unduly exacted in fact we know not. This we
know in learning, that neither a hundred years, nor seven
hundred of non-payment, may debar the right of God's
law. The manner of payment, and person unto whom to
pay, may be in time altered, but the duty cannot by any
means be taken away.

'Item, when they say that when a mortuary is due,
curates sometimes, before they will demand it, will bring
citation for it; and then will not receive the mortuaries
till they may have such costs as they say they have laid
out for the suit of the same; when, indeed, if they would
first have charitably demanded it, they needed not to have
sued for the same, for it should have been paid with
good will:

'We answer that curates thus offending, if they were
known, ought to be punished, but who thus doeth we
know not.

'Item, when they say that divers spiritual persons being presented to benefices within this your realm, we and our ministers do take of them great sums of money and reward; we reply that this is a particular abuse, and he that taketh reward doeth not well; and if any penny be exacted above the accustomed rate and after convenient proportion, it is not well done. But in taking the usual fees for the sealing, writing, and registering the letters, which is very moderate, we cannot think it to be reputed as any offence; neither have we heard any priests in our days complain of any excess therein.

'And when they say in the same article that such as be presented be delayed without reasonable cause, to the intent that we the ordinaries may have the profit of the benefice during the vacation, unless they will pact and convent with us by temporal bonds, whereof some bonds contain that we should have part of the profit of the said benefice, which your said subjects suppose to be not only against right and conscience, but also seemeth to be simony, and contrary to the laws of God:

'To this we do say that a delay without reasonable cause, and for a lucrative intent, is detestable in spiritual men, and the doers cannot eschew punishment: but otherwise a delay is sometimes expedient to examine the clerk, and sometimes necessary when the title is in variance. All other bargains and covenants being contrary to the law ought to be punished, as the quality is of the offence more or less, as simony or inordinate covetousness.

'Item, when they say that we give benefices to our nephews and kinsfolk, being in young age or infants, whereby the cure is not substantially looked into, nor the parishioners taught as they should be; we reply to this that the thing which is not lawful in others is in spiritual men more detestable. Benefices should be disposed of not *secundum carnem et sanguinem, sed secundum merita.* And when there is a default it is not authorized by the clergy as good, but reproved; whereupon in this the clergy is not to be blamed, but the default as it may appear must be laid to particular men.

'And where they say that we take the profit of such benefices for the time of the minority of our said kinsfolk, if it be done to our own use and profit it is not well; *if it be bestowed to the bringing up and use of the same parties,* or applied to the maintenance of the church and God's service, or distributed among the poor, we do not see but that it may be allowed.

'Item, when they say that divers and many spiritual

persons, not contented with the convenient livings and promotions of the church, daily intromit and exercise themselves in secular offices and rooms, as stewards, receivers, auditors, bailiffs, and other temporal occupations, withdrawing themselves from the good contemplative lives that they have professed, not only to the damage but also to the perilous example of your loving and obedient subjects; to this we your bedesmen answer that beneficed men may lawfully be stewards and receivers to their own bishops, as it evidently appeareth in the laws of the church; and we by the said laws ought to have no other. And as for priests to be auditors and bailiffs, we know none such.

'And when, finally, they, in the conclusion of their supplication, do repeat and say that forasmuch as there is at this present time, and by a few years past hath been much misdemeanour and violence upon the one part, and much default and lack of patience, charity, and good will on the other part; and marvellous discord in consequence of the quiet, peace, and tranquillity in which this your realm hath been ever hitherto preserved through your politic wisdom:

''To the first part as touching such discord as is reported, and also the misdemeanour which is imputed to us and our doings, we trust we have sufficiently answered the same, humbly beseeching your Grace so to esteem and weigh such answer with their supplication as shall be thought good and expedient by your high wisdom. Furthermore we ascertain your Grace as touching the violence which they seem to lay to our charge, albeit divers of the clergy of this your realm have sundry times been *rigorously handled, and with much violence entreated by certain ill-disposed and seditious persons of the lay fee, have been injured in their bodies, thrown down in the kennel in the open streets at mid-day,* even here within your city and elsewhere, to the great rebuke and disquietness of the clergy of your realm, the great danger of the souls of the said misdoers, and perilous example of your subjects. Yet we think verily, and do affirm the same, that no violence hath been so used on our behalf towards your said lay subjects in any case; unless they esteem this to be violence that we do use as well for the health of their souls as for the discharge of our duties in taking, examining, and punishing heretics according to the law: wherein we doubt not but that your Grace, and divers of your Grace's subjects, do understand well what charitable entreaty we have used with such as have been before us for the same cause of heresy; and what means we have devised and studied for safeguard specially of their souls; and that charitably, as God be our judge, and without violence as [far as] we could possibly devise. In execution whereof, and also of the laws of the church for repression of sin, and also for reformation of mislivers, it hath been to our great comfort that your Grace hath herein of your goodness, assisted and aided us in this behalf for the zeal and love which your Grace beareth to God's church and to His ministers; specially in defence of His faith whereof your Grace only and most worthily amongst all Christian princes beareth the title and name. And for that marvellous discord and grudge among your subjects as is reported in the supplication of your Commons, we beseech your Majesty, all the premises considered, to repress those that be misdoers; protesting in our behalf that we ourselves have no grudge nor displeasure towards your lay subjects our ghostly children. We intreat your Grace of your accustomed goodness to us your bedemen to continue our chief protector, defender, and aider in and for the execution of our office and duty; specially touching repression of heresy, reformation of sin, and due behaviour and order of all your Grace's subjects, spiritual and temporal; which (no doubt thereof) shall be much to the pleasure of God, great comfort to men's souls, quietness and unity of all your realm; and, as we think, most principally to the great comfort of your Grace's Majesty. Which we beseech lowly upon our knees, so entirely as we can, to be the author of unity, charity, and concord as above, for whose preservation we do and shall continually pray to Almighty God long to reign and prosper in most honourable estate to his pleasure.'

This was the bishops' defence; the best which, under the circumstances, they considered themselves capable of making. The House of Commons had stated their complaints in the form of special notorious facts; the bishops replied with urging the theory of their position, and supposed that they could relieve the ecclesiastical system from the faults of its ministers, by laying the sole blame on the unworthiness of individual persons. The degenerate representatives of a once noble institution could not perhaps be expected to admit their degeneracy, and confess themselves, as they really were, collectively incompetent; yet the defence which they brought forward would have been valid only so long as the blemishes were the rare exceptions in the working of an institution which was still generally beneficent. It was no defence at all when the faults had become the rule, and when there was no security in the system itself for the selection of worth and capacity to exercise its functions. The clergy, as I have already said, claimed the privileges of saints, while their conduct fell below the standard of that of ordinary men; and the position taken in this answer was tenable only on the hypothesis which it, in fact, deliberately asserted, that the judicial authority of the church had been committed to it by God Himself; and that no misconduct of its ministers in detail could forfeit their claims or justify resistance to them.

There is something touching in the bishops' evidently sincere unconsciousness that there could be real room for blame. Warham, who had been Archbishop of Canterbury thirty years, took credit to himself for the reforms which, under the pressure of public opinion he had introduced, in the last few weeks or months; and did not know that in doing so he had passed sentence on a life of neglect. In the opinion of the entire bench no infamy, however notorious, could shake the testimony of a witness in a case of heresy; no cruelty was unjust when there was suspicion of so horrible a crime; while the appointment of minors to church benefices (not to press more closely the edge of the accusation) they admitted while they affected to deny it; since they were not ashamed to defend the appropriation of the proceeds of benefices occupied by such persons, if these proceeds were laid out on the education and maintenance of the minors themselves.

Yet these things were as nothing in comparison with the powers claimed for convocation; and the prelates of the later years of Henry's reign must have looked back with strange sensations at the language which their predecessors had so simply addressed to him. If the canons which convocation might think good to enact were not consistent with the laws of the Realm, 'His Majesty' was desired to produce the wished-for uniformity by altering the laws of the Realm; and although the bishops might not submit their laws to his Majesty's approval, they would be happy, they told him, to consider such suggestions as he might think proper to make. The spirit of the Plantagenets must have slumbered long before such words as these could have been addressed to an English sovereign, and little did the bishops dream that these light words were the spell which would burst the charm, and bid that spirit wake again in all its power and terror.

The House of Commons in the mean time had not been idle. To them the questions at issue were unincumbered with theoretic difficulties. Enormous abuses had been long ripe for dissolution, and there was no occasion to waste time in unnecessary debates. At such a time, with a House practically unanimous, business could be rapidly transacted, the more rapidly indeed in proportion to its importance. In six weeks, for so long only the session lasted, the astonished church authorities saw bill after bill hurried up before the Lords, by which successively the pleasant fountains of their incomes would be dried up to flow no longer; or would flow only in modest rivulets along the beds of the once abundant torrents. The jurisdiction of the spiritual courts was not immediately curtailed, and the authority which was in future to be permitted to convocation lay over for further consideration, to be dealt with in another manner. But probate duties and legacy duties, hitherto assessed at discretion, were dwarfed into fixed proportions,[1] not to touch the poorer laity any more, and bearing even upon wealth with a reserved and gentle hand. Mortuaries were shorn of their luxuriance; when effects were small, no mortuary should be required; when large, the clergy should content themselves with a modest share. No velvet cloaks should be stripped any more from strangers' bodies to save them from a rector's grasp;[2] no shameful battles with apparitors should disturb any more the recent rest of the dead.[3] Such sums as the law would permit should be paid thenceforward in the form of decent funeral fees for householders dying in their own parishes, and there the exactions should terminate.[4]

The carelessness of the bishops in the discharge of their most immediate duties obliged the legislature to trespass also in the provinces purely spiritual, and undertake the discipline of the clergy. The Commons had

---

[1] 21 Hen. VIII. cap. 5. An Act concerning fines and sums of money to be taken by the ministers of bishops and other ordinaries of holy church for the probate of testaments.

[2] HALE, *Precedents*, p. 86. [3] Ibid. p. 63.

[4] 21 Hen. VIII. cap. 6. An Act concerning the taking of mortuaries, or demanding, receiving. or claiming the same.

In Scotland the usual mortuary was a cow and the uppermost cloth or counterpane on the bed in which the death took place. A bishop reprimanding a suspected clergyman for his leanings toward the Reformation, said to him:—

'My joy, Dean Thomas, I am informed that ye preach the epistle and gospel every Sunday to your parishioners, and that ye take not the cow nor the upmost cloth from your parishioners; which thing is very prejudicial to the churchmen. And therefore, Dean Thomas, I would ye took your cow and upmost cloth, or else it is too much to preach every Sunday, for in so doing ye may make the people think we should preach likewise.'—CALDERWOOD, vol. i. p. 126.

The bishop had to burn Dean Thomas at last, being unable to work conviction into him in these matters.

complained in their petition that the clergy, instead of attending to their duties, were acting as auditors, bailiffs, stewards, or in other capacities, as laymen; they were engaged in trade also, in farming, in tanning, in brewing, in doing anything but the duties which they were paid for doing; while they purchased dispensations for non-residence on their benefices; and of these benefices, in favoured cases, single priests held as many as eight or nine. It was thought unnecessary to wait for the bishops' pleasure to apply a remedy here. If the clergy were unjustly accused of these offences, a law of general prohibition would not touch them. If the belief of the House of Commons was well founded, there was no occasion for longer delay. It was therefore enacted[1]—'for the more quiet and virtuous increase and maintenance of divine service, the preaching and teaching the Word of God with godly and good example, for the better discharge of cures, the maintenance of hospitality, the relief of poor people, the increase of devotion and good opinion of the lay fee towards spiritual persons'—that no such persons thenceforward should take any land to farm beyond what was necessary, *bonâ fide*, for the support of their own household; that they should not buy merchandize to sell again; that they should keep no tanneries or brewhouses, or otherwise directly or indirectly trade for gain. Pluralities were not to be permitted with benefices above the yearly value of eight pounds, and residence was made obligatory under penalty in cases of absence without special reason, of ten pounds for each month of such absence. The law against pluralities was limited as against existing holders, each of whom, for their natural lives, might continue to hold as many as four benefices. But dispensations, either for non-residence or for the violation of any other provision of the act, were made penal in a high degree, whether obtained from the bishops or from the court of Rome.

These bills struck hard and struck home. Yet even persons who most disapprove of the Reformation will not at the present time either wonder at their enactment or complain of their severity. They will be desirous rather to disentangle their doctrine from suspicious connexion, and will not be anxious to compromise their theology by the defence of unworthy professors of it.

The bishops were not slow however to sound the note

---

[1] 21 Hen. VIII. cap. 13. An Act that no spiritual person shall take farms; or buy and sell for lucre and profit; or keep tan-houses or breweries. And for pluralities of benefices and for residence.

of alarm with all their power. The Commons, it was exclaimed, in doors and out, were heretics and schismatics;[1]
the cry was heard everywhere, of Lack of faith, Lack of
faith; and the lay peers being constitutionally conservative,
and perhaps instinctively apprehensive of the infectious
tendencies of innovation, it seemed likely for a time that
an effective opposition might be raised in the Upper
House. The clergy commanded an actual majority in that
House from their own body, which they might employ if
they dared; and although they were not likely to venture
alone on so bold a measure, yet a partial support from
the other members was a sufficient encouragement. The
aged Bishop of Rochester was made the spokesman of
the ecclesiastics on this occasion. 'My Lords,' he said,
'you see daily what bills come hither from the Commons'
House, and all is to the destruction of the church. For
God's sake see what a realm the kingdom of Bohemia
was; and when the church went down, then fell the glory
of that kingdom. Now with the Commons is nothing but
Down with the church, and all this meseemeth is for lack
of faith only.'[2] 'In result,' says Hall, 'the acts were sore
debated; the Lords Spiritual would in no wise consent,
and committees of the two Houses sate continually for
discussion.' The spiritualty defended themselves by pre-
scription and usage, to which a Gray's Inn lawyer something insolently answered, on one occasion, 'the usage
hath ever been of thieves to rob on Shooter's Hill, *ergo*,
it is lawful.' 'With this answer,' continues Hall, 'the
spiritual men were sore offended because their doings
were called robberies, but the temporal men stood by their
sayings, insomuch that the said gentleman declared to the
Archbishop of Canterbury, that both the exaction of pro-
bates of testaments and the taking of mortuaries were
open robbery and thefts.'

At length, people out of doors growing impatient, and
dangerous symptoms threatening to show themselves, the
king summoned a meeting in the Star-chamber between
eight members of both Houses. The lay peers, after some
discussion, conclusively gave way; and the bishops, left
without support, were obliged to yield. They signified
their unwilling consent, and the bills, 'something qualified,'
were the next day agreed to—'to the great rejoicing of
the lay people, and the great displeasure of the spiritual
persons.'[3]

Nor were the House of Commons contented with the

[1] HALL, p. 767.   [2] Ibid. p. 766.   [3] Ibid. p. 767.

substance of victory. The reply to their petition had perhaps by that time been made known to them, and at any rate they had been accused of sympathy with heresy, and they would not submit to the hateful charge without exacting revenge. The more clamorous of the clergy out of doors were punished probably by the stocks; from among their opponents in the Upper House, Fisher was selected for especial and signal humiliation. The words of which he had made use were truer than the Commons knew; perhaps the latent truth of them was the secret cause of the pain which they inflicted; but the special anxiety of the English reformers was to disconnect themselves, with marked emphasis, from the movement in Germany, and they determined to compel the offending bishop to withdraw his words.

They sent the speaker, Sir Thomas Audeley, to the king, who 'very eloquently declared what dishonour it was to his Majesty and the realm, that they which were elected for the wisest men in the shires, cities, and boroughs within the realm of England, should be declared in so noble a presence to lack faith.' It was equivalent to saying 'that they were infidels, and no Christians—as ill as Turks and Saracens.' Wherefore he 'most humbly besought the King's Highness to call the said bishop before him, and to cause him to speak more discreetly of such a number as was in the Common House.'[1] Henry consented to their request, it is likely with no great difficulty, and availed himself of the opportunity to read a lesson much needed to the remainder of the bench. He sent for Fisher, and with him for the Archbishop of Canterbury, and for six other bishops. The speaker's message was laid before them, and they were asked what they had to say. It would have been well for the weak trembling old men if they could have repeated what they believed, and had maintained their right to believe it. Bold conduct is ever the most safe; it is fatal only when there is courage but for the first step, and fails when a second is required to support it. But they were forsaken in their hour of calamity, not by courage only, but by prudence, by judgment, by conscience itself. The Bishop of Rochester stooped to an equivocation too transparent to deceive any one; he said that 'he meant only the doings of the Bohemians were for lack of faith, and not the doings of the Commons' House'—'which saying was confirmed by the bishops present.' The king allowed the excuse, and the

[1] HALL, p. 766.

bishops were dismissed; but they were dismissed into ignominy, and thenceforward, in all Henry's dealings with them, they were treated with contemptuous disrespect. For Fisher himself we must feel only sorrow. After seventy-six years of a useful and honourable life, which he might have hoped to close in a quiet haven, he was launched suddenly upon stormy waters, to which he was too brave to yield, which he was too timid to contend against; and the frail vessel, drifting where the waves drove it, was soon piteously to perish.

Thus triumphant on every side, the parliament, in the middle of December, closed its session, and lay England celebrated its exploits as a national victory. 'The king removed to Greenwich, and there kept his Christmas with the queen with great triumph, with great plenty of viands, and disguisings, and .interludes, to the great rejoicing of his people;'[1] the members of the House of Commons, we may well believe, following the royal example in town and country, and being the little heroes of the day. Only the bishops carried home sad hearts within them, to mourn over the perils of the church and the impending end of all things; Fisher, unhappily for himself, to listen to the wailings of the Nun of Kent, and to totter slowly into treason.

Here, for the present leaving the clergy to meditate on their future, and reconsider the wisdom of their answer to the king respecting the ecclesiastical jurisdiction (a point on which they were not the less certain to be pressed, because the process upon it was temporarily suspended), we must turn to the more painful matter which for a time longer, ran parallel with the domestic reformation, and as yet was unable to unite with it. After the departure of Campeggio, the further hearing of the cause had been advoked to Rome, where it was impossible for Henry to consent to plead; while the appearance of the supposed brief had opened avenues of new difficulty which left no hope of a decision within the limits of an ordinary lifetime. Henry was still, however, extremely reluctant[2] to proceed to extremities, and appeal to the

---

[1] HALL, p. 768.

[2] So reluctant was he, that at one time he had resolved, rather than compromise the unity of Christendom, to give way. When the disposition of the court of Rome was no longer doubtful, 'his difficultatibus permotus, cum in hoc statu res essent, dixerunt qui ejus verba exceperunt, post profundam secum de universo negotio deliberationem et mentis agitationem. tandem in hæc verba prorupisse, se primum tentâsse illud divortium persuasum ecclesiam Romanam hoc idem probaturum—quod si ita illa abhorreret ab illâ sententiâ ut nullo

parliament. He had threatened that he would tolerate no delay, and Wolsey had evidently expected that he would not. Queen Catherine's alarm had gone so far, that in the autumn she had procured an injunction from the pope, which had been posted in the churches of Flanders, menacing the king with spiritual censures if he took any further steps.[1] Even this she feared that he would disregard, and in March, 1529-30, a second inhibition was issued at her request, couched in still stronger language.[2] But these measures were needless, or at least premature. Henry expected that the display of temper in the country in the late session would produce an effect both on the pope and on the emperor; and proposing to send an embassy to remonstrate jointly with them on the occasion of the emperor's coronation, which was to take place in the spring at Bologna, he had recourse in the mean time to an expedient which, though blemished in the execution, was itself reasonable and prudent.

Among the many *technical* questions which had been raised upon the divorce, the most serious was on the validity of the original dispensation; a question not only on the sufficiency of the form the defects of which the brief had been invented to remedy; but on the more comprehensive uncertainty whether Pope Julius had not exceeded his powers altogether in granting a dispensation where there was so close affinity. No one supposed that the pope could permit a brother to marry a sister; a dispensation granted in such a case would be *ipso facto* void.—Was not the dispensation similarly void which permitted the marriage of a brother's widow? The advantage which Henry expected from raising this difficulty was the transfer of judgment from the partial tribunal of Clement to a broader court. The pope could not, of course, adjudicate on the extent of his own powers; especially as he always declared himself to be ignorant of the law; and

modo permittendum censeret se nolle cum eâ contendere neque amplius in illo negotio progredi.'

Pole, on whose authority we receive these words, says that they were heard with almost unanimous satisfaction at the council board. The moment of hesitation was, it is almost certain, at the crisis which preceded or attended Wolsey's fall. It endured but for three days, and was dispelled by the influence of Cromwell, who tempted both the king and parliament into their fatal revolt.—POLI *Apologia ad Carolum Quintum.*

[1] LEGRAND, vol. iii. p. 446. The censures were threatened in the first brief, but the menace was withdrawn under the impression that it was not needed.

[2] LEGRAND, vol. iii. p. 446. The second brief is dated March 7, and declares that the king, if he proceeds, shall incur ipso facto the greater excommunication; that the kingdom will fall under an interdict.

the decision of so general a question rested either with a
general council, or must be determined by the consent
of Christendom, obtained in some other manner. If such
general consent declared against the pope, the cause was
virtually terminated. If there was some approach to a
consent against him, or even if there was general uncertainty, Henry had a legal pretext for declining his jurisdiction, and appealing to a council.

Thomas Cranmer, then a doctor of divinity at Cambridge,[1] is said to have been the person who suggested
this ingenious expedient, and to have advised the king,
as the simplest means of carrying it out, to consult in
detail the universities and learned men throughout Europe.
His notorious activity in collecting the opinions may have
easily connected him with the origination of the plan,
which probably occurred to many other persons as well
as to him; but whoever was the first adviser, it was immediately acted upon, and English agents were despatched
into Germany, Italy, and France, carrying with them all
means of persuasion, intellectual, moral, and material,
which promised to be of most cogent potency with lawyers'
convictions.

This matter was in full activity when the Earl of
Wiltshire, Anne Boleyn's father, with Cranmer, the Bishop
of London, and Edward Lee, afterwards Archbishop of
York, were despatched to Bologna to lay Henry's remon-
strances before the emperor, who was come at last in
person to enjoy his miserable triumph, and receive from
the pope the imperial crown. Sir Nicholas Carew, who
had been sent forward a few weeks previously, described
in piteous language the state to which Italy had been
reduced by him. Passing through Pavia, the English
emissary saw the children crying about the streets for
bread, and dying of hunger; the grapes in midwinter rot-
ting on the vines, because there was no one to gather
them; and for fifty miles scarcely a single creature, man
or woman, in the fields. 'They say,' he added, 'and the
pope also showed us the same, that the whole people of
that country, with divers other places in Italia, with war,
famine, and pestilence, are utterly dead and gone.'[2] Such
had been the combined work of the vanity of Francis
and the cold selfishness of Charles; and now the latter
had arrived amidst the ruins which he had made, to receive his crown from the hands of a pope who was true

---

[1] Cranmer was born in 1489, and was thus forty years old when
he first emerged into eminence.
[2] *State Papers*, vol. vii. p. 226.

to Italy, if false to all the world besides, and whom, but two years before, he had imprisoned and disgraced. We think of Clement as the creature of the emperor, and such substantially he allowed himself to be; but his obedience was the obedience of fear to a master whom he hated, and the Bishop of Tarbès, who was present at the coronation, and stood at his side through the ceremony, saw him trembling under his robes with emotion, and heard him sigh bitterly.[1] Very unwillingly, we may be assured, he was compelled to act his vacillating part to England, and England, at this distance of time, may forgive him for faults to which she owes her freedom, and need not refuse him some tribute of sympathy in his sorrows.

Fallen on evil times, which greater wisdom and greater courage than had for many a century been found in the successors of St. Peter would have failed to encounter successfully, Clement VII. remained, with all his cowardice, a true Italian; his errors were the errors of his age and nation, and were softened by the presence, in more than usual measure, of Italian genius and grace. Benvenuto Cellini, who describes his character with much minuteness, has left us a picture of a hot-tempered, but genuine and kind-hearted man, whose taste was elegant, and whose wit, from the playful spirit with which it was pervaded, and from a certain tendency to innocent levity, approached to humour. He was liable to violent bursts of feeling; and his inability to control himself, his gesticulations, his exclamations, and his tears, all represent to us a person who was an indifferent master of the tricks of dissimulation to which he was reduced, and whose weakness entitles him to pity, if not to respect. The papacy had fallen to him at the crisis of its deepest degradation. It existed as a politically organized institution, which it was convenient to maintain, but from which the private hearts of all men had fallen away; and it depended for its very life upon the support which the courts of Europe would condescend to extend to it. Among these governments, therefore, distracted as they were by mutual hostility, the pope was compelled to make his choice; and the fatality of his position condemned him to quarrel with the only prince on whom, at the outset of these complications, he had a right to depend.

---

[1] Je croy qu'il ne feist en sa vie ceremonie qui luy touchast si prés du cœur, ne dont je pense qu'il luy doive advenir moins du bien. Car aucunes fois qu'il pensoit qu'on ne le regardast, il faisoit de si grands soupirs que pour pesante que fust sa chappe, il la faisoit bransler à bon escient.—*Lettre de M. de Gramont, Evesque de Tarbes.* LEGRAND, vol. iii. p. 386.

In 1512, France had been on the point of declaring her religious independence; and as late as 1525, Francis entertained thoughts of offering the patriarchate to Wolsey.[1] Charles V., postponing his religious devotion for the leisure of old age, had reserved the choice of his party, to watch events and to wait upon opportunity; while, from his singular position, he wielded in one hand the power of Catholic Spain, in the other that of Protestant Germany, ready to strike with either, as occasion or necessity recommended. If his Spaniards had annexed the New World to the papacy, his German lanzknechts had stormed the Holy City, murdered cardinals, and outraged the pope's person: while both Charles and Francis, alike caring exclusively for their private interests, had allowed the Turks to overrun Hungary, to conquer Rhodes, and to collect an armament at Constantinople so formidable as to threaten Italy itself, and the very Christian faith. Henry alone had shown hitherto a true feeling for religion; Henry had made war with Louis XII. solely in the pope's quarrel; Henry had broken an old alliance with the emperor to revenge the capture of Rome, and had won Francis back to his allegiance. To Henry, if to any one, the Roman bishop had a right to look with confidence. But the power of England was far off, and could not reach to Rome. Francis had been baffled and defeated, his armies destroyed, his political influence in the Peninsula annihilated. The practical choice which remained to Clement lay only, as it seemed, between the emperor and martyrdom; and having, perhaps, a desire for the nobler alternative, yet being without the power to choose it, his wishes and his conduct, his words to private persons and his open actions before the world, were in perpetual contradiction. He submitted while his heart revolted; and while at Charles's dictation he was threatening Henry with excommunication if he proceeded further with his divorce, he was able at that very time, to say, in confidence, to the Bishop of Tarbès, that he would be well contented if the King of England would marry on his own responsibility,[2] availing himself of any

[1] ELLIS, *Third Series*, vol. ii. p. 98. 'In the letters showed us by M. de Buclans from the emperor, of the which mention was made in ciphers, it was written in terms that the French king would offer unto your Grace the papalite of France vel Patriarchate, for the French men would no more obey the Church of Rome.' Lee to Wolsey.

[2] A ce qu'il m'en a declaré des fois plus de trois en secret, il seroit content que le dit mariage fust ja faict, ou par dispense du Legat d'Angleterre ou autrement; mais que ce ne fust par son autorité, ni aussi diminuant sa puissance, quant aux dispenses, et limitation de droict divin.—*Déchiffrement de Lettres de M. de Tarbès.* LEGRAND, vol. iii. p. 408.

means which he might possess among his own people, so only that he himself was not committed to a consent or the privileges of the papacy were not trenched upon.

Two years later, when the course which the pope would really pursue under such circumstances was of smaller importance, Henry gave him an opportunity of proving the sincerity of this language; and the result was such as he expected it to be. As yet, however, he had not relinquished the hope of succeeding by a more open course.

In March, 1529-30, the English ambassadors appeared at Bologna. Their instructions were honest, manly, and straightforward. They were directed to explain, *ab initio*, the grounds of the king's proceedings, and to appeal to the emperor's understanding of the obligations of princes. Full restitution was to be offered of Catherine's dowry, and the Earl of Wiltshire was provided with letters of credit adequate to the amount.[1] If these proposals were not accepted, they were to assume a more peremptory tone, and threaten the alienation of England; and if menaces were equally ineffectual, they were to declare that Henry, having done all which lay within his power to effect his purpose with the goodwill of his friends, since he could not do as he would, must now do as he could, and discharge his conscience. If the emperor should pretend that he would 'abide the law, and would defer to the pope,' they were to say, 'that the sacking of Rome by the Spaniards and Germans had so discouraged the pope and cardinals, that they feared for body and goods,' and had ceased to be free agents; and concluding finally that the king would fear God rather than man, and would rely on comfort from the Saviour against those who abused their authority, they were then to withdraw.[2] The tone of the directions was not sanguine, and the political complications of Europe, on which the emperor's reply must more or less have depended, were too involved to allow us to trace the influences which were likely to have weighed with him. There seems no primâ facie reason, however, why the attempt might not have been successful. The revolutionary intrigues in England had decisively failed, and the natural sympathy of princes, and a desire to detach Henry from Francis, must have combined to recommend a return to the old cordiality which had so long existed between the sovereigns of England and Flanders. But whatever was the cause, the opening interview assured the Earl of Wiltshire that he had nothing to look for.

[1] LEGRAND, vol. iii. p. 408.   [2] *State Papers*, vol. vii. p. 230.

He was received with distant courtesy; but Charles at once objected even to hearing his instructions, as an interested party.[1] The earl replied that he stood there, not as the father of the queen's rival, but as the representative of his sovereign; but the objection declared the attitude which Charles was resolved to maintain, and which, in fact, he maintained throughout. 'The emperor,' wrote Lord Wiltshire to Henry, 'is stiffly bent against your Grace's matter, and is most earnest in it; while the pope is led by the emperor, and neither will nor dare displease him.'[2] From that quarter, so long as parties remained in their existing attitude, there was no hope. It seems to have been hinted, indeed, that if war broke out again between Charles and Francis, something might be done as the price of Henry's surrendering the French alliance;[3] but the suggestion, if it was made, was probably ironical; and as Charles was unquestionably acting against his interest in rejecting the English overtures, it is fair to give him credit for having acted, on this one occasion of his life, upon generous motives. A respectful compliment was paid to his conduct by Henry himself in the reproaches which he addressed to the pope.[4]

So terminated the first and the last overture on this subject which Henry attempted with Charles V. The ambassadors remained but a few days at Bologna, and then discharged their commission and returned. The pope, however, had played his part with remarkable skill, and by finessing dexterously behind the scenes, had contrived to prevent the precipitation of a rupture with himself. His simple and single wish was to gain time, trusting to accident or Providence to deliver him from his dilemma. On the one hand, he yielded to the emperor in refusing to consent to Henry's demand; on the other, he availed himself of all the intricacies to parry Catherine's demand for a judgment in her favour. He even seemed to part with the emperor on doubtful terms. 'The latter,' said the Bishop of Tarbès,[5] 'before leaving Bologna, desired his Holiness to place two cardinals' hats at his disposal, to enable him to reward certain services.' His Holiness

[1] The Bishop of Tarbès to the King of France. LEGRAND, vol. iii. p. 401.

[2] *State Papers*, vol. vii. p. 234.   [3] Ibid. p. 235.

[4] We demand a service of you which it is your duty to concede; and your first thought is lest you should offend the emperor. We do not blame *him*. That in such a matter he should be influenced by natural affection is intelligible and laudable. But for that very reason we decline to submit to so partial a judgment.—Henry VIII. to the Pope: BURNET'S *Collectanea*, p. 431.

[5] LEGRAND. vol. iii. p. 394.

ventured to refuse. During his imprisonment, he said he
had been compelled to nominate several persons for that
office whose conduct had been a disgrace to their rank;
and when the emperor denied his orders, the pope declared
that he had seen them. The cardinals' hats, therefore,
should be granted only when they were deserved, 'when
the Lutherans in Germany had been reduced to obedience,
and Hungary had been recovered from the Turks.' If
this was acting, it was skilfully managed, and it deceived
the eyes of the French ambassador.

Still further to gratify Henry, the pope made a public
declaration with respect to the dispute which had arisen
on the extent of his authority, desiring, or professing to
desire, that all persons whatever throughout Italy should
be free to express their opinions without fear of incurring
his displeasure. This declaration, had it been honestly
meant, would have been creditable to Clement's courage:
unfortunately for his reputation, his outward and his secret
actions seldom corresponded, and the emperor's agents
were observed to use very dissimilar language in his name.
The double policy, nevertheless, was still followed to secure delay. Delay was his sole aim,—either that Catherine's
death, or his own, or Henry's, or some relenting in one
or other of the two princes who held their minatory arms
extended over him, might spare himself and the church
the calamity of a decision. For to the church any decision
was fatal. If he declared for Charles, England would fall
from it; if for Henry, Germany and Flanders were lost
irrecoverably, and Spain itself might follow. His one hope
was to procrastinate; and in this policy of hesitation for
two more years he succeeded, till at length the patience
of Henry and of England was worn out, and all was ended.
When the emperor required sentence to be passed, he
pretended to be about to yield; and at the last moment,
some technical difficulty ever interfered to make a decision
impossible. When Henry was cited to appear at Rome,
a point of law was raised upon the privilege of kings,
threatening to open into other points of law, and so to
multiply to infinity. The pope, indeed, finding his own
ends so well answered by evasion, imagined that it would
answer equally those of the English nation, and he declared
to Henry's secretary that 'if the King of England would
send a mandate ad totam causam, then if his Highness
would, there might be given so many delays by reason
of matters which his Highness might lay in, and the
remissorials that his Grace might ask, ad partes, that
peradventure in ten years or longer a sentence should not

be given.'[1] In point of worldly prudence, his conduct was unexceptionably wise. Something, however, beyond worldly prudence was demanded of a tribunal which claimed to be inspired by the Holy Ghost.

The dreary details of the negotiations I have no intention of pursuing. They are of no interest to any one, —a miserable tissue of insincerity on one side, and hesitating uncertainty on the other. There is no occasion for us to weary ourselves with the ineffectual efforts to postpone an issue which was sooner or later inevitable.

I may not pass over in similar silence another unpleasant episode in this business,—the execution of Cranmer's project for collecting the sentiments of Europe on the pope's dispensing power. The details of this transaction are not wearying only, but scandalous; and while the substantial justice of Henry's cause is a reason for deploring the means to which he allowed himself to be driven in pursuing it, we may not permit ourselves either to palliate those means or to conceal them. The project seemed a simple one, and likely to be effective and useful. Unhappily, the appeal was still to ecclesiastics, to a body of men who were characterized throughout Europe by a universal absence of integrity, who were incapable of pronouncing an honest judgment, and who courted intimidation and bribery by the readiness with which they submitted to be influenced by them. Corruption was resorted to on all sides with the most lavish unscrupulousness, and the result arrived at was general discredit to all parties, and a conclusion which added but one more circle to the labyrinth of perplexities. Croke,[2] a Doctors' Commons lawyer, who was employed in Italy, described the state of feeling in the peninsula as generally in Henry's favour; and he said that he could have secured an all but universal consent, except for the secret intrigues of the Spanish agents, and their open direct menaces, when intrigue was insufficient. He complained bitterly of the treachery of the Italians who were in the English pay; the two Cassalis, Pallavicino, and Ghinucci, the Bishop of Worcester. These men, he said, were betraying Henry when they were pretending to serve him, and were playing secretly into the hands of the emperor.[3] His private despatches were intercepted, or the contents of them by some means were discovered; for the persons whom he named as inclining against the papal claims, became marked

---

[1] *State Papers*, vol. vii. p. 317.
[2] For Croke's Mission, see BURNET, vol. i. p. 144 e.
[3] *State Papers*, vol. vii. p. 241.

at once for persecution. One of them, a Carmelite friar, was summoned before the Cardinal Governor of Bologna, and threatened with death;[1] and a certain Father Omnibow, a Venetian who had been in active co-operation with Dr. Croke, wrote himself to Henry, informing him in a very graphic manner of the treatment to which, by some treachery, he had been exposed. Croke and Omnibow were sitting one morning in the latter's cell, 'when there entered upon them the emperor's great ambassador, accompanied with many gentlemen of Spain, and demanded of the Father how he durst be so bold to take upon him to intermeddle in so great and weighty a matter, the which did not only lessen and enervate the pope's authority, but was noyful and odious to all Realms Christened.'[2] Omnibow being a man of some influence in Venice, the ambassador warned him on peril of his life to deal no further with such things: there was not the slightest chance that the King of England could obtain a decision in his favour, because the question had been placed in the hands of six cardinals who were all devoted to the emperor: the pope, it was sternly added, had been made aware of his conduct, and was exceedingly displeased, and the general[3] of his order had at the same time issued an injunction, warning all members to desist at their peril from intercourse with the English agents. The Spanish party held themselves justified in resorting to intimidation to defend themselves against English money; the English may have excused their use of money as a defence against Spanish intimidation; and each probably had recourse to their several methods prior to experience of the proceedings of their adversaries, from a certain expectation of what those proceedings would be. Substantially, the opposite manœuvres neutralized each other, and in catholic countries, opinions on the real point at issue seem to have been equally balanced. The Lutheran divines, from their old suspicion of Henry, were more decided in their opposition to him. 'The Italian protestants,' wrote Croke to the king, 'be utterly against your Highness in this cause, and have letted as much as with their power and malice they could or might.'[4] In Germany Dr. Barnes and Cranmer found the

---

[1] Friar Pallavicino to the Bishop of Bath. Rolls House MS.
[2] Croke and Omnibow to the King. Rolls House MS.
[3] Generalis magister nostri ordinis mandavit omnibus suæ religionis professoribus, ut nullus audeat de auctoritate Pontificis quicquam loqui. Denique Orator Cæsareus in talia verba prorupit, quibus facile cognovi ut me a Pontifice vocari studeat et tunc timendum esset saluti meæ. Father Omnibow to Henry VIII. Rolls House MS.
[4] BURNET's Collect. p. 50. Burnet labours to prove that on Henry's

same experience. Luther himself had not forgotten his early passage at arms with the English Defender of the Faith, and was coldly hostile; the German theologians, although they expressed themselves with reserve and caution, saw no reason to court the anger of Charles by meddling in a quarrel in which they had no interest; they revenged the studied slight which had been passed by Henry on themselves, with a pardonable indifference to the English ecclesiastical revolt.

If, however, in Germany and Italy the balance of unjust interference lay on the imperial side, it was more than adequately compensated by the answering pressure which was brought to bear in England and in France on the opposite side. Under the allied sovereigns, the royal authority was openly exercised to compel such expressions of sentiment as the courts of London and Paris desired; and the measures which were taken oblige us more than ever to regret the inventive efforts of Cranmer's genius. For, in fact, these manœuvres, even if honestly executed, were all unrealities. The question at issue was one of domestic English politics, and the metamorphosis of it into a question of ecclesiastical law was a mere delusion. The discussion was transferred to a false ground, and however the king may have chosen to deceive himself, was not being tried upon its real merits. A complicated difficulty vitally affecting the interests of a great nation, was laid for solution before a body of persons incompetent to understand or decide it, and the laity, with the alternative before them of civil war, and the returning miseries of the preceding century, could brook no judgment which did not answer to their wishes.

The French king, contemptuously indifferent to justice, submitted to be guided by his interest; feeling it necessary for his safety to fan the quarrel between Henry and the emperor, he resolved to encourage whatever measures would make the breach between them irreparable. The reconciliation of Herod and Pontius Pilate[1] was the subject of his worst alarm; and a slight exercise of eccle-

---

side there was no bribery, and that the emperor was the only offender; an examination of many MS. letters from Croke and other agents in Italy leads me to believe that, although the emperor only had recourse to intimidation, because he alone was able to practise it, the bribery was equally shared between both parties.

[1] LEGRAND, vol. iii. p. 458. The Grand Master to the King of France:—De l'autre part, adventure il n'est moins a craindre, que le Roy d'Angleterre, irrité de trop longues dissimulations, trouvast moyen de parvenir a ses intentions du consentement de l'Empereur, et que par l'advenement d'un tiers *se fissent amis Herode et Pilate*.

siastical tyranny was but a moderate price by which to ensure himself against so dangerous a possibility.

Accordingly, at the beginning of June, the University of Paris was instructed by royal letters to pronounce an opinion on the extent to which the pope might grant dispensations for marriage within the forbidden degrees. The letters were presented by the grand master, and the latter, in his address to the faculty, maintained at the outset an appearance of impartiality. The doctors were required to decide according to their conscience, having the fear of God before their eyes; and no open effort was ventured to dictate the judgment which was to be delivered.

The majority of the doctors understood their duty and their position, and a speedy resolution was anticipated, when a certain Dr. Beda, an energetic Ultramontane, commenced an opposition. He said that, on a question which touched the power of the pope, they were not at liberty to pronounce an opinion without the permission of his Holiness himself; and that the deliberation ought not to go forward till they had applied for that permission and had received it. This view was supported by the Spanish and Italian party in the university. The debate grew warm, and at length the meeting broke up in confusion without coming to a resolution. Beda, when remonstrated with on the course which he was pursuing, did not hesitate to say that he had the secret approbation of his prince; that, however Francis might disguise from the world his real opinions, in his heart he only desired to see the pope victorious. An assertion so confident was readily believed, nor is it likely that Beda ventured to make it without some foundation. But being spoken of openly it became a matter of general conversation, and reaching the ears of the English ambassador, it was met with instant and angry remonstrance. 'The ambassador,' wrote the grand master to Francis, 'has been to me in great displeasure, and has told me roundly that his master is trifled with by us. We give him words in plenty, to keep his beak in the water; but it is very plain that we are playing false, and that no honesty is intended. Nor are his words altogether without foundation; for many persons declare openly that nothing will be done. If the alliance of England, therefore, appear of importance to your Highness, it would be well for you to write to the Dean of the Faculty, directing him to close an impertinent discussion, and require an answer to the question asked as quickly as possible.'[1] The tone of this letter proves, with sufficient clearness, the true feelings of the French government; but at the moment the alternative suggested by the grand master might not be ventured. Francis could not afford to quarrel with England, or to be on less than cordial terms with it, and for a time at least, his brother sovereigns must continue to be at enmity. The negotiations for the recovery of the French princes out of their Spanish prison, were on the point of conclusion; and, as Francis was insolvent, Henry had consented to become security for the money demanded for their deliverance. Beda had, moreover, injured his cause by attacking the Gallican liberties; and as this was a point on which the government was naturally sensitive, some tolerable excuse was furnished for the lesson which it was thought proper to administer to the offending doctor.

On the seventeenth of June, 1530, therefore, Francis wrote as follows to the President of the Parliament of Paris:—

'We have learnt, to our great displeasure, that one Beda, an imperialist, has dared to raise an agitation among the theologians, dissuading them from giving their voices on the cause of the King of England.—On receipt of this letter, therefore, you shall cause the said Beda to appear before you, and you shall show him the grievous anger which he has given us cause to entertain towards him. And further you shall declare to him, laying these our present writings before him that he may not doubt the truth of what you say, that if he does not instantly repair the fault which he has committed, he shall be punished in such sort as that he shall remember henceforth what it is for a person of his quality to meddle in the affairs of princes. If he venture to remonstrate; if he allege that it is matter of conscience, and that before proceeding to pronounce an opinion it is necessary to communicate with the pope; in our name you shall forbid him to hold any such communication: and he and all who abet him, and all persons whatsoever, not only who shall themselves dare to consult the pope on this matter, but who shall so much as entertain the proposal of consulting him, shall be dealt with in such a manner as shall be an example to all the world. The liberties of the Gallican Church are touched, and the independence of our theological council, and there is no privilege belong-

<hr>

[1] LEONARD, vol. iii. p. 467, &c.

ing to this realm on which we are more peremptorily determined to insist.'[1]

The haughty missive, a copy of which was sent to
England,[2] produced the desired effect. The doctors became obedient and convinced, and the required declaration of opinion in Henry's favour, was drawn up in the
most ample manner. They made a last desperate effort
to escape from the position in which they were placed
when the seal of the university was to be affixed to the
decision; but the resistance was hopeless, the authorities
were inexorable, and they submitted. It is not a little
singular that the English political agent employed on this
occasion, and to whose lot it fell to communicate the result
to the king, was Reginald Pole. He it was, who behind the scenes, and assisting to work the machinery of
the intrigue, first there, perhaps, contracted his disgust
with the cause on which he was embarked. There learning to hate the ill with which he was forced immediately
into contact, he lost sight of the greater ill to which it
was opposed; and in the recoil commenced the first steps
of a career, which brought his mother to the scaffold,
which overspread all England with an atmosphere of
treason and suspicion, and which terminated at last after
years of exile, rebellion, and falsehood, in a brief victory
of blood and shame. So ever does wrong action beget
its own retribution, punishing itself by itself, and wreck-
ing the instruments by which it works. The letter which
Pole wrote from Paris to Henry will not be uninteresting.
It revealed his distaste for his occupation, though prudence held him silent as to his deeper feelings.

'Please it your Highness to be advertised, that the
determination and conclusion of the divines in this university was achieved and finished according to your desired
purpose, upon Saturday last past. The sealing of the same
has been put off unto this day, nor never could be obtained before for any soliciting on our parts which were
your agents here, which never ceased to labour, all that
lay in us, for the expedition of it, both with the privy
president and with all such as we thought might in any
part aid us therein. But what difficulties and stops hath
been, to let the obtaining of the seal of the university,
notwithstanding the conclusion passed and agreed unto
by the more part of the faculty, by reason of such op-
positions as the adversary part hath made to embezzle

[1] Letter from the King of France to the President of the Parliament of Paris. *Rolls House MS.*
[2] Letter from Reginald Pole to Henry VIII. *Rolls House MS.*

the determination that it should not take effect nor go forth in that same form as it was concluded, it may please your Grace to be advertised by this bearer, Master Fox; who, with his prudence, diligence, and great exercise in the cause, hath most holp to resist all these crafts, and to bring the matter to that point as your most desired purpose hath been to have it. He hath indeed acted according to that hope which I had of him at the beginning and first breaking of the matter amongst the faculty here, when I, somewhat fearing and foreseeing such contentions, altercations, and empeschements as by most likelihood might ensue, did give your Grace advertisement, how necessary I thought it was to have Master Fox's presence. And whereas I was informed by Master Fox how it standeth with your Grace's pleasure, considering my fervent desire thereon, that, your motion once achieved and brought to a final conclusion in this university, I should repair to your presence, your Grace could not grant me at this time a petition more comfortable unto me. And so, making what convenient speed I may, my trust is shortly to wait upon your Highness. Thus Jesu preserve your most noble Grace to his pleasure, and your most comfort and honour. Written at Paris, the seventh day of July, by your Grace's most humble and faithful servant, Reginald Pole.'[1]

We must speak of this transaction as it deserves, and call it wholly bad, unjust, and inexcusable. Yet we need not deceive ourselves into supposing that the opposition which was crushed so roughly was based on any principle of real honesty. In Italy, intrigue was used against intimidation. In France intimidation was used against intrigue; and the absence of rectitude in the parties whom it was necessary to influence, provoked and justified the contempt with which they were treated.

The conduct of the English universities on the same occasion was precisely what their later characters would have led us respectively to expect from them. At Oxford the heads of houses and the senior doctors and masters submitted their consciences to state dictation, without opposition, and, as it seemed, without reluctance. Henry was wholly satisfied that the right was on his own side; he was so convinced of it, that an opposition to his wishes among his own subjects, he could attribute only to disloyalty or to some other unworthy feeling; and therefore, while he directed the convocation, 'giving no credence to

<hr>

[1] Pole to Henry VIII. *Rolls House MS.*

of right small learning in regard to the other should be joined with so famous a sort, or in a manner stay their seniors in so weighty a cause. And forasmuch as this, we think, should be no small dishonour to our university there, but most especially to you the seniors and rulers of the same; and as also, we assure you, this their unnatural and unkind demeanour is not only right much to our displeasure, but much to be marvelled of, upon what ground and occasion, they being our mere subjects, should show themselves more unkind and wilful in this matter than all other universities, both in this and all other regions do: we, trusting in the dexterity and wisdom of you and other the said discreet and substantial learned men of that university, be in perfect hope that ye will conduce and frame the said young persons unto order and conformity as it becometh you to do. Whereof we be desirous to hear with incontinent diligence; and doubt you not we shall regard the demeanour of every one of the university according to their merits and deserts. And if the youth of the university will play masteries as they begin to do, we doubt not but they shall well perceive that non est bonum irritare crabrones.[1]

'Given under our hand and seal, at our Castle of Windsor.

'HENRY R.'[2]

It is scarcely necessary to say, that, armed with this letter, the heads of houses subdued the recalcitrance of the overhasty 'youth;' and Oxford duly answered as she was required to answer.

The proceedings at Cambridge were not very dissimilar; but Cambridge being distinguished by greater openness and largeness of mind on this as on the other momentous subjects of the day than the sister university, was able to preserve a more manly bearing, and escape direct humiliation. Cranmer had written a book upon the divorce in the preceding year, which, as coming from a well-known Cambridge man, had occasioned a careful ventilation of the question there; the resident masters had been divided by it into factions nearly equal in number, though unharmoniously composed. The heads of houses, as at Oxford, were inclined to the king, but they were embarrassed and divided by the presence on the same side of the suspected liberals, the party of Shaxton, Latimer, and Cranmer himself. The agitation of many

---

[1] It is not good to stir a hornet's nest.
[2] BURNET'S *Collectanea*, p. 431.

months had rendered all members of the university, young
and old, so well acquainted (as they supposed) with the
bearings of the difficulty, that they naturally resisted, as
at the other university, the demand that their power
should be delegated to a committee; and the Cambridge
convocation, as well as that of Oxford, threw out this resolution when it was first proposed to them. A king's
letter having made them more amenable, a list of the intended committee was drawn out, which, containing Latimer's name, occasioned a fresh storm. But the number
in the senate house being nearly divided, 'the labour of
certain friends' turned the scale; the vote passed, and the
committee was allowed, on condition that the question
should be argued publicly in the presence of the whole
university. Finally, judgment was obtained on the king's
side, though in a less absolute form than he had required,
and the commissioners did not think it prudent to press
for a more extreme conclusion. They had been desired
to pronounce that the pope had no power to permit a
man to marry his brother's widow. They consented only
to say that a marriage within those degrees was contrary
to the divine law; but the question of the pope's power
was left unapproached.[1]

It will not be uninteresting to follow this judgment a
further step, to the delivery of it into the hands of the
king, where it will introduce us to a Sunday at Windsor
Castle three centuries ago. We shall find present there,
as a significant symptom of the time, Hugh Latimer, appointed freshly select preacher in the royal chapel, but
already obnoxious to English orthodoxy, on account of
his Cambridge sermons. These sermons, it had been said,
contained many things good and profitable, 'on sin, and
godliness, and virtue,' but much also which was disrespectful to established beliefs, the preacher being clearly opposed to 'candles and pilgrimages,' and 'calling men unto
the works that God commanded in his Holy Scripture,
all dreams and unprofitable glosses set aside and utterly
despised.' He had, therefore, been cited before consistory
courts and interdicted by bishops, 'swarms of friars and
doctors flocking against Master Latimer on every side.'[2]
This also was to be noted about him, that he was one of
the most fearless men who ever lived. Like John Knox,
whom he much resembled, in whatever presence he might
be, whether of poor or rich, of laymen or priests, of bishops
or kings, he ever spoke out boldly from his pulpit what

<hr>

[1] BURNET's *Collectanea*, p. 48.
[2] Preface to LATIMER's *Sermons*. Parker Society's edition, p. 3.

he thought, directly if necessary to particular persons whom he saw before him respecting their own actions. Even Henry himself he did not spare where he saw occasion for blame; and Henry, of whom it was said that he never was mistaken in a *man*—loving a *man*[1] where he could find him with all his heart—had, notwithstanding, chosen this Latimer as one of his own chaplains.

The unwilling bearer of the Cambridge judgment was Dr. Buckmaster, the vice-chancellor, who, in a letter to a friend, describes his reception at the royal castle.

'To the right worshipful Dr. Edmonds, vicar of Alborne, in Wiltshire, my duty remembered,—

'I heartily commend me unto you, and I let you understand that yesterday week, being Sunday at afternoon, I came to Windsor, and also to part of Mr. Latimer's sermon; and after the end of the same I spake with Mr. Secretary [Cromwell], and also with Mr. Provost; and so after evensong I delivered our letters in the Chamber of Presence, all the court beholding. The king, with Mr. Secretary, did there read them; and did then give me thanks and talked with me a good while. He much lauded our wisdom and good conveyance in the matter, with the great quietness in the same. He showed me also what he had in his hands for our university, according to that which Mr. Secretary did express unto us, and so he departed from me. But bye and bye he greatly praised Mr. Latimer's sermon; and in so praising said on this wise: 'This displeaseth greatly Mr. Vice-Chancellor yonder; yon same,' said he to the Duke of Norfolk, 'is Mr. Vice-Chancellor of Cambridge,' and so pointed unto me. Then he spake secretly unto the said duke, which, after the king's departure, came unto me and welcomed me, saying, among other things, the king would speak with me on the next day. And here is the first act. On the next day I waited until it was dinner time; and so at the last Dr. Butts, [king's physician,] came unto me, and brought a reward, twenty nobles for me, and five marks for the junior proctor which was with me, saying that I should take that for a resolute answer, and that I might depart from the court when I would. Then came Mr. Provost, and when I had shewed him of the answer, he said I should speak with the king after dinner for all that, and so he brought me into a privy place where after dinner he would have me wait. I came thither and he both;

---

[1] 'King Harry loved a man,' was an English proverb to the close of the century. See SIR ROBERT NAUNTON's *Fragmenta Regalia*, London, 1641, p. 14; SOAMES's *Elizabeth*, p. 49, note.

and by one of the clock the king entered in. It was in a gallery. There were Mr. Secretary, Mr. Provost, Mr. Latimer, Mr. Proctor, and I, and no more. The king then talked with us until six of the clock. I assure you he was scarce contented with Mr. Secretary and Mr. Provost, that this was not also determined, *an Papa possit dispensare*. I made the best, and confirmed the same that they had shewed his Grace before; and how it would never have been so obtained. He opened his mind, saying he would have it determined after Easter, and of the same was counselled awhile.

'Much other communication we had, which were too long here to recite. Then his Highness departed, casting a little holy water of the court; and I shortly after took my leave of Mr. Secretary and Mr. Provost, with whom I did not drink, nor yet was bidden, and on the morrow departed from thence, thinking more than I did say; and being glad that I was out of the court, where many men, as I did both hear and perceive, did wonder at me. And here shall be an end for this time of this fable.

'All the world almost crieth out of Cambridge for this act, and specially on me; but I must bear is as well as I may. I have lost a benefice by it, which I should have had within these ten days; for there hath one fallen in Mr. Throgmorton's[1] gift which he hath faithfully promised unto me many a time, but now his mind is turned and alienate from me. If ye go to court after Easter I pray you have me in remembrance. Mr. Latimer preacheth still,—quod æmuli ejus graviter ferunt.

'Thus fare you well. Your own to his power,
'WILLIAM BUCKMASTER.[2]

'Cambridge, Monday after Easter, 1530.'

It does not appear that Cambridge was pressed further, and we may, therefore, allow it to have acquitted itself creditably. If we sum up the results of Cranmer's measure as a whole, it may be said that opinions had been given by about half Europe directly or indirectly unfavourable to the papal claims; and that, therefore, the king had furnished himself with a legal pretext for declining the jurisdiction of the court of Rome, and appealing to a general council. Objections to the manner in which the opinions had been gained could be answered by re-

---

[1] Sir George Throgmorton, who distinguished himself by his opposition to the Reformation in the House of Commons. See vol. iv. Appendix.
[2] BURNET's *Collectanea*, p. 429.

criminations equally just; and in the technical aspect of the question a step had certainly been gained. It will be thought, nevertheless, on wider grounds, that the measure was a mistake; that it would have been far better if the legal labyrinth had never been entered, and if the divorce had been claimed only upon those considerations of policy for which it had been first demanded, and which formed the true justification of it. Not only might a shameful chapter of scandal have been spared out of the world's history, but the point on which the battle was being fought lay beside the real issue. Europe was shaken with intrigue, hundreds of books were written, and tens of thousands of tongues were busy for twelve months weaving logical subtleties, and all for nothing. The truth was left unspoken because it was not convenient to speak it, and all parties agreed to persuade themselves and accept one another's persuasions, that they meant something which they did not mean. Beyond doubt the theological difficulty really affected the king. We cannot read his own book[1] upon it without a conviction that his arguments were honestly urged, that his misgivings were real, and that he meant every word which he said. Yet it is clear at the same time that these misgivings would not have been satisfied, if all the wisdom of the world—pope, cardinals, councils, and all the learned faculties together— had declared against him, the true secret of the matter lying deeper, understood and appreciated by all the chief parties concerned, and by the English laity, whose interests were at stake; but in all these barren disputings ignored as if it had no existence.

It was perhaps less easy than it seems to have followed the main road. The bye ways often promise best at first entrance into them, and Henry's peculiar temper never allowed him to believe beforehand that a way which he had chosen could lead to any conclusion except that to which he had arranged that it should lead. With an intellect endlessly fertile in finding reasons to justify what he desired, he could see no justice on any side but his own, or understand that it was possible to disagree with him except from folly or ill-feeling. Starting always with a foregone conclusion, he arrived of course where he wished to arrive. His 'Glasse of Truth' is a very picture of his mind. 'If the marshall of the host bids us do anything,' he said, 'shall we do it if it be against the great captain? Again, if the great captain bid us do anything,

---

[1] *A Glasse of Truth.*

and the king or the emperor commandeth us to do another, dost thou doubt that we must obey the commandment of the king or emperor, and contemn the commandment of the great captain? Therefore if the king or the emperor bid one thing, and God another, we must obey God, and contemn and not regard neither king nor emperor.' And, therefore, he argued, 'we are not to obey the pope, when the pope commands what is unlawful.'[1] These were but many words to prove what the pope would not have questioned; and either they concluded nothing or the conclusion was assumed.

We cannot but think that among the many misfortunes of Henry's life his theological training was the greatest; and that directly or indirectly it was the parent of all the rest. If in this unhappy business he had trusted only to his instincts as an English statesman; if he had been contented himself with the truth, and had pressed no arguments except those which in the secrets of his heart had weight with him, he would have spared his own memory a mountain of undeserved reproach, and have spared historians their weary labour through these barren deserts of unreality.

[1] *Glasse of Truth*, p. 144.

CHAPTER IV.

The authorities of the church, after the lesson which
they had received from the parliament in its first session,
were now allowed a respite of two years, during which
they might re-consider the complaints of the people, and
consult among themselves upon the conduct which they
would pursue with respect to those complaints. They
availed themselves of their interval of repose in a manner little calculated to recover the esteem which they
had forfeited, or to induce the legislature further to stay
their hand. Instead of reforming their own faults, they
spent the time in making use of their yet uncurtailed
powers of persecution; and they wreaked the bitterness
of their resentment upon the unfortunate heretics, who
paid with their blood at the stake for the diminished re-
venues and blighted dignities of their spiritual lords and
superiors. During the later years of Wolsey's administration, the protestants, though threatened and imprisoned,
had escaped the most cruel consequences of their faith.
Wolsey had been a warm-hearted and genuine man, and
although he had believed as earnestly as his brother
bishops, that protestantism was a pernicious thing, destructive alike to the institutions of the country and to
the souls of mankind, his memory can be reproached with
nothing worse than assiduous but humane efforts for the
repression of it. In the three years which followed his
dismissal, a far more bloody page was written in the
history of the reformers; and under the combined auspices
of Sir Thomas More's fanaticism, and the spleen of the
angry clergy, the stake re-commenced its hateful activity.
This portion of my subject requires a full and detailed
treatment; I reserve the account of it, therefore, for a

separate chapter, and proceed for the present with the progress of the secular changes.

Although, as I said, no further legislative measures were immediately contemplated against the clergy, yet they were not permitted to forget the alteration in their position which had followed upon Wolsey's fall; and as they had shown in the unfortunate document which they had submitted to the king, so great a difficulty in comprehending the nature of that alteration, it was necessary clearly and distinctly to enforce it upon them. Until that moment they had virtually held the supreme power in the state. The nobility, crippled by the wars of the Roses, had sunk into the second place; the commons were disorganized, or incapable of a definite policy; and the chief offices of the government had fallen as a matter of course to the only persons who for the moment were competent to hold them. The jealousy of ecclesiastical encroachments, which had shown itself so bitterly under the Plantagenets, had been superseded from the accession of Henry VII. by a policy of studied conciliation, and the position of Wolsey had but symbolized the position of his order. But Wolsey was now gone, and the ecclesiastics who had shared his greatness while they envied it, were compelled to participate also in his change of fortune.

This great minister, after the failure of a discreditable effort to fasten upon him a charge of high treason,—a charge which, vindictively pressed through the House of Lords, was wisely rejected by the Commons,—had been prosecuted with greater justice for a breach of the law, in having exercised the authority of papal legate within the realm of England. His policy had broken down: he had united against him in a common exasperation all orders in the state, secular and spiritual; and the possible consequences of his adventurous transgression had fallen upon him. The parliaments of Edward I., Edward III., Richard II., and Henry IV. had by a series of statutes pronounced illegal all presentations by the pope to any office or dignity in the Anglican church, under penalty of a premunire; the provisions of these acts extending not only to the persons themselves who accepted office under such conditions, but comprehending equally whoever acknowledged their authority, 'their executors, procurators, fautors, maintainers, and receivers.'[1] The importance attached to these laws was to be seen readily in the fre-

---

[1] 35 Ed. I.; 25 Ed. III. stat. 4; stat. 5, cap. 22; 27 Ed. III. stat. 1; 13 Ric. II. stat. 2, cap. 2; 16 Ric. II. cap. 5; 9 Hen. IV. cap. 8.

quent re-enactment of them, with language of increasing vehemence; and although the primary object was to neutralize the supposed right of the pope to present to English benefices, and although the office of papal legate is not especially named in any one of the prohibitory clauses, yet so acute a canonist as Wolsey could not have been ignorant that it was comprehended under the general denunciation. The 5th of the 16th of Richard II. was in fact explicitly universal in its language, and dwelt especially on the importance of prohibiting the exercise of any species of jurisdiction which could encroach on the royal authority. He had therefore consciously violated a law on his own responsibility, which he knew to exist, but which he perhaps trusted had fallen into desuetude, and would not again be revived. It cannot be denied that in doing so, being at the time the highest law officer of the crown, he had committed a grave offence, and was justly liable to the full penalties of the broken statute. He had received the royal permission, but it was a plea which could not have availed him, and he did not attempt to urge it.[1] The contingency of a possible violation of the law by the king himself had been expressly foreseen and provided against in the act under which he was prosecuted,[2] and being himself the king's legal adviser, it was his duty to have kept his sovereign[3] informed of the true nature of the statute. He had neglected this, his immediate obligation, in pursuit of the interests of the church, and when Henry's eyes were opened, he must justly have resented the betrayal of his confidence. He

[1] CAVENDISH, p. 276.

[2] 13 Ric. II. stat. 2, cap. 2. Et si le Roi envoie par lettre ou en autre maniere a la Courte du Rome al excitacion dascune person, parount que la contrarie de cest estatut soit fait touchant ascune dignité de Sainte Eglise, si celuy qui fait tiel excitacion soit Prelate de Sainte Eglise, paie au Roy le value de ses temporalitees dun an. The petition of parliament which occasioned the statute is even more emphatic: Purveuz tout foitz que par nulle traite ou composition a faire entre le Seint Pere le Pape et notre Seigneur le Roy que riens soit fait a contraire en prejudice de cest Estatute a faire. Et si ascune Seigneur Espirituel ou Temporel ou ascune persone quiconque de qu'elle condition q'il soit, enforme, ensence ou excite le Roi ou ses heirs, l'anientiser, adnuller ou repeller cest Estatut a faire, et de cco soit atteint par due proces du loy que le Seigneur Espirituel eit la peyne sus dite. &c.—*Rolls of Parliament*, Ric. II. 13.

[3] Even further, as chancellor the particular duty had been assigned to him of watching over the observance of the act.

Et le chanceller que pur le temps serra a quelle heure que pleint a luy ou a conseill le Roy soit fait d'ascunes des articles sus ditz par ascune persone que pleindre soy voudra granta briefs sur le cas ou commissions a faire au covenables persones, d'oier et terminer les ditz articles, sur peyne de perdre son office et jamais estre mys en office le Roy et perdra mille livres a lever a l'oeps le Roy si de ce soit atteint par due proces.—*Rolls of Parliament*, Ric. II. 13.

12*

did not consider himself called upon to interfere to shield
his minister from the consequences which he had incurred,
nor is it likely that in the face of the irritation of the
country he could have done so if he had desired. It was
felt, indeed, that the long services of Wolsey, and his
generally admirable administration, might fairly save him
(especially under the circumstances of the case) from extremity of punishment; and if he had been allowed to
remain unmolested in the affluent retirement which was
at first conceded to him, his treatment would not have
caused the stain which we have now to lament on the
conduct of the administration which succeeded his fall.
He indeed himself believed that the final attack upon
him was due to no influence of rival statesmen, but to
the hatred of Anne Boleyn; and perhaps he was not
mistaken. This, however, is a matter which does not
concern us here, and I need not pursue it. It is enough
that he had violated the law of England, openly and
knowingly, and on the revival of the national policy by
which that law had been enacted, he was naturally called
to account and punished.

It will be a question whether we can equally approve
of the enlarged application of the statute which immediately followed. The guilt of Wolsey did not rest with
himself; it extended to all who had recognised him in
his capacity of legate; to the archbishops and bishops, to
the two Houses of Convocation, to the Privy Council, to
the Lords and Commons, and indirectly to the nation itself. It was obvious that such a state of things was not
contemplated by the act under which he was tried, and
where in point of law all persons were equally guilty, in
equity they were equally innocent; the circumstances of
the case, therefore, rendered necessary a general pardon,
which was immediately drawn out. The government, however, while granting absolution to the nation, determined
to make some exceptions in their lenity; and harsh as their
resolution appeared, it is not difficult to conjecture the
reasons which induced them to form it. The higher clergy
had been encouraged by Wolsey's position to commit those
excessive acts of despotism which had created so deep
animosity among the people. The overthrow of the last
ecclesiastical minister was an opportunity to teach them
that the privileges which they had abused were at an end;
and as the lesson was so difficult for them to learn, the
letter of the law which they had broken was put in force
to quicken their perceptions. They were to be punished
indirectly for their other evil doings, and forced to sur-

render some portion of the unnumbered exactions which they had extorted from the helplessness of their flocks.

In pursuance of this resolution, therefore, official notice was issued in December, 1530, that the clergy lay all under a premunire, and that the crown intended to prosecute. Convocation was to meet in the middle of January, and this comforting fact was communicated to the bishops in order to divert their attention to subjects which might profitably occupy their deliberations. The church legislature had sate in the preceding year contemporaneously with the sitting of parliament, at the time when their privileges were being discussed, and when their conduct had been so angrily challenged: but these matters had not disturbed their placid equanimity: and while the bishops were composing their answer to the House of Commons, Convocation had been engaged in debating the most promising means of persecuting heretics and preventing the circulation of the Bible.[1] The session had continued into the spring of 1529-30, when the king had been prevailed upon to grant an order in council prohibiting Tyndale's Testament, in the preface of which the clergy were spoken of disrespectfully.[2] His consent had been obtained with great difficulty, on the representation of the bishops that the translation was faulty, and on their undertaking themselves to supply the place of it with a corrected version. But in obtaining the order, they supposed themselves to have gained a victory; and their triumph was celebrated in St. Paul's churchyard with an auto da fé, over which the Bishop of London consented to preside; when such New Testaments as the diligence of the apparitors could discover, were solemnly burned.

From occupation such as this a not unwholesome distraction was furnished by the intimation of the premunire; and that it might produce its due effect, it was

---

[1] BURNET, vol. iii. p. 77. See a summary of the acts of this Convocation in a sermon of Latimer's preached before the two Houses in 1536. LATIMER'S *Sermons*, p. 45.

[2] The king, considering what good might come of reading of the New Testament and following the same; and what evil might come of the reading of the same if it were evil translated, and not followed; came into the Star Chamber the five-and-twentieth day of May; and then communed with his council and the prelates concerning the cause. And after long debating, it was alleged that the translations of Tyndal and Joy were not truly translated, and also that in them were prologues and prefaces that sounded unto heresy, and railed against the bishops uncharitably. Wherefore all such books were prohibited, and commandment given by the king to the bishops, that they, calling to them the best learned men of the universities, should cause a new translation to be made, so that the people should not be ignorant of the law of God.—HALL, p. 771. And see WARHAM'S *Register* for the years 1529—1531. MS. Lambeth.

accompanied with the further information that the clergy of the province of Canterbury would receive their pardon only upon payment of a hundred thousand pounds—a very considerable fine, amounting to more than a million of our money. Eighteen thousand pounds was required simultaneously from the province of York; and the whole sum was to be paid in instalments spread over a period of five years.[1] The demand was serious, but the clergy had no alternative but to submit, or to risk the chances of the law; and feeling that, with the people so unfavourably disposed towards them, they had no chance of a more equitable construction of their position, they consented with a tolerable grace, the Upper House of Convocation first, the Lower following. Their debates upon the subject have not been preserved. It was probably difficult to persuade them that they were treated with anything but the most exquisite injustice, since Wolsey's legatine faculties had been the object of their general dread; and if he had remained in power, the religious orders would have been exposed to a searching visitation in virtue of these faculties, from which they could have promised themselves but little advantage. But their punishment, if tyrannical in form, was equitable in substance, and we can reconcile ourselves without difficulty to an act of judicial confiscation.

The money, however, was not the only concession which the threat of the premunire gave opportunity to extort; and it is creditable to the clergy that the demand which they showed most desire to resist was not that which most touched their personal interests. In the preamble of the subsidy bill, under which they were to levy their ransom, they were required by the council to designate the king by the famous title which gave occasion for such momentous consequences, of 'Protector and only Supreme Head of the Church and Clergy of England.'[2] It is not very easy to see what Henry proposed to himself by requiring this designation, at so early a stage in the movement. The breach with the pope was still distant, and he was prepared to make many sacrifices before he would even seriously contemplate a step which he so little desired. It may have been designed as a reply to the papal censures: it may have been to give effect to his own menaces, which Clement to the last believed to be no more than words;[3] or perhaps (and this is the most

<hr>

[1] 22 Hen. VIII. cap. 15.   [2] BURNET, vol. iii. p. 78.
[3] *State Papers*, vol. vii. p. 457.

likely) he desired, by some emphatic act, to make his clergy understand the relation in which thenceforward they were to be placed towards the temporal authority. It is certain only that this title was not intended to imply what it implied when, four years later, it was conferred by act of parliament, and when virtually England was severed by it from the Roman communion.

But whatever may have been the king's motive, he was serious in requiring that the title should be granted to him. Only by acknowledging Henry as Head of the Church should the clergy receive their pardon, and the longer they hesitated, the more peremptorily he insisted on their obedience. The clergy had defied the lion, and the lion held them in his grasp; and they could but struggle helplessly, supplicate, and submit. Archbishop Warham, just drawing his life to a close, presided for the last time in the miserable scene, imagining that the clouds were gathering for the storms of the latter day, and that Antichrist was coming in his power.

There had been a debate of three days, whether they should or should not consent, when, on the 9th of February, a deputation of the judges appeared in Convocation, to ask whether the Houses were agreed, and to inform them finally that the king had determined to allow no qualifications. The clergy begged for one more day, and the following morning the bishops held a private meeting among themselves, to discuss some plan to turn aside the blow. They desired to see Cromwell, to learn, perhaps, if there was a chance of melting the hard heart of Henry; and after an interview with the minister which could not have been encouraging, they sent two of their number, the Bishops of Exeter and Lincoln, to attempt the unpromising task. It was in vain; the miserable old men were obliged to return with the answer that the king would not see them—they had seen only the judges, who had assured them, in simple language, that the pardon was not to be settled until the supremacy was admitted. The answer was communicated to the House, and again 'debated.' Submission was against the consciences of the unhappy clergy; to obey their consciences, involved forfeiture of property; and naturally in such a dilemma they found resolution difficult. They attempted another appeal, suggesting that eight of their number should hold a conference with the privy council, and 'discover, if they might, some possible expedient.' But Henry replied, as before, that he would have a clear answer, '*yes,* or *no.*' They might say 'yes,' and their pardon was ready. They might say 'no'—and accept the premunire and its penalties. And now, what should the clergy have done? No very great courage was required to answer, 'This thing is wrong; it is against God's will, and therefore it must not be, whether premunire come or do not come.' They might have said it, and if they could have dared this little act of courage, victory was in their hands. With the cause against them so doubtful, their very attitude would have commanded back the sympathies of half the nation, and the king's threats would have exploded as an empty sound. But Henry knew the persons with whom he had to deal—forlorn shadows, decked in the trappings of dignity—who only by some such rough method could be brought to a knowledge of themselves. 'Shrink to the clergy'—I find in a state paper of the time—'Shrink to the clergy, and they be lions; lay their faults roundly and charitably to them, and they be as sheep, and will lightly be reformed, for their consciences will not suffer them to resist.'[1]

They hesitated for another night. The day following, the archbishop submitted the clause containing the title to the Upper House, with a saving paragraph, which, as Burnet sententiously observes, the nature of things did require to be supposed.[2] 'Ecclesiæ et cleri Anglicani,' so it ran, 'singularem protectorem, et unicum et supremum Dominum, et quantum per legem Christi licet, etiam supremum caput ipsius Majestatem agnoscimus—We recognise the King's Majesty to be our only sovereign lord, the singular protector of the church and clergy of England, and as far as is allowed by the law of Christ, also as our Supreme Head.' The words were read aloud by the archbishop, and were received in silence. 'Do you assent?' he asked. The House remained speechless. 'Whoever is silent seems to consent,' the archbishop said. A voice answered out of the crowd, 'Then are we all silent.' They separated for a few hours to collect themselves. In the afternoon sitting they discussed the sufficiency of the subterfuge; and at length agreeing that it saved their consciences, the clause was finally passed, the Bishop of Rochester, among the rest, giving his unwilling acquiescence.

So for the present terminated this grave matter. The pardon was immediately submitted to parliament, where it was digested into a statute;[3] and this act of dubious

<hr>

[1] Memoranda relating to the clergy. *Rolls House MS.*
[2] BURNET, vol. iii. p. 80.
[3] The King's Highness, having always tender eyes with mercy and

justice accomplished, the Convocation was allowed to return to its usual occupations, and continue the prosecutions of the heretics.

The House of Commons, during their second session, had confined themselves meanwhile to secular business. They had been concerned chiefly with regulations affecting trade and labour; and the proceedings on the premunire being thought for the time to press sufficiently on the clergy, they deferred the further prosecution of their own complaints till the following year. Two measures, however, highly characteristic of the age, must not be passed over, one of which concerned a matter that must have added heavily to the troubles of the Bishop of Rochester at a time when he was in no need of any addition to his burdens.

Fisher was the only one among the prelates for whom it is possible to feel respect. He was weak, superstitious, pedantical; towards the protestants he was even cruel; but he was a singlehearted man, who lived in honest fear of evil, so far as he understood what evil was; and he alone could rise above the menaces of worldly suffering, under which his brethren on the bench sank so rapidly into meekness and submission. We can therefore afford to compassionate him in the unexpected calamity by which he was overtaken, and which must have tried his failing spirit in no common manner.

He lived, while his duties required his presence in London, at a house in Lambeth, and being a hospitable person, he opened his doors at the dinner hour for the poor of the neighbourhood. Shortly after the matter which I have just related, many of these people who were dependent on his bounty were reported to have become alarmingly ill, and several gentlemen of the household sickened also in the same sudden and startling manner. One of these gentlemen died, and a poor woman also died; and it was discovered on inquiry that the yeast which had been used in various dishes had been poisoned. The guilty person was the cook, a certain Richard Rouse:

pity and compassion towards his spiritual subjects, minding of his high goodness and great benignity so always to impart the same unto them, as justice being duly administered, all rigour be excluded; and the great benevolent minds of his said subjects [having been] largely and many times approved towards his Highness, and specially in their Convocation and Synod, now presently being in the Chapter House of Westminster, his Highness, of his said benignity and high liberality, in consideration that the said Convocation has given and granted unto him a subsidy of one hundred thousand pounds, is content to grant his general pardon to the clergy and the province of Canterbury, for all offences against the statute and premunire.—22 Hen. VIII. cap. 15.

and inasmuch as all crimes might be presumed to have
had motives, and the motive in the present instance was
undiscoverable, it was conjectured by Queen Catherine's
friends that he had been bribed by Anne Boleyn, or by
some one of her party, to remove out of the way the
most influential of the English opponents of the divorce.[1]
The story was possibly without foundation, although it is
not unlikely that Fisher himself believed it. The shock
of such an occurrence may well have unsettled his powers
of reasoning, and at all times he was a person whose
better judgment was easily harassed into incapacity. The
origin of the crime, however, is of less importance than
the effect of the discovery upon the nation, in whom horror of the action itself absorbed every other feeling.
Murder of this kind was new in England. Ready as the
people ever were with sword or lance—incurably given
as they were to fighting in the best ordered times—an
Englishman was accustomed to face his enemy, man to
man, in the open day; and the Italian crime (as it was
called) of poisoning had not till recent years been heard
of.[2] Even revenge and passion recognised their own laws
of honour and fair play; and the cowardly ferocity which
would work its vengeance in the dark, and practise destruction by wholesale to implicate one hated person in
the catastrophe was a new feature of criminality. Occurring in a time so excited, when all minds were on the
stretch, and imaginations were feverish with fancies, it
appeared like a frightful portent, some prodigy of nature,
or enormous new birth of wickedness, not to be received
or passed by as a common incident, and not to be dealt
with by the process of ordinary law. Parliament undertook the investigation, making it the occasion, when the
evidence was completed, of a special statute, so remarkable
that I quote it in its detail and wording. The English
were a stern people—a people knowing little of compassion where no lawful ground existed for it; but they were
possessed of an awful and solemn horror of evil things,—
a feeling which, in proportion as it exists, inevitably and
necessarily issues in tempers of iron. The stern man is
ever the most tender when good remains amidst evil, and
is still contending with it; but we purchase compassion for
utter wickedness only by doubting in our hearts whether
wickedness is more than misfortune.

[1] BURNET, vol. i. p. 185.
[2] An instance is reported in the Chronicle of the Grey Friars ten
years previously. The punishment was the same as that which was
statutably enacted in the case of Rouse.

'The King's royal Majesty,' says the 9th of the 22nd of Henry VIII., 'calling to his most blessed remembrance that the making of good and wholesome laws, and due execution of the same against the offenders thereof, is the only cause that good obedience and order hath been preserved in this realm; and his Highness having most tender zeal for the same, considering that man's life above all things is chiefly to be favoured, and voluntary murders most highly to be detested and abhorred; and specially all kinds of murders by poisoning, which in this realm hitherto, our Lord be thanked, hath been most rare and seldom committed or practised: and now, in the time of this present parliament, that is to say, on the eighteenth day of February, in the twenty-second year of his most victorious reign, one Richard Rouse, late of Rochester, in the county of Kent, cook, otherwise called Richard Cook, of his most wicked and damnable disposition, did cast a certain venom or poison into a vessel replenished with yeast or barm, standing in the kitchen of the reverend father in God, John Bishop of Rochester, at his place in Lambeth Marsh; with which yeast or barm, and other things convenient, porridge or gruel was forthwith made for his family there being; whereby not only the number of seventeen persons of his said family, which did eat of that porridge, were mortally infected or poisoned, and one of them, that is to say, Bennet Curwan, gentleman, is thereof deceased; but also certain poor people which resorted to the said bishop's place, and were there charitably fed with the remains of the said porridge and other victuals, were in like wise infected; and one poor woman of them, that is to say, Alice Tryppitt, widow, is also thereof now deceased: Our said sovereign lord the king, of his blessed disposition inwardly abhorring all such abominable offences, because that in manner no person can live in surety out of danger of death by that means, if practices thereof should not be eschewed, hath ordained and enacted by authority of this present parliament, that the said poisoning be adjudged and deemed as high treason; and that the said Richard, for the said murder and poisoning of the said two persons, shall stand and be attainted of high treason.

'And because that detestable offence, now newly practised and committed, requireth condign punishment for the same, it is ordained and enacted by authority of this present parliament that the said Richard Rouse shall be therefore boiled to death, without having any advantage of his clergy; and that from henceforth every wilful murder of any person or persons hereafter to be committed or done by means or way of poisoning, shall be reputed, deemed, and judged in the law to be high treason; and that all and every person or persons which shall hereafter be indicted and condemned by order of the law of such treason, shall not be admitted to the benefit of his or their clergy, but shall be immediately after such attainder or condemnation, committed to execution of death by boiling for the same.'

The sentence was carried into effect[1] in Smithfield, 'on the tenebra Wednesday following, to the terrible example of all others.' The spectacle of a living human being boiled to death, was really witnessed three hundred years ago by the London citizens, within the walls of that old cattle-market; an example terrible indeed, the significance of which is not easily to be exhausted. For the poisoners of the soul there was the stake,[2] for the poisoners of the body, the boiling cauldron,—the two most fearful punishments for the most fearful of crimes. The stake at which the heretic suffered was an inherited institution descending through the usage of centuries; the poisoner's cauldron was the fresh expression of the judgment of the English nation on a novel enormity; and I have called attention to it because the temper which this act exhibits is the key to all which has seemed most dark and cruel in the rough years which followed; a temper which would keep no terms with evil, or with anything which, rightly or wrongly, was believed to be evil, but dreadfully and inexorably hurried out the penalties of it.

Following the statute against poisoning, there stands 'an act for the banishment out of the country of divers outlandish and vagabond people called Egyptians;[3] and attached to it another of analogous import, 'for the repression of beggars and vagabonds, the number of whom, it was alleged, was increasing greatly throughout the country, and much crime and other inconveniences were said to have been occasioned by them. We may regard these two measures, if we please, as a result of the energetic and reforming spirit in the parliament, which was

---

[1] HALL, p. 781.

[2] Most shocking when the *wrong persons* were made the victims; and because clerical officials were altogether incapable of detecting the *right persons*, the memory of the practice has become abhorrent to all just men. I suppose, however, that, if the *right persons* could have been detected, even the stake itself would not have been too tremendous a penalty for the destroying of human souls.

[3] 22 Hen. VIII. cap. 10.

dragging into prominence all forms of existing disorders, and devising remedies for those disorders. But they indicate something more than this: they point to the growth of a disturbed and restless disposition, the interruption of industry, and other symptoms of approaching social confusion; and at the same time they show us the government conscious of the momentous nature of the struggle into which it was launched; and with timely energy bracing up the sinews of the nation for its approaching trial. The act against the gipsies especially, illustrates one of the most remarkable features of the times. The air was impregnated with superstition; in a half consciousness of the impending changes, all men were listening with wide ears to rumours and prophecies and fantastic fore-shadowings of the future; and fanaticism, half deceiving and half itself deceived, was grasping the lever of the popular excitement to work out its own ends.[1] The power which had ruled the hearts of mankind for ten centuries was shaking suddenly to its foundation. The Infallible guidance of the Church was failing; its light gone out, or pronounced to be but a mere deceitful ignis fatuus; and men found themselves wandering in darkness, unknowing where to turn or what to think or believe. It was easy to clamour against the spiritual courts. From men smarting under the barefaced oppression of that iniquitous jurisdiction, the immediate outcry rose without ulterior thought; but unexpectedly the frail edifice of the church itself threatened under the attack to crumble into ruins; and many gentle hearts began to tremble and recoil when they saw what was likely to follow on their light beginnings. It was true that the measures as yet taken by the parliament and the crown professed to be directed, not to the overthrow of the church, but to the re-establishment of its strength. But the exulting triumph of the protestants, the promotion of Latimer to a royal chaplaincy, the quarrel with the papacy, and a dim but sure perception of the direction in which the stream was flowing, foretold to earnest catholics a widely different issue; and the simplest of them knew better than the court knew, that they were drifting from the sure moorings of the faith into the broad ocean of uncertainty. There seems, indeed, to be in religious men, whatever be their creed, and however limited their

<hr>

[1] See a very curious pamphlet on this subject, by SIR FRANCIS PALGRAVE. It is called *The Confessions of Richard Bishop, Robert Seymour, and Sir Edward Neville, before the Privy Council, touching Prophecie, Necromancy, and Treasure-trore.*

intellectual power, a prophetic faculty of insight into the true bearings of outward things,—an insight which puts to shame the sagacity of statesmen, and claims for the sons of God, and only for them, the wisdom even of the world. Those only read the world's future truly who have faith in principle, as opposed to faith in human dexterity; who feel that in human things there lies really and truly a spiritual nature, a spiritual connexion, a spiritual tendency, which the wisdom of the serpent cannot alter, and scarcely can affect.

Excitement, nevertheless, is no guarantee for the understanding; and these instincts, powerful as they are, may be found often in minds wild and chaotic, which, although they vaguely foresee the future, yet have no power of sound judgment, and know not what they foresee, or how wisely to estimate it. Their wisdom, if we may so use the word, combines crudely with any form of superstition or fanaticism. Thus in England, at the time of which we are speaking, catholics and protestants had alike their horoscope of the impending changes, each nearer to the truth than the methodical calculations of the statesmen; yet their foresight did not affect their convictions, or alter the temper of their hearts. They foresaw the same catastrophe, yet their faith still coloured the character of it. To the one it was the advent of Antichrist, to the other the inauguration of the millennium. The truest hearted men on all sides were deserted by their understandings at the moment when their understandings were the most deeply needed: and they saw the realities which were round them transfigured into phantoms through the mists of their hopes and fears. The present was significant only as it seemed in labour with some gigantic issue, and the events of the outer world flew from lip to lip, taking as they passed every shape most wild and fantastical. Until 'the king's matter' was decided, there was no censorship upon speech, and all tongues ran freely on the great subjects of the day. Every parish pulpit rang with the divorce, or with the perils of the catholic faith; at every village ale-house, the talk was of St. Peter's Keys, the sacrament, or of the pope's supremacy, or of the points in which a priest differed from a layman. Ostlers quarrelled over such questions as they groomed their masters' horses; old women mourned across the village shopboards of the evil days which were come or coming; while every kind of strangest superstition, fairy stories and witch stories, stories of saints and stories of devils, were woven in and out and to and fro, like quaint, bewildering arabesques, in the tissue of the general imagination.[1]

These were the forces which were working on the surface of the English mind; while underneath, availing themselves skilfully of the excitement, the agents of the disaffected among the clergy, or the friars mendicant, who to a man were devoted to the pope and to Queen Catherine, passed up and down the country, denouncing the divorce, foretelling ruin, disaster, and the wrath of God; and mingling with their prophecies more than dubious language on the near destruction or deposition of a prince who was opposing God and Heaven. The soil was manured for treason, and the sowers made haste to use their opportunity. Thus especially was there danger in those wandering encampments of 'outlandish people,' whose habits rendered them the ready-made missionaries of sedition; whose swarthy features might hide a Spanish heart, and who in telling fortunes might readily dictate policy.[2] Under the disguise of gipsies, the emissaries of the emperor or the pope might pass unsuspected from the Land's End to Berwick-upon-Tweed, penetrating the secrets of families, tying the links of the catholic organization: and in the later years of the struggle, as the intrigues became more determined and a closer connexion was established between the Continental powers and the disaffected English, it became necessary to increase the penalty against these irregular wanderers from banishment to death. As yet, however, the milder punishment was held sufficient, and even this was imperfectly enforced.[3] The tendencies to treason were still incipient—they were tendencies only which had as yet shown themselves in no decisive acts; the future was uncertain, the action of the government doubtful. The aim was rather to calm down the excitement of the people, and to extinguish with as little violence as possible the means by which it was fed.

Ominous symptoms of eccentric agitation, however, began to take shape in the confusion. A preacher, calling

[1] Miscellaneous Depositions on the State of the Country: *Rolls House MS.*

[2] See the Preamble of the Bill against conjurations, witchcraft, sorceries, and enchantments.—33 Hen. VIII. cap. 8.

Also 'the Bill touching Prophecies upon Arms and Badges.—33 Hen. VIII. cap. 14.

A similar edict expelled the gipsies from Germany. At the Diet of Spires, June 10, 1544.

Statutum est ne vagabundum hominum genus quos vulgo Saracenos vocant per Germaniam oberrare sinatur *usu enim compertum est eos exploratores et proditores esse.—State Papers,* vol. ix. p. 705.

[3] ELLIS, first series, vol. ii. p. 101.

himself the favourite of the Virgin Mary, had started up
at Edinburgh, professing miraculous powers of abstinence
from food. This man was sent by James V. to Rome,
where, after having been examined by Clement, and having sufficiently proved his mission, he was furnished with
a priest's habit and a certificate under leaden seal.[1] Thus
equipped, he went a pilgrimage to Jerusalem, and loaded
himself with palm-leaves and with stones from the pillar
at which Christ was scourged; and from thence making
his way to England, he appeared at Paul's Cross an evident saint and apostle, cursing the king and his divorce,
denouncing his apostacy, and threatening the anger of
Heaven. He was arrested and thrown into prison, where
he remained, as it was believed, fifty days without food,
or fed in secret by the Virgin. At the close of the time
the government thought it prudent to send him back to
Scotland, without further punishment.[2]

Another more famous prophetess was then in the
zenith of her reputation—the celebrated Nun of Kent—
whose cell at Canterbury, for some three years, was the
Delphic shrine of the catholic oracle, from which the
orders of Heaven were communicated even to the pope
himself. This singular woman seems for a time to have
held in her hand the balance of the fortunes of England.
By the papal party she was universally believed to be
inspired. Wolsey believed it, Warham believed it, the
bishops believed it, Queen Catherine believed it, Sir Thomas More's philosophy was no protection to him against
the same delusion; and finally, she herself believed the
world, when she found the world believed in her. Her
story is a psychological curiosity; and, interwoven as it
was with the underplots of the time, we cannot observe
it too accurately.

In the year 1525, there lived in the parish of Aldington, in Kent, a certain Thomas Cobb, bailiff or steward
of the Archbishop of Canterbury, who possessed an estate
there. Among the servants of this Thomas Cobb was a
country girl called Elizabeth Barton—a decent person, so
far as we can learn, but of mere ordinary character, and
until that year having shown nothing unusual in her
temperament. She was then attacked, however, by some
internal disease; and after many months of suffering, she
was reduced into that abnormal and singular condition,
in which she exhibited the phenomena known to modern

<hr>

[1] Bulla pro Johanne Scot, qui sine cibo et potu per centum et sex
dies vixerat.—RYMER, vol. vi. part 2, p. 176.
[2] BUCHANAN, *History of Scotland*, vol. ii. p. 156.

wonder-seekers as those of somnambulism or clairvoyance. The scientific value of such phenomena is still undetermined, but that they are not purely imaginary is generally agreed. In the histories of all countries and of all times, we are familiar with accounts of young women of bad health and irritable nerves, who have exhibited at recurring periods certain unusual powers; and these exhibitions have had especial attraction for superstitious persons, whether they have believed in God, or in the devil, or in neither. A further feature also uniform in such cases, has been that a small element of truth may furnish a substructure for a considerable edifice of falsehood; human credulity being always an insatiable faculty, and its powers being unlimited when once the path of ordinary experience has been transcended. We have seen in our own time to what excesses occurrences of this kind may tempt the belief, even when defended with the armour of science. In the sixteenth century, when demoniacal possession was the explanation usually received even of ordinary insanity, we can well believe that the temptation must have been great to recognise supernatural agency in a manifestation far more uncommon; and that the difficulty of retaining the judgment in a position of equipoise must have been very great not only to the spectators but still more to the subject of the phenomenon herself. To sustain ourselves continuously under the influence of reason, even when our faculties are preserved in their natural balance, is a task too hard for most of us. We cannot easily make too great allowance for the moral derangement likely to follow, when a weak girl suddenly found herself possessed of powers which she was unable to understand. Bearing this in mind, for it is only just that we should do so, we continue the story.

This Elizabeth Barton, then, 'in the trances, of which she had divers and many,[1] consequent upon her illness, told wondrously things done and said in other places whereat she was neither herself present, nor yet had heard no report thereof.' To simple-minded people who believed in Romanism and the legends of the saints, the natural explanation of such a marvel was, that she must be possessed either by the Holy Ghost, or by the devil. The archbishop's bailiff, not feeling himself able to decide in a case of so much gravity, called in the advice of the parish priest, one Richard Masters; and together they observed carefully all that fell from her. The girl had

[1] *Letter of Archbishop Cranmer.*—ELLIS, second series, vol. ii. p. 314.

been well disposed, as the priest probably knew. She had
been brought up religiously; and her mind running upon
what was most familiar to it, 'she spake words of marvellous holyness in rebuke of sin and vice;'[1] or, as another account says, 'she spake very godly certain things
concerning the seven deadly sins and the Ten Commandments.'[2] This seemed satisfactory as to the source of the
inspiration. It was clearly not a devil that spoke words
against sin, and therefore, as there was no other alternative, it was plain that God had visited her. Her powers
were assuredly from heaven; and it was plain, also, by
a natural sequence of reasoning, that she held some divine
commission, of which her clairvoyance was the miracle
in attestation.

An occurrence of such moment was not to be kept
concealed in the parish of Aldington. The priest mounted
his horse, and rode post-haste to Lambeth with the news
to the Archbishop of Canterbury; and the story having
lost nothing of its marvel by the way,[3] the archbishop,
who was fast sinking into his dotage, instead of ordering
a careful inquiry, and appointing some competent person
to conduct it, listened with greedy interest; he assured
Father Richard that 'the speeches which she had spoken
came of God'; and bidding him keep him diligent account
of all her utterances, directed him to inform her in his
name that she was not to refuse or hide the goodness
and works of God.' Cobb, the bailiff, being encouraged
by such high authority, would not keep any longer in his
kitchen a prophetess with the archbishop's imprimatur
upon her; and as soon as the girl was sufficiently recovered
from her illness to leave her bed, he caused her to sit at
his own mess with his mistress and the parson.[4] The
story spread rapidly through the country; inquisitive foolish
people came about her to try her skill with questions;
and her illness, as she subsequently confessed, having then
left her, and as only her reputation was remaining, she
bethought herself whether it might not be possible to preserve it a little longer. 'Perceiving herself to be much
made of, to be magnified and much set by, by reason of
trifling words spoken unadvisedly by idleness of her brain,
she conceived in her mind that having so good success,
and furthermore from so small an occasion, and nothing
to be esteemed, she might adventure further to enterprise,

[1] *Statutes of the Realm.*—25 Hen. VIII. cap. 12.
[2] Extracts from a Narrative containing an Account of Elizabeth
Barton.—*Rolls House MS.*
[3] *Statutes of the Realm.*   [4] *Rolls House MS.*

and essay what she could do, being in good advisement and remembrance.'[1] Her fits no longer recurred naturally, but she was able to reproduce either the reality or the appearance of them; and she continued to improvise her oracles with such ability as she could command, and with tolerable success.

In this undertaking she was speedily provided with an efficient coadjutor. The catholic church had for some time been unproductive of miracles, and as heresy was raising its head and attracting converts, so opportune an occurrence was not to be allowed to sleep. The archbishop sent his comptroller to the Prior of Christ Church at Canterbury, with directions that two monks whom he especially named, Doctor Bocking, the cellarer, and Dan William Hadley, should go to Aldington to observe.[2] At first, not knowing what was before them, both prior and monks were unwilling to meddle with the matter.[3] They submitted, however, 'from the obedience which they owed unto their lord;' and they had soon reason to approve the correctness of the archbishop's judgment. Bocking selected no doubt from previous knowledge of his qualities, was a man devoted to his order, and not overscrupulous as to the means by which he furthered the interests of it. With instinctive perception he discovered material in Elizabeth Barton too rich to be allowed to waste itself in a country village. Perhaps he partially himself believed in her, but he was more anxious to ensure the belief of others, and he therefore set himself to assist her inspiration towards more effective utterance. Conversing with her in her intervals of quiet, he discovered that she was wholly ignorant, and unprovided with any stock of mental or imaginative furniture; and that consequently her prophecies were without body, and too indefinite to be theologically available. This defect he remedied by instructing her in the catholic legends, and by acquainting her with the revelations of St. Brigitt and St. Catherine of Sienna.[4] In these women she found an enlarged reflection of herself; the details of their visions enriched her imagery; and being provided with these fair examples, she was able to shape herself into fuller resemblance with the traditionary model of the saints.

As she became more proficient, Father Bocking extended his lessons to the protestant controversy, initiating his pupil into the mysteries of justification, sacramental

[1] *Rolls House MS.*   [2] *Suppression of the Monasteries,* p. 19.   [3] Ibid.
[4] Proceedings connected with Elizabeth Barton.—*Rolls House MS.*

grace, and the power of the keys. The ready damsel re-delivered his instructions to the world in her moments of possession; and the world discovered a fresh miracle in the inspired wisdom of the untaught peasant. Lists of these pregnant sayings were forwarded[1] regularly to the archbishop, which still possibly lie mouldering in the Lambeth library, to be discovered by curious antiquaries. It is idle to inquire how far she was yet conscious of her falsehood. Conscious wilful deception lies far down the road in a course of this kind; and supported by the assurance of an archbishop, she was in all likelihood deep in lying before she actually knew it. Fanaticism and deceit are strangely near relations to each other, and the deceiver is often the person first deceived, and the last who is aware of the imposture.

The instructions of the Father had made her acquainted with many stories of miraculous cures. The catholic saints followed the type of the apostles, and to heal diseases by supernatural means was a more orthodox form of credential than clairvoyance or second sight. Being now cured of her real disorder, yet able to counterfeit the appearance of it, she could find no difficulty in arranging in her own case a miracle of the established kind, and so striking an incident would answer a further end. In the parish was a chapel of the Virgin, which was a place of pilgrimage; the pilgrims added something to the income of the priest; and if, by a fresh demonstration of the Virgin's presence at the favoured spot, the number of these pilgrims could be increased, they would add more. For both reasons, therefore, the miracle was desired; and the priest and the monk were agreed that any means were justifiable which would encourage the devotion of the people.[2] Accordingly, the girl announced, in one of her trances, that 'she would never take health of her body till such time as she had visited the image of our Lady' in that chapel. The Virgin had herself appeared to her, she said, and had fixed a day for her appearance there, and had promised that on her obedience she would present herself in person and take away her disorder.[3] The day came; and as (under the circumstances) there was no danger of failure, the holy fathers had collected a vast concourse of people to witness the marvel. The girl was conducted to the chapel by a procession of more than two thousand persons, headed by the monk, the clergyman, and many other religious persons, the whole multitude

<hr>

[1] 25 Hen. VIII. cap. 12.   [2] Ibid.   [3] Ibid.

'singing the Litany and saying divers' psalms and orations
by the way.'

'And when she was brought thither[1] and laid before
the image of our Lady, her face was wonderfully disfigured, her tongue hanging out, and her eyes being in a
manner plucked out and laid upon her cheeks, and so
greatly deformed. There was then heard a voice speaking
within her belly, as it had been in a tonne, her lips not
greatly moving: she all that while continuing by the space
of three hours or more in a trance. The which voice,
when it told of anything of the joys of heaven, spake so
sweetly and so heavenly, that every man was ravished
with the hearing thereof; and contrarywise, when it told
anything of hell, it spake so horribly and terribly, that it put
the hearers in a great fear. It spake also many things for
the confirmation of pilgrimages and trentals, hearing of
masses and confession, and many other such things. And
after she had lyen there a long time, she came to herself
again, and was perfectly whole. So this miracle was
finished and solemnly sung; and a book was written of
all the whole story thereof, and put into print; which
ever since that time was commonly sold, and went abroad
among the people.'

The miracle successfully accomplished, the residence
at Aldington was no longer adapted for an acknowledged
and favoured saint. The Virgin informed her that she
was to leave the bailiff and devote herself to her exclusive
service. She was to be Sister Elizabeth, and her especial
favourite; and Father Bocking was to be her spiritual
father. The priory of St. Sepulchre's, Canterbury, was
chosen for the place of her profession; and as soon as
she was established in her cell, she became an established
priestess or prophetess, alternately communicating revelations, or indulging the curiosity of foolish persons, and
for both services consenting to be paid. The church had
by this time spread her reputation through England. The
book of her oracles, which extended soon to a considerable volume, was shown by Archbishop Warham to the
king, who sent it to Sir Thomas More, desiring him to
look at it. More's good sense had not yet forsaken him;
he pronounced it 'a right poor production, such as any
simple woman might speak of her own wit;'[2] and Henry
himself 'esteemed the matter as light as it afterwards
proved lewd.' But the world were less critical censors:
the saintly halo was round her head, and her most trivial

<hr>

[1] *Cranmer's Letter*, ELLIS, third series, vol. iii. p. 315.
[2] More to Cromwell: BURNET'S *Collectanea*, p. 350.

religious men, had great confidence in her, and often resorted to her.[1] They consulted her much as to the will of God touching the heresies and schisms in the realm; and when the dispute arose between the bishops and the House of Commons, they asked her what judgment there was in heaven 'on the taking away the liberties of the church;' to which questions her answers, being dictated by her confessor, were all which the most eager churchman could desire. Her position becoming more and more determined, the eccentric periods of her earlier visions subsided into regularity. Once a fortnight she was taken up into heaven into the presence of God and the saints, with heavenly lights, heavenly voices, heavenly melodies and joys. The place of ascent was usually the priory chapel, to which it was essential, therefore, that she should have continual access: and she was allowed, in consequence, to pass the dormitory door when she pleased—a privilege of which the Statute uncharitably hints that she availed herself for a less respectable purpose. But whatever was her secret conduct, her outward behaviour was in full keeping with her language and profession. She related many startling stories, not always of the most decent kind, of the attempts which the devil made to lead her astray. The devil and the angels were in fact alternate visitors to her cell, and the former, on one occasion, burnt a mark upon her hand, which she exhibited publicly, and to which the monks were in the habit of appealing, when there were any signs of scepticism in the visitors to the priory. On the occasion of these infernal visits, 'great stinking smokes' were seen to issue from her chamber, 'savouring grievously through all the dorture;' with which, however, it was suspected subsequently that a paper of brimstone and assafœtida, found among her property after her arrest, had been in some way connected. We smile at these stories, looking back at them with eyes enlightened by scientific scepticism; but they furnished matter for something else than smiles when the accounts of them could be exhibited by the clergy as a living proof of the credibility of the Aurea Legenda,— when the subject of them could be held up as a witness, accredited by miracles, to the truth of the old faith, a living evidence to shame the incredulity of the protestant

---

[1] 25 Hen. VIII. cap. 12.

sectaries. She became a figure of great and singular significance; a 'wise woman,' to whom persons of the highest rank were not ashamed to have recourse to inquire of her the will of God, and to ask the benefit of her intercessory prayers, for which also they did not fail to pay at a rate commensurate with their credulity.[1]

This position the Nun of Kent, as she was now called. had achieved for herself, when the divorce question was first agitated. The monks at the Canterbury priory, of course, eagerly espoused the side of the queen, and the Nun's services were at once in active requisition. Absurd as the stories of her revelations may seem to us, she had already given evidence that she was no vulgar impostor. and in the dangerous career on which she now entered. she conducted herself with the utmost skill and audacity. Far from imitating the hesitation of the pope and the bishops, she issued boldly, 'in the name and by the authority of God,' a solemn prohibition against the king: threatening that, if he divorced his wife, he should not 'reign a month, but should die a villain's death.'[2] Burdened with this message, she forced herself into the presence of Henry himself;[3] and when she failed to produce an effect

[1] Confessions of Elizabeth Barton.—*Rolls House MS.* Sir Thomas More gave her a double ducat to pray for him and his. BURNET'S *Collectanea,* p. 352. Moryson, in his *Apomaxis,* declares that she had a regular understanding with the confessors at the Priory. When penitents came to confess, they were detained while a priest conveyed what they had acknowledged to the Nun; and when afterwards they were admitted to her presence, she amazed them with repeating their own confessions.

[2] The said Elizabeth subtilly and craftily conceiving the opinion and mind of the said Edward Bocking, willing to please him, revealed and showed unto the said Edward that God was highly displeased with our said sovereign lord the king for this matter; and in case he desisted not from his proceeding in the said divorce and separation. but pursued the same and married again, that then within one month after such marriage, he should no longer be king of this realm; and in the reputation of Almighty God he should not be a king one day nor one hour, and that he should die a villain's death. Saying further. that there was a root with three branches, and till they were plucked up it should never be merry in England: interpreting the root to be the late lord cardinal, and the first branch to be the king our sovereign lord, the second the Duke of Norfolk, and the third the Duke of Suffolk.—25 Hen. VIII. cap. 12.

[3] Revelations of Elizabeth Barton.—*Rolls House MS.* In the epitome of the book of her Revelations it is stated that there was a story in it 'of an angel that appeared, and bade the Nun go unto the king. that infidel prince of England, and say that I command him to amend his life, and that he leave three things which he loveth and pondereth upon, *i. e.,* that he take none of the pope's right nor patrimony from him; the second that he destroy all these new folks of opinion and the works of their new learning; the third, that if he married and took Anne to wife, the vengeance of God should plague him; and as she sayth she shewed this unto the king.'—Paper on the Nun of Kent: *MS. Cotton. Cleopatra,* E 4.

upon Henry's obdurate scepticism, she turned to the hesitating ecclesiastics, and roused their flagging spirits. The archbishop bent under her denunciations, and at her earnest request introduced her to Wolsey, then tottering on the edge of ruin.[1] He, too, in his confusion and perplexity, was frightened, and doubted. She made herself known to the papal ambassadors, and through them she took upon herself to threaten Clement,[2] assuming, in virtue of her divine commission, an authority above all principalities and powers. If it were likely that she could have heard the story of the Maid of Orleans, or heard of her at least as a possible object of imitation, it might be supposed that her imagination tempted her to play again a similar career on an English stage, and that she fancied herself the destined saviour of the Church of Christ, as the Maid had been the saviour of France.

It would indeed be a libel on the fair fame of Joan of Arc, if she were to be compared to a confessed impostor; but Joan of Arc might have been the reality which the Nun attempted to counterfeit; and the history of the true heroine might have suggested easily to the imitator the outline of her part. A revolution had been effected in Europe by a somnambulist peasant girl; another peasant girl, a somnambulist also, might have seen in the achievement which had been already accomplished, an earnest of what might be done by herself. While we call the Nun, too, an impostor, we are bound to believe that she first imposed upon herself, and that her wildest adventures into falsehood were compatible with a belief that she was really and truly inspired. Nothing short of such a conviction would have enabled her to play a part among kings and queens, and so many of the ablest statesmen of that most able age. Nothing else could have tempted her, on the failure of her prophecies, into the desperate

---

[1] ELLIS, third series, vol. ii. p. 137. Warham had promised to marry Henry to Anne Boleyn. The Nun frightened him into a refusal by a pretended message from an angel.—*MS. Cotton. Cleopatra. E 4.*

[2] The Nun hath practised with two of the pope's ambassadors within this realm, and hath sent to the pope that if he did not his duty in reformation of kings, God would destroy him at a certain day which he had appointed. By reason whereof it is supposed that the pope hath showed himself so double and so deceivable to the King's Grace in his great cause of marriage as he hath done, contrary to all truth, justice, and equity. As likewise the late cardinal of England, and the Archbishop of Canterbury, being very well-minded to further and set at an end the marriage which the King's Grace now enjoyeth, according to their spiritual duty, were prevented by the false revelations of the said Nun. And that the said Bishop of Canterbury was so minded may be proved by divers which knew then his towardness.—Narrative of the Proceedings of Elizabeth Barton: *Rolls House MS.*

career of treason into which we are soon to see her launched.

Her proceedings were known partially, but partially only, to the king; and the king seems to have been the only person whose understanding was proof against her influence. To him she appeared nothing worse than an excited fanatic, and he allowed her to go her own way, as the best escapement of a frenzy. Until parliament had declared it illegal to discuss the marriage question further, he interfered with no one, and therefore not with her. If her own word was to be taken, he even showed her much personal kindness, having offered to make her an abbess, which is difficult to believe, especially as she said that she had refused his offer. She stated also that at the time of Lord Wiltshire's mission to the emperor, the Countess of Wiltshire endeavoured to persuade her to accept a place at the court, as a companion to Anne; which again is unsupported by other evidence, and sounds improbable;[1] but it is plain, that until she was found to be meditating treason, she experienced no treatment from the government of which she had cause to complain. And thus for the present we may leave her pursuing her machinations with the Canterbury friars, and return to the parliament.

The second session had been longer than the first; it had commenced on the 16th of January, and continued for ten weeks. On the 30th of March, which was to be its last day, Sir Thomas More came down to the House of Commons, and there read aloud to the members the decision of the various universities on the papal power, and the judgment of European learning on the general question of the king's divorce. The country, he said, was much disturbed, and the king desired them each to report what they had heard in their several counties and towns, 'in order that all men might perceive that he had not attempted this matter of his own will or pleasure, as some strangers reported, but only for the discharge of his conscience and surety of the succession of his realm.'[2] This appears to have been the first time that the subject was mentioned before parliament, and the occasion was reasonably and sensibly chosen. The clergy having possession of the pulpits, had used their opportunity to spread a false impression where the ignorance of the people would allow them to venture the experiment; the king having resolved to fall back upon the support of his subjects, naturally

---

[1] Note of the Revelations of Elizabeth Barton: *Rolls House* MS.
[2] HALL, p. 780.

desired the assistance of the country gentlemen, and the nobles to counteract the efforts of disaffection, and provided them with accurate information in the simplest manner which he could have chosen.

But the desire expressed by Henry was no more than an unnecessary form, for as a body, the educated laity were as earnestly bent upon the divorce as the king himself could be, and might have been trusted to use all means by which to further it. The parliament was prorogued, but the Lords, shortly after the separation, united with such of the Commons as remained in London, to give a proof of their feeling by a voluntary address to the pope. The meaning of this movement was not to be mistaken. On one side, the Nun of Kent was threatening Clement, speaking, perhaps, the feelings of the clergy and of all the women in England; on the other side, the parliament thought well to threaten him, speaking for the great body of English *men*, for all persons of substance and property, who desired above all things peace and order and a secured succession.

The language of this remarkable document[1] was as follows:—

'To the Most Holy Lord our Lord and Father in Christ, Clement, by Divine Providence the seventh of that name, we desire perpetual happiness in our Lord Jesus Christ.

'Most blessed Father, albeit the cause concerning the marriage of the most invincible prince, our sovereign lord, the King of England and of France, Defender of the Faith, and Lord of Ireland, does for sundry great and weighty reasons require and demand the aid of your Holiness, that it may be brought to that brief end and determination which we with so great and earnest desire have expected, and which we have been contented hitherto to expect,

---

[1] RYMER, vol. vi. p. 160. We are left to collateral evidence to fix the place of this petition, the official transcriber having contented himself with the substance, and omitted the date. The original, as appears from the pope's reply (LORD HERBERT, p. 145), bore the date of July 13; and unless a mistake was made in transcribing the papal brief, this was July, 1530. I have ventured to assume a mistake, and to place the petition in the following year, because the judgment of the universities, to which it refers, was not completed till the winter of 1530; they were not read in parliament till March 30, 1531; and it seems unlikely that a petition of so great moment would have been presented on an incomplete case, or before the additional support of the House of Commons had been secured. I am far from satisfied, however, that I am right in making the change. The petition must have been drawn up (though it need not have been presented) in 1530; since it bears the signature of Wolsey, who died in the November of that year.

though so far, vainly, at your Holiness's hands; we have been unable, nevertheless, to keep longer silence herein, seeing that this kingdom and the affairs of it are brought into so high peril through the unseasonable delay of sentence. His Majesty, who is our head, and by consequence the life of us all, and we through him as subject members by a just union annexed to the head, have with great earnestness entreated your Holiness for judgment; we have however entreated in vain: we are by the greatness of our grief therefore forced separately and distinctly by these our letters most humbly to demand a speedy determination. There ought, indeed, to have been no need of this request on our part. The justice of the cause itself, approved to be just by the sentence of so many learned men, by the suffrage of the most famous universities in England, France, and Italy, should have sufficed alone to have induced your Holiness to confirm the sentence given by others; especially when the interests of a king and kingdom are at stake, which in so many ways have deserved well of the apostolic see. This we say ought to have been motive sufficient with you, without need of petition on our part; and if we had added our entreaties, it should have been but as men yielding to a causeless anxiety, and wasting words for which there was no occasion. Since, however, neither the merit of the cause nor the recollection of the benefits which you have received, nor the assiduous and diligent supplications of our prince have availed anything with your Holiness; since we cannot obtain from you what it is your duty as a father to grant; the load of our grief, increased as it is beyond measure by the remembrance of the past miseries and calamities which have befallen this nation, makes vocal every member of our commonwealth, and compels us by word and letter to utter our complaints.

'For what a misfortune is this,—that a sentence which our own two universities, which the University of Paris, and many other universities in France, which men of the highest learning and probity everywhere, at home and abroad, are ready to defend with word and pen, that such sentence, we say, cannot be obtained from the apostolic see by a prince to whom that see owes its present existence. Amidst the attacks of so many and so powerful enemies, the King of England ever has stood by that see with sword and pen, with voice and with authority. Yet he alone is to reap no benefit from his labours. He has saved the papacy from ruin, that others might enjoy the fruits of the life which he has preserved for it. We see not what answer can be made to this; and meanwhile we perceive a flood of miseries impending over the commonwealth, threatening to bring back upon us the ancient controversy on the succession, which had been extinguished only with so much blood and slaughter. We have now a king most eminent for his virtues, and reigning by unchallenged title, who will secure assured tranquillity to the realm if he leave a son born of his body to succeed him. The sole hope that such a son may be born to him lies in the being found for him some lawful marriage into which he may enter; and to such marriage the only obstacle lies with your Holiness. It cannot be until you shall confirm the sentence of so many learned men on the character of his former connexion. This if you will not do, if you who ought to be our father have determined to leave us as orphans, and to treat us as castaways, we shall interpret such conduct to mean only that we are left to care for ourselves, and to seek our remedy elsewhere. We do not desire to be driven to this extremity, and therefore we beseech your Holiness without further delay to assist his Majesty's just and reasonable desires. We entreat you to confirm the judgment of these learned men; and for the sake of that love and fatherly affection which your office requires you to show towards us, not to close your bowels of compassion against us, your most dutiful, most loving, most obedient children. The cause of his Majesty is the cause of each of ourselves; the head cannot suffer, but the members must bear a part. We have all our common share in the pain and in the injury; and as the remedy is wholly in the power of your Holiness, so does the duty of your fatherly office require you to administer it. If, however, your Holiness will not do this, or if you choose longer to delay to do it, our condition hitherto will have been so much the more wretched, that we have so long laboured fruitlessly and in vain. But it will not be wholly irremediable; extreme remedies are ever harsh of application; but he that is sick will by any means be rid of his distemper; and there is hope in the exchange of miseries, when, if we cannot obtain what is good, we may obtain a lesser evil, and trust that time may enable us to endure it.

'These things we beseech your Holiness, in the name of our Lord Jesus Christ, to consider with yourself. You profess that on earth you are His vicar. Endeavour, then, to show yourself so to be, by pronouncing your sentence to the glory and praise of God, and giving your sanction to that truth which has been examined, approved, and after much deliberation confirmed by the most learned men of all nations. We meanwhile will pray the all-good God, whom we know by most sure testimony to be truth itself, that He will deign so to inform and direct the counsels of your Holiness, that we obtaining by your authority what is holy, just, and true, may be spared from seeking it by other more painful methods.'

Thus was the great crisis steadily maturing itself, and the cause by this petition was made to rest upon its proper merits. The justification of the demand for the divorce was the danger of civil war; and into civil war the nation had no intention of permitting themselves to be drifted by papal imbecility. Whatever was the origin of Henry's resolution, it was acted out with calmness, and justified by sober reason; and backed by the good sense of his lay subjects, he proceeded bravely, in spite of excommunication, interdict, and the Nun of Kent, towards the object which his country's interests, as well as his own, required.

It would have been well if his private behaviour as a man had been as unobjectionable as his conduct as a sovereign. Hitherto he had remained under the same roof with Queen Catherine, but with that indelicacy which was the singular blemish on his character, he had maintained her rival in the same household with the state of a princess,[1] and needlessly wounded feelings which he was bound to have spared to the utmost which his duty permitted. The circumstances of the case, if they were known to us, though they could never excuse such a proceeding, might perhaps partially palliate it. Catherine was harsh and offensive, and it was by her own determination, and not by Henry's desire, that she was unprovided with an establishment elsewhere. There lay, moreover, as I have said, behind the scenes a whole drama of contention and bitterness, which now is happily concealed from us; but which being concealed, leaves us without the clue to these painful doings. Indelicate, however, the position given to Anne Boleyn could not but be; and, if it was indelicate in Henry to grant such a position, what shall we say of

---

[1] Mademoiselle de Boleyn est venue; et l'a le Roy logée en fort beau logis; et qu'il a faict bien accoustrer tout auprés du sien. Et luy est la cour faicte ordinairement tous les jours plus grosse que de long temps elle ne fut faicte a la Royne. Je crois bien qu'on veult accoutumer par les petie ce peuple à l'endurer, afin que quand viendra à donner les grands coups, il ne les trouve si estrange. Toutefois il demeure tous jours endurcy, et croy bien qu'il feroit plus qu'il ne faict si plus il avoit de puissance; mais grand ordre se donne par tout.—Bishop of Bayonne to the Grand Master: LEGRAND, vol. iii. p. 231.

the lady who consented, in the presence of her sovereign and mistress, to wear such ignominious splendour?

But in these most offensive relations there was henceforth to be a change. In June, 1531, two months after the prorogation of parliament, a deputation of the privy council went to the apartments of Catherine at Greenwich, and laying before her the papers which had been read by Sir Thomas More to the two Houses, demanded formally, whether, for the sake of the country, and for the quiet of the king's conscience, she would withdraw her appeal to Rome, and submit to an arbitration in the kingdom. It was, probably, but an official request, proposed without expectation that she would yield. After rejecting a similar entreaty from the pope himself, she was not likely, inflexible as she had ever been, to yield, when the pope had admitted her appeal, and the emperor, victorious through Europe, had promised her support. She refused, of course, like herself, proudly, resolutely, gallantly, and not without the scorn which she was entitled to feel. The nation had no claims upon her, and 'for the king's conscience,' she answered, 'I pray God send his Grace good quiet therein; and tell him I say I am his lawful wife, and to him lawfully married; and in that point I will abide till the court of Rome, which was privy to the beginning, hath made thereof a determination and a final ending.'[1] The learned councillors retired with their answer. A more passive resistance would have been more dignified; but Catherine was a queen, and a queen she chose to be; and in defence of her own high honour, and of her daughter's, by no act of hers would she abate one tittle of her dignity, or cease to assert her claim to it. Her reply, however, appears to have been anticipated, and the request was only preparatory to ulterior measures. For the sake of public decency, and certainly in no unkind spirit towards herself, a retirement from the court was now to be forced upon her. At Midsummer she accompanied the king to Windsor; in the middle of July he left her there, and never saw her again. She was removed to the More, a house in Hertfordshire, which had been originally built by George Neville, Archbishop of York, and had belonged to Wolsey, who had maintained it with his usual splendour.[2] Once more an attempt was made to persuade her to submit; but with no better result,

---

[1] HALL, p. 781.

[2] It seems to have been his favourite place of retirement. The gardens and fishponds were peculiarly elaborate and beautiful.—Sir John Russell to Cromwell: *MS. State Paper Office.*

and a formal establishment was then provided for her at
Ampthill, a large place belonging to Henry not far from
Dunstable. There at least she was her own mistress, surrounded by her own friends, who were true to her as
queen, and she attracted to her side from all parts of
England those whom sympathy or policy attached to her
cause. The court, though keeping a partial surveillance
over her, did not dare to restrict her liberty; and as the
measures against the church became more stringent, and
a separation from the papacy more nearly imminent, she
became the nucleus of a powerful political party. Her
injuries had deprived the king and the nation of a right
to complain of her conduct. She owed nothing to England. Her allegiance, politically, was to Spain; spiritually
she was the subject of the pope; and this dubious position
gave her an advantage which she was not slow to perceive.
Rapidly every one rallied to her who adhered to the old
faith, and to whom the measures of the government appeared a sacrilege. Through herself, or through her
secretaries and confessors, a correspondence was conducted which brought the courts of the continent into
connexion with the various disaffected parties in England,
with the Nun of Kent and her friars, with the Poles, the
Nevilles, the Courtenays, and all the remaining faction of
the White Rose. And so first the great party of sedition
began to shape itself, which for sixty years, except in the
shortlived interlude of its triumph under Catherine's
daughter, held the nation on the edge of civil war. We
shall see this faction slowly and steadily organizing itself,
starting from scattered and small beginnings, till at length
it overspread all England and Ireland and Scotland, ex-
ploding from time to time in abortive insurrections, yet
ever held in check by the tact and firmness of the government, and by the inherent loyalty of the English to the
land of their birth. There was a proverb then current that
'the treasons of England should never cease.' It was
perhaps fortunate that the papal cause was the cause of
a foreign power, and could only be defended by a betrayal
of the independence of the country. In Scotland and Ireland the insurrectionists were more successful, being supported in either instance by the national feeling. But the
strength of Scotland had been broken at Flodden; and
Ireland, though hating 'the Saxons' with her whole heart,
was far off and divided. The true danger was at home;

1 Also it is a proverb of old date—'The pride of France, the treason
of England, and the war of Ireland, shall never have end.'—*State Papers*, vol. ii. p. 11.

and when the extent and nature of it is fairly known and weighed, we shall understand better what is called the 'tyranny' of Henry VIII. and of Elizabeth; and rather admire the judgment than condemn the resolution which steered the country safe among those dangerous shoals. Elizabeth's position is more familiar to us, and is more reasonably appreciated because the danger was more palpable. Henry has been hardly judged because he trampled down the smouldering fire, and never allowed it to assume the form which would have justified him with the foolish and the unthinking. Once and once only the flame blazed out; but it was checked on the instant, and therefore it has been slighted and forgotten. But with despatches before his eyes, in which Charles V. was offering James of Scotland the hand of the Princess Mary, with the title for himself of Prince of England and Duke of York[1]— with Ireland, as we shall speedily see it, in flame from end to end, and Dublin castle the one spot left within the island on which the banner of St. George still floated —with a corps of friars in hair shirts and chains, who are also soon to be introduced to us, and an inspired prophetess at their head preaching rebellion in the name of God—with his daughter, and his daughter's mother in league against him, some forty thousand clergy to be coerced into honest dealing, and the succession to the crown floating in uncertainty—finally, with excommunication hanging over himself, and at length falling, and his deposition pronounced, Henry, we may be sure, had no easy time of it, and no common work to accomplish; and all these things ought to be present before our minds, as they were present before his mind, if we would see him as he was, and judge him as we would be judged ourselves.

Leaving disaffection to mature itself, we return to the struggle between the House of Commons and the bishops, which recommenced in the following winter; first pausing to notice a clerical interlude of some illustrative importance which took place in the close of the summer. The

[1] There was a secret ambassador with the Scots king from the emperour, who had long communicated with the king alone in his privy chamber. And after the ambassador's departure the king, coming out into his outer chamber, said to his chancellor and the Earl Bothwell, 'My lords, how much are we bounden unto the emperour that in the matter concerning our style, which so long he hath set about for our honour, that shall be by him discussed on Easter day, and that we may lawfully write ourself Prince of England and Duke of York.' To which the chancellor said, 'I pray God the pope confirm the same.' The Scots king answered, 'Let the emperour alone.'—Earl of Northumberland to Henry VIII.: *State Papers*, vol. iv. p. 599.

clergy, as we saw, were relieved of their premunire on engaging to pay 118,000 pounds within five years. They were punished for their general offences; the formal offence for which they were condemned being one which could not fairly be considered an offence at all. When they came to discuss therefore the manner in which the money was to be levied, they naturally quarrelled among themselves as to where the burden of the fine should fairly rest, and a little scene has been preserved to us by Hall, through which, with momentary distinctness, we can look in upon those poor men in their perplexity. The bishops had settled among themselves that each diocese should make its own arrangements; and some of these great persons intended to spare their own shoulders to the utmost decent extremity. With this object, Stokesley, Bishop of London, who was just then very busy burning heretics, and therefore in bad odour with the people, resolved to call a meeting of five or six of his clergy, on whom he could depend; and passing quietly with their assistance such resolutions as seemed convenient, to avoid in this way the more doubtful expedient of a large assembly.

The necessary intimations were given, and the meeting was to be held on the 1st of September, in the Chapter-house of St. Paul's. The bishop arrived at the time appointed, but unhappily for his hopes, not only the chosen six, but with them six hundred of the clergy of Middlesex, accompanied by a mob of the London citizens, all gathered in a crowd at the Chapter-house door, and clamouring to be admitted.

The bishop, trusting in the strength of the chains and bolts, and still hoping to manage the affair officially, sent out a list of persons who might be allowed to take part in the proceedings, and these with difficulty made their way to the entrance. A rush was made by the others as they were going in, and there was a scuffle, which ended for the moment in the victory of the officials: but the triumph was of brief duration; the excluded clergy were now encouraged by the people; they returned vigorously to the attack, broke down the doors, 'struck the bishop's officers over the face,' and the whole crowd, priests and laity, rushed together, storming and shouting, into the Chapter-house. The scene may be easily imagined; dust flying, gowns torn, heads broken, well-fed faces in the hot September weather steaming with anger and exertion, and every voice in loudest outcry. At length the clamour was partially subdued, and the bishop, beautifully equal to the emergency, arose bland and persuasive.

'My brethren,' he said, 'I marvel not a little why ye be so heady. Ye know not what shall be said to you, therefore I pray you keep silence, and hear me patiently. My friends, ye all know that we be men, frail of condition and no angels; and by frailty and lack of wisdom we have misdemeaned ourselves towards the king our sovereign lord and his laws; so that all we of the clergy were in premunire, by reason whereof all our promotions, lands, goods, and chattels were to him forfeit, and our bodies ready to be imprisoned. Yet his Grace, moved with pity and compassion, demanded of us what we could say why he should not extend his laws upon us.

'Then the fathers of the clergy humbly besought his Grace for mercy, to whom he answered he was ever inclined to mercy. Then for all our great offences we had but little penance; for when he might, by the rigour of his laws, have taken all our livelihoods, he was contented with one hundred thousand pounds, to be paid in five years. And though this sum may be more than we may easily bear, yet, by the rigour of his law, we should have borne the whole burden; whereupon, my brethren, I charitably exhort you to bear your parts of your livelihood and salary towards payment of this sum granted.'[1]

The ingenuity of this address deserved all praise; but the beauty of the form was insufficient to disguise the inconclusiveness of the reasoning. It confessed an offence which the hearers knew to be none; the true provocation which had led to the penalty—the unjust extortion of the high church officials—was ignored. The crowd laughed and hooted. The clergy fiercely tightened their purse-strings, and the bishop was heard out with hardly restrained indignation. 'My lord,' it was shortly answered by one of them, 'twenty nobles a year is but a bare living for a priest. Victual and all else is now so dear that poverty enforceth us to say nay. Besides that, my lord, we never meddled with the cardinal's faculties. Let the bishops and abbots which have offended pay.' Loud clamour followed and shouts of applause. The bishop's officers gave the priests high words. The priests threw back the taunts as they came; and the London citizens, delighting in the scandalous quarrel, hounded on the opposition. From words they passed to blows; the bedell and vergers tried to keep order, but 'were buffeted and stricken,'[2] and the meeting broke up in wild uproar and

[1] HALL, p. 783.
[2] 'The bishop was brought in desperation of his life.'—*Rolls House MS.*, second series, 532. This paper confirms Hall's account in every point.

confusion. For this matter five of the lay crowd and fifteen London curates were sent to the Tower by Sir Thomas More; but the undignified manœuvre had failed, and the fruit of it was but fresh disgrace. United, the clergy might have defied the king and the parliament; but in the race of selfishness the bishops and high dignitaries had cared only for their own advantage. They had left the poorer members of their order with no interest in common with that of their superiors, beyond the shield which the courts consented to extend over moral delinquency; and in the hour of danger they found themselves left naked and alone to bear the storm as they were able.

This incident, and it was perhaps but one of many, is not likely to have softened the disposition of the Commons, or induced them to entertain more respectfully the bishops' own estimate of their privileges. The convocation and the parliament met simultaneously, on the 15th of January, and the conflict, which had been for two years in abeyance, recommenced. The initial measure was taken by convocation, and this body showed a spirit still unsubdued, and a resolution to fight in their own feebly tyrannical manner to the last. A gentleman in Gloucestershire had lately died, by name Tracy. In his last testament he had bequeathed his soul to God through the mercies of Christ, declining the mediatorial offices of the saints, and leaving no money to be expended in masses.[1] Such notorious heresy could not be passed over with impunity; the first step of the assembled clergy[2] was to issue a commission to raise the body and burn it. Their audacity displayed at once the power which they possessed, and the temper in which they were disposed to use it. The Archbishop of Canterbury seems to have been responsible for this monstrous order, which unfortunately was carried into execution before Henry had time to interfere.[3] It was the last act of the kind, however, in which he was permitted to indulge, and the legislature made haste to take away such authority from hands so incompetent to use it. From their debates upon burning the dead Tracy, convocation were proceeding to discuss the possibility of burning the living Latimer,[4] when they were recalled to their senses by a summons to prepare some more reasonable answer than that which the bishops had

<hr>

[1] HALL, p. 796. [2] BURNET, vol. iii. p. 115.
[3] Warham was however fined 300l. for it.—HALL, p. 796. A letter of Richard Tracy, son of the dead man, is in the *MS. State Paper Office*, first series, vol. iv. He says the King's Majesty had committed the investigation of the matter to Cromwell.
[4] LATIMER'S *Sermons*, p. 46.

14 *

made for them on their privilege of making laws. Twenty more years of work were to be lived by Latimer before they were to burn him, and their own delinquencies were for the present of a more pressing nature. The House of Commons at the same time proceeded to frame necessary bills on the other points of their complaint.

The first act upon the roll recalls the Constitutions of Clarendon and the famous quarrel between Becket and the Crown. When catholicism was a living belief, when ordained priests were held really and truly to possess those awful powers which the mystery of transubstantiation assigns to them, they were acknowledged by common consent to be an order apart from the rest of mankind, and being spiritual men, to be amenable only to spiritual jurisdiction. It was not intended that, if they committed crimes, they should escape the retributive consequences of those crimes: offenders against the law might (originally at least) be degraded, if the bishops thought good, and stripped of their commission be delivered thus to the secular arm. But the more appropriate punishment for such persons was of a more awful kind, proportioned to the magnitude of the fault; and was conveyed or held to be conveyed in the infliction of the spiritual death of excommunication. Excommunication was, in real earnest, the death of the soul, at a time when communion with the church was the only means by which it could approach the divine life; and it was a noble thing to believe that there was something worse for a man than legal penalties on his person or on his mortal body; it was beautiful to recognise in an active living form, that the heaviest ill which could befal a man was to be cut off from God. But it is only for periods that humanity can endure the atmosphere of these high altitudes of morality. The early Christians attempted a community of goods, but they were unequal to it for more than a generation. The discipline of catholicism was assisted by superstition,—it remained vigorous for many hundreds of years, but it languished at last; and although there was so great virtue in a living idea, that its forms preserved the reverence of mankind unabated, even when in their effect and working they had become as evil as they once were noble; yet reverence and endurance were at length exhausted, and these forms were to submit to alteration in conformity with the altered nature of the persons whom they affected.

I have already alluded to the abuse of 'benefit of clergy:'[1] we have arrived at the first of those many steps

---

[1] Cap. iii.

by which at length it was finally put away,—a step which did not, however, as yet approach the heart of the evil, but touched only its extreme outworks. The clergy had monopolized the learning of the middle ages, and few persons external to their body being able to read or write, their privileges became co-extensive, as I above stated, with these acquirements. The exemption from secular jurisdiction, which they obtained in virtue of their sacred character, had been used as a protection in villany for every scoundrel who could write his name. Under this plea, felons of the worst kind might claim, till this time, to be taken out of the hands of the lay judges, and to be tried at the bishops' tribunals; and at these tribunals, such a monstrous solecism had catholicism become, the payment of money was ever welcomed as the ready expiation of crime. To prevent the escape of the Bishop of Rochester's cook, who was a 'clerk,' parliament had specially interfered, and sentenced him without trial, by attainder. They now passed a general act, remarkable alike in what it provided as in what, for the present, it omitted to provide.[1] The preamble related the nature of the evil which was to be remedied, and the historical position of it. It dwelt upon the assurances which had been given again and again by the ordinaries that their privileges should not be abused; but these promises had been broken as often as they had been made; so that 'continually manifest thieves and murderers, indicted and found guilty of their misdeeds by good and substantial inquests, and afterwards, by the usages of the common lawes of the land, delivered to the ordinaries as clerks convict, were speedily and hastily delivered and set at large by the ministers of the said ordinaries for corruption and lucre; or else because the ordinaries enclaiming such offenders by the liberties of the church would in no wise take the charges in safe keeping of them, but did suffer them to make their purgation by such as nothing knew of their misdeeds, and by such fraud did annull and make void the good and provable trial which was used against such offenders by the king's law; to the pernicious example, increase, and courage of such offenders, if the King's Highness by his authority royal put not speedy remedy thereto.'

To provide such necessary remedy, it was enacted that thenceforward no person under the degree of subdeacon, if guilty of felony, should be allowed to plead 'his clergy' any more, but should be proceeded against by the ordinary

---

[1] 23 Hen. VIII. cap. 1.

law. So far it was possible to go—an enormous step if we think of what the evil had been; and in such matters to make a beginning was the true difficulty—it was the logical premise from which the conclusion could not choose but follow. Yet such was the mystical sacredness which clung about the ordained clergy, that their patent profligacy had not yet destroyed it—a priest might still commit a murder, and the profane hand of the law might not reach to him.

The measure, however, if imperfect, was excellent in its degree; and when this had been accomplished, the House proceeded next to deal with the Arches Court—the one enormous grievance of the time. The petition of the Commons has already exhibited the condition of this institution; but the act by which the power of it was limited added more than one particular to what had been previously stated, and the first twenty lines of the statute which was now passed[1] may be recommended to the consideration of the modern censors of the Reformation. The framer of the resolution was no bad friend to the bishops, if they had possessed the faculty of knowing who their true friends were, for the statement of complaint was limited, mild, and moderate. Again, as with the 'benefit of clergy,' the real ground for surprise is that any fraction of a system so indefensible should have been permitted to continue. The courts were nothing else but the vicious sources of unjust revenue; and with the opportunity so fairly offered, it is strange indeed that they were not swept utterly away. But sweeping measures have never found favour in England. There has ever been in English legislation, even when most reforming, that temperate spirit of equity which has refused to visit the sins of centuries upon a single generation. The statute limited its accusations to the points which it was designed to correct, and touched these with a hand firmly gentle.

'Whereas great numbers of the king's subjects,' says the preamble, 'as well men, wives, servants, or others dwelling in divers dioceses of the realm of England and Wales, heretofore have been at many times called by citations and other processes compulsory to appear in the Arches, Audience, and other high Courts of the archbishops of this realm, far from and out of the dioceses where such persons are inhabitant and dwelling; and many times to answer to surmised and feigned causes and matters, which

____
[1] 23 Hen. VIII. cap. 9.

have been sued more for vexation and malice than from any just cause of suit; and when certificate hath been made by the sumner's apparitors or any such light litterate person that the party against whom. such citations have been awarded hath been cited or summoned; and thereupon the same party so certified to be cited or summoned hath not appeared according to the certificate, the same party therefore hath been excommunicated, or, at the least, suspended from all divine service; and thereupon, before that he or she could be absolved, hath been compelled, not only to pay the fees of the court whereunto he or she was so called, amounting to the sum of two shillings, or twenty pence at the least; but also to pay to the sumner, for every mile distant from the place where he or she then dwelled unto the same court whereunto he or she was summoned to appear, twopence; to the great charge and impoverishment of the king's subjects, and to the great occasion of misbehaviour of wives, women, and servants, and to the great impairment and diminution of their good names and honesties. Be it enacted——' We ask what?—looking with impatience for some large measure to follow these solemn accusations; and we find parliament contenting itself with forbidding the bishops, under heavy penalties, to cite any man out of his own diocese, except for specified causes (heresy being one of them), and with limiting the fees which were to be taken by the officers of the courts.[1] It could hardly be said that in this parliament there was any bitter spirit against the church. This act showed only mild forbearance and complacent endurance of all tolerable evil.

Another serious matter was dealt with in the same moderate temper. The Mortmain Act had prohibited the church corporations from further absorbing the lands; but the Mortmain Act was evaded in detail, the clergy using their influence to induce persons on their deathbeds to leave estates to provide a priest for ever 'to sing for their souls.' The arrangement was convenient possibly for both parties, or if not for both, certainly for one; but to tie up lands for ever for a special service was not to the advantage of the country; and it was held unjust to allow a man a perpetual power over the disposition of property to atone for the iniquities of his life. But the privilege

---

[1] Be it further enacted that no archbishop, or bishop, official commissary, or any other minister, having spiritual jurisdiction, shall ask. demand, or receive of any of the king's subjects any sum or sums of money for the seal of any citizen, but only threepence sterling.—23 Hen. VIII. cap. 9.

was not abolished altogether; it was submitted only to reasonable limitation. Men might still burden their lands to find a priest for twenty years. After twenty years the lands were to relapse for the service of the living, and sinners were expected in equity to bear the consequence in their own persons of such offences as remained after that time unexpiated.[1]

Thus, in two sessions, the most flagrant of the abuses first complained of were in a fair way of being remedied. The exorbitant charges for mortuaries, probate duties, legacy duties, the illegal exactions for the sacraments, the worst injustices of the ecclesiastical courts, the non-residence, pluralities, neglect of cures, the secular occupations and extravagant privileges of the clergy, were either terminated or brought within bounds. There remained yet to be disposed of the legislative power of the convocation and the tyrannical prosecutions for heresy. The last of these was not yet ripe for settlement; the former was under reconsideration by the convocation itself, which at length was arriving at a truer conception of its position; and this question was not therefore to be dealt with by the legislature.

One more important measure, however, was passed by parliament before it separated, and it is noticeable as the first step which was taken in the momentous direction of a breach with the See of Rome. A practice had existed for some hundreds of years in all the churches of Europe, that bishops and archbishops, on presentation to their sees, should transmit to the pope, on receiving their bulls of investment, one year's income from their new preferments. It was called the payment of annates, or firstfruits, and had originated in the time of the crusades, as a means of providing a fund for the holy wars. Once established, it had settled into custom,[2] and was one of the chief resources of the papal revenue. From England alone, as much as 160,000 pounds had been paid out of the country in fifty years;[3] and the impost was alike oppressive to individuals and injurious to the state. Men were appointed to bishopricks frequently at an advanced age, and dying,

---

[1] 23 Hen. VIII. cap. 10.—By a separate clause all covenants to defraud the purposes of this act were declared void, and the act itself was to be interpreted 'as beneficially as might be, to the destruction and utter avoiding of such uses, intents, and purposes.'

[2] Annates or firstfruits were first suffered to be taken within the realm for the only defence of Christian people against infidels; and now they be claimed and demanded as mere duty only for lucre, against all right and conscience.—23 Hen. VIII. cap. 20.

[3] 23 Hen. VIII. cap. 20.

as they often did, within two or three years of their nomination, their elevation had sometimes involved their
families and friends in debt and embarrassment;[1] while
the annual export of so much bullion was a serious evil
at a time when the precious metals formed the only currency, and were so difficult to obtain. Before a quarrel
with the court of Rome had been thought of as a possible
contingency, the king had laboured with the pope to terminate the system by some equitable composition; and
subsequently cessation of payment had been mentioned
more than once in connexion with the threats of a separation. The pope had made light of these threats, believing
them to be no more than words; there was an opportunity, therefore, of proving that the English government
was really in earnest, in a manner which would touch him
in a point where he was naturally sensitive, and would
show him at the same time that he could not wholly count
on the attachment even of the clergy themselves. For,
in fact, the church itself was fast disintegrating, and the
allegiance even of the bishops and the secular clergy to
Rome had begun to waver: they had a stronger faith in
their own privileges than in the union of Christendom;
and if they could purchase the continuance of the former
at the price of a quarrel with the pope, some among them
were not disinclined to venture the alternative. The
Bishop of Rochester held aloof from such tendencies, and
Warham, though he signed the address of the House of
Lords to the pope, regretted the weakness to which he
had yielded; but in the other prelates there was little
seriousness of conviction; and the constitution of the bench
had been affected also by the preferment of Gardiner and
Edward Lee to the two sees made vacant by the death
of Wolsey. Both these men had been active agents in
the prosecution of the divorce; and Gardiner, followed at
a distance by the other, had shaped out, as the pope grew
more intractable, the famous notion that the English church
could and should subsist as a separate communion, independent of foreign control, self governed, self organized,
and at the same time adhering without variation to catholic doctrine. This principle (if we may so abuse the
word) shot rapidly into popularity: a party formed about
it strong in parliament, strong in convocation, strong out

---

[1] It hath happened many times by occasion of death unto archbishops or bishops newly promoted within two or three years after
their consecration, that their friends by whom they have been holpen
to make payment have been utterly undone and impoverished.—
23 Henry VIII. cap. 20.

of doors among the country gentlemen and the higher clergy—a respectable, wealthy, powerful body, trading upon a solecism, but not the less, therefore, devoted to its maintenance, and in their artificial horror of being identified with heresy, the most relentless persecutors of the protestants. This party, unreal as they were, and influential perhaps in virtue of their unreality, became for the moment the arbiters of the Church of England; and the bishops belonging to it, and each rising ecclesiastic who hoped to be a bishop, welcomed the resistance of the annates as an opportunity for a demonstration of their strength. On this question, with a fair show of justice they could at once relieve themselves of a burden which pressed upon their purses, and as they supposed, gratify the king. Under Anglican influence therefore, while parliament was sitting, the two Houses of Convocation presented an address to the crown for the abolition of the impost, and with it of all other exactions, direct and indirect,—the indulgences, dispensations, delegacies, and the thousand similar forms and processes by which the privileges of the Church of England were abridged for the benefit of the Church of Rome, and weighty injury of purse inflicted both on the clergy and the laity.[1]

The petition demands especial notice, not only because it was the first active movement towards a separation from Rome; but because it originated, not with the king, not with the parliament, not with the people, but with a section of the clergy themselves;[2] who took advantage of the confusion of the time for the advantage of their order, and desired probably to outbid the House of Commons for the king's favour, by volunteering in the opposition to the pope. That they contemplated a conclusive revolt from Rome as a consequence of the refusal to pay annates, appears positively in the close of their address: 'May it please your Grace,' they concluded, after detailing their occasions for complaint, — 'may it please your Grace to cause the said unjust exactions to cease, and to be foredone for ever by act of your high Court of Parliament; and in case the pope will make process against this realm for the attaining those annates, or else will retain bishops' bulls till the annates be paid; forasmuch as the exaction of the said annates is against the law of God and the pope's own laws, forbidding the buying or selling of spiritual gifts or promotions; and forasmuch as all good

---

[1] STRYPE, *Eccles. Mem.*, vol. i. part 2, p. 158.

[2] It is possible, however, that this movement was not spontaneous, and was suggested to the Erastian party by high authority.

Christian men be more bound to obey God than any man; and forasmuch as St. Paul willeth us to withdraw from all such as walk inordinately; may it please your Highness to ordain in this present parliament that the obedience of your Highness and of the people be withdrawn from the See of Rome.'[1]

The king accepted the address, and referred it to the House of Commons, who, more moderate than the clergy, passed the bill which they desired; but passed it only conditionally; leaving power to the crown, if the pope would at length consent to a composition, to settle the matter by amicable arrangement.[2] There was no intention, either in the king or the parliament, of decorating the Anglican clergy with the spoils of the battle, if the battle were really to be fought; and therefore they were in no haste to commence it. The language of the House of Commons contrasted favourably with that of the convocation. It displayed a spirit of equity in place of a spirit of selfishness; and if the Roman consistory would have treated upon the separate question, instead of receiving the mention of it with passionate and angry menaces, the annates could have been disposed of quietly on their own merits, without adding their cumulative weight to the general ground of quarrel.[3]

'Forasmuch,' concluded the statute, 'as the King's Highness and this his high Court of Parliament neither have nor do intend in this or any other like cause any manner of extremity or violence, before gentle courtesy and friendly ways and means be first approved and attempted, and without a very great urgent cause and occasion given to the contrary; but principally coveting to disburden this Realm of the said great exactions and intolerable charges of annates and firstfruits: [the said Court of Parliament] have therefore thought convenient to commit the final order and determination of the premises unto the King's Highness, so that if it may seem to his high wisdom and most prudent discretion meet to move the Pope's Holiness and the Court of Rome, amicably, chari-

---

[1] STRYPE, *Eccles. Mem.*, vol. i. part 2, p. 158.

[2] 23 Hen. VIII. cap. 20.

[3] There was a parliamentary opposition, however, whose views had perhaps to be consulted. Sir George Throgmorton, Sir William Essex, Sir John Giffard, Sir Marmaduke Constable, with many others, spoke and voted in opposition to the government. They had a sort of club at the Queen's Head by Temple Bar, where they held discussions in secret, 'and when we did commence,' said Throgmorton, 'we did bid the servants of the house go out, and likewise our own servants, because we thought it not convenient that they should hear us speak of such matters.'—Throgmorton to the King: *MS. State Paper Office.*

tably, and reasonably, to compound either to extinct the said annates, or by some friendly, loving, and tolerable composition to moderate the same in such way as may be by this his Realm easily borne and sustained, then those ways of composition once taken shall stand in the strength, force, and effect of a law.'[1]

The business of the session was closing. It remained to receive the reply of convocation on the limitation of its powers. The convocation, presuming, perhaps, upon its services on the annates question, and untamed by the premunire, had framed their answer in the same spirit which had been previously exhibited by the bishops. They had re-asserted their claims as resting on divine authority, and had declined to acknowledge the right of any secular power to restrain or meddle with them.[2] The second answer, as may be supposed, fared no better than the first. It was returned with a peremptory demand for submission; and taught by experience the uselessness of further opposition, the clergy with a bad grace complied. The form was again drawn by the bishops, and it is amusing to trace the workings of their humbled spirit in their reluctant descent from their high estate. They still laboured to protect their dignity in the terms of their concession:—

'As concerning such constitutions and ordinances provincial,' they wrote, 'as shall be made hereafter by your most humble subjects, we having our special trust and confidence in your most excellent wisdom, your princely goodness, and fervent zeal for the promotion of God's honour and Christian religion, and specially in your incomparable learning far exceeding in our judgment the learning of all other kings and princes that we have read of; and not doubting but that the same should still continue and daily increase in your Majesty; do offer and promise here unto the same, that from henceforth we shall forbear to enact, promulge, or put in execution any such constitutions and ordinances so by us to be made in time coming, unless your Highness by your Royal assent shall license us to make, promulge, and execute such constitutions, and the same so made be approved by your Highness's authority.

'And whereas your Highness's most honourable Commons do pretend that divers of the constitutions provincial,

---

[1] 23 Hen. VIII. cap. 20.

[2] Printed in STRYPE, *Eccles. Mem.*, vol. i. p. 201. Strype, knowing nothing of the first answer, and perceiving in the second an allusion to one preceding, has supposed that this answer followed the third and last, and was in fact a retractation of it. All obscurity is removed when the three replies are arranged in their legitimate order.

which have been heretofore enacted, be not only much prejudicial to your Highness's prerogative royal, but be also overmuch onerous to your said Commons, we, your most humble servants for the consideration before said, be contented to refer all the said constitutions to the judgment of your Grace only. And whatsoever of the same shall finally be found prejudicial and overmuch onerous as is pretended, we offer and promise your Highness to moderate or utterly to abrogate and anuul the same, according to the judgment of your Grace. Saving to us always such liberties and immunities of this Church of England as hath been granted unto the same by the goodness and benignity of your Highness and of others your most noble progenitors; with such constitutions provincial as do stand with the laws of Almighty God and of your Realm heretofore made, which we most humbly beseech your Grace to ratify and approve by your most Royal assent for the better execution of the same in times to come.'[1]

The acknowledgment appeared to be complete, and might perhaps have been accepted without minute examination, except for the imprudent acuteness of the Lower House of Convocation. As it passed through their hands, they discovered—what had no doubt been intended as a loophole for future evasion—that the grounds which were alleged to excuse the submission were the virtues of the reigning king: and therefore, as they sagaciously argued, the submission must only remain in force for his life. They introduced a limitation to that effect. Some further paltry dabbling was also attempted with the phraseology: and at length, impatient with such dishonest trifling, and weary of a discussion in which they had resolved to allow but one conclusion, the king and the legislature thought it well to interfere with a high hand, and cut short such unprofitable folly. The language of the bishops was converted into an act of parliament; a mixed commission was appointed to revise the canon law, and the clergy with a few brief strokes were reduced for ever into their fit position of subjects.[2] Thus with a moderate hand this great revolution was effected, and, to outward appearance, with offence to none except the sufferers, whose misuse of power when they possessed it deprived them of all sympathy in their fall.

But no change of so vast a kind can be other than a stone of stumbling to those many persons for whom the

<hr>

[1] STRYPE, *Eccles. Mem.*, vol. i. p. 199, &c.
[2] 23 Hen. VIII. cap. 20.

beaten ways of life alone are tolerable, and who, when these ways are broken, are bewildered and lost. Religion, when men are under its influence at all, so absorbs their senses, and so pervades all their associations, that no faults in the ministers of it can divest their persons of reverence; and just and necessary as all these alterations were, many a pious and noble heart was wounded, many a man was asking himself in his perplexity where things would end, and still more sadly, where, if these quarrels deepened, would lie his own duty. Now the Nun of Kent grew louder in her Cassandra wailings. Now the mendicant friars mounted the pulpits exclaiming sacrilege; bold men, who feared nothing that men could do to them, and who dared in the king's own presence, and in his own chapel, to denounce him by name.[1] The sacred associations of twelve centuries were tumbling into ruin; and hot and angry as men had been before the work began, the hearts of numbers sank in them when they 'saw. what was done;' and they fell away slowly to doubt, disaffection, distrust, and at last treason.

The first outward symptom of importance. pointing in this direction, was the resignation of the seals by Sir Thomas More.[2] More had not been an illiberal man; when he wrote the *Utopia*, he seemed even to be in advance of his time. None could see the rogue's face under the cowl clearer than he, or the proud bad heart under the scarlet hat; and few men had ventured to speak their thoughts more boldly. But there was in him a want of confidence in human nature, a scorn of the follies of his fellow creatures which he unwisely indulged, and which, as he became more earnestly religious, narrowed and hardened his convictions, and transformed the genial philosopher into the merciless bigot. 'Heresy' was naturally hateful to him; his mind was too clear and genuine to

[1] STOWE, p. 562.

[2] 'In connexion with the Annates Act, the question of appeals to Rome had been discussed in the present session. Sir George Throgmorton had spoken on the papal side, and in his subsequent confession he mentioned a remarkable interview which he had had with More.

'After I had reasoned to the Bill of Appeals,' he said, 'Sir Thomas More, then being chancellor, sent for me to come and speak with him in the parliament chamber. And when I came to him he was in a little chamber within the parliament chamber, where, as I remember, stood an altar, or a thing like unto an altar, whereupon he did lean and, as I do think, the same time the Bishop of Bath was talking with him. And then he said this to me, I am very glad to hear the good report that goeth of you, and that ye be so good a catholic man as ye be. And if ye do continue in the same way that ye begin, and be not afraid to say your conscience, ye shall deserve great reward of God, and thanks of the King's Grace at length, and much worship to yourself.'—Throgmorton to the King: *MS. State Paper Office.*

allow him to deceive himself with the delusions of Angli-
canism; and as he saw the inevitable tendency of the Reformation to lead ultimately to a change of doctrine, he
attached himself with increasing determination to the cause
of the pope and of the old faith. As if with an instinctive
prescience of what would follow from it, he had from the
first been opposed to the divorce; and he had not concealed his feeling from the king at the time when the
latter had pressed the seals on his unwilling acceptance.
In consenting to become chancellor, he had yielded only
to Henry's entreaties; he had held his office for two years
and a half—and it would have been well for his memory
if he had been constant in his refusal—for in his ineffectual struggles against the stream, he had attempted to
counterpoise the attack upon the church by destroying the
unhappy protestants. At the close of the session, however,
the acts of which we have just described, he felt that he
must no longer countenance, by remaining in an office so
near to the crown, measures which he so intensely dis-
approved and deplored; it was time for him to retire from
a world not moving to his mind; and in the fair tranquillity of his family prepare himself for the evil days
which he foresaw. In May, 1532, he petitioned for permission to resign, resting his request unobtrusively on
failing health; and Henry sadly consented to lose his
services.

Parallel to More's retirement, and though less important, yet still noticeable, is a proceeding of old Archbishop
Warham under the same trying circumstances. In the days
of his prosperity, Warham had never reached to greatness
as a man. He had been a great ecclesiastic, successful,
dignified, important, but without those highest qualities
which command respect or interest. The iniquities of his
spiritual courts were greater than those of any other in
England. He had not made them what they were. They
grew by their own proper corruption; and he was no
more responsible for them than every man is responsible
for the continuance of an evil by which he profits, and
which he has power to remedy. We must look upon him
as the leader of the bishops in their opposition to the
reform; and he was the probable author of the famous
answer to the Commons' petition, which led to such momentous consequences.[1] These consequences he had lived
partially to see. Powerless to struggle against the stream,
he had seen swept away one by one those gigantic privi-

[1] In part of it he speaks in his own person. Vide supra, cap. 3.

leges to which he had asserted for his order a claim divinely sanctioned: and he withdrew himself heartbroken, into his palace at Lambeth, and there entered his solemn protest against all which had been done. Too ill to write, and trembling on the edge of the grave, he dictated to his notaries from his bed these not unaffecting words:—

'In the name of God, Amen. We, William, by Divine Providence Archbishop of Canterbury, Primate of all England, Legate of the Apostolic See, hereby publicly and expressly do protest for ourselves and for our Holy Metropolitan Church of Canterbury, that to any statute passed or hereafter to be passed in this present Parliament, begun the third of November, 1529, and continued until this present time; in so far as such statute or statutes be in derogation of the Pope of Rome or the Apostolic See, or be to the hurt, prejudice, or limitation of the powers of the Church, or shall tend to the subverting, enervating, derogating from, or diminishing the laws, customs, privileges, prerogatives, pre-eminence of liberties of our Metropolitan Church of Canterbury; we neither will, nor intend, nor with clear conscience are able to consent to the same, but by these writings we do dissent from, refuse, and contradict them.'[1]

Thus formally having delivered his soul, he laid himself down and died.

[1] BURNET'S *Collectanea*, p. 435.

CHAPTER V.

Although the king had interfered despotically to control the judgment of the universities, he had made no attempt, as we have seen, to check the tongues of the clergy. Nor if he had desired to check them, is it likely that at the present stage of proceedings he could have succeeded. No law had as yet been passed which made a crime of a difference of opinion on the pope's dispensing powers; and so long as no definitive sentence had been pronounced, every one had free liberty to think and speak as he pleased. So great, indeed, was the anxiety to disprove Catherine's assertion that England was a *locus suspectus*, and therefore that the cause could not be equitably tried there, that even in the distribution of patronage there was an ostentatious display of impartiality. Not only had Sir Thomas More been made chancellor, although emphatically on Catherine's side; but Cuthbert Tunstal, who had been her counsel, was promoted to the see of Durham. The Nun of Kent, if her word was to be believed, had been offered an abbey,[1] and that Henry permitted language to pass unnoticed of the most uncontrolled violence, appears from a multitude of informations which were forwarded to the government from all parts of the country. But while imposing no restraint on the expression of opinion, the council were careful to keep themselves well informed of the opinions which were expressed, and an instrument was ready made to their hands, which placed them in easy possession of what they desired. Among the many abominable practices which had been introduced by the ecclesiastical courts, not the least

[1] Note of the Revelations of Elizabeth Barton: *Rolls House MS.*

hateful was the system of espionage with which they had saturated English society; encouraging servants to be spies on their masters, children on their parents, neighbours on their neighbours, inviting every one who heard language spoken anywhere of doubtful allegiance to the church, to report the words to the nearest official, as an occasion of instant process. It is not without a feeling of satisfaction, that we find this detestable invention recoiling upon the heads of its authors. Those who had so long suffered under it, found an opportunity in the turning tide, of revenging themselves on their oppressors; and the country was covered with a ready-made army of spies, who, with ears ever open, were on the watch for impatient or disaffected language in their clerical superiors, and furnished steady reports of such language to Cromwell.[1]

[1] It has been thought that the Tudor princes and their ministers carried out the spy system to an iniquitous extent,—that it was the great instrument of their Machiavellian policy, introduced by Cromwell, and afterwards developed by Cecil and Walsingham. That both Cromwell and Walsingham availed themselves of secret information, is unquestionable,—as I think it is also unquestionable that they would have betrayed the interests of their country if they had neglected to do so. Nothing, in fact, except their skill in fighting treason with its own weapons, saved England from a repetition of the wars of the Roses, envenomed with the additional fury of religious fanaticism. But the agents of Cromwell, at least, were all volunteers;—their services were rather checked than encouraged; and when I am told, by high authority, that in those times an accusation was equivalent to a sentence of death, I am compelled to lay so sweeping a charge of injustice by the side of a document which forces me to demur to it. 'In the reign of the Tudors,' says a very eminent writer, 'the committal, arraignment, conviction, and execution of any state prisoner, accused or *suspected, or under suspicion of being suspected* of high treason, were only the regular terms in the series of judicial proceedings.' This is scarcely to be reconciled with the 10th of the 37th of Hen. VIII., which shows no desire to welcome accusations, or exaggerated readiness to listen to them.

'Whereas,' says that Act, 'divers malicious and evil disposed persons, of their perverse, cruel, and malicious intents, minding the utter undoing of some persons to whom they have and do bear malice, hatred, and evil will, have of late most devilishly practised and devised divers writings, wherein hath been comprised that the same persons to whom they bear malice should speak traitorous words against the King's Majesty, his crown and dignity, or commit divers heinous and detestable treasons against the King's Highness, where, in very deed, the persons so accused never spake nor committed any such offence; by reason whereof divers of the king's true, faithful, and loving subjects have been put in fear and dread of their lives and of the loss and forfeiture of their lands and chattels. For reformation hereof, be it enacted, that if any person or persons, of what estate, degree, or condition he or they shall be, shall at any time hereafter devise, make, or write, or cause to be made any manner of writing comprising that any person has spoken, committed, or done any offence or offences which now by the laws of this realm be made treason, or that hereafter shall be made treason, and do not subscribe, or cause to be subscribed, his true name to the said writing, and

Specimens of these informations will throw curious light on the feelings of a portion at least of the people. The English licence of speech, if not recognised to the same extent as it is at present, was certainly as fully practised. On the return of the Abbot of Whitby from the convocation at York in the summer of 1532, when the premunire money was voted, the following conversation was reported as having been overheard in the abbey.

The prior of the convent asked the abbot what the news were. 'What news,' said the abbot, 'evil news. The king is ruled by a common——Anne Boleyn, who has made all the spiritualty to be beggared, and the temporalty also. Further he told the prior of a sermon that he had heard in York, in which it was said, when a great wind rose in the west we should hear news. And he asked what that was; and he said a great man told him at York, and if he knew as much as three in England he would tell what the news were. And he said who were they? and he said the Duke of Norfolk, the Earl of Wiltshire, and the common——Anne Boleyn.'[1]

The dates of these papers cannot always be determined; this which follows, probably, is something later, but it shows the general temper in which the clergy were disposed to meet the measures of the government.

'Robert Legate, friar of Furness, deposeth that the monks had a prophecy among them, that 'in England shall be slain the decorate rose in his mother's belly,' and this they interpret of his Majesty, saying that his Majesty shall die by the hands of priests; for the church is the mother, and the church shall slay his Grace. The said Robert maintaineth that he hath heard the monks often say this. Also, it is said among them that the King's Grace was not the right heir to the crown; for that his Grace's father came in by no line, but by the sword. Also, that no secular knave should be head of

within twelve days next after ensuing do not personally come before the king or his council, and affirm the contents of the said writings to be true, and do as much as in him shall be for the approvement of the same, that then all and every person or persons offending as aforesaid, shall be deemed and adjudged a felon or felons; and being lawfully convicted of such offence. after the laws of the realm, shall suffer pains of death and loss and forfeiture of lands, goods, and chattels, without benefit of clergy or privilege of sanctuary to be admitted or allowed in that behalf.'

[1] Accusation brought by Robert Wodehouse, Prior of Whitby, against the Abbot, for slanderous words against Anne Boleyn: *Rolls House MS.*

the church; also that the abbot did know of these treasons, and had made no report thereof.'[1]

Nor was it only in the remote abbeys of the North that such dangerous language was ventured. The pulpit at St. Paul's rang Sunday after Sunday with the polemics of the divorce; and if 'the holy water of the court' made the higher clergy cringing and cowardly, the rank and file, even in London itself, showed a bold English front, and spoke out their thoughts with entire recklessness. Among the preachers on Catherine's side, Father Forest, famous afterward in catholic martyrologies, began to distinguish himself. Forest was warden of a convent of Observants at Greenwich attached to the royal chapel, and having been Catherine's confessor, remained, with the majority of the friars, faithful to her interests, and fearless in the assertion of them. From their connexion with the palace, the intercourse of these monks with the royal household was considerable; their position gave them influence, and Anne Boleyn tried the power of her charms, if possible, to gain them over. She had succeeded with a few of the weaker brothers, but she was unable (and her inability speaks remarkably for Henry's endurance of opposition through the early stages of the controversy) to protect those whose services she had won from the anger of their superiors. One monk in whom she was interested the warden imprisoned,[2] another there was an effort to expel,[3] because he was ready to preach on her side; and Forest himself preached a violent sermon at Paul's Cross, attacking Cromwell and indirectly the king.[4] He was sent for to the court, and the persecuted brothers expected their triumph; but he returned, as one of them wrote bitterly to Cromwell, having been received with respect and favour, as if, after all, the enmity of a brave man found more honour at the court than the complacency of cowardice. Father Forest, says this letter, has been with the king. 'He says he spake with the king for half an hour and more, and was well retained by his Grace; and the King's Grace did send him a great piece of beef from his own table; and also he met with my

<hr>

[1] Deposition of Robert Legate concerning the language of the Monks of Furness: *Rolls House MS.*

[2] ELLIS, third series, vol. ii. p. 254.

[3] Father Forest hath laboured divers manner of ways to expulse Father Laurence out of the convent, and his chief cause is, because he knoweth that Father Laurence will preach the king's matter whensoever it shall please his Grace to command him.—*Ibid.* p. 250.

[4] *Ibid.* p. 251.

Lord of Norfolk, and he says he took him in his arms and bade him welcome.'[1]

Forest, unfortunately for himself, misconstrued forbearance into fear, and went his way at last, through treason and perjury, to the stake. In the mean time the Observants were left in possession of the royal chapel, the weak brother died in prison, and the king, when at Greenwich, continued to attend service, submitting to listen, as long as submission was possible, to the admonitions which the friars used the opportunity to deliver to him.

In these more courteous days we can form little conception of the licence which preachers in the sixteenth century allowed themselves, or the language which persons in high authority were often obliged to bear. Latimer spoke as freely to Henry VIII. of neglected duties, as to the peasants in his Wiltshire parish. St. Ambrose did not rebuke the Emperor Theodosius more haughtily than John Knox lectured Queen Mary and her ministers on the vanities of Holyrood; and catholic priests, it seems, were not afraid to display even louder disrespect.

On Sunday, the first of May, 1532, the pulpit at Greenwich[2] was occupied by Father Peto, afterwards Cardinal Peto, famous through Europe as a catholic incendiary; but at this time an undistinguished brother of the Observants convent. His sermon had been upon the story of Ahab and Naboth, and his text had been, 'Where the dogs licked the blood of Naboth, even there shall they lick thy blood, O king.' The king and all the court were present; the first of May being the great holyday of the English year, and always observed at Greenwich with peculiar splendour. The preacher had dilated at length upon the crimes and the fall of Ahab, and had drawn the portrait in all its magnificent wickedness. He had described the scene in the court of heaven, and spoken of the lying prophets who had mocked the monarch's hopes before the fatal battle. At the end, he turned directly to Henry, and assuming to himself the mission of Micaiah, he closed his address in the following audacious words:—
'And now, O king,' he said, 'hear what I say to thee. I am that Micaiah whom thou wilt hate, because I must tell thee truly that this marriage is unlawful, and I know that I shall eat the bread of affliction and drink the waters of sorrow, yet because the Lord hath put it in my

---

[1] Lyst to Cromwell. ELLIS, third series. vol. ii. p. 255. STRYPE, *Eccles. Memor.*, vol. i. Appendix, No. 47.

[2] See vol. iv. Appendix.

mouth I must speak it. There are other preachers, yea too many, which preach and persuade thee otherwise, feeding thy folly and frail affections upon hopes of their own worldly promotion; and by that means they betray thy soul, thy honour, and thy posterity; to obtain fat benefices, to become rich abbots and bishops, and I know not what. These I say are the four hundred prophets who, in the spirit of lying, seek to deceive thee. Take heed lest thou, being seduced, find Ahab's punishment, who had his blood licked up by the dogs.'

Henry must have been compelled to listen to many such invectives. He left the chapel without noticing what had passed; and in the course of the week Peto went down from Greenwich to attend a provincial council at Canterbury, and perhaps to communicate with the Nun of Kent. Meantime a certain Dr. Kirwan was commissioned to preach on the other side of the question the following Sunday.

Kirwan was one of those men of whom the preacher spoke prophetically, since by the present and similar services he made his way to the archbishopric of Dublin and the bishopric of Oxford, and accepting the Erastian theory of a Christian's duty, followed Edward VI. into heresy, and Mary into popery and persecution. He regarded himself as an official of the state religion; and his highest conception of evil in a Christian was disobedience to the reigning authority. We may therefore conceive easily the burden of his sermon in the royal chapel. 'He most sharply reprehended Peto,' calling him foul names. 'dog, slanderer, base beggarly friar, rebel, and traitor,' saying 'that no subject should speak so audaciously to his prince:' he 'commended' Henry's intended marriage, 'thereby to establish his seed in his seat for ever;' and having won, as he supposed, his facile victory, he proceeded with his peroration, addressing his absent antagonist. 'I speak to thee, Peto,' he exclaimed, 'to thee, Peto, which makest thyself Micaiah, that thou mayest speak evil of kings; but now art not to be found, being fled for fear and shame, as unable to answer my argument.' In the royal chapel at Greenwich there was more reality than decorum. A voice out of the rood-loft cut short the eloquent declamation. 'Good sir,' it said, 'you know Father Peto is gone to Canterbury to a provincial council, and not fled for fear of you; for to-morrow he will return again. In the mean time I am here as another Micaiah, and will lay down my life to prove those things true which he hath taught. And to this combat I challenge thee; thee

Kirwan, I say, who art one of the four hundred into whom the spirit of lying is entered, and thou seekest by adultery to establish the succession, betraying thy king for thy own vain glory into endless perdition.'

A scene of confusion followed, which was allayed at last by the king himself, who rose in his seat and commanded silence. It was thought that the limit of permissible licence had been transcended, and the following day Peto and Elstowe, the other speaker, were summoned before the council to receive a reprimand. Lord Essex told them they deserved to be sewn into a sack and thrown into the Thames. 'Threaten such things to rich and dainty folk, which have their hope in this world,' answered Elstowe, gallantly, 'we fear them not; with thanks to God we know the way to heaven to be as ready by water as by land.'[1] Men of such metal might be broken, but they could not be bent. The two offenders were hopelessly unrepentant and impracticable, and it was found necessary to banish them. They retired to Antwerp, where we find them the following year busy procuring copies of the Bishop of Rochester's book against the king, which was broadly disseminated on the continent, and secretly transmitting them into England; in close correspondence also with Fisher himself, with Sir Thomas More, and for the ill fortune of their friends, with the court at Brussels, between which and the English catholics the intercourse was dangerously growing.[2]

---

[1] STOWE'S *Annals*, p. 562. This expression passed into a proverb, although the words were first spoken by a poor friar; they were the last which the good Sir Humfrey Gilbert was heard to utter before his ship went down.

[2] Vaughan to Cromwell: *State Papers*, vol. vii. p. 489-90. 'I learn that this book was first drawn by the Bishop of Rochester, and so being drawn, was by the said bishop afterwards delivered in England to two Spaniards, being secular and laymen. They receiving his first draught, either by themselves or some other Spaniards, altered and perfinished the same into the form that it now is; Peto and one Friar Elstowe of Canterbury, being the only men that have and do take upon themselves to be conveyers of the same books into England, and conveyors of all other things into and out of England. If privy search be made, and shortly, peradventure in the house of the same bishop shall be found his first copy. Master More hath sent oftentimes and lately books unto Peto, in Antwerp—as his book of the confutation of Tyndal, and of Frith's opinion of the sacrament, with divers other books. I can no further learn of More's practices, but if you consider this well, you may perchance espy his craft. Peto laboureth busylier than a bee in the setting forth of this book. He never ceaseth running to and from the court here. The king never had in his realm traitors like his friars—[Vaughan wrote 'clergy.' The word in the original is dashed through, and 'friars' is substituted, whether by Cromwell or by himself in an afterthought, I do not know]—and so I have always said, and yet do. Let his Grace look well about him, for they seek to devour him. They have blinded his Grace.'

The Greenwich friars, with their warden, went also a bad way. The death of the persecuted brother was attended with circumstances in a high degree suspicious.[1] Henry ordered an enquiry, which did not terminate in any actual exposure; but a cloud hung over the convent, which refused to be dispelled; the warden was deposed, and soon after it was found necessary to dissolve the order.

If the English monks had shared as a body the character of the Greenwich Observants, of the Carthusians of London and Richmond, and of some other establishments, —which may easily be numbered,—the resistance which they might have offered to the government, with the sympathy which it would have commanded, would have formed an obstacle to the Reformation that no power could have overcome. It was time, however, for the dissolution of the monasteries, when the few among them, which on other grounds might have claimed a right to survive, were driven by their very virtues into treason. The majority perished of their proper worthlessness; the few remaining contrived to make their existence incompatible with the safety of the state.

Leaving for the present these disorders to mature themselves, I must now return to the weary chapter of European diplomacy, to trace the tortuous course of popes and princes, duping one another with false hopes; saying what they did not mean, and meaning what they did not say. It is a very Slough of Despond, through which we must plunge desperately as we may; and we can cheer ourselves in this dismal region only by the knowledge that, although we are now approaching the spot where the mire is deepest, the hard ground is immediately beyond.

We shall, perhaps, be able most readily to comprehend the position of the various parties in Europe, by placing them before us as they stood severally in the summer of 1532, and defining briefly the object which each was pursuing.

Henry only, among the great powers, laid his conduct open to the world, declaring truly what he desired, and seeking it by open means. He was determined to proceed with the divorce, and he was determined also to continue the Reformation of the English Church. If consistently with these two objects he could avoid a rupture with the pope, he was sincerely anxious to avoid it. He was ready

<hr>

[1] Ellis. third series, vol. ii. p. 262, &c.

to make great efforts, to risk great sacrifices, to do anything short of surrendering what he considered of vital moment, to remain upon good terms with the See of Rome. If his efforts failed, and a quarrel was inevitable, he desired to secure himself by a close maintenance of the French alliance; and having induced Francis to urge compliance upon the pope by a threat of separation if he refused, to prevail on him, in the event of the pope's continued obstinacy, to put his threat in execution, and unite with England in a common schism. All this is plain and straightforward—Henry concealed nothing, and, in fact, had nothing to conceal. In his threats, his promises, and his entreaties, we feel entire certainty that he was speaking his real thoughts.

The emperor's position also, though not equally simple, is intelligible, and commands our respect. Although if he had consented to sacrifice his aunt, he might have spared himself serious embarrassment; although both by the pope and by the consistory such a resolution would probably have been welcomed with passionate thankfulness; yet at all hazards Charles was determined to make her his first object, even with the risk of convulsing Europe. At the same time his position was encumbered with difficulty. The Turks were pressing upon him in Hungary and in the Mediterranean; his relations with Francis—fortunately for the prospects of the Reformation—were those of inveterate hostility; while in Germany he had been driven to make terms with the protestant princes; he had offended the pope by promising them a general council, in which the Lutheran divines should be represented; and the pope, taught by recent experience, was made to fear that these symptoms of favour towards heresy, might convert themselves into open support.

With Francis the prevailing feeling was rivalry with the emperor, combined with an eager desire to recover his influence in Italy, and to restore France to the position in Europe which had been lost by the defeat of Pavia, and the failure of Lautrec at Naples. This was his first object, to which every other was subsidiary. He was disinclined to a rupture with the pope; but the possibility of such a rupture had been long contemplated by French statesmen. It was a contingency which the pope feared:—which the hopes of Henry pictured as more likely than it was—and Francis, like his rivals in the European system, held the menace of it extended over the chair of St. Peter, to coerce its unhappy occupant into compliance with his wishes. With respect to Henry's divorce, his conduct to the University of Paris, and his assurances repeated voluntarily on many occasions, show that he was sincerely desirous to forward it. He did not care for Henry, or for England, or for the cause itself; he desired only to make the breach between Henry and Charles irreparable; to make it impossible for ever that 'his two great rivals' should become friends together; and by inducing the pope to consent to the English demand, to detach the court of Rome conclusively from the imperial interests.

The two princes who disputed the supremacy of Europe, were intriguing one against the other, each desiring to constitute himself the champion of the church; and to compel the church to accept his services, by the threat of passing over to her enemies. By a dexterous use of the cards which were in his hands, the King of France proposed to secure one of two alternatives. Either he would form a league between himself, Henry, and the pope, against the emperor, of which the divorce, and the consent to it, which he would extort from Clement, should be the cement; or, if this failed him, he would avail himself of the vantage ground which was given to him by the English alliance to obtain such concessions for himself at the emperor's expense as the pope could be induced to make, and the emperor to tolerate.

Such, in so far as I can unravel the web of the diplomatic correspondence, appear to have been the open positions and the secret purposes of the great European powers.

There remains the fourth figure upon the board, the pope himself, labouring with such means as were at his disposal to watch over the interests of the church, and to neutralize the destructive ambition of the princes, by playing upon their respective selfishnesses. On the central question, that of the divorce, his position was briefly this. Both the emperor and Henry pressed for a decision. If he decided for Henry, he lost Germany; if he decided for Catherine, while Henry was supported by Francis, France and England threatened both to fall from him. It was therefore necessary for him to induce the emperor to consent to delay, while he worked upon the King of France; and, if France and England could once be separated, he trusted that Henry would yield in despair. This most subtle and difficult policy reveals itself in the transactions open and secret of the ensuing years. It was followed with a dexterity as extraordinary as its unscrupulousness, and with all but perfect success. That it

failed at all, in the ordinary sense of failure, was due to
the accidental delay of a courier; and Clement, while he
succeeded in preserving the allegiance of France to the
Roman see, succeeded also—and this is no small thing to
have accomplished—in weaving the most curious tissue of
falsehood which will be met with even in the fertile pages
of Italian subtlety.

With this general understanding of the relation between
the great parties in the drama, let us look to their exact
position in the summer of 1532.

Charles was engaged in repelling an invasion of the
Turks, with an anarchical Germany in his rear, seething
with fanatical anabaptists, and clamouring for a general
council.

Henry and Francis had been called upon to furnish a
contingent against Solyman, and had declined to act with
the emperor. They had undertaken to concert their own
measures between themselves, if it proved necessary for
them to move; and in the mean time Cardinal Grammont
and Cardinal Tournon were sent by Francis to Rome, to
inform Clement that unless he gave a verdict in Henry's
favour, the two Kings of France and England, being *une
mesme chose,* would pursue some policy with respect to
him, to which he would regret that he had compelled
them to have recourse. So far their instructions were
avowed and open. A private message revealed the secret
means by which the pope might escape from his dilemma;
the cardinals were to negotiate a marriage between the
Duke of Orleans and the pope's niece (afterwards so in-
famously famous), Catherine de Medicis. The marriage,
as Francis represented it to Henry, was beneath the
dignity of a prince of France, and he had consented to
it, as he professed, only for Henry's sake;[1] but the pope
had made it palatable by a secret article in the engagement, for the grant of the duchy of Milan as the lady's
dowry.

Henry, threatened as we have seen with domestic
disturbance, and with further danger on the side of Scotland, which Charles had succeeded in agitating, concluded
on the 23rd of June, a league, offensive and defensive,
with France, the latter engaging to send a fleet into the
Channel, and to land 15,000 troops in England if the emperor should attempt an invasion from the sea.[2] For the
better consolidation of this league, and to consult upon

[1] *State Papers,* vol. vii. p. 428. LEGRAND, vol. iii.
[2] LORD HERBERT, p. 160. RYMER, vol. vi. part. ii. p. 171.

the measures which they would pursue on the great questions at issue in Christendom, and lastly to come to a final understanding on the divorce, it was agreed further that in the autumn the two kings should meet at Calais. The conditions of the interview were still unarranged on the 22nd of July, when the Bishop of Paris, who remained ambassador at the English court, wrote to Montmorency to suggest that Anne Boleyn should be invited to accompany the King of England on this occasion, and that she should be received in state. The letter was dated from Ampthill, to which Henry had escaped for a while from his Greenwich friars and other troubles, and where the king was staying a few weeks before the house was given up to Queen Catherine. Anne Boleyn was with him; she now, as a matter of course, attended him everywhere. Intending her, as he did, to be the mother of the future heir to his crown, he preserved what is technically called her honour unimpeached and unimpaired. In all other respects she occupied the position and received the homage due to the actual wife of the English sovereign; and in this capacity it was the desire of Henry that she should be acknowledged by a foreign prince.

The bishop's letter on this occasion is singularly interesting and descriptive. The court were out hunting, he said, every day; and while the king was pursuing the heat of the chase, he and Mademoiselle Anne were posted together, each with a crossbow, at the point to which the deer was to be driven. The young lady, in order that the appearance of her reverend cavalier might correspond with his occupation, had made him a present of a hunting cap and frock, a horn and a greyhound. Her invitation to Calais he pressed with great earnestness, and suggested that Marguerite de Valois, the Queen of Navarre, should be brought down to entertain her. The Queen of France being a Spaniard, would not, he thought, be welcome; 'the sight of a Spanish dress being as hateful in the King of England's eyes as the devil himself.' In other respects the reception should be as magnificent as possible, 'and I beseech you,' he concluded, 'keep out of the court *deux sortes de gens*, the imperialists, and the wits and mockers; the English can endure neither of them.'[1]

<hr>

[1] Francis seems to have desired that the intention of the interview should be kept secret. Henry found this impossible. 'Monseigneur,' wrote the Bishop of Paris to the Grand Master, 'quant à tenir la chose secrette comme vous le demandez, il est mal aisé; combien que ce Roy fust bien de cest advis, sinon qu'il le treuve impossible; car a cause de ces provisions et choses, qu'il fault faire en ce Royaulme,

Through the tone of this language the contempt is easily visible with which the affair was regarded in the French court. But for Francis to receive in public the rival of Queen Catherine, to admit her into his family, and to bring his sister from Paris to entertain her, was to declare in the face of Europe, in a manner which would leave no doubt of his sincerity, that he intended to countenance Henry. With this view only was the reception of Anne desired by the King of England; with this view it was recommended by the bishop, and assented to by the French court. Nor was this the only proof which Francis was prepared to give, that he was in earnest. He had promised to distribute forty thousand crowns at Rome, in bribing cardinals to give their voices for Henry in the consistory, with other possible benefactions.[1]

He had further volunteered his good offices with the court of Scotland, where matters were growing serious,

incontinent sera sceu a Londres, et de la par tout le monde. Pourquoy ne faictes vostre compte qu'on le puisse tenir secret.

'Monseigneur, je sçay veritablement et de bon lieu que le plus grant plaisir que le Roy pourroit faire au Roy son frere et a Madame Anne, c'est que le dit seigneur m'escripre que je requiere le Roy son dit frere qu'il veuille mener la dicte Dame Anne avec luy a Callais pour la veoir et pour la festoyer, afin qu'ils ne demeurrent ensembles sans compagnie de dames, pour ce que les bonnes cheres en sont tous jours meilleures: mais il fauldroit que en pareil le Roy menast la Royne de Navarre à Boulogne, pour festoyer le Roy d'Angleterre.

'Quant à la Royne pour rien ce Roy ne vouldroit qu'elle vint: Il hait cest habillement à l'Espagnolle, tant qu'il luy semble veoir un diable. Il desireroit qu'il pleust au Roy mener à Boulogne, messeigneurs ses enfans pour les veoir.

'Surtout je vous prie que vous ostez de la court deux sortes de gens, ceulx qui sont imperiaulx, s'aucuns en y a, et ceux qui ont la reputation d'estre mocqueurs et gaudisseurs,. car c'est bien la chose en ce monde autant haïe de ceste nation.'—Bishop of Paris to the Grand Master: LEGRAND, vol. iii. pp. 555, 556.

[1] Sir Gregory Cassalis to Henry VIII: BURNET'S *Collectanea*, p. 433. Valde existimabam necessarium cum hoc Principe (*i. e.*, Francis) agere ut duobus Cardinalibus daret in mandatis ut ante omnes Cardinalis de Monte meminissent, eique pensionem annuam saltem trium millium aureorum ex quadraginta millibus quæ mihi dixerat velle in Cardinales distribuere, assignaret. Et Rex quidem hæc etiam scribi ad duos Cardinales jussit secretario Vitandri. Quicum ego postmodo super iis pensionibus sermonem habui, cognovique sic in animo Regem habere ut duo Cardinales cum Romæ fuerint, videant, qui potissimum digni hâc Regiâ sint liberalitate; in eosque quum quid in Regno Galliæ ecclesiasticum vacare contigerit ex meritis uniuscujusque pensiones conferantur. Tunc autem nihil in promptu haberi quod Cardinali de Monte dari possit—verum Regio nomine illi de futuro esse promittendum quod mihi certe summopere displicuit; et secretario Vitandri non reticui ostendens pollicitationes hujusmodi centies jam Cardinali de Monte factas fuisse; et modo si iterum fiant nihil effecturas nisi ut illius viri quasi ulcera pertractent; id quod Vitandris verum esse fatebatur pollicitusque est se, quum Rex a venatu rediisset velle ei suadere ut Cardinalem de Monte aliquâ presenti pensione prosequatur; quâ quidem tibi nihil conducibilius aut opportunius fieri possit.

and where his influence could be used to great advantage. The ability of James the Fifth to injure Henry happily fell short of his inclination, but encouraged by secret promises from Clement and from the emperor, he was waiting his opportunity to cross the Border with an army; and in the meantime he was feeding with efficient support a rebellion in Ireland. Of what was occurring at this time in that perennially miserable country I shall speak in a separate chapter. It is here sufficient to mention, that on the 23rd of August, Henry received information that McConnell of the Isles, after receiving knighthood from James, had been despatched into Ulster with four thousand men,[1] and was followed by Mackane with seven thousand more on the 3rd of September.[2] Peace with England nominally continued; but the Kers, the Humes, the Scotts of Buccleugh, the advanced guard of the Marches, where nightly making forays across the Border, and open hostilities appeared to be on the point of explosion.[3] If war was to follow, Henry was prepared for it. He had a powerful force at Berwick, and in Scotland itself a large party were secretly attached to the English interests. The clan of Douglas, with their adherents, were even prepared for open revolt, and open transfer of allegiance.[4] But, although Scottish nobles might be gained over, and Scottish armies might be defeated in the field, Scotland itself, as the experience of centuries had proved, could never be conquered. The policy of the Tudors had been to abstain from aggression, till time should have soothed down the inherited animosity between the two countries; and Henry was unwilling to be forced into extremities which might revive the bitter memories of Flodden. The Northern counties also, in spite of their Border prejudices, were the stronghold of the papal party, and it was doubtful how far their allegiance could be counted upon in the event of an invasion sanctioned by the pope. The hands of the English government were already full without any superadded

---

[1] *State Papers*, vol. iv. p. 612.

[2] Ibid. p. 616.

[3] The *State Papers* contain a piteous picture of this business, the hereditary feuds of centuries bursting out on the first symptoms of ill will between the two governments, with fire and devastation.—*State Papers*, vol. iv. p. 620—644.

[4] If the said Earl of Angus do make unto us oath of allegiance, and recognises us as Supreme Lord of Scotland, and as his prince and sovereign, we then, the said earl doing the premises, by these presents bind ourself to pay yearly to the said earl the sum of one thousand pounds sterling.—Henry VIII. to the Earl of Angus: *State Papers*, vol. iv. p. 615.

embarrassment, and the offered mediation of Francis was gratefully welcomed.

These were the circumstances under which the second great interview was to take place between Francis the First and Henry of England. Twelve years had passed since their last meeting, and the experience which those years had brought to both of them, had probably subdued their inclination for splendid pageantry. Nevertheless, in honour of the occasion some faint revival was attempted of the magnificence of the Field of the Cloth of Gold. Anne Boleyn was invited duly; and the Queen of Navarre, as the Bishop of Paris recommended, came down to Boulogne to receive her. The French princes came also to thank Henry in person for their deliverance out of their Spanish prison; and he too, on his side, brought with him his young Marcellus, the Duke of Richmond, his only son—illegitimate unfortunately—but whose beauty and noble promise were at once his father's misery and pride; giving point to his bitterness at the loss of his sons by Catherine; quickening his hopes of what might be, and deepening his discontent with that which was. If this boy had lived, he would have been named to follow Edward the Sixth in the succession, and would have been King of England;[1] but he too passed away in the flower

[1] There can be little doubt of this. He was the child of the only intrigue of Henry VIII. of which any credible evidence exists. His mother was Elizabeth, daughter of Sir John Blunt, an accomplished and most interesting person; and the offspring of the connexion, one boy only, was brought up with the care and the state of a prince. Henry Fitz Roy, as he was called, was born in 1519, and when six years old was created Earl of Nottingham and Duke of Richmond and Somerset, the title of the king's father.

In 1527, before the commencement of the disturbance on the divorce, Henry endeavoured to negotiate a marriage for him with a princess of the imperial blood; and in the first overtures gave an intimation which could not be mistaken, of his intention, if possible, to place him in the line of the succession. After speaking of the desire which was felt by the King of England for some connexion in marriage of the Houses of England and Spain, the ambassadors charged with the negotiation were to say to Charles, that—

'His Highness can be content to bestow the Duke of Richmond and Somerset (who is near of his blood, and of excellent qualities, and is already furnished to keep the state of a great prince, *and yet may be easily by the king's means exalted to higher things*) to some noble princess of his near blood.'—ELLIS. third series, vol. ii. p. 121.

He was a gallant, high-spirited boy. A letter is extant, from him to Wolsey, written when he was nine years old, begging the cardinal to intercede with the king, 'for an harness to exercise myself in arms according to my erudition in the Commentaries of Cæsar.'—Ibid. p. 119.

He was brought up with Lord Surrey, who has left a beautiful account of their boyhood at Windsor—their tournaments, their hunts, their young loves, and passionate friendship. Richmond married Surrey's sister, but died the year after, when only seventeen; and

of his loveliness, one more evidence of the blight which rested upon the stem of the Tudors.

The English court was entertained by Francis at Boulogne. The French court was received in return at Calais by the English. The outward description of the scene, the magnificent train of the princes, the tournaments, the feasts, the dances, will be found minutely given in the pages of Hall, and need not be repeated here. To Hall indeed, the outward life of men, their exploits in war, and their pageantries in peace, alone had meaning or interest: and the backstairs secrets of Vatican diplomacy, the questionings of opinion, and all the brood of mental sicknesses then beginning to distract the world, were but impertinent interferences with the true business of existence. But the healthy objectiveness of an old English chronicler is no longer possible for us; we may envy where we cannot imitate; and our business is with such features of the story as are of moment to ourselves.

The political questions which were to be debated at the conference, were three; the Turkish Invasion, the General Council, and King Henry's divorce.

On the first, it was decided that there was no immediate occasion for France and England to move. Solyman's retreat from Vienna had relieved Europe from present peril; and the enormous losses which he had suffered, might prevent him from repeating the experiment. If the danger became again imminent, however, the two kings agreed to take the field in person the following year at the head of eighty thousand men.

On the second point they came to no conclusion, but es olved only to act in common.

On the third and most important, they parted with

Surrey revisiting Windsor, recalls his image among the scenes which they had enjoyed together, in the most interesting of all his poems. He speaks of

> The secret grove, which oft we made resound
> Of pleasant plaint and of our ladies' praise;
> Recording oft what grace each one had found,
> What hope of speed, what dread of long delays.
> The wild forest; the clothed holts with green;
> With reins availed, and swift y-breathed horse,
> With cry of hounds, and merry blasts between,
> Where we did chase the fearful hart of force.
> The void walls eke that harboured us each night,
> Wherewith, alas! reviveth in my breast
> The sweet accord, such sleeps as yet delight
> The pleasant dream, the quiet bed of rest;
> The secret thoughts imparted with such trust,
> The wanton talk, the divers change of play,
> The friendship sworn, each promise kept so just,
> Wherewith we past the winter nights away.

a belief that they understood each other; but their memories, or the memory of one of them proved subsequently treacherous; and we can only extract what passed between them out of their mutual recriminations.

It was determined certainly that at the earliest convenient moment, a meeting should take place between the pope and Francis; and that at this meeting Francis should urge in person concession to Henry's demands. If the pope professed himself unable to risk the displeasure of the emperor, it should be suggested that he might return to Avignon, where he would be secure under the protection of France and England. If he was still reluctant, and persisted in asserting his right to compel Henry to plead before him at Rome, or if he followed up his citations by inhibitions, suspensions, excommunications, or other form of censure, Francis declared that he would support Henry to the last, whether against the pope himself or against any prince or potentate who might attempt to enforce the sentence. On this point the promises of the King of France were most profuse and decided; and although it was not expressly stated in words, Henry seems to have persuaded himself that, if the pope pressed matters to extremities, Francis had engaged further that the two countries should pursue a common course, and unite in a common schism. The two princes did in fact agree, that if the general council which they desired was refused, they would summon provincial councils on their own authority. Each of them perhaps interpreted their engagements by their own wishes or interests.[1]

We may further believe, since it was affirmed by Henry, and not denied by Francis, that the latter advised Henry to bring the dispute to a close, by a measure from which he could not recede; that he recommended him to act on the general opinion of Europe that his marriage with Queen Catherine was null, and at once upon his return to England to make Anne Boleyn his wife.[2]

---

[1] Compare LORD HERBERT with A Paper of Instructions to Lord Rochfort on his Mission to Paris: *State Papers*, vol. vii. p. 427, &c.; and A Remonstrance of Francis I. to Henry VIII: LEGRAND, vol. iii. p. 571, &c. It would be curious to know whether Francis ever actually wrote to the pope a letter of which Henry sent him a draft. If he did, there are expressions contained in it which amount to a threat of separation. In case the pope was obstinate Francis was to say, 'Lors force seroit de pourvoir audict affaire, par autres voyes et façons; qui peut etre, ne vous seroint gueres agreable.—*State Papers*, vol. vii. p. 436.

[2] A nostre derniere entrevue sur la fraternelle et familiere communication que nous eusmes ensemble de noz affaires venant aux nostres, Luy declarasmes comme a tord et injustment nous estions affligez, dilayez, et fort ingratement manniez et troublez, en nostre

So far the account is clear. This advice was certainly given, and as certainly Francis undertook to support Henry through all the consequences in which the marriage might involve him. But a league for mutual defence fell short of what Henry desired, and fell short also of what Francis, by the warmth of his manner, had induced Henry for the moment to believe that he meant. It is probable that the latter pressed upon him engagements which he avoided by taking refuge in general professions; and no sooner had Henry returned to England, than either misgivings occurred to him as to the substantial results of the interview, or he was anxious to make the French king commit himself more definitely. He sent to him to beg that he would either write out, or dictate and sign, the expressions which he had used; professing to wish it only for the comfort which he would derive from the continual presence of such refreshing words—but surely for some deeper reason.[1]

Francis had perhaps said more than he meant; Henry supposed him to have meant more than he said. Yet some promise was made, which was not afterwards observed; and Francis acknowledged some engagement in an apology which he offered for the breach of it. He asserted, in defence of himself, that he had added a stipulation which Henry passed over in silence,—that no steps should be taken towards annulling the marriage with Catherine in

dicte graude et pesante matiere de marriage par la particuliere affection de l'empereur et du pape. Lesquelz sembloient par leurs longues retardations de nostre dicte matiere ne sercher autre chose, sinon par longue attente et laps de temps, nous frustrer malicieusement du propoz, qui plus nous induict a poursuivir et mettre avant la dicte matiere; c'est davoir masculine succession et posterite en laquelle nous establirons (Dieu voulant) le quiet repoz et tranquillite de notre royaulme et dominion. Son fraternel, plain, et entier advis (et a bref dire le meilleur qui pourroit estre) ful tel; il nous conseilla de ne dilayer ne protracter le temps plus longuement, mais en toute celerite proceder effectuellement a laccomplisment et consummation de nostre marriage. —Henry VIII. to Rochfort: *State Papers*, vol. vii. p. 428-9.

[1] The extent of Francis's engagements, as Henry represents them, was this:—He had promised qu'en icelle nostre dicte cause jamais ne nous abandonneroit quelque chose que sen ensuyst; ainsi de tout son pouvoir l'establiroit. supporteroit, aideroit et maintiendroit notre bon droict, et le droict de la posterite et succession qui sen pourroit ensuyr; et a tous ceulz qui y vouldroyent mettre trouble, empeschement, encombrance, ou y procurer deshonnenr, vitupere, ou infraction, il seroit enemy et adversaire de tout son pouvoir, de quelconque estat qu'il soit, fust pape ou empereur,—avecques plusieurs autres consolatives paroles. This he wished Francis to commit to paper. Car autant de fois, que les verrions, he says, qui seroit tous les jours, nous ne pourrions, si non les liscent, imaginer et reduire a notre souvenance la bonne grace facunde et geste, dont il les nous prononçait, et estimer estre comme face a face, parlans avecque luy.—*State Papers*, vol. vii. p. 437. Evidently language of so wide a kind might admit of many interpretations.

the English law courts until the effect had been seen of
his interview with the pope, provided the pope on his
side remained similarly inactive.[1] Whatever it was which
he had bound himself to do, this condition, if made at
all, could be reconciled only with his advice that Henry
should marry Anne Boleyn without further delay, on the
supposition that the interview in question was to take
place immediately; for the natural consequences of the
second marriage would involve, as a matter of course,
some speedy legal declaration with respect to the first.
And when on various pretexts the pope postponed the
meeting, and on the other part of his suggestion Henry
had acted within a few months of his return from Calais,
it became impossible that such a condition could be observed. It availed for a formal excuse; but Francis vainly
endeavoured to disguise his own infirmity of purpose behind the language of a negotiation which conveyed, when
it was used, a meaning widely different.

The conference was concluded on the 1st of November,
but the court was detained at Calais for a further fortnight by violent gales in the Channel. In the excited
state of public feeling, events in themselves ordinary assumed a preternatural significance. The friends of Queen
Catherine, to whom the meeting between the kings was
of so disastrous augury, and the nation generally, which
an accident to Henry at such a time would have plunged
into a chaos of confusion, alike watched the storm with
anxious agitation; on the king's return to London, Te
Deums were offered in the churches, as if for his deliverance from some extreme and imminent peril. The Nun
of Kent on this great occasion was admitted to conferences
with angels. She denounced the meeting, under celestial
instruction, as a conspiracy against Heaven. The king,
she said, but for her interposition, would have proceeded,
while at Calais, to his impious marriage;[2] and God was
so angry with him, that he was not permitted to profane
with his unholy eyes the blessed Sacrament. 'It was
written in her revelations,' says the statute of her attainder,
'that when the King's Grace was at Calais, and his Majesty
and the French king were hearing mass in the Church of
Our Lady, that God was so displeased with the King's
Highness, that his Grace saw not at that time the blessed
sacrament in the form of bread, for it was taken away
from the priest, being at mass, by an angel, and was

[1] LEGRAND, vol. iii. p. 571, &c.
[2] Note of the Revelations of Eliz. Barton: *Rolls House MS. Suppression of the Monasteries,* p. 17.

ministered to the said Elizabeth, there being present and invisible, and suddenly conveyed and rapt thence again into the nunnery where she was professed.'[1]

She had an interview with Henry on his return through Canterbury, to try the effect of her Cassandra presence on his fears;[2] but if he still delayed his marriage, it was probably neither because he was frightened by her denunciations, nor from alarm at the usual occurrence of an equinoctial storm. Many motives combined to dissuade him from further hesitation. Six years of trifling must have convinced him that by decisive action alone he could force the pope to a conclusion. He was growing old, and the exigencies of the succession, rendered doubly pressing by the long agitation, required immediate resolution. He was himself satisfied that he was at liberty to marry whom he pleased and when he pleased, his relationship to Catherine, according to his recent convictions, being such as had rendered his connexion with her from the beginning invalid and void. His own inclinations and the interests of the nation pointed to the same course. The King of France had advised it. Even the pope himself, at the outset of the discussion, had advised it also. 'Marry freely,' the pope had said; 'fear nothing, and all shall be arranged as you desire.' He had forborne to take the pope at his word; he had hoped that the justice of his demands might open a less violent way to him; and he had shrunk from a step which might throw even a causeless shadow over the legitimacy of the offspring for which he longed. The case was now changed; no other alternative seemed to be open to his choice, and it was necessary to bring the matter to a close once and for all.

But Henry, as he said himself, was past the age when passion or appetite would be likely to move him, and having waited so many years, he could afford to wait a little longer, till the effects of the Calais conferences upon the pope should have had time to show themselves. In December, Clement was to meet the emperor at Bologna. In the month following, it might be hoped that he would meet Francis at Marseilles or Avignon, and from their interview would be seen conclusively the future attitude of the papal and imperial courts. Experience of the past forbade anything like sanguine expectation; yet it was not impossible that the pope might be compelled at last to yield to the required concessions. The terms of Henry's understanding with Francis were not perhaps made public,

[1] 25 Hen. VIII. cap. 12.
[2] Revelations of Eliz. Barton: *Rolls House MS.*

but he was allowed to dictate the language which the French cardinals were to make use of in the consistory;[1] and the reception of Anne Boleyn by the French king was equivalent to the most emphatic declaration that if the censures of the church were attempted in defence of Catherine, the enforcement of them would be resisted by the combined arms of France and England.

And the pope did in fact feel himself in a dilemma from which all his address was required to extricate him. He had no support from his conscience, for he knew that he was acting unjustly in refusing the divorce; while to risk the emperor's anger, which was the only honest course before him, was perhaps for that very reason impossible. He fell back upon his Italian cunning, and it did not fail him in his need. But his conduct, though creditable to his ingenuity, reflects less pleasantly on his character; and when it is traced through all its windings, few reasonable persons will think that they have need to blush at the causes which led to the last breach between England and the papacy.

From the time of Catherine's appeal and the retirement of Campeggio, Clement, with rare exceptions, had maintained an attitude of impassive reserve. He had allowed judgment to be delayed on various pretexts, because until that time delay had answered his purposes sufficiently. But to the English agents he had been studiously cold, not condescending even to hold out hopes to them that concession might be possible. Some little time before the meeting at Calais, however, a change was observed in the language both of the pope himself and of the consistory. The cardinals were visibly afraid of the position which had been taken by the French king; questions supposed to be closed were once more admitted to debate in a manner which seemed to show that their resolution was wavering; and one day, at the close of a long argument, the following curious conversation took place between some person (Sir Gregory Cassalis, apparently), who reported it to Henry, and Clement himself. 'I had desired a private interview with his Holiness,' says the writer, 'intending to use all my endeavours to persuade him to satisfy your Majesty. But although I did my best, I could obtain nothing from him; he had an answer for everything which I advanced, and it was in vain that I laboured to remove his difficulties. At length, however, in reply to something which I had proposed, he said shortly,—Multo minus scan-

<hr>

dalosum fuisset dispensare cum majestate vestrâ super duabus uxoribus, quam ea cedere quæ ego petebam. It would have created less scandal to have granted your Majesty a dispensation to have two wives than to concede what I was then demanding. As I did not know how far this alternative would be pleasing to your Majesty, I endeavoured to divert him from it, and to lead him back to what I had been previously saying. He was silent for a while, and then, paying no regard to my interruption, he continued to speak of the 'two wives,' admitting however that there were difficulties in the way of such an arrangement, principally it seemed because the emperor would refuse his consent from the possible injury which it might create to his cousin's prospects of the succession. I replied, that as to the succession, I could not see what right the emperor had to a voice upon the matter. If some lawful means could be discovered by which your Majesty could furnish yourself with male offspring, the emperor could no more justly complain than if the queen were to die and the prospects of the princess were interfered with by a second marriage of an ordinary kind. To this the pope made no answer. I cannot tell what your Majesty will think, nor how far this suggestion of the pope would be pleasing to your Majesty. Nor indeed can I feel sure, in consequence of what he said about the emperor, that he actually would grant the dispensation of which he spoke. I have thought it right, however, to inform you of what passed.'[1]

This letter is undated, but it was written, as appears from internal evidence, some time in the year 1532.[2]

---

[1] Letter from ——, containing an account of an interview with his Holiness: *Rolls House MS.*

[2] The proposal was originally the king's (see chapter 2), but it had been dropped because one of the conditions of it had been Catherine's 'entrance into religion.' The pope, however, had not lost sight of the alternative, as one of which, in case of extremity, he might avail himself; and, in 1530, in a short interval of relaxation, he had definitely offered the king a dispensation to have two wives, at the instigation, curiously, of the imperialists. The following letter was written on that occasion to the king by Sir Gregory Cassalis :—

Serenissime et potentissime domine rex, domine mi supreme humillimâ commendatione premissâ, salutem et felicitatem. Superioribus diebus Pontifex secreto, veluti rem quam magni faceret, mihi proposuit conditionem hujusmodi; concedi posse vestræ majestati, ut duas uxores habeat; cui dixi nolle me provinciam suscipere eâ de re scribendi, ob eam causam quod ignorarem an inde vestræ conscientiæ satisfieri posset quam vestra majestas imprimis exonerare cupit. Cur autem sic responderem, illud in causâ fuit, quod ex certo loco, unde quæ Cæsariani moliantur aucupari soleo exploratum certumque habebam Cæsarianos illud ipsum quærere et procurare. Quem vero ad finem id quærant pro certo exprimere non ausim. Id certo totum vestræ prudentiæ considerandum relinquo. Et quamvis dixerim Pontifici, ni-

The pope's language was ambiguous, and the writer did not allow himself to derive from it any favourable augury; but the tone in which the suggestions had been made was by many degrees more favourable than had been heard for a very long time in the quarter from which they came, and the symptoms which it promised of a change of feeling were more than confirmed in the following winter.

Charles was to be at Bologna in the middle of December, where he was to discuss with Clement the situation of Europe, and in particular of Germany, with the desirableness of fulfilling the engagements into which he had entered for a general council.

This was the avowed object of the meeting. But, however important the question of holding council was becoming, it was not immediately pressing; and we cannot doubt that the disquiet occassioned by the alliance of England and France was the cause that the conference was held at so inconvenient a season. The pope left Rome on the 18th of November, having in his train a person who afterwards earned for himself a dark name in English history, Dr. Bonner, then a famous canon lawyer attached to the embassy. The journey in the wild weather was extremely miserable; and Bonner, whose style was as graphic as it was coarse, sent home a humorous account of it to Cromwell.[1] Three wretched weeks the party were upon the road, plunging through mire and water. They reached Bologna on the 8th of December, where, four days after them, arrived Charles V. It is important, as we shall presently see, to observe the dates of these movements. I shall have to compare with them the successive issues of several curious documents. On the 12th of December the pope and the emperor met at Bologna; on the 24th Dr. Bennet, Henry's able secretary, who had been despatched from England to be present at the conference, wrote to report the result of his observations. He had been admitted to repeated interviews with the pope, as well before as after the emperor's arrival; and the language which the former made use of could only be understood, and was of course intended to be under-

hil me de eo scripturum, nolui tamen majestati vestræ hoc reticere; quæ sciat omni me industriâ laborâsse in iis quæ nobis mandat exequendis et cum Anconitano qui me familiariter uti solet, omnia sum conatus. De omnibus autem me ad communes literas rejicio. Optime valeat vestra majestas.—Romæ die xviii. Septembris, 1530.
Clarissimi vestrai Majestatis, Humillimus servus,
GREGORIUS CASSALIS.

—LORD HERBERT, p. 140.
[1] *State Papers*, vol. vii. p. 394, &c.

stood, as expressing the attitude in which he was placing himself towards the imperial faction. Bennet's letter was as follows:—

'I have been sundry and many times with the pope, as well afore the coming of the emperour as sythen, yet I have not at any time found his Holiness more tractable or propense to show gratuity unto your Highness than now of late,—insomuch that he hath more freely opened his mind than he was accustomed, and said also that he would speak with me frankly without any observance or respect at all. At which time, I greatly lamented that (your Highness's cause being so just) no means could be found and taken to satisfy your Highness therein; and I said also that I doubted not but that (if his Holiness would) ways might be found by his wisdom, now at the emperour's being with him, to satisfy your Highness; and that done, his Holiness should not only have your Highness in as much or more friendship than he hath had heretofore, but also procure thereby that thing which his Holiness hath chiefly desired, which is, as he hath said, a universal concord among the princes of Christendom. His Holiness answered, that he would it had cost him a joint of his hand that such a way might be excogitate; and he said also, that the best thing which he could see to be done therein at this present, for a preparation to that purpose, was the thing which is contained in the first part of the cipher.' Speaking of the justness of your

---

¹ The obtaining the opinion in writing of the late Cardinal of Ancona, and submitting it to the emperor. This minister, the most aged as well as the most influential member of the conclave, had latterly been supposed to be inclined to advise a conciliatory policy towards England; and his judgment was of so much weight that it was thought likely that the emperor would have been unable to resist the publication of it, if it was given against him. At the critical moment of the Bologna interview this cardinal unfortunately died: he had left his sentiments, however, in the hands of his nephew, the Cardinal of Ravenna, who, knowing the value of his legacy, was disposed to make a market of it. It was a knavish piece of business. The English ambassadors offered 3000 ducats; Charles bid them out of the field with a promise of church benefices to the extent of 6000 ducats; he did not know precisely the terms of the judgment, or even on which side it inclined, but in either case the purchase was of equal importance to him, either to produce it or to suppress it. The French and English ambassadors then combined, and bid again with church benefices in the two countries, of equal value with those offered by Charles, with a promise of the next English bishopric which fell vacant, and the original 3000 ducats as an initiatory fee. There was a difficulty in the transaction, for the cardinal would not part with the paper till he had received the ducats, and the ambassadors would not pay the ducats till they had possession of the paper. The Italian, however, proved an overmatch for his antagonists. He got his money, and the judgment was not produced after all.—*State Papers*, vol. vii. pp. 397-8, 464. BURNET, vol. iii. p. 108.

cause, he called to his remembrance the thing which he told me two years past; which was, that the opinion of the lawyers was more certain, favourable, and helping to your cause than the opinion of the divines; for he said that as far as he could perceive, the lawyers, though they held quod Papa possit dispensare in this case, yet they commonly do agree quod hoc fieri debeat ex maximâ causâ adhibitâ causæ cognitione, which in this case doth not appear; and he said, that to come to the truth herein he had used all diligence possible, and enquired the opinion of learned men, being of fame and indifferency both in the court here and in other places. And his Holiness promised me that he would herein use all good policy and dexterity to imprint the same in the emperour's head; which done, he reckoneth many things to be invented that may be pleasant and profitable to your Highness; adding yet that this is not to be done with a fury, but with leisure and as occasion shall serve, lest if he should otherwise do, he should let and hinder that good effect which peradventure might ensue thereby.'[1]

This letter has all the character of truth about it. The secretary had no interest in deceiving Henry, and it is quite certain that, whether honestly or not, the pope had led him to believe that his sympathies were again on the English side, and that he was using his best endeavours to subdue the emperor's opposition.

On the 26th of December, two days later, Sir Gregory Cassalis, who had also followed the papal court to Bologna, wrote to the same effect. He, too, had been with the pope, who had been very open and confidential with him. The emperor, the pope said, had complained of the delay in the process, but he had assured him that it was impossible for the consistory to do more than it had done. The opinion of the theologians was on the whole against the papal power of dispensation in cases of so close relationship; of the canon lawyers part agreed with the theologians, and those who differed from them were satisfied that such a power might not be exercised unless there were most urgent cause, unless, that is, the safety of a kingdom were dependent upon it. Such occasion he had declared that he could not find to have existed for the dispensation granted by his predecessor. The emperor had replied that there had been such occasion: the dispensation had been granted to prevent war between Spain and England; and that otherwise great calamities would

---

[1] Bennet to Henry VIII.: *State Papers,* vol. vii. p. 402.

have befallen both countries. But this was manifestly untrue; and his Holiness said that he had answered, It was a pity, then, that these causes had not been submitted at the time, as the reason for the demand, which it was clear that they had not been: as the case stood, it was impossible for him to proceed further. Upon which he added, 'Se vidisse Cæsarem obstupefactum.' 'I write the words,' continued Sir Gregory, 'exactly as the pope related them to me; whether he really spoke in this way, I cannot tell. Of this, however, I am sure, that on the day of our conversation he had taken the blessed sacrament. He assured me further, that he had laboured to induce the emperor to permit him to satisfy your Majesty. I recommended him that when next the emperor spoke with him upon the subject, he should enter at greater length on the question of *justice*, and that some other person should be present at the conference, that there might be no room left for suspicion.'[1]

The manner of Clement was so unlike what Cassalis had been in the habit of witnessing in him, that he was unable, as we see, wholly to persuade himself that the change was sincere: the letter, however, was despatched to England, and was followed in a few days by Bonner, who brought with him the result of the pope's good will in the form of definite propositions—instructions of similar purport having been forwarded at the same time to the papal nuncio in England. The pope, so Henry was informed, was now really well disposed to do what was required: he had urged upon the emperor the necessity of concessions, and the cause might be settled in one of two ways, to either of which he was himself ready to consent. Catherine had appealed against judgment being passed in England, as a place which was not indifferent. Henry had refused to allow his cause to be heard anywhere but in his own realm; pleading first his privilege as a sovereign prince; and secondly, his exemption as an Englishman.[2] The pope, with appearance of openness, now suggested that Henry should either 'send a mandate requiring the remission of his cause to an indifferent place, in which case he would himself surrender his claim to have it tried in the courts at Rome, and would appoint a legate and two auditors to hear the trial elsewhere;' or else, a truce

---

[1] Sir Gregory Cassalis to the King: *Rolls House MS.*, endorsed by Henry, Litteræ in Pontificis dicta declaratoriæ quæ maxime causam nostram probant.

[2] There was a tradition (it cannot be called more), that no Englishman could be compelled against his will to plead at a foreign tribunal. 'Ne Angli extra Angliam litigare cogantur.'

of three or four years being concluded between England, France, and Spain, the pope would 'with all celerity indict a general council, to which he would absolutely and wholly remit the consideration of the question.'[1]

Both proposals carried on their front a show of fair dealing, and if honestly proffered, were an evidence that something more might at length be hoped than words. But the true obstacle to a settlement lay, as had been long evident, rather in the want of an honest will, than in legal difficulties or uncertainty as to the justice of the cause; and while neither of the alternatives as they stood were admissible or immediately desirable, there were many other roads, if the point of honesty were once made good, which would lead more readily to the desired end. Once for all Henry could not consent to plead out of England; while an appeal to a council would occupy more time than the condition of the country could conveniently allow. But the offer had been courteously made; it had been accompanied with language which might be sincere; and the king replied with grace, and almost with cordiality; not wholly giving Clement his confidence, but expressing a hope that he might soon be no longer justified in withholding it. He was unable, he said, to accept the first condition, because it was contrary to his coronation oath; 'it so highly touched the prerogative royal of the realm, that though he were minded to do it, yet must he abstain without the assent of the court of parliament, which he thought verily would never condescend to it.'[2] The other suggestion he did not absolutely reject, but the gathering of a council was too serious a matter to be precipitated, and the situation of Christendom presented many obstacles to a measure which would be useless unless it were carried through by all the great powers in a spirit of cordial unanimity. He trusted therefore that if the pope's intentions were really such as he pretended to entertain, he would find some method more convenient of proving his sincerity.

It was happy for Henry that experience had taught him to be distrustful. Events proved too clearly that Clement's assumed alteration of tone was no more than a manœuvre designed to entice him to withdraw from the position in which he had entrenched himself, and to induce him to acknowledge that he was amenable to an earthly authority exterior to his own realm.[3] In his offer

---

[1] Henry VIII. to the Ambassadors with the Pope: *Rolls House MS.*
[2] Ibid.
[3] So at least the English government was at last convinced, as

to refer the cause to a general council, he proved that he was insincere, when in the following year he refused to allow a council to be a valid tribunal for the trial of it. The course which he would have followed if the other alternative had been accepted, may be conjectured from the measures which, as I shall presently show, he was at this very moment secretly pursuing. Henry, however, had happily resolved that he would be trifled with no further; he felt instinctively that only action would cut the net in which he was entangled; and he would not hesitate any longer to take a step which, in one way or another, must bring the weary question to a close. If the pope meant well, he would welcome a resolution which made further procrastination impossible; if he did not mean well, he could not be permitted to dally further with the interests of the English nation. Within a few days, therefore, of Bonner's return from Bologna, he took the final step from which there was no retreat, and 'somewhere about St. Paul's day,'[1] Anne Boleyn received the prize for which she had thirsted seven long years, in the hand of the King of England. The ceremony was private. No authentic details are known either of the scene of it or the circumstances under which it took place; but it is said to have been performed by the able Rowland Lee, Bishop of Lichfield, summoned up for the purpose from the Welsh Marches, of which he was warden. It was done, however—in one way or other finally done—the cast was thrown, and a match was laid to the train which now at length could explode the spell of intrigue, and set Henry and England free.

We have arrived at a point from which the issue of the labyrinth is clearly visible. The course of it has been very dreary; and brought in contact as we have been with so much which is painful, so much which is discreditable to all parties concerned, we may perhaps have lost our sense of the broad bearings of the question in indiscriminate disgust. It will be well, therefore, to pause for a moment to recapitulate those features of the story which are the main indications of its character, and may serve to guide our judgment in the censure which we shall pass.

appears in the circular to the clergy, printed in BURNET's *Collectanea*, p. 447, &c. I try to believe, however, that the pope's conduct was rather weak than treacherous.

[1] So at least Craumer says; but he was not present, nor was he at the time informed that it was to take place.—ELLIS, first series, vol. ii. p. 32. The belief, however, generally was, that the marriage took place in November; and though Cranmer's evidence is very strong, his language is too vague to be decisive.

It may be admitted, or it ought to be admitted, that
if Henry VIII. had been contented to rest his demand for
a divorce merely on the interests of the kingdom, if he
had forborne, while his request was pending, to affront
the princess who had for many years been his companion
and his queen; if he had shown her that respect which
her high character gave her a right to demand, and which
her situation as a stranger ought to have made it impossible to him to refuse; his conduct would have been
liable to no imputation, and our sympathies would without
reserve have been on his side. He could not have been
expected to love a person to whom he had been married
as a boy for political convenience, merely beause she was
his wife; especially when she was many years his senior
in age, disagreeable in her person, and by the consciousness of it embittered in her temper. His kingdom demanded the security of a stable succession; his conscience,
it may not be doubted, was seriously agitated by the loss
of his children; and looking upon it as the sentence of
Heaven upon a connexion, the legality of which had from
the first been violently disputed, he believed that he had
been living in incest, and that his misfortunes were the
consequence of it. Under these circumstances he had a
full right to apply for a divorce.[1]

The causa urgentissima of the canon law for which,
by the pope's own showing, the dispensing powers had
been granted to him, had arisen in an extreme form; and
when the vital interests of England were sacrificed to the
will of a foreign prince, sufficient reason had arisen for
the nation to decline submission to so emphatic injustice,
and to seek within itself its own remedies for its own
necessities. These considerations must be allowed all their
weight: except for them, it is not to be supposed that
Henry would have permitted private distaste or inclination
to induce him to create a scandal in Europe. In his conduct, however, as in that of most men, good was chequered
with evil, and sincerity with self-deception. Personal feeling can be traced from the first, holding a subsidiary, indeed, but still an influential place, among his motives;

---

[1] Individual interests have to yield necessarily and justly to the
interests of a nation, provided the conduct or the sacrifice which the
nation requires is not sinful. That there would have been any sin on
Queen Catherine's part if she had consented to a separation from the
king, was never pretended; and although it is a difficult and delicate
matter to decide how far unwilling persons may be compelled to do
what they ought to have done without compulsion, yet the will of a
single man or woman cannot be allowed to constitute itself an irre-
movable obstacle to a great national good.

and exactly so far as he was influenced by it, his course was wrong, as the consequence miserably proved. The position which, in his wife's presence, he assigned to another woman, however he may have persuaded himself that Catherine had no claim to be considered his wife, admits neither of excuse nor of palliation; and he ought never to have shared his throne with a person who consented to occupy that position. He was blind to the want of delicacy in Anne Boleyn, because, in spite of his chivalry, his genius, his accomplishments, in his relations with women he was without delicacy himself. He directed, or attempted to direct, his conduct by the broad rules of what he thought to be just. In the wide margin of uncertain ground where rules of action cannot be prescribed, and where men must guide themselves by consideration for the feelings of others, he—so far as women were concerned—was altogether or almost a stranger. Such consideration is a virtue which can be learned only in the society of equals, where necessity obliges men to practise it. Henry had been a king from his boyhood; he had been surrounded by courtiers who had anticipated all his desires; and exposed as he was to an ordeal from which no human being could have escaped uninjured, we have more cause, after all, to admire him for those excellences which he conquered for himself, than to blame the defects which he retained.

But if in his private relations the king was hasty and careless, towards the pope, to whom we must now return, he exhausted all resources of forbearance: and although, when separation from Rome was at length forced upon him, he then permitted no half measures, and swept into his new career with the strength of irresistible will, it was not till he had shown resolution no less great in the endurance of indignity; and of the three great powers in Europe, the prince who was compelled to break the unity of the catholic church, was evidently the only one who was capable of real sacrifices to preserve it unbroken. Clement comprehended his reluctance, but presumed too far upon it; and if there was sin in the 'great schism' of the Reformation, the guilt must rest where it is due. We have now to show the reverse side of the transactions at Bologna, and explain what a person wearing the title of his Holiness, in virtue of his supposed sanctity, had been secretly doing.

In January, 1532, some little time before his conversation with Sir Gregory Cassalis on the subject of the two wives, the pope had composed a pastoral letter to Henry, which had never been issued. From its contents it would seem to have been written on the receipt of some indignant remonstrance of Queen Catherine, in which she had complained of her desertion by her husband, and of the public position which had been given to her rival. She had supposed (and it was the natural mistake of an embittered and injured woman) that Anne Boleyn had been placed in possession of the rights of an actual, and not only of an intended wife; and the pope, accepting her account of the situation, had written to implore the king to abstain, so long as the cause remained undetermined, from creating so great a scandal in Christendom, and to restore his late queen to her place at his side. This letter, as it was originally written, was one of Clement's happiest compositions.[1] He abstained in it from using any expression which could be construed into a threat: he appealed to Henry's honourable character, which no blot had hitherto stained; and dwelling upon the general confusion of the Christian world, he urged with temperate earnestness the ill effects which would be produced by so open a defiance of the injunctions of the Holy See in a person of so high a position. So far all was well. Henry had deserved that such a letter should be written to him; and the pope was more than justified in writing it. The letter, however, as we know, produced no effect, and on the 15th of November, three days before Clement's departure to Bologna, where he pretended (we must not forget) that he considered Henry substantially right; he added a postscript, in a tone not contrasting only with his words to the ambassadors, but with the language of the brief itself.

Again urging Henry's delinquencies, his separation from his wife, and the scandal of his connexion with another person, he commanded him, under penalty of excommunication, within one month of the receipt of those injunctions, to restore the queen to her place, and to abstain thenceforward from all intercourse with Anne Boleyn pending the issue of the trial. 'Otherwise,' the pope continued, 'when the said term shall have elapsed, we pronounce thee, Henry King of England, and the said Anne, to be *ipso facto* excommunicate, and command all men to shun and avoid your presence; and although our mind shrinks from allowing such a thought of your Serenity, although by ourselves and by our auditory of the Rota an inhibition has been already issued against you; although the act of which you are suspected be in itself

---

[1] It is printed by LORD HERBERT, and in LEGRAND, vol. iii.

forbidden by all laws human and divine, yet the reports which are brought to us do so move us, that once more we do inhibit you from dissolving your marriage with the aforesaid Catherine, or from continuing process, in your own courts, of divorce from her. And we do also hereby warn you, that you presume not to contract any new marriage with the said or with any other woman; we declare such marriage, if you still attempt it, to be vain and of none effect, and so to be regarded by all persons in obedience to the Apostolic see.'[1]

An inhibitory mandate, was a natural consequence of the conference of Calais, provided that the pope intended to proceed openly and uprightly; and if it had been sent upon the spot, Henry could have complained of nothing worse than of an honourable opposition to his wishes. But the mystery was not yet exhausted. The postscript was not issued, it was not spoken of; it was carried secretly to Bologna, and it bears at its foot a further date of the 23rd of December, the very time, that is to say, at which the pope was representing himself to Bennet as occupied only in devising the best means of satisfying Henry, and to Sir Gregory Cassalis, as so convinced of the justice of the English demands, that he had ventured in defence of them to the edge of rupture with the emperor.

It might be urged that he was sincere both in his brief and in his conversation; that he believed that a verdict ought to be given, and would at last be given, against the original marriage, and that therefore he was the more anxious to prevent unnecessary scandal. Yet a menace of excommunication couched in so haughty a tone, could have been honestly reconciled with his other conduct, only by his following a course with respect to it which he did not follow—by informing the ambassadors openly of what he had done, and transmitting his letter through their hands to Henry himself. This he might have done; and though the issue of such a document at such a time would have been open to question, it might nevertheless have been defended. His Holiness, however, did nothing of the kind. No hint was let fall of the existence of any minatory paper; he sustained his pretence of good will, till there was no longer any occasion for him to counterfeit; and two months later the brief suddenly appeared on the doors of the churches in Flanders.

Henry at first believed it to be a forgery. One forged

<hr>

[1] LEGRAND, vol. iii. p. 558, &c.

brief had already been produced by the imperialists in the course of their transactions, and he imagined that this was another; even his past experience of Clement had not prepared him for this last venture of effrontery; he wrote to Bennet, enclosing a copy, and requiring him to ascertain if it were really genuine.[1]

The pope could not deny his hand, though the exposure, and the strange irregular character of the brief itself troubled him, and Bonner, who was again at the papal court, said that 'he was in manner ashamed, and in great perplexity what he might do therein.'[2]

His conduct will be variously interpreted, and to attempt to analyse the motives of a double-minded man is always a hazardous experiment; but a comparison of date, the character of Clement himself, the circumstances in which he was placed, and the retrospective evidence from after events, points almost necessarily to but one interpretation. It is scarcely disputable that, frightened at the reception of Anne Boleyn in France, the pope found it necessary to pretend for a time an altered disposition towards Henry; and that the emperor, unable to feel wholly confident that a person who was false to others was true to himself, had exacted the brief from him as a guarantee for his good faith; Charles, on his side, reserving the publication until Francis had been gained over, and until Clement was screened against the danger which he so justly feared, from the consequences of the interview at Calais.

There was duplicity of a kind; this cannot be denied; and if not designed to effect this object, this object in fact it answered. While Clement was talking smoothly to Bennet and Cassalis, secret overtures were advanced at Paris for a meeting at Nice between the pope, the emperor, and the King of France, from which Henry was to be excluded.[3] The emperor made haste with con-

---

[1] Ye may show unto his Holiness that ye have heard from a friend of yours in Flanders lately, that there hath been set up certain writings from the See Apostolic, in derogation both of justice and of the affection lately showed by his Holiness unto us; which thing ye may say ye can hardly believe to be true, but that ye reckon them rather to be counterfeited. For if it should be true, it is a thing too far out of the way, specially considering that you and other our ambassadors be there, and have heard nothing of the matter. We send a copy of these writings unto you, which copy we will in no wise that ye shall show to any person which might think that ye had any knowledge from us nor any of our council, marvelling greatly if the same hath proceeded indeed from the pope; [and] willing you expressly not to show that ye had it of us.—*State Papers*, vol. vii. p. 421.

[2] Ibid. p. 454.

[3] Sir John Wallop to Henry: Ibid. p. 422.

cessions to Francis, which but a few months before would have seemed impossible. He withdrew his army out of Lombardy, and left Italy free; he consented to the marriage which he had so earnestly opposed between Catherine de Medici and the Duke of Orleans, agreeing also, it is probable, to the contingency of the Duchy of Milan becoming ultimately her dowry. And Francis having coquetted with the proposal for the Nice meeting,[1] not indeed accepting, but not absolutely rejecting it, Charles consented also to waive his objections to the interview between Francis and the pope, on which he had looked hitherto with so much suspicion; provided that the pope would bear in mind some mysterious and unknown communication which had passed at Bologna.[2]

Thus was Francis won. He cared only, as the pope had seen, for his own interests; and from this time he drew away, by imperceptible degrees, from his engagements to England. He did not stoop to dishonour or treacherous betrayal of confidence, for with all his faults he was, in the technical acceptation of the misused term, a gentleman. He declined only to maintain the attitude which, if he had continued in it, would have compelled the pope to yield; and he no longer even seemed to make concessions to Henry the price of preserving France in allegiance to the Holy See. Nor need we regret that Francis shrank from a resolution which Henry had no right to require of him. To have united with France in

---

[1] Francis represented himself to Henry as having refused with a species of bravado. 'He told me,' says Sir John Wallop, 'that he had announced previously that he would consent to no such interview, unless your Highness were also comprised in the same; and if it were so condescended that your Highness and he should be then together, yet you two should go after such a sort and with such power that you would not care whether the pope and emperor would have peace or else *coups the baston*.'—Wallop to Henry, from Paris, Feb. 22. But this was scarcely a complete account of the transaction; it was an account only of so much of it as the French king was pleased to communicate. The emperor was urgent for a council. The pope, feeling the difficulty either of excluding or admitting the protestant representatives, was afraid of consenting to it, and equally afraid of refusing. The meeting proposed to Francis was for the discussion of this difficulty; and Francis, in return, proposed that the great Powers, Henry included, should hold an interview, and arrange beforehand the conclusions at which the council should arrive. This naïve suggestion was waived by Charles, apparently on grounds of religion. LORD HERBERT, Kennet's Edit. p. 167.

[2] The emperor's answer touching this interview is come, and is, in effect, that if the pope shall judge the said interview to be for the wealth and quietness of Christendom, he will not be seen to dissuade his Holiness from the same; but he desired him to remember what he showed to his Holiness when he was with the same, at what time his Holiness offered himself for the commonwealth to go to any place to speak with the French king.—Bennet to Henry VIII.: *State Papers*, vol. vii. p. 464.

a common schism at the crisis of the Reformation would have only embarrassed the free motions of England; and two nations, whose interests and whose tendencies were essentially opposite, might not submit to be linked together by the artificial interests of their princes. The populace of England were unconsciously on the rapid road to protestantism. The populace of France were fanatically catholic. England was to go her way through a golden era of Elizabeth to Cromwell, the Puritans, and a protestant republic; a republic to be perpetuated, if not in England herself, yet among her great children beyond the sea. France was to go her way through Bartholomew massacres and the dragonnades to a polished Louis the Magnificent, and thence to the bloody Medea's cauldron of Revolution, out of which she was to rise as now we know her. No common road could have been found for such destinies as these; and the French prince followed the direction of his wiser instincts when he preferred a quiet arrangement with the pope, in virtue of which his church should be secured by treaty the liberties which she desired, to a doubtful struggle for a freedom which his people neither wished nor approved. The interests of the nation were in fact his own. He could ill afford to forsake a religion which allowed him so pleasantly to compound for his amatory indulgences by the estrapade[1] and a zeal for orthodoxy.

It became evident to Henry early in the spring that he was left substantially alone. His marriage had been kept secret with the intention that it should be divulged by the King of France to the pope when he met him at Marseilles; and as the pope had pretended an anxiety that either the King of England should be present in person at that interview, or should be represented by an ambassador of adequate rank, a train had been equipped for the occasion, the most magnificent which England could furnish. Time, meanwhile, passed on; the meeting, which was to have taken place first in January, and then in April, was delayed till October, and in the interval the papal brief had appeared in Flanders; the queen's pregnancy could not admit of concealment; and the evident proof which appeared that France was no longer to be

---

[1] The estrapade was an infernal machine introduced by Francis into Paris for the better correction of heresy. The offender was slung by a chain over a fire, and by means of a crane was dipped up and down into the flame, the torture being thus prolonged for an indefinite time. Francis was occasionally present in person at these exhibitions, the executioner waiting his arrival before commencing the spectacle.—*History of the Protestants in France*, by G. DE FELICE.

depended upon, convinced the English government that
they had nothing to hope for from abroad, and that Henry's
best resources were to be found, where in fact they had
always been, in the strength and affection of his own
people.

From this choking atmosphere, therefore, we now turn
back to England and the English parliament; and the
change is from darkness to light, from death to life.
Here was no wavering, no uncertainty, no smiling faces
with false hearts behind them; but the steady purpose of
resolute men, who slowly, and with ever opening vision,
bore the nation forward to the fair future which was already dawning.

Parliament met at the beginning of February, a few
days after the king's marriage, which, however, still remained a secret. It is, I think, no slight evidence of the
calmness with which the statesmen of the day proceeded
with their work, that in a session so momentous, in a
session in which the decisive blow was to be struck of
the most serious revolution through which the country as
yet had passed, they should have first settled themselves
calmly down to transact what was then the ordinary
business of legislation, the struggle with the vital evils of
society. The first nine statutes which were passed in this
session were economic acts to protect the public against
the frauds of money-making tradesmen; to provide that
shoes and boots should be made of honest leather; that
food should be sold at fair prices, that merchants should
part with their goods at fair profits; to compel, or as far
as the legislature was able to do it, to compel all classes
of persons to be true men; to deal honestly with each
other, in that high Quixotic sense of honesty which requires good subjects at all times and under all circumstances
to consider the interests of the commonwealth as more
important than their own. I have already spoken of this
economic legislation, and I need not dwell now upon details of it; although under some aspects it may be thought
that more which is truly valuable in English history lies
in these unobtrusive statutes than in all our noisy wars,
reformations, and revolutions. The history of this as of
all other nations (or so much of it as there is occasion
for any of us to know), is the history of the battles which
it has fought and won with evil; not with political evil
merely, or spiritual evil; but with all manifestations whatsoever of the devil's power. And to have beaten back,
or even to have struggled against and stemmed in ever
so small a degree those besetting basenesses of human

nature, now held so invincible that the influences of them are assumed as the fundamental axioms of economic science; this appears to me a greater victory than Agincourt, a grander triumph of wisdom and faith and courage than even the English constitution or the English liturgy. Such a history, however, lies beside the purpose which I may here permit myself; and the two acts with which the session closed, alone in this place require our attention.

The first of these is one of the many 'Acts of Apparel,' which are to be found in the early volumes of the statute book. The meaning of these laws becomes intelligible when we reflect upon the condition of the people. The English were an organized nation of soldiers; they formed an army perpetually ready for the field, where the degrees were determined by social position; and the dresses prescribed to the various orders of society were the graduated uniforms which indicated the rank of the wearers. When every man was a soldier, and every gentleman was an officer, the same causes existed for marking, by costume, the distinctions of authority, which lead to the answering differences in the modern regiments.

The changing condition of the country at the time of the Reformation, the growth of a middle class, with no landed possessions, yet made wealthy by trade or other industry, had tended necessarily to introduce confusion; and the policy of this reign, which was never more markedly operative than during the most critical periods of it, was to reinvigorate the discipline of the feudal system; and pending the growth of what might better suit the age, pending the great struggle in which the nation was engaged, to hold every man at his post. The statute specifies its object, and the motives with which it was passed.

'Whereas,' says the preamble, 'divers laws, ordinances, and statutes have been with great deliberation and advice provided and established for the necessary repressing and avoiding the inordinate excess daily more and more used in the sumptuous and costly array and apparel accustomably worn in this realm, whereof hath ensued, and daily do chance such sundry high and notable inconveniences as be to the great and notorious detriment of the commonweal, the subversion of politic order in knowledge and distinction of people according to their preeminence and degrees, to the utter impoverishment and undoing of many light and inexpert persons inclined to pride, the mother of all vices: Be it enacted,"[1]—but I need not enter into the particulars of the uniforms worn by the nobles and gentlemen of the court of Henry VIII.; the temper, not the detail, is of importance; and of the wisdom or unwisdom of such enactments, we who live in a changed age should be cautious of forming a hasty opinion. The ends which the old legislation proposed to itself, have in later ages been resigned as impracticable. We are therefore no longer adequate judges how far those ends may in other times have been attainable, and we can still less judge of the means through which the attainment of them was sought.

The second act of which I have to speak is open to no such ambiguity; it remains among the few which are and will be of perpetual moment in our national history. The conduct of the pope had forced upon the parliament the reconsideration of the character of his supremacy; and when the question had once been asked, in the existing state of feeling but one answer to it was possible.

The authority of the church over the state, the supreme kingship of Christ, and consequently of him who was held to be Christ's vicar, above all worldly sovereignties, was an established reality of mediæval Europe. The princes had with difficulty preserved their jurisdiction in matters purely secular; while in matters spiritual, and in that vast section of human affairs in which the spiritual and the secular glide one into the other, they had been compelled—all such of them as lay within the pale of the Latin communion—to acknowledge a power superior to their own. To the popes was the ultimate appeal in all causes of which the spiritual courts had cognizance. Their jurisdiction had been extended by an unwavering pursuit of a single policy, and their constancy in the twelfth century was rewarded by absolute victory. In England, however, the field was no sooner won than it was again disputed, and the civil government gave way at last only when the danger seemed to have ceased. So long as the papacy was feared, so long as the successors of St. Peter held a sword which could inflict sensible wounds, and enforce obedience by penalties, the English kings had resisted both the theory and the application. While the pope was dangerous he was dreaded and opposed. When age had withered his arm, and the feeble lightnings flickered in harmless insignificance, they consented to withdraw their watchfulness, and his supremacy was si-

---

[1] 24 Hen. VIII. cap. 13.

lently allowed as an innocent superstition. It existed as
some other institutions exist at the present day, with a
merely nominal authority; with a tacit understanding, that
the power which it was permitted to retain should be
exerted only in conformity with the national will.

Under these conditions the Tudor princes became loyal
subjects to the Holy See, and so they would have will-
ingly remained, had not Clement, in an evil hour for
himself, forgotten the terms of the. compact. He laid
upon a legal fiction a strain which his predecessors, in
their palmiest. days, would have feared to attempt; and
the nation, after grave remonstrance, which was only received with insults, exorcised the chimæra with a few resolute words for ever. The parliament, in asserting the
freedom of England, carefully chose their language. They
did not pass a new law, but they passed an act declaratory merely of the law which already existed, and which they
were vindicating against illegal encroachment. 'Whereas,'
says the Statute of Appeals, 'by divers sundry old authentic histories and chronicles, it is manifestly declared
and expressed. that this realm of England is an empire,
and so hath been accepted in the world; governed by
one supreme head and king, having the dignity and royal
estate of the imperial crown of the same; unto whom a
body politic compact of all sorts and degrees of people,
divided in terms by names of spiritualty and temporalty,
be bound and ought to bear, next to God, a natural and
humble obedience: he being also institute and furnished
by the goodness and sufferance of Almighty God with
plenary, whole, and entire power, pre-eminence, and authority, prerogative and jurisdiction, to render and yield
justice and final determination to all manner of folk resident or subject within this his realm, without restraint
or provocation to any foreign prince or potentate of the
world: the body spiritual whereof having power when
any cause of the law divine happened to come in question,
or of spiritual learning, [such cause being] declared, interpret, and shewed by that part of the body politic called
the spiritualty, now usually called the English church;
(which also hath been reported and also found of that
sort, that both for knowledge, integrity, and sufficiency
of numbers, it hath been always thought to be, and is
also at this hour sufficient and meet of itself, without
the interfering of any exterior person or persons, to declare and determine all such doubts, and to administer
all such offices and duties as to the administration of
their rooms spiritual doth appertain): and the laws tem-

poral, for trial of property of lands and goods, and for the conservation of the people of this realm in unity and peace, having been and yet being administered, adjudged, and executed by sundry judges and administers of the said body politic called the temporalty: and seeing that both these authorities and jurisdictions do conjoin together for the due administration of justice, the one to help the other: and whereas the king's most noble progenitors, and the nobility and commons of this said realm at divers and sundry parliaments, as well in the time of King Edward I., Edward III., Richard II., Henry IV., and other noble kings of this realm, made sundry ordinances, laws, and provisions for the conservation of the prerogatives, liberties, and pre-eminences of the imperial crown of this realm, and of the jurisdiction spiritual and temporal of the same, to keep it from the annoyance as well of the see of Rome as from the authority of other foreign potentates attempting the diminution or violation thereof, as often as from time to time any such annoyance or attempt might be known or espied: and notwithstanding the said good statutes and ordinances, and since the making thereof, divers inconveniences and dangers not provided for plainly by the said statutes, have risen and sprung by reason of appeals sued out of this realm to the see of Rome, in causes testamentary, causes of matrimony and divorce, right of tithes, oblations, and obventions, not only to the great inquietation, vexation, trouble, costs, and charges of the King's Highness, and many of his subjects and residents in this his realm; but also to the delay and let of the speedy determination of the said causes, for so much as parties appealing to the said court of Rome most commonly do the same for the delay of justice; and forasmuch as the great distance of way is so far out of this realm, so that the necessary proofs, nor the true knowledge of the causes, can neither there be so well known, nor the witnesses so well examined there as within this realm, so that the parties grieved by means of the said appeals be most times without remedy; in consideration hereof, all testamentary and matrimonial causes, and all suits for tithes, oblations, and obventions shall henceforth be adjudged in the spiritual and temporal courts within the realm, without regard to any process of foreign jurisdiction, or any inhibition, excommunication, or interdict. Persons procuring processes, inhibitions, appeals, or citations from the court of Rome, as well as their fautors, comforters, counsellors, aiders and abettors, all and every of them shall incur the penalties of premunire; and in all such cases as have hitherto admitted of appeal to Rome, the appeals shall be from the Archdeacon's court to the Bishop's court, from the Bishop's court to that of the Archbishop, and no further.'[1]

There are two aspects under which this statute may be regarded, as there were two objects for which it was passed. Considered as a national act, few persons will now deny that it was as just in itself as it was politically desirable. If the pope had no jurisdiction over English subjects, it was well that he should be known to have none; if he had, it was equally well that such jurisdiction should cease. The question was not of communion between the English and Roman churches, which might or might not continue, but which this act would not affect. The pope might still retain his rights of episcopal precedency, whatever those might be, with all the privileges attached to it. The parliament merely declared that he possessed no right of interference in domestic disputes affecting persons and property.

But the act had a special as well as a national bearing, and here it is less easy to arrive at a just conclusion. It destroyed the validity of Queen Catherine's appeal; it placed a legal power in the hands of the-English judges to proceed to pass sentence upon the divorce; and it is open to the censure which we ever feel entitled to pass upon a measure enacted to meet the particular position of a particular person. When embarrassments have arisen from unforeseen causes, we have a right to legislate to prevent a repetition of those embarrassments. Our instincts tell us that no legislation should be retrospective, and should affect only positions which have been entered into with a full knowledge at the time of the condition of the laws.

The statute endeavours to avoid the difficulty by its declaratory form; but again this is unsatisfactory; for that the pope possessed some authority was substantially acknowledged in every application which was made to him; and when Catherine had married under a papal dispensation, it was a strange thing to turn upon her, and to say, not only that the dispensation in the particular instance had been unlawfully granted, but that the pope had no jurisdiction in the matter by the laws of the land which she had entered.

On the other hand, throughout the entire negotiations King Henry and his ministers had insisted jealously on

<hr>

[1] 24 Hen. VIII. cap. 12.

the English privileges. They had declared from the first that they might, if they so pleased, fall back upon their own laws. In desiring that the cause might be heard by a papal legate in England, they had represented themselves rather as condescending to a form than acknowledging a right; and they had, in fact, in allowing the opening of Campeggio's court, fallen, all of them, even Henry himself, under the penalties of the statutes of provisors. The validity of Catherine's appeal they had always consistently denied. If the papal jurisdiction was to be admitted at all, it could only be through a minister sitting as judge within the realm of England; and the maxim, 'Ne Angli extra Angliam litigare cogantur,' was insisted upon as the absolute privilege of every English subject.

Yet, if we allow full weight to these considerations, a feeling of painful uncertainty continues to cling to us; and in ordinary cases to be uncertain on such a point is to be in reality certain. The state of the law could not have been clear, or the statute of appeals would not have been required; and explain it as we may, it was in fact passed for a special cause against a special person; and that person a woman.

How far the parliament were justified by the extremity of the case is a further question, which it is equally difficult to answer. The alternative, as I have repeatedly said, was an all but inevitable civil war, on the death of the king; and practically, when statesmen are entrusted with the fortunes of an empire, the responsibility is too heavy to allow them to consider other interests. Salus populi suprema lex, ever has been and ever will be the substantial canon of policy with public men, and morality is bound to hesitate before it censures them. There are some acts of injustice which no national interest can excuse, however great in itself that interest may be, or however certain to be attained by the means proposed. Yet government, in its simplest form, is to an extent unjust; it trenches in its easiest tax on natural right and natural freedom; it trenches further and further in proportion to the emergency with which it has to deal. How far it may go in this direction, or whether Henry VIII. and his parliament went too far, is a difficult problem; their best justification is an exceptive clause introduced into the act, which was intended obviously to give Queen Catherine the utmost advantage which was consistent with the liberties of the realm. 'In case,' says the concluding paragraph, 'of any cause, or matter, or contention now depending for the causes before rehearsed, or that hereafter shall come into contention for any of the same causes in any of the foresaid courts, which hath, doth, shall, or may touch the king, his heirs or successors, kings of this realm; that in all or every such case or cases the party grieved as aforesaid shall or may appeal from any of the said courts of this realm, to the spiritual prelates and other abbots and priors of the Upper House, assembled and convocate by the king's writ in convocation.'[1] If Catherine's cause was as just as catholics and English high churchmen are agreed to consider it, the English church might have saved her. If Catherine herself had thought first or chiefly of justice, she would not perhaps have accepted the arbitration of the English convocation; but long years before she would have been in a cloister.

Thus it is that while we regret, we are unable to blame; and we cannot wish undone an act, to have shrunk from which might have spared a single heart, but *might* have wrecked the English nation. We increase our pity for Catherine because she was a princess. We measure the magnitude of the evils which human beings endure by their position in the scale of society; and misfortunes which private persons would be expected to bear without excessive complaining, furnish matter for the lamentation of ages when they touch the sacred head which has been circled with a diadem. Let it be so. Let us compensate the queen's sorrows with unstinted sympathy; but let us not trifle with history, by confusing a political necessity with a moral crime.

The English parliament, then, had taken up the gauntlet which the pope had flung to it with trembling fingers: and there remained nothing but for the Archbishop of Canterbury to make use of the power of which by law he was now possessed. And the time was pressing, for the new queen was enceinte, and further concealment was not to be thought of. The delay of the interview between the pope and Francis, and the change in the demeanour of the latter, which had become palpably evident, discharged Henry of all promises by which he might have bound himself; and to hesitate before the menaces of the pope's brief would have been fatal.

The act of appeals being passed, convocation was the authority to which the power of determining unsettled points of spiritual law seemed to have elapsed. In the month of April, therefore, Cranmer, now Archbishop of

---

[1] 24 Hen. VIII. cap. 12.

Canterbury,[1] submitted to it the two questions, on the resolution of which the sentence which he was to pass was dependent.

The first had been already answered separately by the bench of bishops and by the universities, and had been agitated from end to end of Europe—was it lawful to marry the widow of a brother dying without issue, but having consummated his marriage; and was the Levitical prohibition of such a marriage grounded on a divine law, with which the pope could not dispense, or on a canon law of which a dispensation was permissible?[2]

The pope had declared himself unable to answer; but he had allowed that the general opinion was against the power of dispensing,[3] and there could be little doubt, therefore, of the reply of the English convocation, or at least of the upper house. Fisher attempted an opposition; but wholly without effect. The question was one in which the interests of the higher clergy were not concerned, and they were therefore left to the dominion of their ordinary understandings. Out of two hundred and sixty-three votes, nineteen only were in the pope's favour.[4]

The lower house was less unanimous, as might have been expected, and as had been experienced before; the opposition spirit of the English clergy being usually then, as much as now, in the ratio of their poverty. But there too the nature of the case compelled an overwhelming majority.[5] It was decided by both houses that Pope Julius, in granting a licence for the marriage of Henry and Catherine, had exceeded his authority, and that this marriage was therefore, *ab initio*, void.

The other question to be decided was one of fact; whether the marriage of Catherine with Prince Arthur had or had not been consummated, a matter which the Catholic divines conceived to be of paramount importance,

---

[1] He had been selected as Warham's successor, and had been consecrated on the 30th of March, 1533. On the occasion of the ceremony when the usual oath to the Pope was presented to him, he took it with a declaration that his first duty and first obedience was to the crown and laws of his own country. It is idle trifling to build up, as too many writers have attempted to do, a charge of insincerity upon an action which was forced upon him by the existing relation between England and Rome. The Act of Appeals was the law of the land. The separation from the papacy was a contingency which there was still a hope might be avoided. Such a protest as Cranmer made was therefore the easiest solution of the difficulty. See it in STRYPE'S *Cranmer*, Appendix, p. 683.

[2] BURNET, vol. iii. pp. 122-3.

[3] Bennet to Henry VIII.: *State Papers*, vol. vii. p. 402. Sir Gregory Cassalis to the same: *Rolls House MS.*

[4] BURNET, vol. iii. p. 123.   [5] Ibid. vol. i. p. 210.

but which to few persons at the present day will seem of any importance whatsoever. We cannot even read the evidence which was produced without a sensation of disgust, although in those broader and less conscious ages the indelicacy was less obviously perceptible. And we may console ourselves with the hope that the discussion was not so wounding as might have been expected to the feelings of Queen Catherine, since at all official interviews, with all classes of persons, at all times and in all places, she appeared herself to court the subject.[1] There is no occasion in this place to follow her example. It is enough that Ferdinand, at the time of her first marriage, satisfied himself, after curious inquiry, that he might hope for a grandchild; and that the fact of the consummation was asserted in the treaty between England and Spain, which preceded the marriage with Henry, and in the supposed brief of Pope Julius which permitted it.[2] We cannot in consequence be surprised that the convocation accepted the conclusion which was sanctioned by so high authority, and we rather wonder at the persistency of Catherine's denials. With respect to this vote, therefore, we need notice nothing except that Dr. Clerk, Bishop of Bath and Wells,[3] was one of an exceedingly small minority, who were inclined to believe that the denial might be true, and this bishop was one of the four who were associated with Cranmer when he sate at Dunstable for the trial of the cause.

The ground being thus opened, and all preparations being completed, the archbishop composed a formal letter to the king, in which he dwelt upon the uncertain prospects of the succession, and the danger of leaving a question which closely affected it so long unsettled. He expatiated at length on the general anxiety which was felt throughout the realm, and requested permission to employ the powers attached to his office to bring it to some conclusion. The recent alterations had rendered the archbishop something doubtful of the nature of his position; he was diffident and unwilling to offend; and not clearly knowing in the exercise of the new authority which had been granted to him, whether the extension of his power was accompanied with a parallel extension of liberty in

[1] See *State Papers*, vol. i. pp. 415, 420, &c.
[2] BURNET's *Collectanea*, p. 22. It is very singular that in the original Bull of Julius, the expression is 'forsan consummavissetis;' while in the brief, which, if it was genuine, was written the same day, and which, if forged, was forged by Catherine's friends, there is no forsan. The fact is stated absolutely.
[3] LORD HERBERT, p. 163. BURNET, vol. iii. p. 123.

making use of it, he wrote two copies of this letter, with slight alterations of language, that the king might select between them the one which he would officially recogniee. Both these copies are extant; both were written the same day from the same place; both were folded, sealed, and sent. It seems, therefore, that neither was Cranmer furnished beforehand with a draught of what he was to write; nor was his first letter sent back to him corrected. He must have acted by his own judgment; and a comparison of the two letters is singular and instructive. In the first he spoke of his office and duty in language, chastened indeed and modest, but still language of independence; and while he declared his unwillingness to 'enterprise any part of that office' without his grace's favour obtained, and pleasure therein first known, he implied nevertheless that his request was rather of courtesy than of obligation, and had arisen rather from a sense of moral propriety than because he might not legally enter on the exercise of his duty without the permission of the crown.[1]

The moderate gleam of freedom vanishes in the other copy under a few pithy changes, as if Cranmer instinctively felt the revolution which had taken place in the relations of church and state. Where in the first letter he asked for his grace's favour, in the second he asked for his grace's favour *and licence*—where in the first he requested to know his grace's pleasure as to his proceeding, in the second he desired his most excellent majesty to *license* him to proceed. The burden of both letters was the same, but the introduction of the little word license changed all. It implied a hesitating belief that the spiritual judges might perhaps thenceforward be on a footing with the temporal judges and the magistrates; that under the new constitution they were to understand that they held their offices not directly under God as they had hitherto pretended, but under God through the crown.

The answer of Henry indicated that he had perceived the archbishop's uncertainty; and that he was desirous by the emphatic distinctness of his own language to spare him a future recurrence of it. He accepted the deferential version of the petition; but even Cranmer's anticipation of what might be required of him had not reached the reality. In running through the preamble, the king flung into the tone of it a character of still deeper humi-

---

[1] *State Papers*, vol. i. pp. 390, 391.

lity;[1] and he conceded the desired licence in the following imperial style. 'In consideration of these things,'—*i.e.* of the grounds urged by the archbishop for the petition—'albeit we being your King and Sovereign, do recognise no superior on earth but only God, and not being subject to the laws of any earthly creature; yet because ye be under us, by God's calling and ours, the most principal minister of our spiritual jurisdiction within this our Realm, who we think assuredly is so in the fear of God, and love towards the observance of his laws, to the which laws, we as a Christian king have always heretofore, and shall ever most obediently submit ourself, we will not therefore refuse (our pre-eminence, power, and authority to us and to our successors in this behalf nevertheless saved) your humble request, offer, and towardness—that is, to mean to make an end according to the will and pleasure of Almighty God in our said great cause of matrimony, which hath so long depended undetermined, to our great and grievous unquietness and burden of our conscience. Wherefore we, inclining to your humble petition, by these our letters sealed with our seal, and signed with our sign manual, do license you to proceed in the said cause, and the examination and final determination of the same; not doubting but that ye will have God and the justice of the said cause only before your eyes, and not to regard any earthly or worldly affection therein; for assuredly the thing which we most covet in the world, is so to proceed in all our acts and doings as may be the most acceptable to the pleasure of Almighty God our Creator, to the wealth and honour of us, our successors and posterity, and the surety of our Realm, and subjects within the same.'[2]

The vision of ecclesiastical independence, if Cranmer had indulged in it, must have faded utterly before his eyes on receiving this letter. As clergy who committed felony were no longer exempted from the penalties of their crimes; so henceforward the courts of the clergy were to fall into conformity with the secular tribunals. The temporal prerogatives of ecclesiastics as a body whose authority over the laity was countervailed with no reciprocal obligation, existed no longer. This is what the language of the king implied. The difficulty which the

[1] Ye therefore duly recognising that it becometh you not, being our subject, to enterprize any part of your said office in so weighty and great a cause pertaining to us being your prince and sovereign, without our licence obtained so to do; and therefore in your most humble wise ye supplicate us to grant unto you our licence to proceed—*State Papers*, vol. i. p. 392.

[2] Ibid.

persons whom he was addressing experienced in realizing the change in their position, obliged him to be something emphatic in his assertion of it; and it might be imagined at first sight, that in insisting on his superiority to the officers of the spiritual courts, he claimed a right to dictate their sentences. But to venture such a supposition would be to mistake the nature of English sovereignty and the spirit of the change. The supreme authority in England was the law; and the king no more possessed, or claimed a power of controlling the judgment of the bishops or their ministers, than he could interfere with the jurisdiction of the judges of the bench. All persons in authority, whether in church or state, held their offices thenceforth by similar tenure; but the rule of the proceedings in each remained alike the law of the land, which Henry had no more thought of superseding by his own will than the most constitutional of modern princes.

The closing sentences of his reply to Cranmer are striking, and it is difficult to believe that he did not mean what he was saying. From the first step in the process to the last, he maintained consistently that his only object was to do what was right. He was thoroughly persuaded that the course which he was pursuing was sanctioned by justice—and persons who are satisfied that he was entitled to feel such persuasion, need not refuse him the merit of sincerity, because (to use the language which Cromwell used at the fatal crisis of his life[1]) 'It may be well that they who medelle in many matters are not able to answer for them all.'

Cranmer, then, being fortified with this permission, and taking with him the Bishops of London, Winchester, Lincoln, and Bath and Wells (the latter perhaps having been chosen in consequence of his late conduct in the convocation, to give show of fairness to the proceeding), went down to Dunstable and opened his court there. The queen was at Ampthill, six miles distant, having entered on her sad tenancy, it would seem, as soon as the place had been evacuated by the gaudy hunting party of the preceding summer. The cause being undecided, and her title being therefore uncertain, she was called by the safe name of 'the Lady Catherine,' and under this designation she was served with a citation from the archbishop to appear before him on Saturday, the 10th of May. The bearers of the summons were Sir Francis Bryan (an unfortunate choice, for he was cousin of the new queen, and

______

[1] Cromwell to the king on his committal to the Tower: BURNET, *Collectanea*, p. 500.

insolent in his manner and bearing), Sir Thomas Gage, and Lord Vaux. She received them like herself with imperial sorrow. They delivered their message; she announced that she refused utterly to acknowledge the competency of the tribunal before which she was called; the court was a mockery; the archbishop was a shadow.[1] She would neither appear before him in person, nor commission any one to appear on her behalf.

The court had but one course before it—she was pronounced contumacious, and the trial went forward. None of her household were tempted even by curiosity to be present. 'There came not so much as a servant of hers to Dunstable, save such as were brought in as witnesses;' some of them having been required to give evidence in the re-examination which was thought necessary, as to the nature of the relation of their mistress with her first boy husband. As soon as this disgusting question had been sufficiently investigated, nothing remained but to pronounce judgment. The marriage with the king was declared to have been null and void from the beginning, and on the 23rd of May, the archbishop sent to London the welcome news that the long matter was at an end.[2]

---

[1] So at least she called him a few days later.—*State Papers*, vol. i. p. 420. We have no details of her words when she was summoned, but only a general account of them.—*State Papers*, vol. i. pp. 394-5.

[2] The words of the sentence may be interesting:—'In the name of God, Amen. We, Thomas, by Divine permission Archbishop of Canterbury, Primate of all England, and Legate of the Apostolic See, in a certain cause of enquiry of and concerning the validity of the marriage contracted and consummated between the most potent and most illustrious Prince, our Sovereign Lord, Henry VIII., by the grace of God King of England and France, Defender of the Faith, and Lord of Ireland, and the most serene princess, Catherine, daughter of his Most Catholic Majesty, Ferdinand, King of Spain, of glorious memory, we proceeding according to law and justice in the said cause which has been brought judicially before us in virtue of our office, and which for some time has lain under examination, as it still is, being not yet finally determined and decided; having first seen all the articles and pleas which have been exhibited and set forth of her part, together with the answers made thereto on the part of the most illustrious and powerful Prince, Henry VIII.; having likewise seen and diligently inspected the informations and depositions of many noblemen and other witnesses of unsuspected veracity exhibited in the said cause; having also seen and in like manner carefully considered not only the censures and decrees of the most famous universities of almost the whole Christian world, but likewise the opinions and determinations both of the most eminent divines and civilians, as also the resolutions and conclusions of the clergy of both Provinces of England in Convocation assembled, and many other wholesome instructions and doctrines which have been given in and laid before us concerning the said marriage; having further seen and in like manner inspected all the treaties and leagues of peace and amity on this account entered upon and concluded between Henry VII., of immortal fame, late King of England, and the said Ferdinand, of glorious memory, late King of Spain; having besides seen and most carefully weighed all and every

It was over;—over at last; yet so over, that the conclusion could but appear to the losing party a fresh injustice. To those who were concerned in bringing it to pass, to the king himself, to the nation, to Europe, to every one who heard of it at the time, it must have appeared, as it appears now to us who read the story of it, if a necessity, yet a most unwelcome and unsatisfying one. That the king remained uneasy is evident from the efforts which he continued to make, or which he allowed to be made, notwithstanding the brief of the 23rd of December,

of the acts, debates, letters, processes, instruments, writs, arguments, and all other things which have passed and been transacted in the said cause at any time; in all which thus seen and inspected, our most exact care in examining, and our most mature deliberation in weighing them hath by us been used, and all other things have been observed by us, which of right in this matter were to be observed; furthermore, the said most illustrious Prince, Henry VIII., in the forementioned cause, by his proper Proctor having appeared before us, but the said most serene Lady Catherine in contempt absenting herself (whose absence we pray that the divine presence may compensate) [cujus absentia Divinâ repleatur præsentiâ. Lord Herbert translates it, 'whose absence may the Divine presence attend,' missing, I think, the point of the Archbishop's parenthesis] by and with the advice of the most learned in the law, and of persons of most eminent skill in divinity whom we have consulted in the premises, we have found it our duty to proceed to give our final decree and sentence in the said cause, which, accordingly, we do in this manner.

'Because by acts, warrants, deductions, propositions, exhibitions, allegations, proofs and confessions, articles drawn up, answers of witnesses, depositions, informations, instruments, arguments, letters, writs, censures, determinations of professors, opinions, councils, assertions, affirmations, treaties, and leagues of peace, processes, and other matters in the said cause, as is above mentioned, before us laid, had, done, exhibited, and respectively produced, as also from the same and sundry other reasons, causes, and considerations, manifold arguments, and various kinds of proof of the greatest evidence, strength, and validity, of which in the said cause we have fully and clearly informed ourselves, we find, and with undeniable evidence and plainness see that the marriage contracted and consummated, as is aforesaid, between the said most illustrious Prince, Henry VIII., and the most serene Lady Catherine, was and is null and invalid, and that it was contracted and consummated contrary to the law of God: therefore, we, Thomas, Archbishop, Primate, and Legate aforesaid, having first called upon the name of Christ for direction herein, and having God altogether before our eyes, do pronounce sentence, and declare for the invalidity of the said marriage, decreeing that the said pretended marriage always was and still is null and invalid; that it was contracted and consummated contrary to the will and law of God, that it is of no force or obligation, but that it always wanted, and still wants, the strength and sanction of law; and therefore we sentence that it is not lawful for the said most illustrious Prince, Henry VIII., and the said most serene Lady Catherine, to remain in the said pretended marriage; and we do separate and divorce them one from the other, inasmuch as they contracted and consummated the said pretended marriage de facto, and not de jure; and that they so separated and divorced are absolutely free from all marriage bond with regard to the foresaid pretended marriage, we pronounce, and declare by this our definitive sentence and final decree, which we now give, and by the tenour of these present writings do publish. May 23rd, 1533.— BURNET'S *Collectanea*, p. 68, and LORD HERBERT.

to gain the sanction of the pope. That the nation was uneasy, we should not require the evidence of history to tell us. 'There was much murmuring in England,' says Hall, 'and it was thought by the unwise that the Bishop of Rome would curse all Englishmen; that the emperor and he would destroy all the people.' And those who had no such fears, and whose judgment in the main approved of what had been done, were scandalized at the presentation to them at the instant of the publication of the divorce, of a new queen, four months advanced in pregnancy. This also was a misfortune which had arisen out of the chain of duplicities, a fresh accident swelling a complication which was already sufficiently entangled. It had been occasioned by steps which at the moment at which they were ventured, prudence seemed to justify; but we the more regret it, because, in comparison with the interests which were at issue, the few months of additional delay were infinitely unimportant.

Nevertheless, we have reason to be thankful that the thing, well or ill, was over; seven years of endurance were enough for the English nation, and may be supposed to have gained even for Henry a character for patience. In some way, too, it is needless to say, the thing must have ended. The life of none of us is long enough to allow us to squander so large a section of it struggling in the meshes of a law-suit; and although there may be a difference of opinion on the wisdom of having first entered upon ground of such a kind, few thinking persons can suggest any other method in which either the nation or the king could have extricated themselves. Meanwhile, it was resolved that such spots and blemishes as hung about the transaction should be forgotten in the splendour of the coronation. If there was scandal in the condition of the queen, yet under another aspect that condition was matter of congratulation to a people so eager for an heir; and Henry may have thought that the sight for the first time in public of so beautiful a creature, surrounded by the most magnificent pageant which London had witnessed since the unknown day on which the first stone of it was laid, and bearing in her bosom the long hoped-for inheritor of the English crown, might induce a chivalrous nation to forget what it was the interest of no loyal subject to remember longer, and to offer her an English welcome to the throne.

In anticipation of the timely close of the proceedings at Dunstable, notice had been given in the city early in May, that preparations should be made for the coronation on the first of the following month. Queen Anne was at Greenwich, but, according to custom, the few preceding days were to be spent at the Tower; and on the 19th of May, she was conducted thither in state by the lord mayor and the city companies, with one of those splendid exhibitions upon the water which in the days when the silver Thames deserved its name, and the sun could shine down upon it out of the blue summer sky, were spectacles scarcely rivalled in gorgeousness by the world-famous wedding of the Adriatic. The river was crowded with boats, the banks and the ships in the pool swarmed with people; and fifty of the great barges formed the procession, all blazing with gold and banners. The queen herself was in her own barge, close to that of the lord mayor; and in keeping with the fantastic genius of the time, she was preceded up the water by 'a foyst or wafter full of ordnance, in which was a great dragon continually moving and casting wildfire, and round about the foyst stood terrible monsters and wild men, casting fire and making hideous noise.'[1] So, with trumpets blowing, cannon pealing, the Tower guns answering the guns of the ships, in a blaze of fireworks and splendour, she was borne along to the great archway of the Tower, where the king was waiting on the stairs to receive her.

And now let us suppose eleven days to have elapsed, the welcome news to have arrived at length from Dunstable, and the fair summer morning of life dawning in treacherous beauty after the long night of expectation. No bridal ceremonial had been possible; the marriage had been huddled over like a stolen love-match, and the marriage feast had been eaten in vexation and disappointment. These past mortifications were to be atoned for by a coronation pageant which the art and the wealth of the richest city in Europe should be poured out in the most lavish profusion to adorn.

On the morning of the 31st of May, the families of the London citizens were stirring early in all houses. From Temple Bar to the Tower, the streets were fresh strewed with gravel, the footpaths were railed off along the whole distance, and occupied on one side by the guilds, their workmen, and apprentices, on the other by the city constables and officials in their gaudy uniforms, 'with their staves in hand for to cause the people to keep good room and order.'[2] Cornhill and Gracechurch-street had dressed their fronts in scarlet and crimson, in arras

---

[1] HALL.   [2] Ibid.

and tapestry, and the rich carpet-work from Persia and the East. Cheapside, to outshine her rivals, was draped even more splendidly in cloth of gold, and tissue, and velvet. The sheriffs were pacing up and down on their great Flemish horses, hung with liveries, and all the windows were thronged with ladies crowding to see the procession pass. At length the Tower guns opened, the grim gates rolled back, and under the archway in the bright May sunshine, the long column began slowly to defile. Two states only permitted their representatives to grace the scene with their presence—Venice and France. It was, perhaps, to make the most of this isolated countenance, that the French ambassador's train formed the van of the cavalcade. Twelve French knights came riding foremost in surcoats of blue velvet with sleeves of yellow silk, their horses trapped in blue, with white crosses powdered on their hangings. After them followed a troop of English gentlemen, two and two, and then the Knights of the Bath, 'in gowns of violet, with hoods purfled with miniver like doctors.' Next, perhaps at a little interval, the abbots passed on, mitred in their robes; the barons followed in crimson velvet, the bishops then, and then the earls and marquises, the dresses of each order increasing in elaborate gorgeousness. All these rode on in pairs. Then came alone Audeley, lord-chancellor, and behind him the Venetian ambassador and the Archbishop of York; the Archbishop of Canterbury, and Du Bellay, Bishop of Bayonne and of Paris, not now with bugle and hunting-frock, but solemn with stole and crozier. Next, the lord mayor, with the city mace in hand, and Garter in his coat of arms; and then Lord William Howard—Belted Will Howard, of the Scottish Border, Marshal of England. The officers of the queen's household succeeded the marshal in scarlet and gold, and the van of the procession was closed by the Duke of Suffolk, as high constable, with his silver wand. It is no easy matter to picture to ourselves the blazing trail of splendour which in such a pageant must have drawn along the London streets,—those streets which now we know so black and smoke-grimed, themselves then radiant with masses of colour, gold, and crimson, and violet. Yet there it was, and there the sun could shine upon it, and tens of thousands of eyes were gazing on the scene out of the crowded lattices.

Glorious as the spectacle was, perhaps however, it passed unheeded. Those eyes were watching all for another object, which now drew near. In an open space behind the constable there was seen approaching 'a white chariot,' drawn by two palfreys in white damask which swept the ground, a golden canopy borne above it making music with silver bells: and in the chariot sat the observed of all observers, the beautiful occasion of all this glittering homage; fortune's plaything of the hour, the Queen of England—queen at last—borne along upon the waves of this sea of glory, breathing the perfumed incense of greatness which she had risked her fair name, her delicacy, her honour, her self-respect, to win; and she had won it.

There she sate, dressed in white tissue robes, her fair hair flowing loose over her shoulders, and her temples circled with a light coronet of gold and diamonds—most beautiful—loveliest—most favoured perhaps, as she seemed at that hour, of all England's daughters. Alas! 'within the hollow round' of that coronet—

> Kept death his court, and there the antick sate,
> Scoffing her state and grinning at her pomp.
> Allowing her a little breath, a little scene
> To monarchize, be feared, and kill with looks,
> Infusing her with self and vain conceit,
> As if the flesh which walled about her life
> Were brass impregnable; and humoured thus,
> Bored through her castle walls; and farewell, Queen.

Fatal gift of greatness! so dangerous ever! so more than dangerous in those tremendous times when the fountains are broken loose of the great deeps of thought; and nations are in the throes of revolution;—when ancient order and law and tradition are splitting in the social earthquake; and as the opposing forces wrestle to and fro, those unhappy ones who stand out above the crowd become the symbols of the struggle, and fall the victims of its alternating fortunes. And what if into an unsteady heart and brain, intoxicated with splendour, the outward chaos should find its way, converting the poor silly soul into an image of the same confusion,—if conscience should be deposed from her high place, and the Pandora box be broken loose of passions and sensualities and follies; and at length there be nothing left of all which man or woman ought to value, save hope of God's forgiveness.

Three short years have yet to pass, and again, on a summer morning, Queen Anne Boleyn will leave the Tower of London—not radiant then with beauty on a gay errand of coronation, but a poor wandering ghost, on a sad tragic errand, from which she will never more return, passing away out of an earth where she may stay no longer, into a Presence where, nevertheless, we know that all is well—for all of us—and therefore for her.

But let us not cloud her shortlived sunshine with the shadow of the future. She went on in her loveliness, the peeresses following in their carriages, with the royal guard in their rear. In Fenchurch-street she was met by the children of the city schools; and at the corner of Grace-church-street a masterpiece had been prepared of the pseudo-classic art, then so fashionable, by the merchants of the Styll-yard. A Mount Parnassus had been constructed, and a Helicon fountain upon it playing into a basin with four jets of Rhenish wine. On the top of the mountain sat Apollo with Calliope at his feet, and on either side the remaining Muses, holding lutes or harps, and singing each of them some 'posy' or epigram in praise of the queen, which was presented, after it had been sung, written in letters of gold.

From Gracechurch-street the procession passed to Leadenhall, where there was a spectacle in better taste, of the old English catholic kind, quaint perhaps and forced, but truly and even beautifully emblematic. There was again a 'little mountain,' which was hung with red and white roses; a gold ring was placed on the summit, on which, as the queen appeared, a white falcon was made to 'descend as out of the sky'—'and then incontinent came down an angel with great melody, and set a close crown of gold upon the falcon's head; and in the same pageant sat Saint Anne with all her issue beneath her; and Mary Cleophas with her four children, of the which children one made a goodly oration to the queen, of the fruitfulness of Saint Anne, trusting that like fruit should come of her.'[1]

With such 'pretty conceits,' at that time the honest tokens of an English welcome, the new queen was received by the citizens of London. These scenes must be multiplied by the number of the streets, where some fresh fancy met her at every turn. To preserve the festivities from flagging, every fountain and conduit within the walls ran all day with wine; the bells of every steeple were ringing; children lay in wait with songs, and ladies with posies, in which all the resources of fantastic extravagance were exhausted; and thus in an unbroken triumph—and to outward appearance received with the warmest affection

---

[1] HALL, p. 801. Hall was most likely an eye-witness, and may be thoroughly trusted in these descriptions. Whenever we are able to test him, which sometimes happens, by independent contemporary accounts, he proves faithful in the most minute particulars.

—she passed under Temple Bar, down the Strand by Charing Cross to Westminster Hall. The king was not with her throughout the day; nor did he intend to be with her in any part of the ceremony. She was to reign without a rival, the undisputed sovereign of the hour.

Saturday being passed in showing herself to the people, she retired for the night to 'the king's manour house at Westminster,' where she slept. On the following morning, between eight and nine o'clock, she returned to the hall, where the lord mayor, the city council, and the peers were again assembled, and took her place on the high dais at the top of the stairs under the cloth of state; while the bishops, the abbots, and the monks of the abbey formed in the area. A railed way had been laid with carpets across Palace Yard and the Sanctuary to the abbey gates, and when all was ready, preceded by the peers in their robes of parliament, the Knights of the Garter in the dress of the order, she swept out under her canopy, the bishops and the monks 'solemnly singing.' The train was borne by the old Duchess of Norfolk her aunt, the Bishops of London and Winchester on either side 'bearing up the lappets of her robe.' The Earl of Oxford carried the crown on its cushion immediately before her. She was dressed in purple velvet furred with ermine, her hair escaping loose, as she usually wore it, under a wreath of diamonds.

On entering the abbey, she was led to the coronation chair, where she sat while the train fell into their places, and the preliminaries of the ceremonial were despatched. Then she was conducted up to the high altar, and anointed Queen of England, and she received from the hands of Cranmer, fresh come in haste from Dunstable, with the last words of his sentence upon Catherine scarcely silent upon his lips, the golden sceptre, and St. Edward's crown.

Did any twinge of remorse, any pang of painful recollection, pierce at that moment the incense of glory which she was inhaling? Did any vision flit across her of a sad mourning figure which once had stood where she was standing, now desolate, neglected, sinking into the darkening twilight of a life cut short by sorrow? Who can tell? At such a time, that figure would have weighed heavily upon a noble mind, and a wise mind would have been taught by the thought of it, that although life be fleeting as a dream, it is long enough to experience strange vicissitudes of fortune. But Anne Boleyn was not noble and was not wise,—too probably she felt nothing

but the delicious, all-absorbing, all-intoxicating present,
and if that plain, suffering face presented itself to her
memory at all, we may fear that it was rather as a foil
to her own surpassing loveliness. Two years later, she
was able to exult over Catherine's death; she is not likely
to have thought of her with gentler feelings in the first
glow and flush of triumph.

We may now leave these scenes. They concluded in
the usual English style, with a banquet in the great hall,
and with all outward signs of enjoyment and pleasure.
There must have been but few persons present, however,
who did not feel that the sunshine of such a day might
not last for ever, and that over so dubious a marriage no
Englishman could exult with more than half a heart. It
is foolish to blame lightly actions which arise in the midst
of circumstances which are and can be but imperfectly
known; and there may have been political reasons which
made so much pomp desirable. Anne Boleyn had been
the subject of public conversation for seven years, and
Henry, no doubt, desired to present his jewel to them in
the rarest and choicest setting. Yet to our eyes, seeing,
perhaps, by the light of what followed, a more modest
introduction would have appeared more suited to the
doubtful nature of her position.

At any rate we escape from this scene of splendour
very gladly as from something unseasonable. It would
have been well for Henry VIII. if he had lived in a world
in which women could have been dispensed with; so ill,
in all his relations with them, he succeeded. With men
he could speak the right word, he could do the right
thing; with women he seemed to be under a fatal necessity of mistake.

It was now necessary, however, after this public step,
to communicate in form to the emperor the divorce and
the new marriage. The king was assured of the rectitude
of the motives on which he had himself acted, and he
knew at the same time that he had challenged the hostility of the papal world. Yet he did not desire a quarrel
if there were means of avoiding it; and more than once
he had shown respect for the opposition which he had
met with from Charles, as dictated by honourable care
for the interests of his kinswoman. He therefore, in the
truest language which will be met with in the whole long
series of the correspondence, composed a despatch for his
ambassador at Brussels, and expressed himself in a tone
of honest sorrow for the injury which he had been compelled to commit. Neither the coercion which the em-

peror had exerted over the pope, nor his intrigues with his subjects in Ireland and England, could deprive the nephew of Catherine of his right to a courteous explanation; and Henry directed Doctor Nicholas Hawkins in making his communication 'to use only gentle words;' to express a hope that Charles would not think only of his own honour, but would remember public justice; and that a friendship of long standing, which the interests of the subjects of both countries were concerned so strongly in maintaining, might not be broken. The instructions are too interesting to pass over with a general description. After stating the grounds on which Henry had proceeded, and which Charles thoroughly understood, Hawkins was directed to continue thus:—

'His Highness is not ignorant what respect is due unto the world. How much he hath laboured and travailed therein he hath sufficiently declared and showed in his acts and proceedings. If he had contemned the order and process of the world, or the friendship and amity of your Majesty, he needed not to have sent so often to the pope and to you both, nor continued and spent his time in delays. He might have done what he has done now, had it so liked him, with as little difficulty as now, if without such respect he would have followed his pleasure.'

The minister was then to touch the pope's behaviour and Henry's forbearance, and after that to say:—

'Going forward in that way his Highness saw that he could come to no conclusion; and he was therefore compelled to step right forth out of the maze, and so to quiet himself at last. And is it not time to have an end in seven years? It is not to be asked nor questioned whether the matter hath been determined after the common fashion, but whether it hath in it common justice, truth, and equity. For observation of the common order, his Grace hath done what lay in him. Enforced by necessity he hath found the true order which he hath in substance followed with effect, and hath done as becometh him. He doubteth not but your Majesty, remembering his cause from the beginning hitherto, will of yourself consider and think, that among mortal men nothing should be immortal; and suits must once have an end, si possis recte, si non quocunque modo. If his Highness cannot as he would, then must he do as he may; and he that hath a journey to be perfected must, if he cannot go one way, essay another. For his matter with the pope, he shall deal with him apart. Your Majesty he taketh for his friend, and as to a friend he openeth these matters to you, trusting to find your Majesty no less friendly than he hath done heretofore.'[1]

If courtesy obliged Henry to express a confidence in the stability of the relations between himself and Charles, which it was impossible that he could have felt, yet in other respects this letter has the most pleasant merit of honesty. Hawkins was so much overcome by 'the sweetness of it,' that 'he nothing doubted if that the emperor read the same, by God's grace he should be utterly persuaded;' and although in this expectation he was a little over sanguine, as in calmer moments he would have acknowledged, yet plain speech is never without its value; and Charles himself after he had tried other expedients, and they had not succeeded with him, found it more prudent to acquiesce in what could no longer be altered, and to return to cordiality.

For the present he remained under the impression that by the great body of the English the divorce was looked upon with coldness and even with displeasure, that the king was supported only by the complacency of a few courtiers, and that the nation were prepared to compel him to undo the wrong which had been inflicted upon Catherine and the princess. So he was assured by the Spanish party in England; so all the disaffected assured him, who were perhaps themselves deceived. He had secured Ireland, and Scotland also in so far as James's promises could secure it;[2] and he was not disposed to surrender for the present so promising a game till he had tried his strength and proved his weakness. He replied coldly to Hawkins, 'That for the King of England's amity he would be glad thereof, so the said king would do works according. The matter was none of his; but the lady, whose rights had been violated, was his aunt and an orphan, and that he must see for her, and for her daughter his cousin.'[3]

The scarcely ambiguous answer was something softened the following day; perhaps only, however, because it was too plain a betrayal of his intentions. He communicated at once with Catherine, and Henry speedily learnt the nature of the advice which he had given to her. After the coronation had passed off so splendidly, when no disturbance had risen, no voice had been raised for her or for her daughter, the poor queen's spirit for the moment had sunk; she had thought of leaving the country, and flying

<hr>

[1] FOXE, vol. v. p. 111.
[2] Northumberland to Henry VIII. *State Papers*, vol. iv. pp. 598-9.
[3] Hawkins to Henry VIII. *State Papers*, vol. vii. p. 488.

with the Princess Mary to Spain. The emperor sent to urge her to remain a little longer, guaranteeing her, if she could command her patience, an ample reparation for her injuries. Whatever might appear upon the surface, the new queen, he was assured, was little loved by the people, and 'they were ready to join with any prince who would espouse her quarrel.'[1] All classes, he said, were agreed in one common feeling of displeasure. They were afraid of a change of religion; they were afraid of the wreck of their commerce; and the whole country was fast ripening towards insurrection. The points on which he relied as the occasion of the disaffection betrayed the sources of his information. He was in correspondence with the regular clergy through Peto at Antwerp, and through his Flemish subjects with merchants of London. Among both these classes, as well as among the White Rose nobles, he had powerful adherents; and it could not have been forgotten in the courts, either of London or Brussels, that within the memory of living men, a small band of exiles, equipped by a Duke of Burgundy, had landed at a Yorkshire village, and in a month had revolutionized the kingdom.

In the eyes of Charles there was no reason why an attempt which had succeeded once might not succeed again under circumstances seemingly of far fairer promise. The strength of a party of insurrection is a power which official statesmen never justly comprehend. It depends upon moral influences, which they are professionally incapable of appreciating. They are able complacently to ignore the existence of substantial disaffection though all society may be undermined; they can build their hopes, when it suits their convenience, on the idle trifling of superficial discontent. In the present instance there was some excuse for the mistake. That in England there really existed an active and organized opposition, prepared, when opportunity offered, to try the chances of rebellion, was no delusion of persons who measured facts by their desires; it was an ascertained peril of serious magnitude, which might be seriously calculated upon; and if the experiment was tried, reasonable men might fairly be divided in opinion on the result to be expected.

In the mean time the government had been obliged to follow up the coronation of the new queen by an act which the situation of the kingdom explained and excused; but which, if Catherine had been no more than a private

---

[1] BURNET, vol. iii. p. 115.

person, would have been wanton cruelty. Among the
people she still bore her royal title; but the name of
queen, so long as she was permitted to retain it, was an
allowed witness against the legality of the sentence at
Dunstable. There could not be 'two queens' in England,[1]
and one or other must retire from the designation. A
proclamation was therefore issued by the council, declaring,
that in consequence of the final proofs that the Lady
Catherine had never been lawfully married to the king,
she was to bear thenceforward the title which she had
received after the death of her first husband, and be called
the Princess Dowager.

Harsh as this measure was, she had left no alternative
to the government by which to escape the enforcement
of it, by her refusal to consent to any form of compromise. If she was queen, Anne Boleyn was not queen. If
she was queen, the Princess Mary remained the heir to
the crown, and the expected offspring of Anne would be
illegitimate. If the question had been merely of names,
to have moved it would have been unworthy and wicked;
but where respect for private feeling was incompatible
with the steps which a nation felt necessary in order to
secure itself against civil convulsions, private feeling was
compelled not unjustly to submit to injury. Mary, though
still a girl, had inherited both her father's will and her
mother's obstinacy. She was in correspondence, as we
have seen, with the Nun of Kent, and aware at least, if
she was not further implicated in it, of the conspiracy to
place her on the throne. Charles was engaged in the
same designs; and it will not be pretended that Catherine
was left without information of what was going forward,
or that her own conduct was uninfluenced by policy.
These intrigues it was positively necessary to stifle, and
it was impossible to leave a pretext of which so powerful
a use might be made in the hands of a party whose object was not only to secure to the princess her right to
succeed her father, but to compel him by arms either to
acknowledge it, or submit to be deposed.[2]

Our sympathies are naturally on the side of the weak
and the unsuccessful. State considerations lose their force
after the lapse of centuries, when no interests of our own
are any longer in jeopardy; and we feel for the great
sufferers of history only in their individual capacity, without recalling or caring for the political exigencies to
which they were sacrificed. It is an error of disguised

---

[1] *State Papers*, vol. i. p. 398.
[2] Papers relating to the Nun of Kent. *Rolls, House MS.*

selfishness, the counterpart of the carelessness with which in our own age, when we are ourselves constituents of an interested public, we ignore what it is inconvenient to remember.

Thus, therefore, on one hot Midsummer Sunday in this year 1533, the people gathering to church in every parish through the English counties, read nailed upon the doors, a paper signed Henry R., setting forth that the Lady Catherine of Spain, heretofore called Queen of England, was not to be called by that title any more, but was to be called Princess Dowager, and so to be held and esteemed. The proclamation, we may suppose, was read with varying comments; of the reception of it in the northern counties, the following information was forwarded to the crown. The Earl of Derby, lord-lieutenant of Yorkshire, wrote to inform the council that he had arrested a certain 'lewd and naughty priest,' James Harrison by name, on the charge of having spoken unfitting and slanderous words of his Highness and the Queen's Grace. He had taken the examination of several witnesses, which he had sent with his letter, and which were to the following effect:—

Richard Clarke deposeth that the said James Harrison reading the proclamation, said that Queen Catherine was queen, Nan Bullen should not be queen, nor the king should be no king but on his bearing.

William Dalton deposeth, that in his hearing the above-named James said, I will take none for queen but Queen Catherine—who the devil made Nan Bullen, that hoore, queen? I will never take her for queen—and he the said William answered, 'Hold thy peace, thou wot'st not what thou sayest—but that thou art a priest I should punish thee, that others should take example.'

Richard Sumner and John Clayton depose, that they came in company with the said James from Perbalt to Eccleston, when the said James did say, 'This is a marvellous world—the king will put down the order of priests and destroy the Sacrament, but he cannot reign long, for York will be in London hastily.'[1]

Here was the later growth of the spirit which we saw a few months previously in the monks of Furness. The mutterings of discontent had developed into plain open treason, confident of success, and scarcely caring to conceal itself—and Yorkshire was preparing for rebellion and 'the Pilgrimage of Grace.'

---

[1] ELLIS, first series, vol. ii. p. 43.

There is another quarter also into which we must follow the proclamation, and watch the effect of the royal order in a scene where it is well that we should for a few moments rest. Catherine was still at Ampthill, surrounded by her own attendants, who formed an inner circle, shielding her retirement against impertinent curiosity. She rarely or never allowed herself to be seen; Lord Mountjoy, with an official retinue, was in attendance in the house; but the occupation was not a pleasant one, and he was as willing to respect the queen's seclusion as she to remain secluded. Injunctions arrived however from the court at the end of June, which compelled him to request an interview; a deputation of the privy council had come down to inform the ex-queen of the orders of the government, and to desire that they might be put in force in her own family. Aware probably of the nature of the communication which was to be made to her, she refused repeatedly to admit them to her presence. At length, however, she nerved herself for the effort, and on the 3rd of July Mountjoy and the state commissioners were informed that she was ready to receive them.

As they entered her room she was lying on a sofa. She had a bad cough, and she had hurt her foot with a pin, and was unable to stand or walk. Her attendants were all present by her own desire; she was glad to see around her some sympathizing human faces, to enable her to endure the cold hard eyes of the officials of the council.

She inquired whether the message was to be delivered in writing or by word of mouth.

They replied that they had brought with them instructions which they were to read, and that they were further charged with a message which was to be delivered verbally. She desired that they would read their written despatch. It was addressed to the Princess Dowager, and she at once excepted to the name. She was not Princess Dowager, she said, but queen, and the king's true wife. She came to the king a clear maid for any bodily knowledge of Prince Arthur; she had borne him lawful issue and no bastard, and therefore queen she was, and queen she would be while she lived.

The commissioners were most likely prepared for this objection, and continued, without replying, to read. The paper contained a statement of worn-out unrealities; the old story of the judgment of the universities and the learned men, the sentence of convocation, and of the houses of parliament; and, finally, the fact of substantial importance, that the king acting as he believed according to the laws of God, had married the Lady Anne Boleyn, who was now his lawful wife, and anointed Queen of England.

Oh yes, she answered when they had done, we know that, and 'we know the authority by which it has been done—more by power than justice.' The king's learned men were learned heretics; the honest learning was for her. As for the seals of the universities, there were strange stories about the way in which they had been obtained. The universities and the parliament had done what the king bade them; and they had gone against their consciences in doing it; but it was of no importance to her*—she was in the hands of the pope, who was God's vicar, and she acknowledged no other judge.

The commissioners informed her of the decision of the council that she was no longer to bear the title of queen. It stood, they said, neither with the laws of God nor man, nor with the king's honour, to have two queens named within the realm; and in fact, there was but one queen, the king's lawful wife, to whom he was now married.

She replied shortly that she was the king's lawful queen, and none other. There was little hope in her manner that anything which could be said would move her; but her visitors were ordered to try her to the uttermost.

The king, they continued, was surprised that she could be so disobedient; and not only that she was disobedient herself, but that she allowed and encouraged her servants in the same conduct.

She was ready to obey the king, she answered, when she could do so without disobeying God; but she could not damn her soul even for him. Her servants, she said, must do the best they could; they were standing round her as she was speaking; and she turned to them with an apology, and a hope that they would pardon her. She would hinder her cause, she said, and put her soul in danger, if on their account she were to relinquish her name, and she could not do it.

The deputation next attempted her on her worldly side. If she would obey, they informed her that she would be allowed not only her jointure as Princess Dowager and her own private fortune, but all the settlements which had been made upon her on her marriage with the king.

She 'passed not upon possessions, in regard of this matter,' she replied. It touched her conscience, and no worldly considerations were of the slightest moment.

In disobeying the king, they said, seeing that she was none other than his subject, she might give cause for dissension and disturbance, and she might lose the favour of the people.

She 'trusted not,' she replied—she 'never minded it, nor would she'—she 'desired only to save her right; and if she should lose the favour of the people in defending that right, yet she trusted to go to heaven cum famâ et infamiâ.'

Promises and persuasions being unavailing, they tried threats. She was told that if she persisted in so obstinate a course, the king would be obliged to make known to the world the offers which he had made to her, and the ill reception which they had met with—and then he would perhaps withdraw those offers, and conceive some evil opinions of high displeasure towards her.

She answered that there was no manner of offers neither of lands nor goods that she had respect unto in comparison of her cause—and as to the loss of the king's affection, she trusted to God, to whom she would daily pray for him.

The learned council might as well have reasoned with the winds, or threatened the waves of the sea. But they were not yet weary, and their next effort was as foolish as it was ungenerous. They suggested, 'that if she did reserve the name of queen, it was thought that she would do it of a vain desire and appetite of glory; and further, she might be an occasion that the king would withdraw his love from her most dear daughter the Lady Princess, which should chiefly move her, if none other cause did.'

They must have known little of Catherine, if they thought she could be influenced by childish vanity. It was for no vain glory that she cared, she answered proudly; she was the king's true wife, and her conscience forbade her to call herself otherwise; the princess was his true begotten child; and as God hath given her to them, so for her part she would render her again. In conclusion, she declared, that neither for daughter, family, nor possessions, would she yield in her cause; she made a solemn protestation, calling on every one present to bear witness to what she said, that the king's wife she was, and such she would take herself to be, and that she would never surrender the name of queen till the pope had decided that she must relinquish it.

So ended the first interview. Catherine before the commissioners left her, desired to have a copy of the proposals which they had brought, that she might translate and send them to Rome. This was brought the next day and they were re-admitted. She requested to see the report which they intended to send to the council of the preceding conversation. It was placed in her hands; and as she read it and found there the name of Princess Dowager, she took a pen and dashed out the words, the mark of which indignant pen-stroke may now be seen in the very letter from which this account is taken.[1] With the accuracy of the rest she appeared to be satisfied—only when she found again their poor suggestion that she was influenced by vanity, she broke out with a burst of passionate indignation.

'I would rather be a poor beggar's wife,' she said, 'and be sure of heaven, than queen of all the world, and stand in doubt thereof by reason of my own consent. I stick not so for vain glory but because I know myself the king's true wife—and while you call me the king's subject, I was his subject while he took me for his wife. But if he take me not for his wife, I came not into this Realm as merchandize, nor to be married to any merchant; nor do I continue in the same but as his lawful wife, and not as a subject to live under his dominion otherwise. I have always demeaned myself well and truly towards the king—and if it can be proved that either in writing to the pope or any other, I have either stirred or procured anything against his Grace, or have been the means to any person to make any motion which might be prejudicial to his Grace or to his Realm, I am content to suffer for it. I have done England little good, and I should be sorry to do it any harm. But if I should agree to your motions and persuasions, I should slander myself, and confess to have been the king's harlot for twenty-four years. The cause, I cannot tell by what subtle means, has been determined here within the king's Realm, before a man of his own making, the Bishop of Canterbury, no person indifferent I think in that behalf; and for the indifference of the place, I think the place had been more indifferent to have been judged in hell; for no truth can be suffered here, whereas the devils themselves I suppose do tremble to see the truth in this cause so sore oppressed.'[2]

Most noble, spirited, and like a queen. Yet she would

---

¹ *Cotton. MS.* Otho X, p. 199. *State Papers*, vol. i. p. 397.
² *State Papers*, vol. i. p. 403.

never have been brought to this extremity, and she would have shown a truer nobleness, if four years before she could have yielded at the pope's entreaty on the first terms which were proposed to her. Those terms would have required no humiliating confessions; they would have involved no sentence on her marriage nor touched her daughter's legitimacy. She would have broken no law of God, nor seemed to break it. She was required only to forget her own interests; and she would not forget them, though all the world should be wrecked by her refusal. She denied that she was concerned in 'motions prejudicial to the king or to the Realm,' but she must have placed her own interpretation on the words, and would have considered excommunication and interdict a salutary discipline to the king and parliament. She knew that this sentence was imminent, that in its minor form it had already fallen; and she knew that her nephew and her friends in England were plotting to give effect to the decree. But we may pass over this. It is not for an English writer to dwell upon those faults of Catherine of Arragon, which English remorse has honourably insisted on forgetting. Her injuries, inevitable as they were, and forced upon her in great measure by her own wilfulness, remain the saddest spots upon the pages of our history.

One other brief incident remains to be noticed here, to bring up before the imagination the features of this momentous summer. It is contained in the postscript of a letter of Cranmer to Hawkins the ambassador in Germany; and the manner in which the story is told is no less suggestive than the story itself.

The immediate present, however awful its import, will ever seem common and familiar to those who live and breathe in the midst of it. In the days of the September massacre at Paris, the theatres were open as usual: men ate, and drank, and laughed, and cried, and went about their common work, unconscious that those days which were passing by them, so much like other days, would remain the *dies nefasti*, accursed in the memory of mankind for ever. Nothing is terrible, nothing is sublime in human things, so long as they are before our eyes. The great man has so much in common with men in general, the routine of daily life, in periods the most remarkable in history, contains so much that is unvarying, that it is only when time has done its work, and all which was unimportant has ceased to be remembered, that such men and such times stand out in their true significance. It

might have been thought that to a man like Cranmer,
the court at Dunstable, the coronation of the new queen,
the past out of which these things had risen, and the
future which they threatened to involve, would have
seemed at least serious; and that, engaged as he had
been as a chief actor, in a matter which, if it had done
nothing else, had broken the heart of a high-born lady
whom once he had honoured as his queen, he would have
been either silent about his exploits, or if he had spoken
of them, would have spoken not without some show of
emotion. We look for a symptom of feeling, but we do
not find it. When the coronation festivities were concluded, he wrote to his friend an account of what had
been done by himself and others in the light gossiping
tone of easiest content; as if he were describing the
common incidents of a common day. It is disappointing,
and not wholly to be approved of. Still less can we approve of the passage with which he concludes his letter.

'Other news we have none notable, but that one Frith,
which was in the Tower in prison,[1] was appointed by the
King's Grace to be examined before me, my Lord of London, my Lord of Winchester, my Lord of Suffolk, my Lord
Chancellor, and my Lord of Wiltshire; whose opinion
was so notably erroneous that we could not dispatch him,
but were fain to leave him to the determination of his
ordinary, which is the Bishop of London. His said opinion
is of such nature, that he thought it not necessary to be
believed as an article of our faith that there is the very
corporeal presence of Christ within the host and sacrament
of the altar; and holdeth on this point much after the
opinion of Œcolampadius.

'And surely I myself sent for him three or four times
to persuade him to leave that imagination. But for all
that we could do therein, he would not apply to any
counsel. Notwithstanding now he is at a final end with
all examinations; for my Lord of London hath given sentence, and delivered him to the secular power when he
looketh every day to go unto the fire. And there is also
condemned with him one Andrew a tailor for the self-same
opinion; and thus fare you well.'[2]

---

[1] Cromwell had endeavoured to save Frith, or at least had been
interested for him. Sir Edmund Walsingham, writing to him about
the prisoners in the Tower, says:—'Two of them wear irons, and Frith
weareth none. Although he lacketh irons, he lacketh not wit nor
pleasant tongue. His learning passeth my judgement. Sir, as ye said,
it were great pity to lose him if he may be reconciled.'—Walsingham
to Cromwell: *MS. State Paper Office*, second series, vol. xlvi.

[2] ELLIS, first series, vol. ii. p. 40.